PRAISE FO

Turn the page for more praise . . .

THE
WALKING

Bentley Little

A SIGNET BOOK

SIGNET
Published by New American Library, a division of
Penguin Group (USA) Inc., 375 Hudson Street,
New York, New York 10014, USA
Penguin Group (Canada), 90 Eglinton Avenue East, Suite 700, Toronto,
Ontario M4P 2Y3, Canada (a division of Pearson Penguin Canada Inc.)
Penguin Books Ltd., 80 Strand, London WC2R 0RL, England
Penguin Ireland, 25 St. Stephen's Green, Dublin 2,
Ireland (a division of Penguin Books Ltd.)
Penguin Group (Australia), 250 Camberwell Road, Camberwell, Victoria 3124,
Australia (a division of Pearson Australia Group Pty. Ltd.)
Penguin Books India Pvt. Ltd., 11 Community Centre, Panchsheel Park,
New Delhi - 110 017, India
Penguin Group (NZ), cnr Airborne and Rosedale Roads, Albany,
Auckland 1310, New Zealand (a division of Pearson New Zealand Ltd.)
Penguin Books (South Africa) (Pty.) Ltd., 24 Sturdee Avenue,
Rosebank, Johannesburg 2196, South Africa

Penguin Books Ltd., Registered Offices:
80 Strand, London WC2R 0RL, England

Frist published by Signet, an imprint of New American Library,
a division of Penguin Group (USA) Inc.

First Printing, November 2000
20 19 18 17 16 15 14 13 12 11 10 9 8 7

Copyright © Bentley Little, 2000
All rights reserved

Ⓟ REGISTERED TRADEMARK—MARCA REGISTRADA

Printed in the United States of America

PUBLISHER'S NOTE
This is a work of fiction. Names, characters, places, and incidents either are the
product of the author's imagination or are used fictitiously, and any resemblance
to actual persons, living or dead, business establishments, events, or locales is
entirely coincidental.

The publisher does not have any control over and does not assume any responsibility for author or third-party Web sites or their content.

For Don Cannon,
the only bookseller who matters
(better late than never).

Prologue

John Hawks died and kept walking.

They had not expected it, but neither did it take them totally by surprise. Garden was the first to notice, and he ran breathlessly into the kitchen to tell his father and his uncle. "I think Grampa's dead!" he called.

His father sucked in his breath. "Has he . . . Is he . . . ?"

"He's still walking."

They went outside to see, standing together on the porch, letting the old screen door slam loudly against its frame behind them. Sure enough, John Hawks was walking purposefully through the desert around the house, maneuvering through the obstacle course of saguaro and cholla and ocotillo just as he had for the past two weeks. From this vantage point, it was impossible to tell whether he was dead or not.

Robert Hawks put his arms protectively around his son's shoulders and turned toward his brother. "Cabe, check it out."

Cabe shook his head. "I ain't—"

"Check it out."

The two brothers looked at each other for a moment, then Cabe glanced away. "All right." He took a few tentative steps down the porch steps as their father disappeared behind the back of the house. He wiped his hands nervously on his jeans, then hurried across the dirt to where a slight groove had been worn into the ground.

Garden watched his uncle plant his feet firmly in the center of the narrow track and face the direction from which the old man would come. He was afraid, and he could tell from the way his father's fingers gripped his shoulders that his father was afraid, too.

John Hawks had started walking the night after his fever broke. At first they'd thought that the sickness had passed. When they heard the creak of his bedsprings, heard his footsteps on the hardwood floor, they assumed that he'd gotten up and out of bed because he was all right. But when he strode straight through the kitchen and outside without so much as a word, when they saw the almost complete lack of expression on his skeletal face, the glassy stare of his pale eyes, they knew something was wrong. Robert and Cabe had run out after him, trying to find out what was going on, but the old man had begun circling around the house, bumping into the cottonwood tree, stepping through jojoba bushes, apparently oblivious to his surroundings. They had followed him around the house once, twice, three times, yelling at him, demanding his attention, but it was clear that he was not going to talk to them. They were not even sure he understood the words they screamed. The only thing they were sure of was that he was still sick. And that, for some reason, he could not stop walking.

They hadn't tried to talk to him since, and they had not tried to stop him. There was something so terrifying about the way he endlessly circled the house, something so utterly wrong and beyond their understanding, that they had thought it best to wait it out. Robert had assigned each of them watches, and for the first couple of days they stuck faithfully to the schedule, although Cabe's nighttime vigil had since been abandoned.

They hadn't expected the old man to last long. He was sick, he was old, he was frail, and he hadn't eaten since before his fever broke. But he'd continued to walk. Three days.

Five days. A week. Two weeks. They'd expected him to die—had hoped, had *prayed*, for him to die—but he had not. His condition worsened. He grew thinner, sicklier. But he continued to walk.

Now he *had* died.

And he continued to walk.

The old man strode back around the corner of the house toward them, and Garden felt his father's grip tighten as Cabe moved forward. His uncle put both hands out in front of him, and Garden saw him reach out and grab the old man's arms, then jump immediately away, uttering a frightened yelp.

John Hawks continued to walk.

"What was it?" Robert demanded.

"His skin's cold," Cabe said. His voice was high and frightened. "It's cold and dry."

"Grampa's dead," Garden repeated.

Cabe hurried back onto the porch and stood next to them. "What're we going to do?" he asked. He sounded as though he was about to cry.

"Exactly what we been doin'. Nuthin'."

"But we gotta do something! We gotta tell someone! We can't—"

"We can't what? You got any ideas?" Robert glared at his brother. "Huh?"

Cabe didn't answer.

"Nuthin' we can do."

"But he's dead! Daddy's dead!"

"Yeah," Robert said quietly. "That he is."

Garden went to bed early that night, and he lay awake in the darkness, listening. In the front room, his father and his uncle were sorting through Grampa's stuff. He'd helped them clean out the old man's room earlier, taking out the boxes of dried roots and twigs and branches, the bottles of powder, the small stuffed animals, the pages of drawings, everything.

Now he stared up at the open beams of the low bedroom ceiling, at the gossamer layers of cobweb stretching across the black corners, silver white in the refracted moonlight. He could hear his father and uncle arguing, his uncle saying that they should have called on Lizabeth weeks ago to find out what was going on, his father replying that the last thing that would help them out with this problem would be calling in a witchwoman.

"What is all this stuff?" Cabe asked. Garden heard him pick up something heavy wrapped in crinkly paper and drop it on the table.

"You know damn well what it is."

There was a pause. "But we don't know nuthin' about this."

"It's our fault. We should've listened to him."

Garden sat up in bed and pulled aside the blue cloth curtain that covered his window. There was a strong wind outside, and from the look of the sky in the north there was a sandstorm coming. Already he could hear the hissing rustle of small grains hitting the glass. He squinted his eyes, trying to see through the dust.

Grampa walked by, his clothes blowing in the wind, billowing outward, his head moving neither to the right nor to the left but staring fixedly ahead.

Garden let the curtain fall. He could hear the wind growing stronger, its rhythms more insistent. He didn't know what was happening, but he was scared. He didn't think Grampa was going to kill him or hurt him in any way, didn't think he'd attack him or his father or his uncle, didn't think Grampa was going to do anything except walk forever in endless circles around the house. But somehow that was more frightening.

"What if he's there for years?" Cabe asked. "What if he

keeps doing this until there's nuthin' left of him and he's just a skeleton or something?"

Garden didn't hear his father's answer. He didn't want to hear. He pulled the blanket over his head. He fell asleep listening to the drone of their voices in the front room as they discussed what to do.

He dreamed about skeletons walking in sandstorms.

He dreamed about Grampa.

In the morning he was gone.

As simple as that.

He had continued walking purposefully around the house until at least after midnight, when Robert and Cabe finally went to bed, impervious to the sandstorm, his torn clothes whipping around him in ragged tatters, but when the sun came up he was no longer there.

They searched their property, walked through the gullies and washes of the surrounding desert, but found no trace of John Hawks. Cabe had wanted to call it a day before noon, thankful that his dead father had disappeared, and Robert would have been inclined to follow his brother's wishes on this one, but Garden insisted that they keep looking.

Several hours later, they found a torn piece of blue shirt cloth on the spiny arm of a saguaro. The sandstorm had wiped out all traces of footprints, but judging by the direction in which the cactus stood in relation to the house, they assumed that the dead man was walking toward the lake. Cabe went back for the truck while Garden and his father waited in place, in the dubious shade of the cactus, and soon the three of them were speeding across the unpaved road that led to the lake.

They arrived just as John Hawks stepped into the water.

Cabe opened his door and jumped out of the driver's seat, while Robert scrambled out of the passenger side. Garden followed his father, leaving the door open behind him. They ran to the edge of the lake.

"Daddy!" Robert called.

But the dead man did not turn around. Neck stiff, head unmoving, proceeding forward at the same indefatigable pace in which he had circled the house for so long, he walked into the lake until just his head and then just his hair were above water. And then he was gone.

They stood there for a while, waiting to see if he came out again, waiting to see if perhaps the lake was just another barrier he had to pass through and if he would emerge on the other shore, but he did not reappear. The sun dipped low in the west, and it was almost dark when they finally decided to head for home. Garden was not sure how his father and uncle felt—both of them seemed more sad than scared now, and more relieved than sad—but he himself was still worried.

He did not think it was over yet.

After graduating from high school, Garden went on to the junior college in Globe. It was a two-hour drive from home, but he had purposely scheduled all of his classes for Tuesdays and Thursdays, so it wasn't quite as bad as it could have been. For an elective his second semester, he decided to take a scuba diving course, and he received an A for his pool work, a B for his solo dive in Apache Lake, and got an A-minus out of the course.

That summer he told his father that he wanted to dive in Wolf Canyon.

"The lake?" Robert said, frowning.

"I want to see what happened to Grampa."

They had not talked of John Hawks since the day he had disappeared. They had not reminisced about either the good times or the bad times, had avoided completely the subject of the walking. Robert and Cabe had not even finished going through all of his old things. They had thrown away boxes unopened, tossed all loose items without looking at them.

None of them had ever gone back to the lake.

Robert stared at his son. "No," he said flatly.

"I'm going with you or without you."

"You can't!"

"I will."

Cabe walked into the kitchen from outside. He sat down tiredly in the chair opposite his brother. "What's all this about?"

"Garden wants to scuba dive in the lake. He wants to look for Daddy."

Cabe sighed. "We all want to know," he said. "You do, too. Admit it." He looked at Garden. "I'm coming with you."

"Cabe—"

"It's time."

"The water's muddy," Robert said. "You won't be able to see nuthin'."

Garden licked his lips. "I'll be able to see."

They went out on a Saturday, borrowing a boat from Jim Holman, Garden bringing equipment from school. They were all nervous, and though the night before they had spent hours going over plans for the dive, discussing each possibility, mapping out a strict timetable, they were now almost silent, talking only to ask for equipment or instructions.

Garden went over the side at ten o'clock sharp.

The orders were strict. Since neither his father nor his uncle knew anything about scuba diving, he was on a line, the line connected to a winch. If he did not check in every five minutes with the prearranged signals, if he did not surface five minutes before the hour limit of his air supply, they were to haul him up.

The two men waited, silently pacing the deck of the boat.

The first signal arrived on time.

As did the second and the third.

Then he was up.

Garden pulled himself onto the boat, flipping over the low side wall of the craft, tearing off his face mask and spitting water out of his mouth. He was breathing heavily, his face was white, and he appeared to be panicked.

"What is it?" Robert demanded, crouching next to his son. "What did you see?"

Garden caught his breath. He looked from his uncle to his father and back again.

"What's happening?" Cabe asked.

Garden closed his eyes. "He's still down there," he said. "And he's walking."

Now

1

"I knew it." Sanderson kept repeating the words like a litany. "I knew it."

Miles Huerdeen did not look at his client's face. Instead, he focused his attention on the contents of the folder spread out over the top of the desk: photos of Sanderson's wife walking arm in arm with the purchasing agent of his company, credit card carbons from the hotel, a copy of a dinner bill, a list of phone charges for the past two months.

"I knew it."

This was the part of the job Miles hated the most. The investigation itself was always fun, and as long as he didn't think about the consequences, he enjoyed his work. But he did not like to see the pain that was caused his clients by the information he gathered. He hated even being the messenger of that hurt. It was one of the paradoxes of this job that the work which was most rewarding was that which was most devastating to the people who hired him.

He glanced up at Sanderson. He always felt as though he should say something to comfort his clients, to somehow apologize for the facts he presented to them. But instead, he stood there poker-faced, feigning an objectivity he did not feel.

Sanderson looked at him with eyes that were a memory away from tears. "I knew it."

Miles said nothing, looked down embarrassedly at the desk.

He was relieved when Sanderson finally left.

The detective business was nothing like the way it was portrayed in movies. Miles hadn't really expected it to be, but he hadn't known what to expect when he made the decision to become a private investigator, when he'd forsaken his business classes and enrolled in his first criminology course. He'd known it wasn't going to be Phillip Marlowe time—glamorously seedy office, shady clientele, fast and loose women—but he'd half expected Jim Rockford. Instead, he'd ended up working in an environment not very far removed from the one in which he would have found himself had he continued to major in business.

Only he now made a hell of a lot less money.

At least he was working for a real detective agency, and not an insurance company, as so many of his fellow graduates were doing. He might be entrenched amid the trappings of a corporate world—desk cubicle in a high-rise office, quotas and timetables he had to meet—but sometimes he was allowed to go out in the field, follow people around, take clandestine photos. Sometimes he could *pretend* he was Phillip Marlowe.

Phillip Marlowe with medical insurance and a good dental plan.

He filled out the form for billable hours, and sent it in an interoffice envelope along with a labor distribution time sheet to the bookkeeper. There was nothing more he could do here this afternoon, so he decided to leave a little early. He had to stop by the library tonight anyway, which would make up for any work-hour discrepancy.

He waved to Naomi the receptionist as he waited for the elevator. "I'm out of here," he said.

She smiled at him. "You're dust in the wind?"

"I'm a puff of smoke. I'm history. I'm gone."

The elevator arrived, and he gave her a James Dean low sign as the metal doors closed.

Outside, the air was cold, or as cold as it got in Southern California. Miles put his hands in the pockets of his jacket. As he walked next door to the parking lot, his breath blew out in puffs of white steam before dissipating in the breeze. It had rained sometime since lunch. He hadn't noticed it while in the office, but now he saw that the streets were slick and cinematically reflective. The water and rain puddles made it seem more Christmassy to him, made the tinsel trees on the lampposts and the small blinking multicolored lights outlining the doors and windows of the buildings seem not quite so inappropriate, lending the entire street a festive holiday air.

He'd been feeling kind of Scroogy about Christmas this year, though he wasn't sure why. Usually Christmas was his favorite season. He loved everything about it: loved hearing the same damn Christmas carols played in each store he went inside, loved the repeats of the old television specials, loved buying presents, loved receiving presents. Most of all, he loved the decorations. Though he did not contradict his friends when they complained that stores put out their decorations too early, that the whole season was far too commercialized, he secretly would have been happy had decorations gone up before Halloween. He saw nothing wrong with making the Christmas season last even longer.

But this year, for some reason, he'd felt a little out of it. Though he'd seen the decorations, heard the music, even started buying some of his presents, it hadn't seemed like Christmas to him. He'd kept waiting for the feeling to kick in.

Now it had.

He walked between a Mercedes and a BMW to his old Buick, humming "Rudolph the Red-Nosed Reindeer" under his breath.

His father was sleeping on the couch when he arrived home, lying on his side in a modified fetal position, one arm curled under his head like a pillow, the other hanging loosely over the edge of the sofa. He was snoring softly, a sound barely audible over the voices of the newscasters on the television. Miles stood there for a moment, looking down at his dad. People were supposed to look younger when they slept. They were supposed to look peaceful, innocent, childlike. But his father looked older. Awake, his features reflected his relatively youthful mental state. But asleep, Bob Huerdeen looked every bit of his seventy-one years. His skin, a leathery cross-hatching of lines and wrinkles, sagged shapelessly over his thin cheeks; his discolored scalp could be seen through the thin back-comb of sparse gray hair. The expression on his face was one of resignation and tired defeat.

This was what his dad would look like when he was dead, Miles thought. In his mind, he saw his father lying in a casket, eyes closed, arms folded across his chest, the expression on his lifeless face the same unhappy one he wore now.

The image disturbed him, and though he had not intended to wake his father up, he walked across the room and turned on the light, noisily announcing his presence with a series of false coughs.

Rubbing his eyes, coughing himself, Bob sat up. He blinked back the light, then glanced over at his son. "Home already?"

"It's after six."

Bob rubbed his eyes. "I had that nightmare again."

"What nightmare?"

"The one I told you about."

"You didn't tell me anything."

"I told you last week. The one about the tidal wave."

Miles frowned. "A recurring dream?"

"It is now."

"Tell me again."

Bob shook his head. "I knew you never listened to me."

"I listen. I just forgot."

"I'm in the kitchen, cooking myself breakfast. Pancakes.

I look out the window and I see a tidal wave coming toward me. It's already crashed, and now it's a wall of white water and it's knocking over buildings and houses and everything in its way. I try to run, but it's like my feet are stuck to the floor. I can't move. Then the wave hits, and I'm thrown against the wall, only the wall's no longer there. Nothing's there, and I'm struggling underwater, trying to hold my breath until I reach the surface, but there is no surface. The wave keeps moving, and I'm trapped inside it, being carried along, tumbling over and over, and I can feel my lungs and stomach start to hurt, and I open my mouth because I can't keep it shut anymore and I have to breathe, and water floods down my throat, and I can feel myself dying. And then I wake up."

"Wow."

"It seemed damn real, let me tell you. Both times."

"Jesus. You ever have a recurring dream before?"

"Not that I remember."

Miles smiled. "Maybe we really are going to have a tidal wave or an earthquake or something."

His father chuckled. "Knock that crap off."

But the old man didn't sound as derisive as Miles would have expected, and for some reason he found that unsettling.

After dinner, Miles did the dishes, then told his dad that he had to go to the library and do some research.

"You're not doing it online?"

"Sometimes you need an actual book."

His father nodded. "Mind if I tag along?"

"No problem," Miles said, but he was surprised. He couldn't remember the last time his dad had been to the library. Hell, he couldn't remember the last time the old man had read a book all the way through. Ever since they'd gotten cable, his father had given up the paperback westerns that had previously occupied his spare time and had not even bothered to finish the business magnate biography through which he'd been slogging. Now, when he wasn't out playing poker with his buddies or going to senior citizen meetings, his dad lay on the couch watching old B-movies and reruns of forty-year-old TV shows.

Miles picked up his wallet and keys from the breakfront. "There something you need to get?"

"Just thought I'd look around. Can't tell what I might find."

"Let's go."

They walked out to the Buick, and for once his dad didn't put up a fight and demand to drive. Thank God. His father's reflexes and road-handling skills had declined precipitously over the past few years, and if there were some way to contact the DMV and get a man's driver's license revoked, Miles would've turned his father in without a second thought. He could only hope that when his father had to get his license renewed next year, he would fail the test.

The library was surprisingly crowded for a weeknight. Students primarily. Most of them Asian. Aside from the occasional runaway, he seldom came into contact with kids these days, and his perception of the younger generation was formed mostly by movies and television. Which was why it surprised him to see what looked like normal, happy, well-adjusted teenagers laughing quietly, talking together in low voices, and copying notes while sitting around large round tables piled with books.

Perhaps society wasn't doomed after all.

His father immediately wandered away, and Miles headed over to the bank of monitors and keyboards that had replaced the card catalog. It still felt strange to him to be using a computer in a library, and though the machines were part of both his work and his everyday life, he mourned its intrusion into this world. It seemed incongruous to him. And unnecessary. There'd been an article last week in the *Los*

Angeles Times about magnetic storage media and the rapid pace of technological change. The gist of the article was that storing information on computer discs or CDs required translating technology—a machine to read the encrypted information and translate it into words—and that things were moving so quickly that a lot of information was being saved in dying formats and would be impossible to retrieve even ten years hence. Written words, however, needed no interpretive mechanism, and information stored in books and printed on acid-free paper would remain easily accessible far longer than those using newer storage methods.

Which made him wonder why the library had ever scrapped its card catalog, a series of beautiful oak cabinets that were not only functional but added immeasurably to the library's ambience.

Sighing, Miles sat down on a stool. He had jotted down several keywords, and he went down the list, typing them in and then writing down each book and periodical reference that appeared. He was working on a case for Graham Donaldson, one of his oldest clients, a lawyer who was currently filing a discrimination suit on behalf of an African American man who'd been fired by Thompson Industries. Miles had already gotten some information from an inside source at the corporation, but he wanted to bolster it with some background. None of the information he'd received from the source was admissible in court, but then Graham was gambling that the case wouldn't even reach that stage. Thompson was extraordinarily concerned about its public image, and Graham was counting on a settlement. Just in case, though, he needed some fallback data.

It was amazing how easy it was to dig up background information. People on the outside always thought he spent his time walking city streets, canvassing neighborhoods, interviewing people, paying bribes for info, using hidden mikes and cameras to listen in on conversations. But sometimes a short trip to the library and a few hours of reading provided him with everything he needed. That wasn't the case here, but he did find two books and one article in a business journal that would prove useful.

His father was already through, sitting on a bench near the front counter, and the old man stood, silently handing Miles his pile of books. Miles gave the librarian his card and glanced down at the titles his dad had chosen: *Past Lives, Future Lives*; *Perception and Precognition*; *Witchcraft and Satanism in Early America*; and *The Prophecies of Nostradamus*. He frowned but didn't say anything until the two of them were outside and in the car. Strapping on his shoulder harness, he casually motioned toward the materials between them. "What is this all about?" he asked.

"What?"

"Your books."

"Do I have to have my reading list approved by you?"

"No, but—"

"Okay then."

"But you've never been interested in the occult."

"I am now." The old man looked at him stubbornly, but for an instant the defensiveness faltered. A flicker of uncertainty—fear?—crossed his father's features, but it was gone before it really registered.

"What's going on?" Miles asked.

"Nothing."

"It's not nothing."

"Just drop it, okay?"

There was anger in his father's voice, and Miles held up a hand in surrender. "Okay. God, I wasn't trying to make a federal case out of it."

But he thought of his father's dream and felt uneasy. He was used to working on hunches, following feelings, but it was usually in the pursuit of facts, and it was the nebulous occult aspect of this that troubled him.

He backed out of his parking spot and pulled onto the street, heading toward home.

His father changed the subject. "I know you're not seeing anyone right now, but do you have any prospects?"

"What?" Miles looked at him, surprised. "What brought this on?"

"I'm just curious. It's not natural for a full-grown man not to be interested in sex."

"First of all, I don't even want to talk about this with you, and, second of all, who says I'm not interested?"

"You don't seem like it."

"I'm going through a dry spell right now."

"Awful long dry spell."

"Why are you suddenly so concerned about my love life?"

"A man gets to a certain age, he wants to know that his son will be settled and happy and taken care of when he's gone."

When he's gone.

Maybe his father hadn't changed the subject after all.

Miles kept his tone light. "You planning to die on me?"

"I'm just asking." Bob grinned. "Besides, no man likes to think that he's been a failure as a father, that he's raised a son who's a pathetic loser and can't even get a date."

"Who can't get a date?"

"When's the last time you went out?"

"Well, there was Janice. That was almost a kind of sort of semi-date. In a way."

"She was married! And you just went out to lunch!"

"She wasn't married. She had a boyfriend."

"Same difference." Bob shook his head. "Thank God you're not on a ball team. I've never seen a man strike out as much as you."

"It's not that bad."

"What about Mary?"

Miles' face clouded over. "I haven't seen her in a long time."

"That's what I mean. Why don't you call her up, ask her out?"

Miles shook his head. "I can't. I couldn't. Besides, she's probably seeing someone else by now."

"Maybe not. Maybe she's in the same boat you are. Who knows? Maybe she's just waiting for you to call."

Miles said nothing. He couldn't tell his dad that Mary was not waiting for him to call, that he had seen her outside a movie theater several months ago, dressed to the hilt, looking gorgeous, laughing happily and intimately touching a tall athletic-looking man wearing an expensive sports coat.

"You can't tell," Bob prodded. "Call her and see. It can't hurt."

It could hurt, though, Miles thought. He turned away. "No, Dad. I'm not calling her."

"You'll be alone until you die."

"I can live with that."

Bob sighed. "That's the sad part. I think you could."

They drove in silence for several blocks, and it was Bob who finally broke the silence. "You'll never do better than Claire. You know that, don't you?"

Miles nodded, staring straight ahead. "I know that."

"You should have never let that girl go."

"I didn't let her go. She wanted out, she wasn't happy, we got a divorce."

"You could've fought a little harder."

Miles didn't reply. He'd thought the same thing himself. Many times. He'd agreed to the divorce, but he hadn't wanted it. He'd loved her then, and he probably still loved her now, though he told himself that he didn't. It had been five years since the final papers had come through, and not a day went by that he didn't think about her. In small ways usually—a brief second wondering what she'd say about this or that—

but she'd remained in his life as a ghost, a conscience, a measuring stick in his mind if not a physical presence.

The truth was, they probably did not have to get divorced. No other people were involved, no other lovers on either of their parts. Her sole complaint with him was that he had too little time for her, that he cared more about his job than he did about his marriage. It wasn't true, but he knew why she felt that way, and it would have been easy for him to correct. If he had just been willing to bend a little, to admit his mistakes, to stop bringing work home, to spend more time with her and be a little more demonstrative with his feelings, they would have been able to survive. He'd known that even then, but some small stubborn part of him had kept him from doing so, had insisted that though the fault was his own, it was her responsibility to solve the problem. If she really loved him, she would understand and forgive him, she would put up with anything he did and be grateful. She was already meeting him more than halfway, but he thought she should have gone *all* the way, and their problems had escalated from there. Divorce had been the ultimate outcome, and though it was not something he had wanted, he had been unwilling to avoid it.

Miles glanced over. His father was still looking at him.

He sighed. "Dad, it's been a long day. Let's just drop it, okay?"

Bob held up his hands in disingenuous innocence. "Okay. Fine."

They pulled into the driveway, and Miles parked the car, pulled the emergency brake. Bob picked up his stack of books before getting out, and once again Miles' gaze was drawn to the volumes.

Witchcraft and Satanism in Early America.

He picked up his own materials and followed his father into the house.

Instead of camping out on the couch as he usually did

and falling asleep to the sounds of sitcoms, Bob retired to his room, bidding his son good night and closing and locking the door.

The Prophecies of Nostradamus.

Miles still felt uneasy, and though he got himself a beer and sat on the couch for a couple of hours, trying to sort through the information he'd gathered, he could not really concentrate, and he gave it up early, going to bed well before his usual time of eleven o'clock.

But he couldn't sleep.

After tossing and turning for what seemed like an eternity, he got up, turned on the small television on his dresser, watched part of an exercise infomercial, then turned it off and walked over to the window, staring out through the crack in the curtains at the cloud-shrouded winter moon.

He thought about Claire, wondered if she was sleeping right now.

Wondered who she was sleeping with.

He glanced back at the empty bed. It had been a long time since he'd had sex. And he missed it. He tried to recall what Claire looked like naked, tried to bring to mind the specifics of her form, but time had blurred her body into the generic. Hell, he could not even recall any details about Mary. He remembered places and positions, but the sensual knowledge ordinarily borne of intimacy was not there. Perversely, he could see clearly in his mind the nude form of Cherise, a one-night stand from three years ago.

Sighing, he walked back over to the bed. He masturbated joylessly, perfunctorily, and finally fell asleep thinking of tidal waves and witches and dreams that predicted the end of the world.

2

Miles felt tired the next morning when he went to work, and it was noticeable enough that Hal commented on it when they met in the elevator.

"Looks like you just came back from a long night at the prison orgy."

Miles smiled wryly. "Thanks."

"To quote the great Dionne Warwick, that's what friends are for."

"You have food in your beard," Miles told him.

The burly detective quickly ran his fingers through his thick facial hair. "Gone?"

Miles grinned. "I lied."

"Jackass."

The doors opened on their floor, and Hal stepped out of the elevator first. He waved to Naomi at the front desk. "Honeybunch! How are you this beautiful morning?"

The receptionist was on the phone, and she frowned at him as she put her caller on hold. She put down the handset and looked from Hal to Miles. "I know it's foolish to ask, but did either of you read the memo yesterday?"

"What memo?" they said in unison.

Hal looked at Miles, chuckled. "Great minds think alike."

Naomi smiled tolerantly. "The memo that was placed in your boxes, the memo stating that the phones will be out of service this morning. They're rewiring for the computers and putting in new fiber-optic lines. They should be finished around eleven or twelve, but until then everything has to go through me. My line and the pay phone are the only two in service."

"Guess I didn't read that one," Miles admitted.

Hal shook his head. "Great. I have about a gazillion calls to make."

"Better break out those quarters," the receptionist said sweetly "I can't tie up my line."

"Thanks." Hal lumbered off toward his cubicle.

Naomi picked up the handset. "Oh," she said to Miles, almost as an afterthought. "You have a client. She's been waiting about ten minutes. Said Phillip Emmons recommended you."

Miles nodded in thanks as she pressed a button on the phone and began talking once again. He strode down the wide central aisle toward his workstation. Phillip Emmons. Old Phil could always be counted on to throw some work his way. It had been awhile since he'd seen his friend, and he promised himself that he'd give Phil a call later in the week and the two of them would get together.

The woman waiting in the client's chair of his cubicle sat perfectly still, staring out the windows of the office at the Hollywood hills. A pretty brunette, wearing a tight blouse with no bra and a short trendy skirt, she saw him coming and stood at his approach, extending a hand.

Raymond Chandler time.

"My name's Marina Lewis."

He shook her hand. "Miles Huerdeen." The first thing he noticed was a wedding ring, and his hopes, faint as they were, faded. He smiled, motioned for her to sit. "What can I do for you, Ms. Lewis?"

"Call me Marina."

"Marina."

She waited for him to settle in behind his desk, then took a deep breath. "Phillip Emmons recommended you. I mentioned to him that I was looking for someone . . . that I needed some help . . ."

"What's the problem?" Miles said gently.

She cleared her throat. "My father is being stalked, but the police refuse to do anything about it."

Miles nodded calmly, professionally, but inside he was

revved up. Finally a real case. In pulp fiction terms: a gorgeous dame and a targeted old man. What more could he ask for? "Who's after your father?" Miles asked.

"We don't know. That's what we want you to find out."

"How do you know he's being stalked?"

"We weren't, at first. I mean, there were little clues. He'd come home and the back door would be unlocked, though he was sure that he had locked it. Stuff like that. Things that could have been imagination or coincidence. But last week, right before we came out here to visit him, he got a phone call from a woman who said he was marked for death. She described the inside of his house perfectly, like she'd been there, and said she was going to kill him in his sleep. And then, a few days later, she called again and started saying weird stuff about things that no one would know but people in our family. Then, two days ago, he was nearly run over by a black car with blacked-out windows that swerved to hit him as he was crossing the street. He only escaped by leaping onto the sidewalk and jumping into the doorway of a jewelry store."

"You told this to the police?"

She nodded.

"What did they say?"

She opened her small handbag, drew out a card, and passed it across the desk to him. "I talked to this guy, Detective Madder, and he said there was nothing they could do until something more concrete occurred. He wrote down the information about the phone call, took a description of the car, and then basically told us that it was going in a file and wasn't going to be acted on. Then he gave me this card and told me to keep him informed. My father didn't even want to go to the police, I convinced him to, and after that he became adamant about handling this by himself. So I'm here on my own. He doesn't know anything about this."

"We can't provide protection," Miles said. "We're an investigative firm, not a security company—"

"I know," she interrupted. "I just want you to find out who's doing this and why. After that we'll either go to the police with what we have or . . . or figure out something else."

Find out who's doing this and why.

As juvenile and stupid as it was, he felt energized. He was in his own movie now, and this made up for all those boring bureaucratic cases he was ordinarily forced to handle. He took out a pen and notebook. "Your father lives where?"

"Santa Monica. 211 Eighth Street."

"And you and your husband?"

"Arizona. We're only out here for a few weeks. My husband's a writer, and he's meeting with some movie people about optioning his book."

"So how much longer will you be staying in California?"

"Probably another week or so." She paused. "Unless something else happens. I'm a teacher and I'm supposed to be back at work on January second, but if my dad's in danger . . ."

"We'll try to clean this up quickly." Miles smiled at her and she smiled back. "Your husband's a writer, huh? I assume that's how you met Phil Emmons."

Her face brightened. "Yes! Phillip's been a godsend. Gordon met him at a horror convention in Phoenix last year, and he's the one who helped him find a movie agent. We're only out here today because of Phillip."

Miles smiled. "Yeah. He's quite a guy."

Marina cleared her throat embarrassedly. "He mentioned something about 'reasonable rates.' I don't know how much you charge, but we can't afford too much. If you could give me an . . . estimate, let me know what we're looking at . . ."

"Don't worry about it. We—"

Naomi stuck her head around the corner of the cubicle. "Miles, phone."

He raised his hand. "I'm with a client. Get a number and tell them that I'll call them back."

"Miles, it's an emergency. Your father. He's in the hospital."

He was instantly up and out of his chair. "Take care of her!" he shouted to Hal, motioning back toward his cubicle as he ran up the aisle toward the front desk. His heart seemed to have stopped, and his chest hurt by the time he reached Naomi's chair because he'd been holding his breath. He let out a huge exhalation of air, reached over the desk, and grabbed the phone, pressing the blinking light on the console. "Hello?"

"Mr. Huerdeen?"

His heart was pumping again. Not just pumping, *pounding*. He could barely hear over the sound of the blood thumping in his head. "What is it? What's happened?"

"I'm sorry, Mr. Huerdeen, but your father has had a stroke."

Stroke.

It was not something he had expected, not anything he had ever thought about or even considered. Miles' mouth felt dry, and for a second he was afraid that he'd forgotten how to speak, but the words finally came out, weak and fearful. "How . . . how did it happen?"

"He was at a grocery store when he collapsed. The manager immediately called the paramedics, and they rushed him here. We found your name and this contact number in his wallet."

"Oh, God," Miles breathed. "Oh, Jesus." He leaned back against the wall for support, closing his eyes. He had a sudden picture in his mind of his father reaching for a can of soup and falling on the linoleum floor, taking shelves of groceries down with him, dying among strangers who had come to the store to buy food and were now dispassionately watching an old man take his last breath on their way to the produce department.

"He's stable right now, but he's not conscious, and we're keeping him monitored in the CCU. He's most likely suffered some brain damage, although we won't know the extent of it until—"

"What hospital?" Miles demanded.

"St. Luke's on—"

"I'll be right there." Miles slammed down the phone just as Naomi reached her desk. "Have Hal take over that client for me." He hit the elevator's Down button. "I'm not sure when I'll be back."

"Is your father all right?"

"He's had a stroke." Miles slammed his palm against the button again, as if trying to hurry the elevator, but when there was no immediate response, he sprinted toward the stairwell door. "I'll call!" he yelled back to Naomi.

And then he was in the stairwell, taking the steps two at a time, leaping the last few to each landing. On the ground floor, he dashed through the building's lobby and out to his car in the adjacent lot.

St. Luke's. That was over on Winnetka, close to home. His dad had probably been shopping at Ralph's.

Somehow, knowing where it had happened, knowing the physical layout of the location, brought it home to him, made it more immediate, less abstract, and the panic flared within him. Thankfully, though, it did not seem to impair his judgment or coordination. He did not have to fumble through his key ring to find the car key, did not have to work with shaking hands to get the car started. If anything, he seemed to be thinking clearer than usual. Everything seemed to be in sharp focus, he had total control over his movements and thought processes, and he sped out of the parking lot, past

a Salvation Army Santa, and onto Wilshire, zooming effort-
lessly into a convenient hole in the traffic.

His luck did not hold.

All of the streets leading to the Ventura freeway seemed
to be under construction, and it was like one of those horrific stress dreams. He'd sit in congestion for two blocks,
then finally turn down a side street until he hit another major
thoroughfare, only to have the same thing happen all over
again. It took him twenty minutes to drive six miles, and by
the time he reached the freeway, he was a nervous wreck.
His jaw hurt from clenching his muscles, and through his
mind ran the dozens of death scenarios he'd imagined while
waiting for stoplights to change.

It was clear sailing from then on out, however, and ten
minutes later, he was in the hospital elevator, heading up to
the Critical Care Unit. His chest felt tight, and though he
knew it was only from stress, he could not help thinking
that if he was having a heart attack, this was the best place
for it to happen.

There was a nurses station backed by a wall of monitors
just past the elevator, and Miles quickly walked over to the
one person who looked up at his entrance, a young Asian
man wearing blue scrubs. "I'm looking for my father, Bob
Huerdeen. He had a stroke and he's supposed to be in the
CCU."

It came out as a single frightened sentence, and he was
half expecting to be told the worst, but the man was nodding before he'd even finished speaking, walking quickly
around the counter to join Miles. "He's in room twelve. Follow me."

Room twelve was halfway down the hallway and, like
seemingly all of the other rooms on this floor, had a big
window opening onto the corridor so that the medical personnel passing by could do instant visual checks on the patients inside. Miles saw his father before he even walked

into the room. The old man was hooked up to machines, IV tubes had been inserted into one extended arm, and he lay there, still and unmoving, eyes closed, as though he was dead.

Miles followed the—intern? doctor? nurse? attendant?—through the open doorway into the room. He'd steeled himself for an onslaught of emotion, but none came. There was no sadness, no tears, no anger, only the same fear, dread, and panic that he'd been experiencing since Naomi first told him his father was in the hospital.

Inside, the room was silent, the only sound the persistent beep of heart-monitoring equipment. Miles cleared his throat before speaking, and the noise was deafening in the stillness. When he spoke, his voice was a reverent whisper. "Are you the doctor?"

The other man shook his head, whispering also. "I'm an intern. The doctor is on his rounds. He should be back in fifteen minutes or so, but I could get him if you want."

"So there's nothing . . . life-threatening? I mean, my dad doesn't have to have emergency surgery or something?"

"Your father almost died. Could have died. As it is, he may have suffered some serious brain damage. But we have him on a blood thinner, and he's being given medication that will break down any clots."

Miles shook his head. "I'm sorry. I don't understand. Is that what caused the stroke?"

"A stroke usually occurs when blockage in one of the arteries breaks off, travels through the bloodstream, and becomes lodged in one of the blood vessels of the brain. This is what happened to your father. There's not much we can do about the stroke that already occurred, although the doctor will talk to you more about that when he sees you. The anticoagulant and blood thinner he's being administered are to prevent additional strokes. They often come in waves, the clots dislodging sequentially or in pieces, or dislodging other blockages farther down the line, and this hopefully will prevent that from occurring."

Miles was listening, but he was looking at his father. He turned back toward the intern only when the other man stopped speaking.

"Would you like me to get the doctor?"

"Yes," Miles admitted. "Would you?"

The intern smiled. "I'll be back in a few minutes."

There was a chair against the wall by the foot of the bed, and Miles pulled it to his dad's side, sitting down. Lying there, eyes closed, a tube shoved up his nose, the man on the bed did not even look like his father. Not only did he seem older and thinner, but the features of his face appeared to be altered. His nose looked larger than it did ordinarily, his chin longer and more pointed. The teeth that were exposed between pale, partially open lips were much too big and much too white, out of proportion with the rest of the face. Only the single exposed hand, connected to the arm in which bottled nutrients and medication were being intravenously fed, seemed familiar.

He recognized that hand.

The sight of it, for some reason, brought on the tears that previously wouldn't come. Looking at the veined, mottled skin, the bony, excessively lined knuckles, he could conjure up images of the past that were not prompted by the still face, the sheeted body. He saw that hand helping him climb the metal ladder out of the YMCA pool, spanking him when he shot the Werthers' dog in the butt with a BB gun, showing him how to tie knots for his Boy Scouts merit badge, dribbling a basketball.

It was this that made him cry, that triggered the emotional outburst for which he'd been prepared.

He touched his dad's hand, patted it, held it.

And when the doctor came in, five minutes later, he was still crying.

Then

1

The girl sat trembling in the darkness, her frightened features only partially illuminated by the flickering orange glow of the fireplace. Her hands were clasped tightly together, and though her fingers moved nervously, they did not leave her lap.

"There is nothing to be afraid of," William said kindly. He smiled at the girl, trying to calm her nerves, but this only seemed to make her more agitated. "It will not be painful," he told her. "It is a very simple procedure."

The girl's hands clenched and unclenched in her lap. Under any other circumstances she would probably be very pretty. Now she just looked troubled and scared. She took a deep breath, a sound audible even over the crackle of the burning log in the fireplace. "Will—" she began. She coughed nervously, cleared her throat. "Will you have to see me?"

William shook his head. "Not if you don't want me to," he said softly. "But I must warn you that it will come out. I can take care of that for you, but if you do not want me to see you, you will have to get rid of it yourself." He paused for a moment to let his words sink in. "It will be embarrassing for you, but it will be easier if I do it all. I promise I will not look at you as a man. If it makes you feel any better, I have seen many other young women the same way."

"Who?" the girl asked, her fear temporarily overtaken by curiosity.

William shook his head. "I cannot tell you."

She thought for a moment, then met his eyes for the first time. "You will not tell about me, either?"

"Not upon pain of death." He stood, went to the window, parted the curtain. The land outside was empty, tall grasses swaying in the chill winter wind that blew across the plains. In the distance, the flickering gaslights of town shone like yellow stars at the edge of the horizon. He let the curtain fall and walked across the room to the series of shelves next to the bed. Taking out a match, he struck it against the log wall and lit a candle.

He had a bad feeling about this. As he'd told the girl, he'd done this many times before, but this was different. He could sense it. He'd been run out of towns in the past, had been whipped and beaten. But that was not what was coming here, that was not what he foresaw happening. No, this was something else.

And it frightened him.

The girl's name was Jane, and, like all of them, she was in love. She had given herself to the boy, though her father wanted her betrothed to another—perhaps *because* her father wanted her betrothed to another—and thanks to that one encounter was now with child. She was not yet showing, but she had not been visited by the menses twice now, and as innocent as she was supposed to be, she knew what that meant.

Like many of them, she had been on the verge of killing herself when a friend of a friend told Jane about him, and William had received a hurriedly written note the next day, a badly misspelled missive begging him to put an end to her condition.

As always, he had agreed to do so.

And that had led her here, to his hut, in the middle of the night.

He knew that what he was about to do was illegal. And he had been beaten and chased in the past not only for performing such an act but for the *way* in which he performed it.

For using magic.

He looked around his little room. He had been here for over a year. It was the longest time he'd spent anywhere since leaving the East, and he liked the place, liked the people. He'd become a member of this community, and the suspicions that had always seemed to grow up around him elsewhere had failed to materialize here. He had helped some girls, even helped a few men, but this was a strongly Christian town, and those mores had kept people from talking.

That was about to end. He knew it, he *sensed* it, and that made him sad.

It was also going to end badly.

Violently.

And that scared him.

William forced himself to smile reassuringly at Jane, who was still sitting primly in the small chair, her hands clasping and unclasping nervously on her lap.

"I'd like you to move over to the bed," he suggested. "And you'll have to remove your clothing."

Jane nodded, stood. Her hands were trembling. She took off her coat, took off her dress, took off her undergarments. She was crying as she placed her clothing on the chair, sobbing by the time she lay down on the bed. Her legs and feet were pressed tightly together, and standing to the side of the bed, William cleared his throat to get her attention and motioned with his hand that she was to spread her legs open.

She did so, sobbing loudly now, her hands held over her face so she could not see him, as if, by shielding her face she could shield the rest of her body.

He set the candle on her stomach, carefully placed a rag between her legs. Closing his eyes, he concentrated for a moment, gathering the strength he needed. As always, it started with a tingle deep in his midsection, a fluttering of the heart that grew into a warm vibration and spread outward through his body, through his limbs, into his head, lighting up the world inside his brain.

He opened his eyes, and the room was tinged with extra color. Everything had a halo about it, auras of different tint that emanated from the walls, from the floor, from the ceiling, from the furniture, and especially, from the girl.

Her head was bathed in yellow, most of her body in blue, but both the candle on her stomach and her abdomen had auras of gray.

William took a deep breath, then slowly passed his hands over her abdomen, muttering the Words that would terminate her pregnancy. From the hairy cleft between her legs came a small trickle of blood that was immediately soaked up by the rag. Jane was still crying, but from shame and humiliation. It was obvious that she felt no pain.

Once more his hands passed over her, and this time a gloppy mess spilled out from between her legs onto the rag, a bloody mass of undistinguishable flesh that he quickly covered and took away. He tossed the entire rag in the fire, said a few Words, then turned back toward the girl. "It is over," he told her. "You may dress."

She took her hands from her face, and the expression he saw, in the second before he turned away to give the girl her privacy, was one of surprise. She had not known it was over because she had not even known it had started.

He heard from behind him the creak of bed and floorboard, the rustle of clothes. It was not over yet, however. His premonition of lurking disaster had not abated one whit, and though the auras were fading before his eyes, though the tingle in his body had subsided into almost nothing, he still had the sense that something was wrong, that what had transpired here tonight would lead to . . . to . . .

To what?

Death.

Yes, death. Whether his own or Jane's he did not know, but he tried to hurry her up, tried to get the girl out the door and back on the path to town before anything occurred. She tried to pay him, offered to work off her debt to him for his kindness and help, but he told her he would accept no payment. He did this because he wanted to help her, not because he wanted anything for himself. She did not fight him but allowed herself to be hurried out.

He watched her through the window as she sprinted back toward town, moonlight illuminating her form until she hit a small dip in the trail and faded into the shadows.

William poured himself some tea from the kettle above the fire and sat in the chair, waiting, but his sense of foreboding did not go away. He was debating whether to saddle up and ride off for a few days, maybe spend a week or so in the hills until whatever this was had passed, when he heard noises from outside.

Someone knocked on the door.

This is it.

He nearly spilled the tea on his lap, getting up, but he managed to avoid burning himself and placed the cup on the mantel above the fireplace.

The knock came again, louder, stronger, not the friendly sound of a neighbor's tapping hand but the hard, demanding rap of wood on wood. William walked across the room, pulled back the bolt, and opened the door.

Six or seven men stood on the porch, ax handles and shotguns in hand. Even backlit by the moon, their forms in silhouette, their faces bathed in darkness, William could see defensiveness in their postures, anger in the way they held their weapons. Beneath everything, he could sense their fear.

He had been through all of this before.

"Come in," he said, feigning a camaraderie he did not feel.

"We didn't come for no visit," the closest man said.

William recognized the low rough voice of Calhoun Stevens, Jane's father. The big man stepped over the threshold. "We know what you did."

"And we know what you is!" came the jittery voice of an old man at the back.

"I have no idea what you're talking about," William lied.

Stevens raised his ax handle threateningly. "I know my daughter was here tonight. I know what you did to her!"

Jane could not have told, William realized. These men could not have been gathered and ridden out here in that short time. It had to have been her friend, the one who'd given her his name.

The men pushed forward. Stevens slammed his ax handle against the cabin wall. "We're here to make sure you can never do anything like that again."

"We know what you is!" the man in back repeated.

There was going to be no easy way out of this, William understood. These men had not come to talk, and they were not prepared to listen. They were obviously afraid of him, and they'd obviously had to build themselves up to this. As they pressed farther into the room, he could smell whiskey breath.

He could use their fear against them.

It was his last chance to avoid violence.

He stood straight and moved next to the fire, aware of the image the flickering orange flames would produce. "You know what I am?" he said. "Then, you know what I can do."

He concentrated, caused the flames to leap and grow in a roaring whoosh that sped up the chimney.

The men, all of the men except Stevens, stumbled backward.

"She's my daughter!" Stevens said, advancing.

William stood still, gathering his strength, hoping he wouldn't have to use the magic, knowing he would. "I have not touched your daughter." He glanced quickly around the room, taking inventory, deciding what he would need to take with him, what he could afford to leave. He would miss this place.

Stevens swung at him.

William ducked, expecting it. The ax handle knocked down the mantel above the fireplace, the objects atop it clattering and breaking on the wooden floor. Before the big man could attack again, William waved his hand and caused the ax handle to fly from Stevens' hand.

"Stop right now," he warned. "Leave my house or I will not be responsible." From the corner of his eye, he saw a couple of the men nearest the door edge their way back outside. No one was rushing forward to help Stevens.

His muscles were shaking. Anger and power coursed through him. When he saw that Stevens had no intention of leaving or backing off, when he saw that the father's rage and pride were running too high, William steeled himself.

Stevens rushed him. "Die, witch!"

He'd clearly expected his friends to help, but as William began chanting some of the Words, as the fireplace roared again and a green flame leapt out and struck Stevens full in the face, the other men fled, scrambling to get out the door.

William continued chanting and the green flame grew, spreading down the big man's body, engulfing him, freezing him in place. Beneath the sickly illumination of the unnatural fire, Stevens' body blackened, crumpled, started to melt.

William looked out the open door at the men and horses running away, their forms little more than scrambling shadows in the moonlight. They'd scurry back to town, and soon they'd be back, with more men, more weapons. The righteous townspeople marching forth to put an end to the evil witch and his black arts.

All because a girl had fallen in love with someone other than the boy her father wanted her to marry.

And he had helped her.

William sighed.

He'd thought this kind of persecution was over, that the hatred and horror of the old days had faded.

But it wasn't, it hadn't, it never would.

The green flames were gone, and he stared down at the twisted black lump that had once been a body, thinking of his mother. He remembered the way she had looked at the stake, remembered the panicked expression on her doomed face, remembered the way her eyes had scanned over him without recognition, mistaking him for merely another face in the hostile crowd that was putting her to death. "Run!" the man with the torch had ordered her, and she had run in place as the fire caught, as first the kindling and then the bigger branches had begun to burn. She had continued to run as the sack dress she was wearing ripped open, had continued to run naked as around her the blaze grew.

He touched the twisted form with his foot. In his mind, as clear as if it had been yesterday, he heard the sound of his mother screaming as the flames scorched her skin, as her legs blackened and she started to burn. He'd wanted her to save herself, to use whatever magic she had left and kill however many men she could, and he had not understood at the time why she'd gone down passively, why she hadn't struck back.

But he knew now that she'd done it for him. Any indication that the judge was right, that she really *was* a witch, would have ensured that he, too, would be put to the stake. But dying this way had kept alive a flicker of doubt in the townspeople's minds, had guaranteed him life.

Men like Stevens and his friends had killed his mother, and though he understood that they feared what they did not understand, it did not excuse their actions. He felt no qualms about putting an end to Stevens' life. It had been kill or be killed—as it was so often out here in the territories—and he would do the same thing over again if given the chance.

But he had no time to dally. They would be back. He gathered his bag of writings and powders, took whatever food and clothing he could fit onto the horse, and headed out. He considered torching the house, leaving behind no evidence, but then they'd know for sure he'd fled. This way they'd search the house and the property before giving chase. It would buy him some time.

He ran the horse at first, but then slowed it to a trot. If the gathering posse really wanted, he knew, they would be able to overtake him. Maybe not the first day. But the second. Or the third. And he thought it better to appear less desperate. Let them know he was leaving, but also let them think that he was not afraid, that he was confident enough of his powers that he did not need to run.

From behind him, he heard the sound of a shotgun, its thunderous blast amplified and echoing in the cold winter night. He told the horse it was nothing and made the animal continue forward at its leisurely pace. Even if one of the men was shooting at him—which he doubted—none of the bullets would find their mark. The first thing he had done was cloak himself in a protective spell that was strong enough to shield him from all but a direct blow with a handheld weapon.

Ahead of him was blackness.

Behind him echoed the sound of another shotgun blast.

He looked up at the position of the moon. It was after midnight, he realized. It was Christmas. When the sun rose, the men behind him would be opening presents, giving thanks to God, going to church.

He sighed. It didn't matter.

He continued slowly forward into the darkness.

It wasn't a day he recognized anyway.

Now

1

The body was torn in half lengthwise. *Literally* torn. Like a piece of paper. With the entire right side of the connected head, torso and abdomen pulled down so that the man's left half and right halves were touching only at the feet.

He had never seen or heard of anything like this happening before, and Miles stared with revulsion and horror at the spilled guts and broken bits of bone that littered the bloody hardwood floor. He felt like throwing up, and it was only through an effort of sheer will that he managed to keep down his breakfast.

It was the smell that was the worst, the disgusting stench of bile and excrement and bodily fluids. He was forced to hold his hand over his nose, and he wished that the policemen and forensic experts would offer him a surgical mask like the ones they were wearing.

Graham Donaldson had called him, and Graham stood next to him now, watching as the police dusted for fingerprints, collected trace evidence, and photographed the crime scene. Miles didn't know why the lawyer wanted him here— as a witness perhaps, as a nonofficial observer—but Graham was a friend, and he had come automatically.

He had not been prepared for what he'd found.

A criminalist crouched near the shattered left half of the head and gathered a sample of blood from the brain cavity. Miles turned away. His noirish fantasies had sometimes involved murder cases, but those dreams had crashed to earth in the first second he'd seen the body—or what was left of it. He realized how lucky he was to be working in a downtown office suite with computers and ergonomic office furniture and nice clean paperwork.

He'd never complain about being a glorified clerk again.

Miles turned to Graham. "So why, exactly, am I here?"

The lawyer shrugged. "I thought you might be able to help me find out who did this. I figured it'd be better if you were at the scene and could oversee what the cops were doing rather than simply read about it afterward and look at pictures."

At this, two of the nearest policemen turned toward them. Graham ignored the hostile stares. "I need to know if it was someone from or someone hired by Thompson."

Miles turned back toward the body. Montgomery Jones was supposed to have met Graham at Jerry's Famous Deli in the Valley to go over their strategy before heading over to a deposition session with Thompson's lawyers. Miles had managed to dig up some pretty good statistical dirt on the company's minority hiring practices, as well as a rather incriminating quote from Thompson's CEO, and Graham had been excited about his client's chances for a settlement and was anxious to discuss it with him.

Only Montgomery had never shown.

His body had been found, two hours later, here, in the old carriage house near the Whittier Narrows dam.

"I have no legal status here," Miles pointed out. "They told me to stay behind the tape, and I have to—"

"I know that," Graham snapped. "Don't talk to me about 'legal status.' "

Miles raised an eyebrow.

"I'm sorry," the lawyer apologized. "It's just . . . It's a stressful situation. I know you can't go conducting a private investigation of your own. You weren't even hired by him or technically working for him. You're working for me. But

I was hired by him, and I mean to see that his killer is brought to justice."

"The cops seem to be doing a thorough job."

"I just wanted you as a witness in case they weren't. I don't know what I'm going to do or how I'm going to handle this, and I want to make sure all my bases are covered from the beginning."

It was what he'd figured, and Miles nodded, satisfied. He glanced around the carriage house, at the antique horse carts and livery, at the huge barnlike doors. Were the doors open all the time? There didn't seem to be any padlocks or locks of any sort, and the chain-link fence around the Whittier Narrows recreation area had been breached in several places. Anyone could have come in here.

Thompson Industries could be playing hardball, but somehow Miles didn't think so. Ruthless businessmen they might be, but he didn't think they could afford the public relations nightmare of being associated with a criminal act. Particularly not one this heinous.

Besides, even if they were into this stuff, they would've been more discreet. Montgomery would not have been so publicly dispatched. He would have just disappeared.

This wasn't the work of a corporation trying to avoid a lawsuit, this was the work of . . . of what?

A monster, was his first thought, but that didn't make any sense. There were no such things as monsters. Still, he could not imagine how this could have been done, how a person or even a gang of people could have physically accomplished this act, and the only image that would come to mind when he looked at Montgomery's torn form was that of an overgrown Frankenstein, a huge, grotesque creature angrily grabbing the man and tearing him in two.

Goose bumps cascaded down the skin of his arms.

The two of them stood there for a moment, watching the police at work.

"You don't think it's connected to Thompson," Graham asked, "do you?"

Miles looked at him. "Do you?"

The lawyer shook his head. "I don't know *what* did this."

Miles parked his car on the street instead of in the lot, pulling into an empty space in a green twenty-minute zone. He just needed to grab some files and addresses, to rush in and rush out, and he didn't want to waste any more time. The trip out to Whittier had cost half the day, and he had to tie up several loose ends on old cases before getting to the stalking of Marina Lewis' father.

He got out of the car, walked into the building. He felt tired, and he understood for the first time how cops and lawyers, psychiatrists and doctors became burned out. Death was draining. Between his father and Montgomery Jones, he'd seen enough of sickness, death, and dying to last a lifetime.

He punched the button for the elevator. The doors slid open immediately, and he rode up to the agency's office. He closed his eyes. He could not get the image of Montgomery's body out of his mind, and he realized that he knew something about himself he hadn't known this morning when he woke up: he was not cut out to have a high-stress job. He was not one of those people who rose to a challenge, who thrived under pressure. It was a sobering thought, and as the elevator doors opened, he understood that despite his petty complaints, he was generally content with his lot in life. He didn't want to be a real detective, he didn't want to solve real crimes. He wanted work that was mildly interesting, mildly stimulating.

He nodded to Naomi, Hal, Tran, and Vince, walked straight over to his cubicle, grabbed the folders he needed, and headed back down the elevator and outside.

He'd called Marina Lewis last night and apologized for

the delay, asking if she'd rather have the case transferred to Hal or one of the other investigators, but she'd been understanding and assured him that she'd rather the case remain with him.

He'd talked to her father Liam over the phone, and the old man had been a cipher. He realized Marina was the one pushing the investigation, that her father didn't want to talk about the subject or face it, and Miles wondered why. He had the feeling that the old man knew more than he was telling, and Miles had decided to interview some of Liam's friends to find out whether he'd revealed anything to them.

He got into the car and quickly sorted through the top folder on his pile. The Gonzalez divorce.

It was going to be a long day.

After work, he went to the hospital.

His father's condition had changed little since the first day, and while his dad didn't seem in imminent danger of dying, it was clear that he was not going to recover to the extent that Miles had initially hoped.

As always, the corridor leading to the CCU was crowded with doctors and nurses and interns, but he'd been here so often over the past few days that no one stopped him and several people actually smiled and nodded. He walked up to his father's open door, took a deep breath to fortify himself, and peeked inside. If his father was asleep, he'd wait in the hallway. He didn't want to disturb him. But Bob was wide awake and staring at the television mounted on the wall.

Miles walked into the room. The sound of the monitoring equipment hooked up to his father was louder than the muted noise of the TV. He looked up. *Oprah* was on. His dad hated *Oprah*. Miles searched around until he found the remote control, and changed the channel to the local news program Bob ordinarily watched.

He sat down on the chair next to his father's bed. He forced himself to smile. "Hey, Dad, how's it going?"

Bob's hand reached out and grabbed his own with a surprisingly strong grip. He tried to talk. He could speak only in a whisper and only without moving his lips, the words emerging from remembered rhythms of breath. Miles leaned closer to his father, placing his ear next to the old man's mouth. "What is it?"

"Eeeeeee . . . Eeeeear."

"Ear?"

"Eeeeeee . . . Eeeeear."

E Ear? Miles frowned. It didn't make any sense.

"Eeeeeee . . . Eeeeear."

He patted his father's shoulder. "It's okay, Dad." He felt bone beneath the skin beneath the covers. It was a disconcerting sensation, made even more so by the incomprehensibility of Bob's speech.

"Eeeeeee . . . Eeeeear," his father repeated.

Miles did not know what to say, and he kept patting his father's bony shoulder and saying, "It's all right, Dad. It's all right." He realized that since Bob probably wasn't going to die from this stroke, he would be coming home at some point. Miles felt horribly out of his depth, unable to deal with the responsibilities that would entail. The only reason he was coping even now was because the hospital was taking care of his dad's physical needs, monitoring him. He had no idea how he would go about taking care of his father on his own.

It would be one thing if Bonnie were here to help him, but his sister had not even bothered to come down and see their dad. That was to be expected, but it still pissed him off. She'd called, of course, but only once, and it hadn't seemed to occur to her that perhaps her father would like to see her or that perhaps Miles himself would like a little moral support.

As always, she was thinking only of herself, of what was convenient for *her.*

"I-uh?" his father whispered.

Miles

He squeezed Bob's hand. "I'm here, Dad."

His father nodded, almost smiled, and his head sank back onto the pillow. He closed his eyes.

Miles found himself thinking of Claire. His ex-wife and his father had always gotten along great, and he considered calling her. She'd probably want to know what was happening. But he knew he would not be able to bring himself to do it. Even after all this time the wounds were still raw, and the only reason he had even thought of phoning Claire was because of some harebrained idea in the back of his mind that this would lead to some sort of reconciliation, that this would bring her back and that somehow they'd get together again and live happily ever after. It wasn't for his father's sake that he had considered calling her, it was for his own, and that was why he could not contact her.

That and the fact that he didn't want to discover how she was incredibly happy with her new life and involved with a guy she loved more than anything in the world.

"I-uh?"

"Yeah, Dad."

Miles started talking. He gave his father a rundown on his day, keeping out the gruesome details of the morning. Carrying on a one-way conversation was awkward, and he was not good at it, but his father's firm squeeze told him that the effort was appreciated, and he racked his brain trying to think of things to keep on talking about. Eventually, he started making things up, and around that time Bob finally drifted off to sleep.

Miles slipped carefully out of his chair and made his way across the hall to the monitoring station. "Is Dr. Yee here?" he asked a nurse.

"He's coming back for his rounds later, but I think he's out right now. Do you want me to page him?"

Miles shook his head. "That's okay. I'll wait and catch him when he comes back."

An intern standing behind the nurse looked up. "Maybe I can help you."

"I just have a question about my father I'd like to ask Dr. Yee."

"Which room is your father in?"

"Twelve."

"Oh, yes. Mr. Huerdeen. I'm familiar with the case. What would you like to know?"

"I was just wondering if he's . . . going to be going home. I mean eventually, not right away."

"He'll probably be going home next week. He doesn't require life support or continued treatment, and to be honest, there's not a lot we can do for him at this point. He'll be prescribed anticoagulant medication, and we'll probably enroll him in our stroke-recovery program, which involves informational classes for the family as well as physical therapy for the patient. As you know, your father's right side has been affected by his stroke, and the rehab will be concentrating on retraining his mind and body to adapt to their post-stroke condition.

"But the fact is, he'll need full-time care. He'll need a live-in nurse, someone with professional training. I don't know what type of insurance your father has—"

Miles cut him off. "That's not a problem."

"Are you sure? I hope so, but I'd suggest you look into the details of your father's plan. A lot of these senior health plans let the HMOs determine the course of treatment rather than the patient's doctor, which means that they have standardized solutions to every problem and a set amount they'll pay for each illness or disability. I'm not saying that's what your father has, but if it is, you're going to be facing some major, major medical bills."

Miles drove home feeling depressed. He wasn't the happiest guy on the planet even under the best of circumstances, but now he felt as though the weight of the world was on his shoulders. His life seemed oppressive, stifling, and instead of going straight home, he drove aimlessly toward the Hollywood hills, cruising over the narrow winding canyon streets, concentrating on the road, trying not to think about his father, his job, or anything remotely related to his life.

Luckily, his father's insurance covered everything. Bob had worked in the aerospace industry during the boom years and had retired when pension benefits were at their peak, so he wasn't locked into an HMO and could pick his own doctor. As Miles sorted through the documents and policy statements, he learned that not only would the insurance company pay a hundred percent of the hospital bill, it would also cover ninety percent of the rehab costs.

He wished his own insurance coverage was even half this good, and he longed for those bygone days when employers actually took care of their employees rather than giving them the shaft.

The shaft.

Did anyone even use that phrase anymore?

He sighed. Another sign of encroaching old age.

It was Saturday, and after visiting with his dad, Miles went down, policies in hand, to talk to the hospital's "patient representative." The representative, Teri, bore more than a slight resemblance to Claire, and like his ex-wife she seemed at once sympathetic and capable. She efficiently sorted through the documents he gave her, made a few phone calls, and within an hour everything was set.

"They'll be sending a nurse—or a 'caregiver,' as I think they prefer to be called—out to your house this afternoon at two. As I'm sure you heard from that last phone call, the hospital no longer provides in-home care to our patients directly. We've contracted with another company for that service. Everything is coordinated through here, however, so if you have any problems, come and see me and we'll get them straightened out."

Miles nodded.

"The caregiver will be dropping by today just to introduce herself, to explain a little bit about what she does and when she'll be coming over permanently."

"She won't be living with us, will she?"

"That can be arranged if it becomes necessary, but at this time Dr. Yee does not think your father requires round-the-clock professional care. So no. She'll probably come in the morning, stay the day, and you'll be responsible for watching your father at night, which shouldn't be too hard since he'll be sleeping then. But the caregiver will explain more about that to you this afternoon. Mostly, she'll be coming by to see the layout of your house, determine if there needs to be any modifications in your father's bed or other furniture. Things like that." She smiled. "As I said, if there are any problems, just give me a call."

Miles left the hospital shortly after speaking with Dr. Yee on his afternoon rounds and hurried home. A pretty, youngish red-haired woman who looked like a country music singer was already waiting for him, leaning against the hood of her Camry, a brown briefcase at her feet. He parked on the street, got out of the car, and walked toward her. "Hello," he said. "I'm Miles Huerdeen."

"My name's Audra? Audra Williams? I'm the home health nurse assigned to your father?"

She had a pronounced Southern accent that made statements sound like questions, and though he ordinarily had a prejudice against such a manner of talking—its speakers always sounded stupid to him—Audra exuded an air of confidence and competence, and as she began explaining what she did and how she would be assisting his father, he stopped even noticing her accent.

The two of them walked through the house, Audra jotting down notes in a leather-bound organizer. In Bob's room, she stated that she would be ordering a new bed for him, an adjustable hospital bed, and then she added on her list a special mattress and a meal tray. Miles didn't know if any of these accessories were covered by insurance, but he nodded in agreement.

They finished up in the living room, where she gave him a stack of pamphlets as well as a video on home health care. He led her to the door and was about to say good-bye when Audra turned toward him. "Mr. Huerdeen?"

"Yes?"

"I just want you to know that I'm a Christian? I'd like to get that straight from the beginning? I'm a God-fearing woman? I am here to provide a service to your family in this, your hour of need, but I am born-again, and I think you should know that up front?"

That came out of nowhere.

She looked at him expectantly, and Miles maintained the strained smile on his face.

A God-fearing woman.

Why would a woman who defined herself as Christian *fear* God? Shouldn't she love God? He never had been able to understand the bizarre system of interlocking, overlapping rewards, promises, and prohibitions that born-again Christians used to guide their lives.

He considered replacing Audra, asking for someone else. That was why she'd warned him, and it was a considerate thing to do. Especially in this situation. A born-againer, he knew, would really annoy the hell out of his dad. Of course, he and his dad would annoy the hell out of anyone even remotely religious, and Miles thought that maybe his father would like that. It might boost his spirits to be involved in a little bloodless battle now and then.

He smiled at the nurse. "Audra?" he said. "I'm glad you'll be here."

2

The next day was the second Sunday of the month. Miles had learned from Marina Lewis that although her father wasn't going to be there this weekend, he ordinarily sold Amberolas at the Rose Bowl's monthly flea market. He'd worked for forty years as a lathe operator in a machine shop, but after retirement, looking for something to do with his time and in need of a few extra bucks, he'd started buying and restoring antique phonographs. Marina said that most of his friends these days were fellow antique sellers.

She had no specific names to give him, and once again her father was being peculiarly uncooperative, so Miles' bare-bones plan was to go to the swap meet and ask around until he found someone who knew Liam Connor.

He stopped by the hospital first to see his dad, stayed until he'd had a chance to talk to Dr. Yee, and then headed up the side streets toward Pasadena, avoiding the freeways that were being earthquake retrofitted.

Wind overnight had blown away most of the smog, and the sky above the Rose Bowl was actually blue. Miles paid an outrageous six dollars to park in a vacant lot next to the Bowl, and when he got out of the climate-controlled car, he found that the outside air was cool and reasonably seasonal.

He walked through the gates toward the gigantic jumble of vendors, customers, and browsers that ringed the stadium. He felt like a real detective today, as though he was actually doing some investigating, and that, combined with the clean cool air, gave him a rare feeling of well-being.

He pushed through a wall of moms with strollers and

stopped in front of the first table. "Excuse me," he asked the hunched old man standing behind a display of glass milk bottles. "Do you know Liam Connor?"

The old man looked at him, through him, then turned away, not answering.

Miles resisted the temptation to knock one of the milk bottles to the ground and instead looked around the collection of dealers to see if there were any sellers of antique phonographs in this area. He figured vendors were probably grouped by category. Unfortunately, this section seemed to be mostly knickknacks, bottles and china, and he made his way through the crowd, glancing around as he headed down the east side of the Rose Bowl.

The placement of sellers followed no logical order, he discovered almost instantly. It was pure luck that the vendors near the entrance had exhibited similar wares, because as he moved deeper into the flea market, he saw furniture next to jewelry, vintage clothing next to farm implements. And the place was massive. It would probably take all day to find someone who knew Marina's father.

Still, he thought his idea of finding another seller of phonographs was a good one, and he walked up and down the aisles, looking for Victrolas or Amberolas or other types of old record players.

He passed a lot of tables covered with antique toys—apparently a hot trend among current collectors—and several of the so-called antiques were things he'd had as a child. He saw his old James Bond lunch pail selling for fifty dollars, his Hot Wheel Supercharger for thirty-five. He wandered past boxes of *Life* magazines, stacks of old Beatle albums. Next to an Aurora Wolfman model he saw a Fred Flintstone Pez dispenser. One of the small candies was pushed halfway out, and Fred's head was tilted slightly back, making it look as though his throat had been slit.

Miles looked away. Montgomery Jones' death the other

day had affected him more than he'd thought. Now he was even ascribing malevolent meaning to Pez dispensers.

Which reminded him that he should call Graham. He hadn't talked to the lawyer since leaving the crime scene, but the murder had somehow been kept out of the papers and off the TV news, and Miles wanted to know if that was Graham's doing or if Thompson had pulled some strings. He also wanted to know if the lawyer wanted him to pursue his investigation of the company or if everything was now in the hands of the police.

Miles kept walking. Ahead was a blanket spread on the ground atop which were old Victrola speaker horns. A heavily bearded, grossly overweight man with a long, greasy ponytail sat in a metal folding chair behind the blanket, polishing what looked like a miniature speaker horn.

"Excuse me," Miles said. The man looked up. "Do you know Liam Connor?"

"Liam? Sure. You want his card?"

"No, I want to ask you a few questions about him."

The man's expression shut down. What had been willing helpfulness became blank neutrality. "Sorry. Can't help you."

"I'm not a cop," Miles quickly explained. "I'm a private investigator. I've been hired by Mr. Connor's daughter to investigate a possible stalker. Mr. Connor has apparently been followed and harassed recently, and his daughter is worried. I was wondering if he'd talked to you about any of this or if he'd mentioned any enemies that he might have."

"Liam?" The man let out a loud, gruffly obnoxious laugh that caused most of the browsers nearby to look in his direction. "Liam doesn't have an enemy in this world!"

Miles smiled thinly. "Apparently he does."

The laughter died. "Seriously? Someone's stalking him?"

"We think so."

"Why? To . . . kill him?"

"That's what I'm trying to find out. If you could just tell me whether he's talked to you about—"

"Wait a minute. Why are you asking me what *he* talked about? Why don't you ask him?" The man looked at Miles suspiciously. "You're investigating *him*, aren't you?"

"No, I assure you, his daughter hired me—"

"His daughter's probably after his money or something." The man shook his head. "Nope. If Liam ain't talking, I ain't talking." He picked up the rag he'd placed on his lap and started polishing the small horn he'd been working on.

Miles knew better than to press the man, and he peeled off a card, dropped it on the blanket. "This is legit. Call Mr. Connor and ask him if you want. And if you think of something, give me a call."

The man just looked at him. He didn't reach down to pick up Miles' card, but he didn't tear it up either. Miles hoped that the man would keep it and change his mind.

Several other vendors knew Liam, and two of them were more than willing to talk, but neither of them seemed to have heard anything or noticed any unusual behavior on his part recently.

It was nearly three o'clock when Miles made his way dejectedly back out to the car. He knew no more now than he had when he'd first arrived. The whole day had been a waste, and he wanted to just go home and take a nap. But instead he stopped by the hospital, and he held his father's hand and listened to his unintelligible whispers and lied to the old man that everything was going to be all right.

3

Derek Baur woke up knowing that he would die today.

He'd dreamed the night before about Wolf Canyon, and in the dream the people in the water had been his family: his parents, his sister, his brothers. He hadn't thought of Wolf

Canyon for years, decades, and that should have tipped him off that there was something amiss, but the premonition was not so logical, was not tied to a story line or a series of images or a specific dream scape. It was not something he had been told, not something he had concluded or deducted.

He just knew.

And he was ready.

He'd turned eighty-six last March, and his wife, his friends, even his son, had all died years before. He was the last, and he had long since given up all pretense of interest in this life. There was no longer anything he enjoyed, nothing he looked forward to. Death was the only thing left.

How would it come? Derek wondered. Gently, in his sleep? Violently? Or somewhere in the middle, like a heart attack or stroke?

He had given a lot of thought to the subject, and he had concluded that there was no pleasant way to die. In his mid-fifties he had almost choked to death on a piece of steak in a restaurant, before Emily had pounded him on the back and dislodged the obstruction in his throat. Though the entire incident had lasted only a few seconds, to him it had felt interminable. Time was subjective, and he had realized ever since that while a death might be considered "quick" if measured objectively by the clock, to the victim it might seem to take forever.

So while he was ready to die, he did not relish the process.

He rolled over, pulled open the drape. Outside, the Michigan landscape was covered with snow. In the rest home's parking lot, the cars looked like a row of igloos more than motor vehicles.

He was still staring out the window when Jimmy, the new attendant, brought in his breakfast. And he had not moved by the time the attendant returned to collect the tray and untouched dishes a half hour later.

"Not hungry, Mr. Baur? I'm gonna have to report you, you know."

Derek did not even bother to respond.

Why eat when he was going to die?

He would be glad to put an end to this existence. He was not mistreated here, but he hated the rest home, hated the indignity of it and the cold feeling of having paid caretakers rather than family surrounding him.

At least he could still get around—even if it was with the aid of a walker. Plenty of other residents in the home, many younger than himself, could not even get out of bed, and were stuck full-time in their rooms.

He would have taken his life long ago if that had been his situation.

Of course, most of those people didn't have any way *to* take their own lives.

He spent the morning staring out at the snow. Sometime before noon one of the doctors came in to speak with him— apparently Jimmy had made good on the threat to report him—and since Derek was not in the mood for a lecture or lengthy discussion, he agreed with everything the doctor said and promised to eat his lunch. Jimmy returned soon after with a food tray, looking smug, and Derek ignored him. He ate his lunch and was once again silent as the attendant took the tray, leaving him alone. After a short, painful trip to the bathroom, Derek relocated himself to the room's chair and spent the afternoon looking through magazines. Waiting.

He wondered how it was going to come.

There was no doubt in his mind that he would die today. He was not a religious man, but he knew there were things in this world that he did not understand—

Wolf Canyon

—that he would never understand, and he trusted the knowledge that had been supplied to him. He waited for death to arrive.

But sleep arrived first, and as the magazine slipped from his fingers, as he felt himself beginning to drop off, he wondered if he was going to wake up again or if this was it.

He did wake up. He awoke from another Wolf Canyon dream, one in which he was trapped in a house as the waters rose, his feet stuck to the floor as if they had been set in cement, resisting his efforts to pull them free and escape. He jerked awake just as he was starting to swallow water and drown.

He opened his eyes to see Joe, the night attendant, standing in front of him with a dinner tray. "Sorry to disturb you, Mr. Baur, but it's suppertime. You want to eat here at your chair today?"

Derek nodded, not trusting himself to speak. He was surprised to be alive, and for the first time he questioned whether his premonition was correct. Maybe he wasn't going to die yet. Maybe his mind was just going.

He picked at his food, then pushed the tray aside and, after another trip to the bathroom, settled back into his bed, staring out at the snowy landscape until he fell asleep.

The room was black when he awoke—pitch-black, much darker than he had ever seen it—and he wondered for a moment if he had gone blind. The darkness was uniform, with no light anywhere, and only by reaching over to the nightstand, feeling for his watch, and pressing the button on the timepiece to illuminate the numbers, did he know he still possessed his sight.

He felt for the curtain, pulled it aside. He understood that the lights in the home were all off. But where were the lights outside? The streetlamps were out and the house across the road was dark. There was no moon. It was as if every possible source of illumination—save for his watch—had been extinguished.

Maybe there'd been a blackout.

A blackout. It made sense, but . . . but it didn't *feel* right.

He didn't understand why, but in the same way that he knew he was destined to die today, he knew that this darkness had been brought about for his benefit.

In fact, the two were related.

Yes, they were. How he didn't know, but he did know that the lights were off because of him, *for* him, and that his death would take place in the darkness.

For the first time he felt fear. He was afraid to die, he realized. He did not want to die. Not this way.

He pressed the buzzer next to his bed to call an attendant. He waited for what seemed like forever, pressing the buzzer several more times in the interim, but no attendant came. He did not even hear the sound of anyone in the hallway. The entire rest home was silent, and the lack of noise seemed ominous to him. Maybe death had come for them all tonight. Maybe everyone else in the building had been killed, and he was the last one left. Maybe the murderer was playing with him, toying with him, before coming in to slit his throat.

Derek sat up painfully. His muscles always seemed to be at their lowest ebb in the middle of the night. As usual, he'd laid his walker against the side of the bed, and he reached for it, bending awkwardly, trying to grab hold of the cold metal top bar. It took him several moments to find it, and by the time he did he was sweating—not just from exertion but from fear. Something was definitely wrong here, something was fundamentally off. There was no sound in the room, in the building, save his own labored breathing, and there was still no light either inside or outside the rest home.

He'd changed his mind. He was *positive* he did not want to die. And while there might be no pleasant way to go, some ways were definitely worse than others. Much, much worse.

He could still see nothing, but there was a sense of movement in the blackness, and he knew with a certainty he could not explain that he was not alone in the room, that there was something in here with him.

Something not human.

There was another sound now besides his breathing—the hiss of piss as he peed his pants in terror. He threw himself out of bed, the walker clutched tightly, and headed toward where he knew the door had to be. He expected at any moment to feel a clawed hand on his shoulder, but he concentrated on moving, walking, getting out of here, not allowing himself to dwell on the other possible outcomes of this situation. He wanted to cry out for help, but he was not sure there was any help to be had, and he was hoping that this darkness was just as disorienting to whatever was after him.

His walker hit a barrier, the wall, and Derek reached out to touch, feeling to the left and to the right until he found a crack, a hinge, and, finally, a knob.

He grasped the knob, turned it.

Or tried to.

The door was locked.

From the outside.

Was that something that was done every night? He didn't think so, but he wasn't sure. The only thing he was sure of was that he was now trapped in here with whatever was trying to kill him.

There was a . . . a *slumping* sound, the noise of something large moving forward through the room, forcing its weight across the floor toward him.

He wished to God the room had remained silent. He didn't want to think about what kind of form went with that sound. He wanted only to find a way to escape, a way to get out of here before—

The bathroom!

Yes! If he could make it to the bathroom without being caught, he could lock himself in until morning. Maybe the monster could break down the door, but his chances were better in there than they were out here.

The monster?

He had no problem with that word.

The bathroom was to the right, and he started toward it. He did not have to face forward as he moved—his walker met obstructions before he did—so he kept swiveling his head around, looking from one section of the room to the other. The darkness was still almost total, but his eyes seemed to be adjusting to the lack of light because there was an area now less black than the room around it, a rounded, shapeless mass that drew ever closer to him and looked somehow as though it was made out of ice.

His heart was pounding loud enough to drown out that horrible slumping sound. He tried to hurry but—

Damn this walker!

—was not able to move any faster than he did ordinarily. His old bones and feeble muscles were unwilling to grant him any favors even in this time of crisis.

His walker hit the wall. He looked forward, and was promptly grabbed from behind.

This is it, he thought.

The hand that covered his mouth was cold, freezing cold, and hard.

Ice.

He thought of Wolf Canyon.

Ice, it occurred to him, was made of water.

And then the cold hand forced itself into his mouth and down his throat.

Then

1

These were bad times, especially for his kind.

It was almost as if the old days had returned.

William talked to the wolves as he traveled, and the ravens. They told him of burnings and hangings that were occurring on an almost regular basis in the scattered settlements of the territories. The stories chilled him. He would have been better off having been born into one of the Indian tribes, where his powers and abilities would be, if not understood, at least respected and appreciated. But he was white-skinned, and as such was fated to live within the world of the fair, that irrationally rational culture that believed only in one unseen, uninvolved God and attributed anything even remotely supernatural to the work of Satan.

He traveled by day, slept at night, and tried to ignore the horrible sounds he heard in the darkness, the moans and wails that came from no man, no animal, no wind but seemed to emanate from the land itself. There were Bad Places in the territories, places where neither white man nor Indian had settled, where even animals would not live. He passed through these on his way from one temporary home to another, and there was a voice in the Bad Places that spoke to him, a uniform voice that was the same in the Dakotas as it was in Wyoming, a voice he found at once tempting and terrifying, a seductive presence that pleaded with him to give up his sense of self, to abandon his small meaningless life and become one with the land.

He did not stay long in one place, not after what he'd done to Jane Stevens' father back in Sycamore. He thought of his mother and remembered how difficult life had been for him as a child, but if anything, settlements in the West were less tolerant than the more sophisticated and civilized cities of the East. The people here were less modern, less educated, filled with the superstitious dread that had afflicted their forefathers, indiscriminately afraid of anything they did not understand.

So he kept moving, living in Deadwood, in Cheyenne, in Colorado Springs, staying just long enough to make some money and load up on supplies, not long enough to arouse suspicion. He tried to stick to trading and trapping and other respectable ways of making a living, but somehow someone would always find out who he was, what he could do, and he'd end up helping them out.

These days he always left immediately after that.

He was by nature and necessity a solitary man, used to being alone. He was also, like his mother before him, familiar with forces unseen. But often, as he traveled across the great expanses, he was afraid. Moving through this vast country, he realized how small and insignificant he was, how puny and limited was his power, his gift. A heavy, brooding untapped energy lay beneath the surface of this rugged country. It ran in continuous currents beneath his feet, in veins the size of rivers. It hung thick in the oppressive silence of the windless air. He could sense it in the huge dark mountains that hunkered waiting on the horizon, in the thick stands of ancient trees, which were home to far more than animals. And the Bad Places . . .

They scared him.

He'd been traveling west now for over a month, nearly

losing himself in the mountains, coming through only with the help of the ravens. His supplies were almost gone, but he had some pelts he could trade, and he found a trail through the foothills that connected to a wagon-rutted road on the plain. He followed the setting sun, and on his first night on the plain he could see, maybe one or two days ahead, the small twinkling lights of what looked like a fairly large town.

He felt nothing beneath his feet, heard no voices, and he slept peacefully next to his untethered horse, not waking up until dawn.

The town was neither as far away as it looked nor as big as he'd hoped, and William knew by mid-morning that he'd reach it some time in the early afternoon. The knowledge did not excite him as much as it should have, however, and he did not know whether his trepidation came from a legitimate premonition or merely reflected his disappointment at not finding a bigger settlement after all this time alone.

The sun was straight up when he reached the graveyard.

The witch graveyard.

It was several miles away from the town, out of sight of even a rooftop or flagpole, far away from the regular cemetery. It had not been fenced and had no headstones to mark the grave sites—witches did not deserve such amenities—but it was clearly a burial tract. Rectangular indentations in the barren soil, sunken from the packing of weather, identified the individual plots. A rusty pick and broken-handled shovel were embedded in the hard ground next to what was obviously the most recent grave.

William stopped his horse. No weeds grew within the graveyard, he noticed. Nothing grew. The desert bushes and cactus that rimmed the periphery of the spot were all dead and had turned a peculiar orangish brown.

From the branch of a lifeless tree nearby hung the frayed end of a thick rope.

"Bastards," William said to himself.

He dismounted, leaving his horse to graze among the low clumps of pale weeds that grew next to the wagon trail. He could feel the power here. Not the wild power of the land, but a familiar pleasant tingle in the air that he recognized as the energy of fellow witches.

The energy was dead, though. It was like the lingering smell of a campfire that remained in the air long after the flames had been put out, and he felt an odd sadness settle over him even as he enjoyed the warm, stimulating aura.

He walked slowly past the unmarked graves, the intentionally anonymous resting places of men and women who had once been vibrant individuals, who had been no more good or evil than the general population, but who had been condemned to death because they possessed abilities that most people were too frightened to even try and understand. It was happening all over, this killing of their kind, and if it continued, soon there would be none of them left. They would be exterminated in America just as they had been exterminated in Europe.

He stared down at a recent grave, one that still retained a slightly raised rectangular outline. Was this to be his fate as well? Did his future lie in an unmarked grave in a cursed and segregated graveyard? It was what had happened to his mother. He did not even know where she was buried. No one had ever told him.

He took off his hat, wiped the sweat from his forehead. What kind of life was this? He stared up at the cloudless sky.

Why had he been born a witch?

It was the same question he always asked himself, and as always, he had no answer.

He put his hat back on and walked over to his horse. Taking the reins, he grabbed the horn and pulled himself onto the saddle.

As if the graveyard had not been enough of a deterrent, there was an explicit warning posted on a leaning sign next to the road leading toward town:

WITCHES WILL BE EXECUTED

William stopped the horse, looked at the sign, then glanced ahead, but the ramshackle huts that marked the outskirts of the settlement several miles down the road were obscured by watery heat waves stretching across the length of the plain.

He wondered how long the sign had been in place, how many had ignored its warning, its promise, and continued on regardless.

What they needed, he thought, was someplace of their own, land in which they were in charge and they made the rules, somewhere away from everything else where they could live in peace and be free from persecution.

It sounded like a fantasy, a dream, but he'd heard that the Mormons were making for themselves just such a place, that their prophet had led them across the desert sands to a special spot their God had picked out for them, a place where they could live among their own kind and be free to practice their own ways.

His people could do the same. Such an idea was not inconceivable.

But they were so hard to find these days. The ones who had not been killed had gone into hiding, fleeing like himself into the wilderness or keeping secret their true natures amid the normal residents of their communities.

He looked again at the sign—

WITCHES WILL BE EXECUTED

—then bade his horse turn around. He was getting no concrete feelings from up ahead, but the graveyard and the sign were warning enough, and even without a definite reading he could tell that this was one town he did not want to visit.

He would return to the foothills and then travel south through them until he was far enough away from this nameless community to once again head west. He would trade his pelts elsewhere, in a bigger settlement, one where he would be less likely to be noticed.

Just in case, he cloaked himself in a protective spell, then pushed his horse into galloping back toward the hills.

Now

1

Muzak carols over hard-to-hear speakers. Decorations that were nothing more than products sold inside the stores they adorned. A skinny Hispanic Santa Claus kids could meet only if their parents paid to have their picture taken with him.

Miles stood unmoving in the center of the jostling crowd. Christmas seemed cheap and depressingly pointless to him this year, its practitioners yuppified and smugly materialistic. Ordinarily, he rejoiced in the trappings of the season, but all of the joy had gone out of it for him. It reminded him of Halloween, a grassroots celebration that had been turned into a buying contest by the newly affluent.

He was at the mall to purchase presents, but he realized that he didn't really have any presents to buy. A few small tokens for people at the office, gifts for his sister and her family. That was it. He had no wife, no girlfriend, no significant other, and though he usually celebrated the holiday with his dad, there was a distinct possibility that his father might not even be here come Christmas day.

Happy holidays.

Miles sat down heavily on a bench in front of Sears, feeling as if a great weight had been placed upon his shoulders. He understood now why people buried themselves in their work. It kept them from having to deal with the depressing realities of their lives.

Claire had never been one to look back, to dwell on past

mistakes. She had told him once that life was a ride and all you could do was hold on, face forward, and see it out to the end. It was too painful looking at where you'd been or where you were. The best thing to do was hang on and enjoy the next curve, the next hill, the next drop, the next . . . anything.

He found himself wondering if she still adhered to that philosophy. Did that mean that she never thought about him, never had any memories, good or bad, of their marriage, of the time they'd spent together?

The thought depressed the hell out of him.

Feeling empty, feeling numb, he stared blankly into the crowd of holiday shoppers. The people he saw were almost indistinguishable in their happiness, and he envied them.

He leaned back on the bench against the brick wall of Sears, looking at the rush of people. Gradually, one face began to differentiate itself from the rest, a wrinkled old lady's visage that drew his attention because her gaze remained fully, unwaveringly focused on him.

Miles blinked, caught off guard.

The woman broke from the rest of the crowd, heading straight over to his bench.

He shivered involuntarily, a slight chill passing through him as his eyes met hers. There was something wrong here. As a private investigator, he dealt in facts. He didn't believe in intuition or ESP or anything he couldn't see, hear, or record. But the apprehension he felt was not the result of conscious thought or decision. It was visceral and instinctive.

The old lady stood before him, dressed in clothes that did not match. "Bob!" she said, grinning broadly.

The effect was unnerving. That huge smile seemed incongruous on the small wrinkled face. It reminded him of something in his childhood, something he could not remember but that he knew had frightened him, and again a chill passed through his body.

"Bob!"

He forced himself to look at the old lady. "I'm sorry," he said. "You have me confused with someone else."

"Bob Huerdeen!"

The hair prickled on the back of his neck. This was too weird.

"Who are you?" he asked.

"It's me, Bob! You know me!"

"I don't know you and I'm not Bob." He took a deep breath, decided to admit it. "I'm Bob's son, Miles."

She leaned forward conspiratorily, pressing her ancient face almost against his. He smelled medicine and mouthwash. "She's going after the dam builders, too, Bob. Not just us." She backed away, nodding to herself, still grinning though the edges of the smile were starting to fade.

The old lady was crazy. Either senile or schizo. She had obviously known his father at some point, and she had enough brain cells left to be able to spot the family resemblance, but other than that, she was off the deep end.

He stood, hoping he'd be able to make excuses and just walk away, but prepared to confront her if necessary. "I'm sorry," he said. "I have to go."

She reached out, grabbed the sleeve of his jacket. "It's not just us, Bob! It's the dam builders, too!"

"I know," he said politely. "But I really do have to go."

"Don't let her catch you, Bob! Don't let her catch you!"

"I won't," he promised, pulling away.

He thought she'd pursue him, badgering him all the way about her crazy concerns, but she let him go, remained standing in front of the Sears bench, and he hurried toward the mall exit, more rattled by the old lady than he wanted to admit.

* * *

Darkness.

Low whispers.

Miles held his breath, listened. He had only awakened because he'd drunk too much tonight and desperately had to take a leak. Ordinarily, he slept straight through until morning. He'd even slept through two major earthquakes. But tonight his bladder had woken him up, and he had heard the sound of breathy, hushed voices in the otherwise silent house.

Again, low whispers.

He still felt a little light-headed—the effects of the alcohol had not entirely worn off—and at first he thought he'd imagined the sounds. But when he sat up and concentrated and could still hear them, he started to think that he was not alone.

He could not make out what was being said, but he thought he heard his father's name in the whispers, and for some reason that made him think of the old lady in the mall.

He got quickly out of bed, turned on the light, threw open his bedroom door.

Silence.

He stood there for a moment, listening, unmoving. Whatever had been there was now gone, and he waited another minute or two before deciding that he'd been right the first time and had imagined the sounds. God knows, he'd drunk enough last night to induce hallucinations. That and the stress would make anyone start hearing voices.

He walked down the hall to the bathroom.

His father was coming home tomorrow . . . today. Audra had prepared the bedroom for him, had helped install the new bed and other medical amenities, and she'd be meeting them both at the hospital, coming home with them to help his dad get settled in. Bob was better. He'd definitely improved since those first few days, and he was actually able to talk now, though his speech was still somewhat unclear.

But he wasn't well, and despite Audra's cheery promises, Miles knew he never would be again. This was the best he was ever going to be. Most likely, he would have a series of increasingly debilitating strokes over the next year or two before all of the shocks to his system finally wore his body out completely.

Miles examined his face in the bathroom mirror as he took a piss. He looked tired and haggard. Granted, it was after midnight, but the toll taken on his appearance was not one of sleep deprivation. It was stress, pure and simple. He found himself wondering if he would have to set his alarm from now on in order to check on his dad in the middle of the night. Maybe he'd even have to wake up and give his father some sort of medication at strange ungodly hours. No matter what, he had the feeling he wouldn't be getting a full night's sleep from now on.

It would have been easier if Bob had died instantly.

He felt guilty for even having such a thought, selfish for putting his own concerns above the well-being of his father, but this late at night he was incapable of lying to himself, and he had to admit that he dreaded the prospect of taking care of an invalid.

He flushed the toilet, walked back down the hall to the bedroom.

He figured he'd lay awake all night, tossing and turning, unable to stop the flood of negative scenarios in his brain, but he was asleep almost before his head hit the pillow.

In the second before he succumbed, he thought he heard the whispers again.

He thought he heard his father's name.

Miles was awakened by the alarm, and he followed his usual routine: showering and shaving before going out to the kitchen and making his breakfast.

His plan was to work in the morning and take the afternoon off. He'd been taking a lot of time off lately, and while the agency was pretty lenient and understanding, he felt guilty. Of course, he had never used a sick day in all the time he'd worked there, so these absences were long overdue; but he felt bad about it nonetheless.

It was cold and foggy out, and as he ate a breakfast of toast and coffee and watched the morning news, the traffic reporter identified accidents and Sig alerts on the 5, 10, and 710 freeways. He decided to take surface streets to the office, and he ate more quickly than usual, wanting to give himself an extra fifteen minutes.

The car was covered with condensation, and he threw the briefcase in the car and washed the vehicle's windows off with the hose. In Anaheim, where he'd grown up, foggy mornings had always smelled of stewed tomatoes from the Hunt factory in adjacent Fullerton. Although ordinarily there was no odor, fog seemed to draw out the scent and disperse it. Now, even after all these years, every time he saw fog and did not smell tomatoes, he could not help thinking that there was something wrong.

Everyone else must have seen the same traffic report he had because the streets were crowded, and even with the lead time he was nearly twenty minutes late for work.

Hal chided him for showing up at all. "I used to think you were just a workaholic. Now I know you're a souless automaton. What kind of lunatic would come into the office on the day his dad was being released from the hospital after having a major stroke?"

"Me," Miles told him.

"That's sad, bud. That's really sad."

The truth was, he should have stayed home. He had a lot of things to do here, but he got none of them done. He found it nearly impossible to concentrate on anything work-related, and he ended up staring out the window at the fog.

Hal left the office for an hour or so, and while he was

gone, Naomi came over to tell him that no one would care if he took off.

Miles gave her a grateful smile. "I'm fine."

She shook her head, rushing quickly back to her desk to answer a ringing phone. "Stubborn," she said. "You are so stubborn."

When Hal returned, Miles was again staring absently out at the fog.

"You still here?" he said. "I thought Naomi was going to tell you to go home."

"She did."

Hal snorted. "Typical."

Miles examined the pencil he was twirling in his fingers. "Do you believe in the supernatural?"

Though he did not look over at Hal, he could feel the bearded man's scowl. "What are you talking about? You mean, like ghosts and demons and crap?"

"Yeah." He continued to look at the pencil. "You've been in this business a long time. Haven't you ever come across something you didn't understand or couldn't explain?"

"Why? What happened?"

"Nothing. I'm just wondering."

"You're not just wondering. What is it?"

Miles put the pencil down, looked over at his friend. "All right, it's my dad. Ever since he had that stroke he's been . . . different."

"Well, of course—"

"No, it's not that. It's something else. It's like . . . I don't know. Sometimes it just seems like he's a different person. He looks like my dad and he sounds like my dad, but every once in a while we'll be talking and something will change. I don't know how to put it any better than that. Something shifts. It's nothing concrete, nothing specific, but I just *feel* something."

"Sounds like you're the one with the problem, not him."

Miles sighed. "Maybe so . . . maybe so. Last night I could have sworn I heard voices in the house. Whispering voices. And they were saying my dad's name."

"Voices like what? Like ghosts?"

Miles shrugged. "I guess."

"You are going off the deep end."

"I'm probably just afraid of my dad coming home. It was all right, him being in the hospital. That's where you're supposed to be if you're sick. But now he'll be home, where he used to be when he was well, and he'll still be sick. I think I'm just freaked about those two worlds colliding."

"That's why you're here today?"

"Probably."

"You know, I used to wonder what would happen if my wife got a brain tumor."

Miles smiled wryly. "You've always been a barrel of fun."

"I'm serious. What if she lived but it changed her personality, made her into a completely different person? Would I still love her?"

"A *shallow* barrel of fun."

"No. Because I'm not sure if I love her personality, the person I know, the person she is now, or if I love some nebulous spirit that is her true essence, something unique that would still be there even if her personality did a complete one-eighty. You know what I mean? It's a question of faith, I guess. Do I think she's just a sum of her experiences and genetics and the chemicals that determine her behavior, and it's that surface woman I love, or do I think she has a soul? Is it that soul I love? Do you see what I'm getting at?"

Miles nodded, sighed. "I'm afraid I do."

Hal walked over, clapped him on the back. "Don't worry, bud. You can hack it."

"I just wish I didn't have to."

Hal headed off to the break room, and Miles leaned back in his chair, staring up at the acoustic tiled ceiling. He had not admitted it to himself until he'd said it, but there *was* something different about his dad these days, something that try as he might he could not attribute to the stroke.

The phone on his desk rang, and Miles picked it up. "Hello?"

"Mr. Huerdeen?" It was Marina Lewis.

"I told you, Miles."

"I need you to come over to my father's house," she said. "Now."

There was an urgency in her voice he hadn't heard before, a tightness that sounded like barely controlled panic. "What is it?" he asked, though he knew she was not going to answer.

"I don't want to talk over the phone."

"I'll be right there."

"Do you need the address?"

"I have it. Give me twenty minutes."

He opened his lower desk drawer, grabbed his mini-tape recorder, threw it into his briefcase along with an extra notebook. He checked the clock. Ten-fifteen. His dad wasn't scheduled to be released until two. He should have plenty of time.

"I won't be back," he told Naomi. "Anything important, leave a message."

She smiled softly at him. "Good luck, Miles. I hope your father's okay."

All the way to Santa Monica, he wondered what it was that Marina couldn't tell him over the phone. She'd sounded freaked, as though she'd discovered something she hadn't been prepared for and didn't want to deal with.

Liam Connor lived in an older neighborhood of single-family Spanish-style homes with white stucco walls and red tile roofs. The lawns were all neatly mowed and nicely manicured, and the juxtaposition of the elderly residents' boat-like Buicks and dusty Pontiacs with their younger neighbors' well-polished Mercedes Benzes and BMWs made it clear that this was a street on the rise.

Marina and a young man Miles assumed to be her husband walked out as he pulled into the driveway. They'd obviously been waiting for him, and they reached his car before he finished opening the door.

Marina tried to smile. "Thank you for coming out Mr. . . . uh, Miles."

He nodded at her, smiled politely at the man.

"Gordon," the man said. "I'm Marina's husband."

Miles glanced toward the house. "Is your father here?" he asked.

Marina and her husband shared a glance.

He caught it, and his antennae immediately went up. "Did something happen to him?"

Marina shook her head. "No. Nothing like that."

"What is it, then? What couldn't you tell me over the phone?"

"It's . . . it's something he did. Something he wrote. We have to show you." The two of them started across the lawn toward the house.

Miles followed. "Is your father here?" he asked again.

"He's in his room," Gordon said. "He . . . he doesn't want to see you."

They walked inside. The interior of the house was hipper than Miles had expected. Instead of framed family photographs and reproductions of generic landscape paintings in the living room, there was an original abstract expressionist painting on one wall, a grouping of antique western memorabilia on another. The furniture was low and modern, and there was an enormous large-screen TV. The hardwood floor gleamed to perfection.

"I still don't understand why your father won't cooperate with this investigation. You said he felt threatened. He even went to the police. How did he go from that point to being totally uninterested in finding whoever's harassing him?"

"I don't understand it either," Marina admitted. "But . . ." she trailed off.

"But what?" he prodded.

"But you have to see what he wrote."

She and Gordon led him into what looked like a den or office: a small cramped room filled with overflowing shelves and boxes piled atop a worktable, everything dominated by a massive old-fashioned rolltop desk.

"It's there," Gordon said, pointing.

Miles walked over to the desk. On top of a manual type-writer was what looked like handwritten notes on a yellow legal pad.

"What do you make of it?"

The note was a list of names Liam had obviously drawn up. Miles picked up the pad and quickly scanned the list.

His gaze locked on a name in the middle, his pulse rac-ing.

Montgomery Jones.

He turned toward Marina and her husband. "What is this?"

Marina faced him, looking pale. "That's what we want to know."

"Did you ask your father about it?"

"He won't talk." She took a deep breath. "I recognized that one guy's name, the one who was killed, and that's why I called you. Gordon and I thought that there might be some connection between the woman or whoever's stalking Dad and the person who killed that man."

"Do you think we should go to the police?" Gordon asked.

"Definitely," Miles said. "But don't get your hopes up. It can't hurt to let them know, put them on alert, but they prob-ably won't do anything. In the meantime, I'll try to track down the names on this list. Obviously, your father knows of some connection between all these people. He seems to think he knows why this other man was killed and why he's being stalked—"

"But he won't tell."

"Then, you need to try and get him to tell. He might not be the only one in danger here. These others might be at risk as well. Tell him that by not cooperating, he may cost some of these people their lives."

"We'll try," Gordon promised.

"But he's stubborn."

Miles looked at the list again, frowned. He thought Graham had kept all mention of Montgomery Jones' death out of the press. He turned toward Marina. "You said you saw his name in the paper?"

"No. On TV. *Extra*."

Extra? Graham had kept news of the killing out of the legitimate media, but it had made its way onto tabloid television?

"I remembered his name because I couldn't forget the way he died." She shivered. "Filled up with ice and drowned? What a horrible way to go."

"Filled up with ice and drowned? What are you talking about?" Something suddenly occurred to him. He cocked his head. "*Who* are you talking about?"

"Derek Baur."

Derek Baur?

There were two of them.

Miles felt his pulse rate accelerate again. "Another man on this list, Montgomery Jones, was also killed recently. Torn in half. Up by the Whittier Narrows dam."

Marina looked at her husband, all of the color draining from her face.

"I don't know what's happening or what this is all about, but I suggest you get your father out here so we can try to talk some sense into him."

She nodded and hurried off down the hall.

"Can I take this to photocopy?" Miles asked Gordon. "I'll give it back to you."

"Take it and keep it."

"You'll need it to show the police."

Gordon nodded. "Yeah," he said. "Okay." He ran a hand through his hair. "Jesus."

"We'll get to the bottom of this," Miles promised.

Gordon looked as though he was about to say something, but at that moment Marina pulled Liam into the room. She faced Miles. "Tell him!" she demanded, pointing at her father. "He won't listen to me. Maybe he'll listen to you."

"Two of the men on this list are dead," Miles said. "One, Montgomery Jones, was torn in half over in Whittier. I saw the body. I was there. The other man, Derek Baur—"

"In Michigan," Marina said.

"—was somehow filled with ice and drowned. If you know anything about either of these deaths, you'd better speak up because you and the other people on that list may be in danger, too."

Liam shook his head.

"Damn it, Dad!"

"Well, you obviously know of something that all of these people have in common. There's *some* reason you put them on this list. If you could just tell us—"

"No."

He was surprised by the vehemence of the old man's response. It was impossible, he knew, and it made no sense, but Liam was acting guilty, as though he were in some way responsible for the deaths.

Miles spoke to him as though addressing a small child. "Your daughter hired me to find out who has been harassing you, who has been stalking you. I'll find out with or without your assistance, but your help would be greatly appreciated. It would also be in your own best interest since you are the subject of this harassment. It also appears that your life is in danger. I have agreed that your daughter and son-in-law should go to the police with this list—"

"No!" He glared at Marina. "You have no right!"

She was practically in tears. "Stop being so stubborn!" she screamed at him. "This is your life we're talking about!"

"Yes!" he shouted back. "*My* life!"

Miles backed off, staying out of it. Marina and her father yelled at each other for several more minutes before he finally stalked off. A door slammed down the hall.

Marina ran out of the room crying.

"I'll find a copy shop, make a quick Xerox, and bring this back," Miles told Gordon. "After that, I'll try to track these people down. You go to the police."

Gordon nodded.

"I have some personal business to attend to this afternoon, but I'll give you a call later this evening and we'll see where we stand."

"Thanks," Gordon said.

Miles offered him a wry smile. "That's what I get paid for."

He drove off, found a Sav-On Drugstore, made an overpriced 25-cent copy of the list, and brought it back. Marina, who was now settled and sipping coffee in the kitchen, looked at him before he left, her eyes still red. "I'm sorry about my father," she said. "He's just so stubborn. Maybe he'll break down a little later."

But she was wrong, Miles thought, driving home. He'd gotten a look at the old man's face when he'd described to him the deaths of the two men.

Her father wasn't stubborn.

He was scared.

2

The kids were gone, off to a lunch meeting with Gordon's agent, and Liam made sure there was no one waiting for him outside, made sure the street was free of unknown vehicles and pedestrians, before venturing out of the house. He'd promised Marina he wouldn't leave the yard, but he'd broken a lot of promises lately, and the more he broke the easier it was to do.

There'd been six calls last night. It was the same woman, and though he knew he'd never heard her voice before, he could not shake the feeling that he knew who she was. Or that he should. Her identity bugged him, and he'd lain awake long after he'd finally taken the phone off the hook, trying to figure out where he should know her from and why.

Her last call, at midnight, had been the worst. "I'll pull your cock out through your asshole," she'd said, and for some reason her voice at that moment had reminded him of his mother's.

He'd given up nothing to either that obnoxious private dick—and the word served double duty here—or the police detective who came by later. They'd tried to crack him, and Marina had jumped all over him, yelling, crying, using every piece of emotional artillery at her disposal, but he had refused to cooperate. He didn't know what was happening, but he knew it was connected with the dam, with the town, and what had happened all those years ago in Arizona.

That was why he didn't want any cops or detectives poking their noses into this.

That was why he wanted Marina kept completely out of it.

Liam walked down the street toward Pacific Coast Highway and the beach. He desperately needed a smoke, but needed to buy a pack of cigarettes. For the past twenty years Marina had bought into the lie that he'd quit smoking—just as her mother had—and he did not want her to find out that he hadn't. So he'd waited until she was out of the house. The liquor store was only a few blocks away, on PCH, and he'd be able to walk there, have a leisurely smoke, and walk back before Marina and Gordon even reached their restaurant. Hell, he could probably sneak a few backyard puffs after his own lunch and have time to rinse his mouth out with Listerine before they returned.

As usual, the coast highway was crowded. Cars were zooming by almost too quickly to see, and even though it was December and chilly, the beach was crowded with wet-suited surfers and narcissistic bodybuilders. On this side of the highway, the typical assortment of the drunk and the displaced, the homeless and the unemployed, were sitting on broken benches or lying on dead grass in the unmaintained lot that was supposed to be a park.

Liam walked past the park, past Bunny's Bar, past the alley, to the entrance of the liquor store. He bought a pack of Marlboro Lites, took one of the books of free matches from the open box next to the register, and lit up as soon as he stepped outside.

He breathed deeply, inhaled. The sun on his face, warm smoke in his lungs ... it didn't get any better than this.

He looked up, exhaled into the air.

And tilted his head down to see a squat dirty woman wearing several layers of filthy ragged clothes standing directly before him.

It was as if she'd appeared out of nowhere, and only the calming influence of the cigarette kept him from visibly reacting. Though he'd never seen the woman before, there was an expression of familiarity on her face, something that made him think she had been looking for him, and he felt the first faint stirrings of fear in his chest.

He looked around, muscles tensing as he tried to spot anyone suspicious on the sidewalk or in the storefronts.

The woman pointed an accusatory finger at him. "How many were there?" she demanded.

He shook his head.

"How many were there?"

"I don't know what you're talking about," Liam said, backing away. But he did. She'd come out of the blue, her words apropos of nothing, yet he understood to what she was referring and it frightened him to the bone.

He should have listened to his daughter.

He never should have left the house.

He walked around the woman, back the way he'd come. Ahead in the park he could see several raggedy men looking in his direction, waiting for him to approach. There was something threatening in the way they stood, and he turned up the alley, deciding to take a long cut home. He wasn't sure what was happening, but once again he thought of the dam, the town, and he found himself hurrying between the buildings, anxious to get away from these homeless people.

Halfway up the alley, he almost tripped over a bum's legs sticking out from behind a trash dumpster. He stopped short, and the bum looked up at him, smiling with brown tobacco-stained teeth. "Wolf Canyon," he rasped.

Liam tossed his cigarette and started running. His heart was pounding, and right now he wanted only to get home. A dark shape lurched at him from the back entrance of an apartment complex, and he had time to register that it was probably female before his feet were carrying him up the alley and past the ill-kept backyard of an old house that had been converted into a beauty salon.

He heard shouts, running footsteps, and he glanced over his shoulder as he ran. Five or six homeless people were following him now, and though his lungs were hurting from lack of breath and it felt as though his heart was going to attack him, he increased his speed. He was embarrassed, ashamed of his fear and cowardice, but he knew his feelings were legitimate. What was going on here made no sense on any rational level, but made perfect sense in the fun house universe in which he'd found himself since receiving that first threatening phone call.

The increasingly loud sounds of footfalls made him speed up yet again. His muscles were straining, and he knew he could not keep this up for any length of time. He burst out of the alley and onto a residential street, the street next to his own, and that gave him an extra burst of energy.

He did not stop or slow down to see if he was still being followed. Though he knew how ridiculous he must look, he ran with all his might, wheezing and panting past well-manicured lawns and spotless driveways toward the end of the block. He did not know why he was being chased or how these street people were connected to the dam, to the town, to what had happened, but he accepted that they were. He was not one to dismiss things that weren't supposed to be able to happen—not after all he'd seen.

He reached his street, reached his house. Dashing up the walk, he finally allowed himself a quick look behind him. As he'd half expected, no one was following. They'd either given up, or he'd lost or outrun them. He exhaled deeply, an honest-to-God sigh of relief.

Then an extraordinarily tall man wearing a torn T-shirt and woolen earmuffs rounded the far corner onto the street, and Liam ducked quickly inside the house, heart pounding.

Wolf Canyon.

He locked the door and leaned against it, trembling. The phone rang a second later, making him jump, but he made no effort to answer it, and though he stopped counting at fifty, the ringing continued on.

Then

1

Jeb Freeman bedded down for the night in a ravine.

He'd been traveling all day, stopping only for two short rests, heading south as he had been for the past week. His feet hurt. Sam, his mount, had died two days ago, and Jeb had been walking ever since, carrying his own bedroll and saddlebag. He'd been hoping to make it as far as the mountains by nightfall, but the terrain was rougher than he'd expected, and it became clear near sundown that he would not reach his goal today. He would have preferred to remain up top, to not have to waste time hiking down into the ravine and back up again tomorrow morning, but the winds here were fierce at night, and since he no longer had a tent, the only way to stay out of them was to stay below them.

There were a few dead branches on the rocky sandy floor, swept there by the last flash flood, and he gathered them up. He made a circle of stones, then placed half of the branches inside, dumping the other half a few feet away. He laid out his bedroll. A hard piece of almost unchewable salt pork was his supper, and he washed it down with a single sip of warm water from his canteen.

Nightfall lingered up on top, but it came swift and sure in the ravines, and his camp was swathed in darkness even as the western sky above remained orange.

There was no sound but the birthing winds above, no scuttle of rats, no cawing of birds, no noise from anything alive. Not only were there no people in this forsaken country, there were not even any animals.

Crouching down, he sprinkled a pinch of bone dust on the branches, dramatically waved his hand over them, and spoke a few words. The fire started.

He sighed. Reduced to performing parlor tricks without an audience.

He made the fire turn blue, then green, but it did not dispel the melancholy that had come over him. He had always been something of a loner, but he had never really been alone before. Not truly alone. If he had not always had living companions, he had always been able to communicate with dead ones, to conjure up the spirits of those who had passed on, to discuss his life with those who had finished theirs.

But here he was too far out. No people had lived here, no people had died here. He could communicate with no one. He was all by himself.

He stared into the rainbow-colored fire, surrounded by silence.

Eventually, he went to sleep.

Above the ravine, the night wind howled.

He met William the next day.

Jeb felt him before he saw him, sensed his presence, and he was filled with a grateful anticipation that was almost joy. He could not remember the last conversation he'd had, and it had been weeks since he'd even seen another human being.

And this man was one of his own.

Jeb continued south, his pace swifter than it had been since Sam's death. The land here was raw and hard and open, not blunted and covered and soft like the land in the East. It was what made the west frightening. And exciting.

The world here seemed to go on forever, and only the lack of companionship had kept it from being a paradise.

A person was dwarfed by this landscape, but Jeb did not need to see the man to know where he was. He could *feel* him, and when he sensed that the man had stopped, was waiting for him to catch up, Jeb increased his speed even more, practically running across the flat ground toward the mountains.

He found the man sitting underneath a low tree at the mouth of a canyon, his horse drinking from a muddy pool. The man stood, shook the dust off his clothes, and walked forward, hand extended. "Glad to finally meet you," he said. "I'm William. William Johnson. I'm a witch."

William, it turned out, had been aware of his presence for days, and Jeb chose to think that it was because his own skills were rusty, because he hadn't been using them lately, that he had not been aware of William until he was practically upon him.

He had met other witches before, but in towns, in cities, and there'd always been a sort of implied acknowledgment of their kinship, a tacit understanding that they recognized each other but were not going to consort with each other so that no suspicions would be raised.

But out here they were all alone, with no one else around for hundreds of miles, and he and William were able to speak openly about things that had always before been only hinted about or left unsaid. It was a strange and unsettling experience, and at first Jeb was wary about saying too much, being too explicit, for fear that William was trying to trick him into revealing incriminating details about himself, trap him into giving away secrets. He knew intellectually that that was not the case—William was a witch just like himself—but the emotional prohibitions were still there, and only after his new companion had told his story, had revealed far more than Jeb would have ever dreamed of sharing with a stranger, did Jeb feel comfortable enough to relax and really talk.

They had a lot in common. William had traveled throughout the territories, living for a time in various settlements, keeping to himself when he could, providing help when asked. He'd removed unwanted pregnancies, performed small healings, made the infertile fertile. And he'd been punished for it: harassed, attacked, exiled.

Much as Jeb had himself.

They'd both tried their best to fit in, and had both been found out every time, persecuted for their natures, for who they were and could not help being, by the intolerant men and women who claimed to be speaking for God.

He told William about Carlsville, about Becky, the girl he'd loved who had betrayed him. He had never told this to anyone else, but he already felt closer to William than he had to anyone since . . . well, since Becky, and it felt good to talk about it, to clear his chest.

He explained how he'd moved to Carlsville after his father's very public death back in the appropriately named town of Lynchburg. He'd escaped his father's fate for the simple reason that he had not been home when the mob showed up to the door of their house, and he'd lain low and headed west, traveling as far away from Virginia as quickly as possible. He'd finally stopped running in Missouri, deciding to settle in the beautiful town of Carlsville, where he was fortunate enough to find work as an apprentice blacksmith.

He was still in his teens then, and he portrayed himself as a young man with no parents who had escaped from a tyrannical orphanage back East. The blacksmith, and indeed the entire town, welcomed him with open arms, treating him as one of their own. He was given a room at the stable, took his meals with the blacksmith's family, and went to church with everyone on Sundays.

He also fell in love with Becky, Reverend Faron's daughter.

From the beginning, Becky exhibited an interest in him that went beyond the merely solicitous. He found her very attractive as well, and discovered as they talked after church services that he enjoyed being with her. Of course, the fact that she was a minister's daughter meant that he had to be extra careful. He could not exhibit any abilities that were even slightly out of the ordinary, had to pretend not to know things that he knew, not to believe things he believed.

Becky sensed in him something that no one else did, a darkness, she called it, and she confessed quite often that this was what had first attracted her. She said there was an enigma at the core of his being, a mysteriousness to the seeming straightforwardness of his past that no one in town had caught, and she was intrigued by that. The more time they spent together, the closer they became, and a year after he'd first arrived in Carlsville she revealed that she loved him.

He discovered that he loved her too. It was not something he'd been looking for, not even something he'd wanted, but somehow it had happened, and soon after he told her, he proposed to her, and they made plans to get married.

One evening they were lying by the creek that ran through the woods just south of town, talking, touching, looking up at the stars. The conversation faded away, and they lay there for a few moments in silence, listening to the high, clear babble of the creek. Becky seemed more subdued than usual, and he was about to ask her if there was anything the matter when she sat up, facing him. "Do you love me?" she asked.

He laughed. "You know I do."

"Can we tell each other anything?"

"Anything and everything."

She thought for a moment, then took a deep breath. The hand that touched his was trembling. "I'm not . . . pure," she said. The story came out in a torrent, a nonstop jumble of words that flowed over each other and on to the next like the water in the creek: "I wanted to tell you so many times, but I did not know how and it never seemed to be the right time. My father took me against my will. After my mother died. It was only once and I hated it, and he performed penance afterward and we both prayed, but it happened and I'd change that if I could but I can't. No one else knows and I promised him I would never tell another living soul, but I love you and I can't start off our marriage with a lie, and you'd find out anyway, so I thought I'd better tell you."

By this time she was sobbing on his shoulder. "Don't hate me," she cried. "I don't want you to hate me."

"Shhh," he hushed her. "Of course I don't hate you."

"I couldn't stand it if you hated me."

"I don't hate you."

"But you don't love me anymore."

"Of course I love you." He tried to smile, though it felt as if his heart had been ripped open. He gave her a quick kiss on the top of the head, smelled the fragrance of her hair. "Anything and everything, remember?"

"It only happened once, and it's over now. He apologized and I pretended to forgive and forget, I *tried* to forgive and forget, but I didn't, I couldn't, and I've been worried ever since because I knew this day would come. I knew I'd meet a man I loved and he'd find out I wasn't pure. I even thought of what I'd tell him. I had a big story all worked out. A lie."

"Shhh," Jeb said. "Shhhh."

She was silent for a moment, and when she spoke again her voice was low. "I thought of killing him." Her eyes met Jeb's. "He knew what he was doing even while he was doing it, and no matter how much he prays or apologizes, it still happened, and we both know it, and I know that every time we're alone together, we're both thinking about it. So I've thought of killing him many times, but ... but somehow I can't do it. I still *want* to kill him, but I know I won't. He's my father."

She exhaled when she was through, as though a great weight had just been taken from her shoulders. She let out a small harsh laugh. "I never thought I'd admit *that* to anybody."

He didn't know what to do, so he just kept holding her, and when she started crying again, sobbing into his shoulder, he held her tighter.

Eventually the crying stopped, and she pulled back, kissed him on the lips. "I love you so much."

"I love you, too."

"Now it's your turn," she said.

"What?"

She touched his face. "Come on. I want to know your big secret. You've been keeping something from me, and I want to know what it is."

"There is no big secret. My life's an open book."

"With some missing pages." She stood up on her knees, pretended to point a gun at him. "Come on, buster. Admit it." Her face was still red from crying, her cheeks glistening with the wetness of tears, and she looked so sad and lost and alone that it damn near broke his heart.

So he told her.

He did not tell her everything, did not go into detail, but he told her that he had powers, that his father had had powers, and that they had both used those powers to help people. He explained that others had not understood, had feared and hated them, that his father had been killed and he himself had only narrowly escaped the same fate.

He told her he was a witch, though he did not use the word.

She seemed subdued, her reaction not what he had expected. In fact, he did not know that she had a reaction. She was neither understanding and supportive nor horrified and angry. Instead she was politely quiet, pensive, and though that worried him at first, when she gave him a quick kiss before they parted and said, "I love you," he knew that all she needed was a little time to get used to the idea.

He felt good that he'd unburdened himself, freer than he had since living with his father, and he fell into a quick and easy sleep.

The blacksmith awakened him. "Get up!" he whispered. "They're coming after you."

Jeb stirred groggily, blinking against the lamplight. "What? . . . Who?"

"Reverend Faron's gathering up a posse, and they're coming to get you. They're going to string you up."

She'd told her father.

He felt as if his guts had been yanked out of his chest, and only at that moment did he realize how much he truly loved her.

He'd escaped—with the help of the blacksmith, who understood what he was and didn't care—and he'd been on the move ever since.

"Maybe it wasn't her," William offered. "Maybe someone else found out. Maybe—"

"It was her."

Even now the wounds still hurt. Just talking about those memories had dredged up the emotions that went with them, and Jeb found himself wondering where Becky was now, what she was doing, who she was with, what she was like.

"I've never been in love," William said sadly.

They were both walking, William leading his horse, and Jeb looked over at him. "Never?"

The other man shook his head, started to say something,

then thought the better of it. Jeb waited for him to say something else, but he did not.

They continued on in silence.

They came upon the monster in the late afternoon.

The beast was dead, its corpse rotting in the sun, but even in death it was a fearsome sight to behold. They were well up the canyon by this time, fenced in between high rock walls that blocked out half the sky, and they saw the oversize body lying in the dry creek bed well before they reached it. They could both sense the undiluted malevolence of the creature's lingering presence, like the smell of a skunk that remained long after the animal had gone, and the horse seemed to sense it too because William had to talk to the animal to keep it from bolting.

They approached the body warily. It was easily as big as three men, both in height and width, and was vaguely human in form, but there were claws instead of hands at the ends of the excessively long arms, and what remained of the head was unlike anything Jeb had ever seen. Like the rest of its body, the monster's head appeared to have been deflated, like a balloon, black rotting skin hanging loosely off an interior frame of bone, but even in this ruined shape, he could see that there was hair where there should not have been, eyes and nose that should not have been on any living creature, and far, far too many teeth.

Long teeth.

Pointed teeth.

The very air here felt heavy, and Jeb turned toward William. "What do you think it is?" he asked, his voice hushed.

William shook his head, not taking his eyes off the monster. He bent forward to look more closely.

Jeb shivered. The canyon seemed suddenly far too small, far too narrow, and he looked up at the top of the rock walls to see if there were any more of these creatures about. He didn't *feel* the presence of anything else here, but he did not trust his own instincts, and he glanced both up and down the canyon.

"It didn't die naturally," William said. "Something killed it. It looks like its insides were eaten out. Or sucked out through this hole at the top of the back."

"What could kill something like this?"

William looked at him. "I don't think we want to know."

Jeb wanted to get out of the mountains immediately, but though it was a small range, there was no way they could make it through before tomorrow or the day after, and they were forced to set up camp on a flattened ridge. At least they were out of the canyon. He would have rather walked through the night and taken his chances with the cliffs and the darkness than sleep in that cursed place.

Whatever could bring down a monster like that could have them for dessert, but they both wove protective spells around the camp and decided to take turns standing watch for the night, prepared to either flee or fight at the first sign of anything unusual.

Jeb's watch was first, but he saw nothing, heard nothing, and, though he kept his senses wide open, felt nothing. The horse, too, seemed calm. As far as he could tell, they were alone in this place, and he hoped that it remained that way. At least until morning.

He woke William when the moon was halfway across the sky, and the two of them switched places. He knew he had to rest for the grueling trek tomorrow, but he was not at all tired and was not sure he would be able to sleep.

He was out almost immediately after his head hit the saddlebag.

He dreamed of a town in which all of the houses were identical and where at sunset a dwarf roamed the community, placing metal spoons on the porches of those who would die before dawn. He was living in one of the houses and was awakened in the middle of the night by a mysterious sound and went outside to investigate. But when he walked onto the porch, he felt something cold and hard touch his toes, heard a clattering noise. He looked down to see that he'd accidentally kicked a rusted metal spoon off the porch. There was a snickering from the bushes, and when he looked more closely, he saw the face of a dwarf grinning evilly up at him.

He awoke in the morning feeling unrested. William had already conjured a fire and was making coffee with some muddy water he'd found in a barely trickling creek a little farther along the trail. They drank their breakfast, packed up, and set out, both of them wanting to escape from these mountains as quickly as possible.

They did not speak much that day, or that night when they camped in a narrow ravine between two tall cliffs. It was as if a spell had been cast on them, even though they had carefully protected themselves.

The next day they left the mountains and it felt to Jeb as though he had awakened from a bad dream. The feelings that had been following him faded, and even the memory of the monster seemed not as sharp. He recognized the sensation. It was the exhilaration one felt after averting disaster. He had guiltily experienced a variation of it upon escaping Lynchburg and avoiding his father's fate, and he knew that this sudden lifting of dread was due not to any magic but to simple human emotion.

They'd had two days to think about what they'd come across back in the canyon, and while he himself had not been able to piece together any solutions, William struck him as a more pensive sort, a deep thinker, and he turned toward his newfound friend. "What do you think killed that monster?" he asked.

William shook his head, and Jeb understood that he did not want to talk about it.

That was fine with him.

The landscape flattened out, and on this side of the mountains it seemed far less desolate. There were trees here. Bushes and grass. There were still no signs of people, not even Indians, but other signs of life greeted them—birds circling in the sky, squirrels scampering along the ground, the far-off roar of bear. Though this was still uncharted territory, they felt as though they were easing back into the known world.

Their self-imposed silence ended as well, and they began to talk again. They spoke of places they'd been, sights they'd seen along the way. Jeb had no destination, was not heading anywhere in particular, but William seemed to know where he wanted to go; his new friend had some sort of plan or specific intent.

He asked William. "Where are we headed?"

"South."

"I mean, where in particular?"

"Where were *you* headed when we met?"

Jeb shrugged. "No place."

William nodded. "That is the trouble with our kind, isn't it? We're never heading *to* something, we're always heading *away* from something."

"We have no choice. That's the way things are."

William was silent for a moment. "There are other persecuted people," he said finally. "People who have made a fresh start here in the West, who have built their own communities, away from everyone else, where no one bothers them. I've been thinking for some time that we could do the same. This is a land of opportunity because it is new and open, ready to be molded into whatever shape its settlers choose. It is not bound by the models of the past. It does not have to conform to any preexisting notion of what society should be. And it is big enough to support all."

Jeb suddenly understood what he was getting at. "A . . . town?" he said incredulously. "You're talking about a town of witches?"

"Why not? There is going to be an entire Mormon Territory. Why not at least a town for us?" Smiling, he sidled next to his horse and withdrew from the saddlebag a letter, imprinted with the seal of the government of the United States. "I've already written to Washington, and Fenton Barnes, the man to whom I wrote, has talked to the president about my idea."

"The president? Of the country?"

"The government is worried that the violence out here will scare people away, worried that Mexico will be able to exploit this country's divisions to its advantage. A lot of that violence is directed at us, at the Mormons, at those who are . . . different, and if they can keep us separated from the rest of the population by giving us our own lands, and thus retain at least the appearance of national unity . . ." He shrugged. "Well, they think it's worth it."

"So what does that mean? They're going to give us land in order to start our own town?"

William nodded. "Yes. Our own town, with our own local government and local laws. We'll be a recognized community, sanctioned by the federal government, segregated and protected by presidential order from the type of persecution we have faced in the past." He smiled, passed Jeb the letter. "This is the authorization for me to take possession of the land in the name of our people."

"Where is it?" Jeb asked. "Where is this place?"

William looked at him. "In Arizona Territory. A place called Wolf Canyon."

Now

1

He didn't realize until he woke up on Christmas morning that he had forgotten to even buy a tree.

Miles walked out to the kitchen, made coffee. All of the decorations were still in the garage, and he had not bothered to put up lights either. He was tempted to pretend this was just an ordinary day, that there was no Christmas this year, but when he turned on the TV and saw carolers singing in the New York snow as part of a prerecorded *Today* show celebration, he knew he would not be able to do that.

He *had* bought his father some presents, and though he had not yet wrapped them, he did so now. Being such a serious Christian, he'd expected Audra to take the day off, but the nurse had promised to come in, informing him that she would merely arrive a few hours later than usual. He'd bought Audra a present, too. Two presents, actually. One from him and one from his father. He wrapped those as well, inexpertly attempting to cover an awkwardly shaped wicker basket filled with various teas and an unboxed faux crystal vase with what was left of last year's festive snowman paper.

Leaving the nurse's gifts on the coffee table, Miles carried his father's presents back to his room, filling his voice with a false Christmas cheer that was the furthest thing away from what he actually felt: "Merry Christmas, Dad!"

Bob awoke with a blink of his eyes but virtually no movement of his body. He tried to smile, but it looked more like a painful grimace, and when he attempted to adjust himself and use his one good arm to push himself into a sitting position, the effort only served to list him to the left.

Miles placed the packages at the foot of the bed, then helped shift his father back into position. He placed the bed controls in Bob's good hand and waited while the top half of the bed rose into an upright position.

"I hate this shit," his father said in the slurred whisper that was now his permanent voice, and the annoyance in his words was so pure that Miles could not help but smile. Whatever else the stroke had done, it had not affected his dad's personality.

"Merry Christmas," Miles said again.

"I don't know how merry it is."

"But it's Christmas, and, look, I've come bearing gifts!" He picked up the first package and placed it on his father's chest, letting him look at it for a moment before picking it up once more and carefully unwrapping it. "What do we have here, huh?" He opened the box, let his father watch. "Boots, Dad. Cowboy boots. You know those ones you saw last summer but were too cheap to buy?"

Bob said nothing, but Miles saw the glint of a tear in his eye, and he suddenly felt a little choked up himself. He quickly moved on to the next present.

"Hey, what's this?" He unwrapped the gift. "A Louis L'Amour book!"

He felt a hand grab his wrist. His father's hand, surprisingly strong. He looked over at Bob's face and saw tears rolling freely down his cheeks. "Thank you," his father whispered.

Miles suddenly realized that his dad had not expected them to be celebrating Christmas this year. He probably hadn't expected to even be here for Christmas, and Miles understood how much this meant to him. He was glad that he'd bought the presents and wished that he'd made an effort to decorate the house. He should have thought more about his father's feelings and tried to make this year just like every other.

"You're a good son," Bob said, relaxing his grip. "I want you to know that. Just because I don't say it all the time doesn't mean I don't think it."

The lump in his throat returned, and Miles' eyes were watering with the threat of tears. "Thanks, Dad." He swallowed hard, maintained his smile and picked up another package. "Let's see what we have here."

There were two more presents to go, far less than they usually had, but a decent number under the circumstances. After Miles cleared the wrapping paper off the covers and scrunched it in the trash, his dad waved him back over.

"Look under the bed," Bob whispered. "I had Audra buy me something for you."

This was a complete surprise, and Miles crouched down, felt under the bed, and brought forth a rather large and heavy gift whose careful wrapping betrayed a female hand.

"Open it," his father said.

Miles ripped the red and green paper to reveal a boxed turntable.

"I found it several months ago and had Audra go get it for me. I know you have a lot old records you can't play because your stereo just has a CD. So I thought you might like this."

It was the best present his father had ever given him, not only because it was something he really wanted and would use but because of the thought put into it and the effort required to get it. His dad's presents usually consisted of items from Sears that he himself wanted, and Miles was impressed that he'd actually been thinking about the turntable for some time, that he'd noticed it and remembered it.

"Thanks," he said. "This is great."

"Merry Christmas, boy." Bob pressed a button, lowering

the bed, apparently tired already, and Miles decided to let him alone for a while.

"I'll go heat up the coffee," he said.

Bob closed his eyes. "That sounds good."

He was snoring even before Miles left the room.

That, Miles thought, was one of the most disconcerting aftereffects of the stroke: the abrupt changes, the immediate shift from happy to sad, from wide awake to tired, with no cooling-down period, no time allotted for any gradations in between.

He walked out to the kitchen.

Bonnie called around eleven, pretending as though there was nothing wrong. She thanked him for the presents he'd sent, asked perfunctorily how Dad was, then went on to tell him of the morning of gift unwrapping they'd had at her house and the huge turkey dinner she was preparing. Gil even came on the line for a second with some generic holiday greetings, and Miles responded in kind. He had never much liked his brother-in-law, but he'd always been able to maintain a polite facade, and he did so now as well. After Gil hung up the other phone, Miles asked his sister if she'd like to talk to Dad, and she felt obliged to say yes. When he went back, checked, and told her that their father was still asleep, though, he could tell she was relieved. He said he'd call back later, when Dad was awake, and the two of them hung up, exchanging inanities.

A short time later, he heard the whir of the bed motor from the bedroom, and he went back to let his father know that Bonnie had called.

Bob smiled. "How's our old friend Gil?" he whispered.

"He can still go from man to wuss in three seconds."

Bob laughed. Or tried to. But the laugh became a cough, and the cough got stuck somewhere in his throat and all that came out of his father's grimacing mouth was a hard, harsh wheeze.

The two of them were still talking about Bonnie and Gil when Audra showed up with a premade Christmas dinner: microwavable plates of turkey, mashed potatoes, stuffing, and a plastic sack filled with salad. Miles was genuinely touched, and after he gave the nurse her presents and watched her unwrap them, she heated up the food. He sat in a chair next to the bed, eating, while Audra cut up his father's turkey into small easily digestible pieces and carefully fed them to him.

As he'd suspected, Audra and his father had not initially gotten along, although in recent days they seemed to have reached a kind of truce. As he'd hoped, that confrontation seemed to have energized his father, who had been making much better progress than expected—particularly in regard to his speech. Twice a week he still went to the hospital for tests and therapy, and while there was no change in his long-term prognosis, the doctor and the therapists admitted that in the short term, he was making excellent progress.

Miles finished his meal and walked out to the kitchen to put his plate in the sink. When he returned, Audra was just getting up from her chair next to the bed. Her face was red as she strode wordlessly out of the room.

Miles frowned. "What did you say to her, Dad?"

He was too far away to hear the answer, so he sat down in the nurse's chair and asked again. "What did you say?"

"I asked if it was true that in Japan they have vending machines that sell soiled panties," his father whispered. "I heard that they do."

Miles blinked, stunned, then laughed out loud. It had been a long time since he'd laughed, and he was probably over-reacting, investing the comment with more humor than it probably warranted, but it felt good to laugh and he seemed to have no control of it anyway, and he just rode the wave and enjoyed the feeling.

His father grinned.

No, the stroke had not changed Bob's personality one bit.

Miles grasped his dad's good hand, held it, squeezed. From the kitchen he heard the angry sound of a cupboard slamming.

He smiled. Taking everything into consideration, it wasn't such a bad Christmas after all.

2

L.A. was once again showing its true colors after its traditional New Year's false front, slumping back into smog as though the maintenance of that perfect-blue-sky ruse for even one day had zapped all its energy. The San Gabriel Mountains were entirely hidden behind a wall of white, and even the Hollywood hills were little more than a faint outline in the haze. As usual, the weatherman on the early morning newscast had said that it was going to be "a beautiful day."

Miles walked into the break room, where Hal and Tran were comparing holidays. Tran had hosted his wife's massive Catholic family in his tiny little duplex, and the place had gotten so crowded and claustrophobic and Christian that Tran, a lax Buddhist, had spent most of Christmas day smoking in the backyard, trying to avoid his in-laws.

Hal and his wife spent the day together in their Sherman Oaks home, their son and his current girlfriend stopping by later for an uneventful visit. It was Christmas Eve day that Hal's usual series of misadventures had occurred, and Miles and Tran listened and laughed as the detective hilariously recounted how he had driven all over creation, looking for the jewelry box his wife wanted, before finally finding one at an independent discount house that he'd investigated last year for fencing stolen property. He'd bought it, intending to find another once the holidays were over and switch the two without his wife knowing, turning in the stolen one to the police and telling them where he'd purchased it.

Tran nodded at him. "So how was your Christmas, Miles?"

"As well as could be expected under the circumstances."

Both Tran and Hal nodded solemnly, understandingly, neither willing to chance a follow-up comment.

Miles felt awkward, and he found himself suddenly inventing a deadline that wasn't there, pretending that he needed to get back to his desk.

He sat down, shuffled through his papers, happy to have something to do, feeling far too comfortable being alone at his desk than he knew he should be.

Although Marina and her husband had gone back to Arizona, and her father refused to speak with him, Miles was still on the case, and for that he was grateful. He sorted through the files until he found theirs, withdrawing the list Liam had made up. He'd been systematically trying to locate all of the men on the list, although so far he'd found none. He'd been hoping to work with the police on this, utilize some of their resources, but to his surprise and consternation, the detective assigned to Liam's case was supremely uninterested. Miles had a few contacts downtown, among the police brass—and the firm itself had many more—and he planned to speak to them and get the case transferred to another detective.

He spent the morning scanning phone directories and doing Internet searches. He was rewarded just after noon with the address and phone number of Hubert P. Lars, now living in Palm Springs. When he attempted to call Hubert, however, a recording informed him: "This number is no longer in service. Please check the number and dial again."

Miles called one more time, just to make sure he hadn't

accidentally punched in a wrong digit, but when the same recording came on the line, he hung up, feeling troubled. The image in his mind was of Hubert P. Lars lying dead on the floor of a long, low desert ranch house. He was half tempted to speed down to Palm Springs and check, but it was two hours away, and he knew his time would be much better spent trying to find addresses and phone numbers for the rest of the people on Liam's list.

He stayed late, and the sun was a smog-shrouded orange glow at the edge of the horizon when he finally pulled into his driveway. Miles grabbed the Taco Bell sack from the seat next to him, got out of the car and used his key to unlock the front door. He was greeted by darkness. And silence. No lights were on in the house, and he did not hear the everpresent sound of the television. "Audra?" he called tentatively. "You here? Audra?"

There was no answer.

He suddenly realized why the house was silent.

His father had died.

"Dad!" He dropped the sack on the coffee table and ran through the living room, his heart pounding so hard that it felt as though it was going to burst through his rib cage.

He dashed into the hall. The hall tree had been shoved in front of the door to his father's room as if to barricade it, and a love seat and chair from the back bedroom had been placed next to the hall tree to reinforce the barricade. It made no sense, but he didn't stop and try to analyze it or figure out why it had been done.

From inside the room he heard the sound of rapid footsteps that rapped against the hardwood floor. They seemed unnaturally loud in the silent house.

"Dad!"

There was no answering reply, only the footsteps. Boot heels on wood.

Miles pushed the love seat aside, pulled the chair and hall tree away from the door. He saw a paper towel, a bottle and syringe lying between the legs of the hall tree. His father's medication, abandoned.

"Dad!" He pushed open the door.

His father was naked, wearing only cowboy boots, and walking in a circle around the periphery of the room. The nightstand was knocked over, as was a chair. Both the bed and the dresser had been shoved away from their usual positions against the wall and were skewed at odd angles against bunched-up sections of throw rug, creating a path next to the wall through which his father could walk. Miles saw bloody bruises on his father's thigh and midsection where he had obviously smacked against the bed and dresser, moving them not intentionally but through sheer stubborn repetition.

"Dad!" he called again.

But he did not rush forward. Something about the scene kept him back. His father's eyes were closed, he saw. The old man's skin was bluish and pasty.

Bob walked between the dresser and the wall, toward him, past him. This close, Miles could see the utter lack of expression on his dad's face, the complete absence of any sign of life or personality.

His father was dead.

He knew it, felt it, understood it, but Bob continued walking, continued on his circular track around the edge of the room. Miles did not know what was happening or why or what to do. This was like something out of *The Twilight Zone,* and he stood there, stunned. He knew he should be scared, but for some reason he wasn't, and when his father came around again, Miles grabbed him around the chest, pinning the old man's arms to his sides. His father's skin felt cold and spongy, rubbery. Miles held his dad tightly, trying to keep him in place, but his father was stronger in death than he had ever been in life, and with only a moment's delay, he broke through his son's restraint and continued his nonstop stride around the periphery of the room.

"Stop!" Miles called, but Bob gave no indication that he had heard.

The dead can't hear, Miles thought.

He hurried out of the room and back down the hall. Audra had to have reported what was happening, an ambulance was probably on its way right now, but he dialed 9-1-1 anyway and was transferred instantly from an emergency operator to a police dispatcher.

He started talking immediately, before the dispatcher had said a word: "My name's Miles Huerdeen. I'm at 1264 Monterey Street, Los Angeles, and my dad is dead. I just came home and found him. He had a stroke and was incapacitated, but now he's walking around the bedroom, and I need someone to come over and take care of him." He was aware of how ridiculous he sounded, and he knew as soon as he said it that he should have kept that part quiet, let the paramedics find out for themselves when they arrived, but he was obviously more freaked than he'd thought, because he had a need to get the information out, he wanted to explain what was really going on.

He wanted someone else to know.

Besides, the police needed to decide how to handle his father, whether to take him to a hospital or the morgue.

The dispatcher was confused. "Your father had a stroke—?"

"No, he died!"

"I thought you said he was walking."

"He is!"

The voice took on a stiff authoritarian formality. "Mr. Huerdeen—"

"He's dead, I told you! And he's still walking around the room!"

"Mr. Huerdeen, I suggest *you* take a walk. We don't have time for these games. Thank y—"

"This isn't a game, goddammit!"

"Then, I suggest you take advantage of our referral service to find the mental health clinic nearest your home. I will connect you." There was an abrupt click, and then a recorded voice came on the line, informing him that if he was thinking about suicide, he should press the number one. If he was suffering from spousal abuse . . .

He hung up the phone, chastising himself for not taking the dispatcher's name. He could not hear it from here, but in his mind he heard the sound of boot heels on wood, and for the first time the creepiness of it all hit home. Father or not, he was alone in the house with a dead man—

a zombie

—and his first priority was to find someone to help him do something about it. He thought for a moment, then reached for his personal phone book. He dialed his friend Ralph Barger, who worked at the county coroner's office. Ralph would know how to handle this.

Luckily for him, Ralph was in, and Miles explained the situation as calmly and rationally as he could. His friend did not interrupt and did not treat him as though he were crazy or drunk but took him seriously and wrote down the address and promised to be there with a wagon and a couple of assistants within the half hour.

After hanging up, Miles called Graham. He might need a lawyer on this. He had no idea what was happening here, but it was doubtlessly unprecedented, and that always meant tangling with the law. The attorney, for once, did not have to be paged but actually answered his phone, and as soon as Miles explained the situation, he promised to be right over.

"You're not pulling my leg, are you? This is on the level?"

"On the level."

"Holy shit. I have to see this for myself."

"Then, get your ass over here."

Miles considered calling Hal, getting some of the other detectives in on this, but decided against it. At least for now.

He hung up the phone, looked around the darkened house. Where was Audra? he wondered. Had she just run off?

Or had his father killed her?

It was clear by now that she had not called the police or any authorities—or if she had, they had treated her information the same way they had treated his. Had she simply abandoned her post and rushed home or to the hospice agency? Or had something happened to her, and was her body still in the house? She must have been the one who had barricaded his father's door, so he most likely hadn't been able to do anything to her, but the truth was that Miles was way out of his depth here. For all he knew, his father was possessed by some malevolent spirit or demon that had also done away with the nurse.

He needed to search the house.

He was a lot more leery about leaving the living room than he had been before. Night had fallen, and though he'd turned on a few of the lights, most of the house was still in darkness. Logically, he knew that his father had died when it was still light outside. Audra had probably taken off sometime this afternoon.

But the fact that she did not appear to have called anyone indicated the possibility that she had never left at all.

He looked down the partially lighted hallway at the moved barricade, feeling a chill creep up his back.

Maybe he should wait until Ralph and the coroner's men arrived.

No. If there was a chance that the nurse was still in the house, that something had happened to her and he could help, he needed to find her.

He took a quick peek into the kitchen, flipping on the lights. Nothing. He went back down the hall, looked into the bathroom, the closet, his office. All empty.

The door to his father's room was still open, and he could not help looking in. Bob was still walking around the room, dead, naked, wearing cowboy boots. His father turned, and Miles saw the unseeing eyes in that unmoving face, and he looked away, hurrying down the hall to check out the last room, his own bedroom.

He was prepared for the worst—the nurse's body, eviscerated on his bed, torn in half like Montgomery Jones—but when he turned on the light there was nothing. Thank God. The master bathroom too was empty, and he at least had the satisfaction of knowing that Audra had escaped the house.

Leaving the lights on, he walked back to his father's room, standing there for a second, watching. He could still feel the cold sponginess of that skin against his hands, and he realized that though this body was moving, animated, he did not consider it his father. It was a shell, energized but empty, and whatever spark or essence had been Bob, it was gone.

He returned to the living room, turned on the television to provide some noise and give the house some sense of life, and waited.

Ralph and two other men from the coroner's office arrived first, around twenty minutes later, and Graham arrived soon after. Both of his friends, and the coroner's assistants, were visibly shaken by the sight of Bob pacing the periphery of his room. Ralph asked a series of rapid-fire questions as he put on gloves and a surgical mask: When did he have the stroke? What was the extent of the brain damage? Was he sure Bob was dead?

Miles gave a quick rundown of his father's recent medical history, described the way he had come home and found the barricaded door and the abandoned house.

Covered and protected, Ralph and his assistants walked into the bedroom. The two men held his father while Ralph injected the body with some sort of drug, sticking the needle in his upper arm because that portion of his body showed no attempt at movement. The moment he was through, he backed away. The two men continued to hold him, visibly straining against the forward motion of Bob's still moving feet.

A few seconds later, his father slumped forward. Ralph took over from one of the men, a young husky intern named Murdock, and held Bob up until the assistant returned with a gurney. Ralph helped lay the body down, then let the other two men strap it in.

"What was that you gave him?" Miles asked.

"It's a very powerful muscle relaxant."

"Is he . . . dead?"

Ralph nodded, the expression on his face one of extreme weariness. "Oh, yes. He's dead."

"What do you think happened?"

His friend shrugged. "I don't know."

"You ever seen anything like this?"

Ralph shook his head. "I have to admit, I haven't."

Miles looked back at Graham. "Keep this out of the *Weekly World News*."

"Tell it to your doctor friend. If there are any leaks, they'll come from the coroner's office, not me."

He faced Ralph. "Can we keep this quiet?"

"Definitely. At least until we figure out what it is. We don't want people panicking." He took off his gloves. "You know, I should be doing cartwheels over this. Something this rare doesn't come along in . . . well, it never comes along, to be honest about it. This is a coroner's wet dream: something that's never been encountered before, a chance to get in all the journals. And as deputy assistant coroner, hell, this a career maker."

"But . . ." Miles prodded.

"But I'm not happy. I'm not excited."

He looked at Miles. "I'm scared."

Miles shivered, looked over at Graham. Ordinarily, this would be the lawyer's cue to make some cynical, wiseass remark. But Graham merely looked pensive.

"What are you going to do?" Miles asked.

"I don't know. We'll take him in, but obviously I'm not going to do an autopsy if he's still moving. I'll call Bill and the chief, let them in on it, see what they come up with. For now, I guess we'll bring your father to the morgue, give him a private room, keep him strapped down and see what happens when the drugs wear off. You want to come along? You're welcome to ride in the wagon."

Miles looked back at Graham.

The lawyer tried to smile, only partially pulled it off. "I think we'll follow in my car," he said.

Miles awoke from a nightmare in which he was being chased through a maze by a jogging mummy with the rotting face of Liam Connor. He sat up, blinked. It was light outside, and one look at the clock told him that he was supposed to have been at work two hours ago. He had not called the office or anyone from it, and he quickly reached across the bed, grabbed the phone, and called Naomi. He explained that his dad died and asked her to patch him through to either Perkins or Miller, but she told him she'd take care of it, just do what he had to do, call in when he could, all their prayers were with him.

"Thanks," he said gratefully.

The next call was to the coroner's office. Ralph was still there, sounding dead tired, and he said there'd been no change. His father was still deceased.

And there was still muscle movement in the legs.

Miles asked what he'd been afraid to ask the night before. "So does this mean he's a zombie?"

"I don't know what it means," Ralph admitted. "None of us here do."

Miles got up, took a shower, made himself some coffee. He was at loose ends and had no idea what he was supposed to do next. Ordinarily, he'd contact a mortuary, call friends and family, but right now everything was up in the air. He should definitely call his sister, he knew, but he didn't want to worry her, and decided to wait until their father was really and truly dead.

Really and truly dead.

He shook his head. He had the feeling that he was supposed to understand what was happening here. On some level perhaps he did, but any connections between his father's un-death and any related information in his own brain remained stubbornly buried. He found himself thinking about his dad's recurring dream, about the occult books he'd checked out of the library. Had Bob known what was going to happen? Had he somehow been preparing himself? And, if so, why hadn't he let Miles in on the secret?

His father was—had been?—nothing if not organized, and a copy of his will, the title to his car, a breakdown of all his assets, and a key to a safety deposit box were in the desk folder marked DEATH that he had shown Miles long before the stroke.

The safety deposit box, Miles assumed, contained the

original will and assorted other documents, perhaps some family photos or heirlooms. Valuables. Checking it out would at least give him something to do, so he drove down to the bank. He was led into a vault by an elderly female teller who removed a long metal box from its niche in the wall and set it down on a table. Both he and the teller inserted their keys to unlock the box, then he thanked the woman, waiting until she had left the room before pulling up the lid.

Miles blinked in confusion. The box was filled with phials of powders and strange-looking roots floating in small bottles of clear liquid. There were branches and leaves in sealed plastic bags, a necklace of teeth, what looked like a dried, flattened frog.

He stared, unmoving, thrown off balance by the sheer unanticipated lunacy of it all. Where were the documents he'd been expecting? The insurance policies? The letters? The family heirlooms?

And what the hell was all this crap?

None of the bags or bottles were labeled, but there was about them the aura of the occult, something that under the present circumstances did not exactly fill him with joy. The necklace of teeth was particularly disturbing, and he tried to think of why his father had such a thing, where he could have gotten it.

Gingerly, he took the items out of the box, spreading them out on the fake wood of the table. The teeth rattled in his shaking hand. He dropped the rough dusty frog. The materials looked like magic paraphernalia to him, the sort of stuff that was used to cast spells and concoct potions.

A chain of thoughts passed through his head.

Magic.

Voodoo.

Zombies.

He thought of his dead dad, walking around the disrupted bedroom, and he stared down at the bizarre paraphernalia on the table. His eyes were drawn once again to the necklace of teeth. He didn't like this. He didn't like this at all.

And he sat alone in the vault, feeling very empty and very, very cold.

3

Fred Tunney awoke in the middle of the night to see a woman at the foot of his bed, a beautiful woman with long straight black hair, a perfect smile, and the most evil eyes he had ever beheld.

He knew instantly who she was, and he said her name, though he had never before met her, had never before seen her and had only heard about her from his parents.

Her smile grew wider and the smile, he saw, was evil too.

He was frightened, of course, and surprised, but this had not come entirely out of the blue. For the past several months, he'd been dreaming about the old days, about the town, about magic, and about a wall of water that he could not escape and that bore down on him as his feet remained cemented to the floor of his bedroom.

Now she was here.

His parents had always feared this would happen, and no matter how far they had run, the specter of the town and the curse had followed them, had hung over everything they'd done. He himself had never believed any of it, had thought they were overreacting, but he had been only a child when they left the town, and obviously they had possessed knowledge he had not.

He knew that now.

Fred sat up against the headboard, not taking his eyes

off the woman. He could feel the power radiating from her, washing over him in waves that were the sensory equivalent of darkness. He was chilled to the bone, afraid in a way that he had never thought possible.

She spoke his name.

"Fred."

The fact that she knew who he was terrified him even more, and he pulled his knees up, preparing to throw off the covers and run like hell out of the room.

She was too fast for him, though. In one fluid movement she was around the side of the bed and next to him, cutting off his avenue of escape. He could feel the coldness coming off her, and he looked up, into those horribly evil eyes, and he knew that he was only the latest victim. She was coming for all of them, one at a time, coming after all of the residents of the town, all of the residents who had escaped.

Her smile broadened as if in acknowledgment, and in a flash of insight that came from somewhere other than himself, he understood that she was not just coming for them. She was after the builders, too. All of the government people who'd worked on the project.

A thought intruded on his mind. No, not a thought. An image. A headless body lying in a watery tomb.

"Fred," she said again.

And reached for him.

He tried to call on his powers, tried to fight her off, but it had been too long and he had forgotten how. She only smiled at his attempts, mocking them. So he tried to attack her physically, kicking off his blanket, kicking out at her, but despite her apparent solidity, she was not really there. She was a shade, a projection, and he understood suddenly why she had come.

She wanted him to get her out.

She wanted him to help resurrect her.

As soon as the knowledge came, it was accompanied by the certainty that he was going to die.

He tried to run through her, toward the door, toward the hallway outside and freedom. While she was not solid, she had substance. It was as if he hit a wall of ice, and the impact was accompanied by a feeling of deep, dark despair so powerful that it sent him staggering back to the bed.

The expression on her face altered. Her features did not change in any way, did not become monstrous or deformed, but they did not have to. The look on her face was so malevolent, so unlike anything he had ever seen before or even imagined, that he felt his heart leap inside his chest.

Felt the coldness nestle around it.

Felt the pain spread through his left side as he fell to the floor gasping, trying to breathe.

He was having a heart attack. She stood there, looking down at him, watching as excruciating pain spread throughout his body, as the tears came to his eyes and the agony was replaced by an even worse numbness.

She faded away silently, smiling, leaving behind only a cold spot in a room that was growing increasingly dark to him.

Gasping, he tried to move, tried to sit up, tried to reach the phone on the nightstand, but the pain was unbearable, and he could not even move his arm.

The world turned black, disappeared.

He died.

And then he started walking.

4

Russ Winston stared out of his office window toward the mall, the white phallic spire of the Washington Monument just barely visible over the top of the generic government building across the street. Outside, the sky was clear blue and cloudless, the January air cool and crisp.

On days like today he regretted ever having taken a desk job. He wished he had not allowed himself to be promoted through the ranks of the department and was still working outside. Back at Yellowstone, perhaps. Or Arches. Or Zion. Or . . .

No.

Not Wolf Canyon.

Anyplace but there.

An involuntary shiver passed through him, and he swiveled his chair, looking away from the window. He was too old for the outdoors now anyway. Hell, he was too old for the job he had. Retirement age had come and gone two presidents ago, and he was lucky to have enough pull in the department to be able to remain on even in this position.

Russ looked at the framed photo of the president mounted on the opposite wall. He tried to think of something else, but he no longer had the control of his thoughts that he once had, and against his will, his mind kept coming back to Wolf Canyon.

It had been his first government job. His previous experience had been in construction and cement contracting, and because of that he'd been assigned to one of the big dam projects out West. He'd worked there for nearly a decade, moving up the on-site hierarchy through aptitude and a series of fortuitous friendships to the position of shift supervisor.

They were damming the Rio Verde at the foot of Wolf Canyon. Another, smaller dam had been constructed twenty miles up the river, at the canyon's head, some twenty years before, but it was determined that the reservoir would not be sufficient for Arizona's needs even ten years hence. Another, much bigger dam was needed, one that could also be used to generate electricity for the town of Rio Verde and the other desert communities spread out across this portion of the state. So the river was diverted, its output cut back to a mere trickle while they completed the project.

There was a town in the canyon between the two dams, a small remote community that had to be evacuated under eminent domain, and the residents screamed bloody murder about being moved, lodging complaint after complaint in Washington, being granted extension after extension, though the outcome of this battle was already a foregone conclusion.

But other than that, it had been smooth sailing, and Russ had enjoyed his dam days. He liked the warm western sun, liked the rugged landscape, liked the easy camaraderie he shared with the other workers.

Only afterward, after it had happened, after it was all over, had his perspective changed.

Then the horror set in.

He had spent the rest of his life denying what had occurred, avoiding any thought of it, and while he had remained in the West for most of his career, even when he transferred to Interior, he had never again gone back to Arizona. Not even to see the Grand Canyon.

He preferred to block out that part of his life.

But he had been thinking about Wolf Canyon more and more often lately. He told himself that it was because he was getting old, because he was surveying his life and trying to sort through it, the good and the bad, to see how the balance sheet of his actions added up. That was a part of it, of course. But something else was involved as well. Something he couldn't quite put his finger on.

And that worried him.

On the way home from work, Russ stopped off at the market and bought a quart of chocolate milk for Cameron. His grandson had seemed somewhat down this past week, and he knew it was because the boy sensed that they would soon be leaving. His father was working again, and it was only a matter of time before he and his parents would be able to move out of Russ's house and back into a place of their own.

Maybe chocolate milk would cheer him up.

Lily was cooking dinner when he arrived home, and he smiled at his daughter-in-law, gave her a quick pat on the back as he put the milk into the fridge. "Where's Cameron?"

"Playing," she said. "He's around."

"If you see him first, tell him I bought him some chocolate milk."

She gave Russ a grateful smile. "Thanks, Dad."

"What are grandfathers for?" He walked back out to the living room and turned on the television to catch the local news. He watched it for a few minutes before becoming disgusted with the anchors' incessant chatter and the parade of soft nonstories, and switched the channel to CNN.

Behind him, he heard a thump, and he glanced over his shoulder, over the back of the couch, to see the door to the garage fly open. Cameron dashed out and slammed the door immediately, throwing his body against the door as if to prevent someone from opening it and entering.

Russ stood, frowning. "What the—?"

Cameron's face was white. "Grampa!"

He felt a sinking in his stomach, a tightening in his chest as he walked around the couch to where his grandson stood leaning against the door, panting. "What is it?"

"There's something in the garage! I think it's a monster!"

Tom walked in at precisely that moment, throwing his keys on the entryway table, and Russ quickly called his son over. "Cameron says there's something in the garage."

"A monster! It tried to attack me!"

Tom gave Russ an amused kids-say-the-darnedest-thing look over the boy's head, and pried Cameron away from the door. "Don't worry, sport. We'll find it. Whatever it is."

Russ was not so sanguine. Maybe it was because he'd

been thinking about Wolf Canyon, but he could not entirely dismiss the boy's fears, and his feelings as Tom opened the door and peered into the semidarkness were closer to his grandson's than his son's.

There was a clatter of paint cans from across the garage.

Russ's heart leaped in his chest. He looked over at Tom, and his son hesitated a moment before reaching around the side of the wall and grabbing the long handle of a shovel.

"Stay out," Tom told Cameron. "Let your grandpa and me handle this." He handed Russ the shovel, picked up a broom for himself.

Something made of glass fell and shattered on the cement floor.

The light in the garage was on, but it was a weak bare bulb hanging down from the center of the ceiling, and it was almost useless. Tom tried flipping the switch to open the big garage door and let in some of the fading outdoor light, but there was no response. The garage door opener seemed to be broken.

"Keep the door open," Tom instructed his son. "But stay in the living room. Don't come in."

The boy nodded.

"What do you think it is?" Russ asked.

"It's a monster!" Cameron piped up.

"Probably just a possum or a raccoon or something."

In the city? Russ wanted to say, but he kept quiet, and the two of them walked slowly forward. They could now see the overturned paint cans and the shattered glass from an old Coke bottle.

Russ found that his palms were sweating, and he was having a hard time breathing. He didn't quite know what had gotten into him. He had cleared vermin out of toolsheds and storage compartments a hundred times, had lived in the wilderness with all sorts of creatures during his early days at Interior.

But this, he sensed, was different.

"Maybe a dog got in here," Tom suggested. "Maybe he snuck in somehow when the door was open and got trapped."

"Maybe," Russ said doubtfully.

But it was not a dog.

It was a monster.

They found it on top of the newspapers stacked for recycling, a terrible thing of fur and feathers, a small misshapen creature with the eyes of a man and the teeth of a beast. It was a frightening sight to behold, and it screeched at them, an abomination from hell that began jumping up and down on the papers, gibbering in a way that almost made it seem as though it were speaking a language.

Tom backed up, whirled toward the still-open door to the living room. "Get out of the house," he ordered Cameron. "You and your mom get out of the house and go next door and call 911."

The boy stood in place, not moving, eyes wide open.

"Now!"

Cameron ran to do as he was told, and the door closed, leaving the garage in almost complete darkness. The bulb barely illuminated the empty concrete directly beneath it, let alone the side of the garage where the papers were stacked.

Tom held out his broom, moving gingerly, careful not to make any sudden movements.

"Maybe we should get out of here, too," Russ suggested. "If both doors are closed, that should trap it until the authorities come."

"Maybe there's another exit—" Tom began.

And the monster screamed.

It was a sound like nothing they had ever heard, and both Russ and Tom jumped back, Russ practically stumbling over an old box of books in his way. He turned, was about to hurry out of the garage, when he saw movement out of the corner of his eye. He swiveled his head to look.

And the creature flew at him.

They did not have enough time to react. Russ tried to fight it off with the shovel, and Tom tried to bat it away with the broom, but it was a whirling dervish of claws and teeth and skinny deformed legs, and neither of them could get it off him.

He felt talons slash skin, felt the stabbing of pain, the wetness of blood.

He dropped the shovel and tried to use his hands to pull the creature off, but his fingers could get no purchase, met only insubstantial feather and slippery scaly flesh, and then his wrists were sliced open, and he fell to the ground. Dimly, he was aware of the fact that Tom's broom was beating against his head, trying to dislodge the monster.

Then he saw those human eyes staring into his own, heard a long low chuckle.

And it ripped out his throat.

Then

1

There were six of them already.

It was not yet a town, not even a hamlet, really, but it was a community, a community of six, and the beginning of a real settlement.

William finished drawing water from the well and carried the bucket back to the house. He poured some in the washbasin, then carried the bucket over to the small kitchen space, where he placed it on the floor next to the sink. He stared out the window at Marie, weaving spells over the vegetables in the garden, and he smiled, feeling good.

They had three houses built. The two women shared one, while the four men doubled up in the other two. He and Jeb lived in the first house they'd built, the smallest house, and though the single room was somewhat confining, they were used to it and would be able to put up with the situation as long as necessary.

Sleeping arrangements were going to change soon, he knew. Olivia and Martin were now a couple and were planning to get married and move in together. That meant they would probably need another house—unless Marie wanted to room with one of the men, which he doubted.

Their first order of business, though, was a barn. The animals were all still with them, bound by magic, but it would be nice if they had some shelter as well. He knew the horses had already been complaining about it, and he had promised the animals that something would be done.

They also needed a dry place to store seeds and tools and some of the implements that were now sharing space inside the homes.

After the barn and the new house?

Who knew? But he was leaning toward a store, a common building where goods could be stored and distributed. The community wasn't big enough yet to really justify such an operation, but more were on the way, and he had the feeling that it soon would be. He envisioned the town as he had first imagined it, with a livery and a saloon, with a library and theater, with a park where children could play and a school where they could learn. One day, he knew, this would be a city, a city with plumbing and law enforcement and all of the amenities of modern life.

And everyone in it would be a witch.

Marie saw him through the window, smiled, waved. He waved back.

The days here were spent working, trying to carve out a life in this canyon. At night they spoke with spirits. There'd been others on this land before, Indians, and though they did not always understand these ghosts from another culture, their presence was still welcome and reassuring.

Particularly after passing through the Bad Lands.

The Bad Lands.

William shivered just to think of it. He knew that settlers called the area around Deadwood the Badlands, but that was different. That was merely a description of geology. The land he and Jeb had come through . . .

Those were *bad* lands.

It was long after the monster in the mountains, yet still a week or so away from Arizona Territory. They'd been traveling almost due south, then suddenly they were walking west, though they hadn't changed directions. They both realized it almost at once, and they stopped. William looked around, and realized that there *were* no directions here.

It made no sense. The sun rose in the east and set in the west, and everything could be calculated from that. Only . . .

Only the sun here seemed different. There appeared to be a uniform brightness in the sky, a vaguely defined whiteness that provided illumination but took no specific shape. They could not make out a sun and thus could not determine in which direction it was headed.

Without warning, William's horse reared up behind him. He and Jeb fell back, startled, and the horse suddenly bolted, running away. He called to it, tried to summon it, and they both chased it, but the animal was gone and would not return. The last view he had of his old companion was of the creature tearing crazily across the semidesert in an indistinguishable direction.

Saying nothing to each other, the two of them gathered what they could from the few supplies that had been thrown from the horse's back and silently continued on.

The land grew rougher, the pockmarked plain degenerating into numerous finger canyons, and soon they were wandering between walls of rounded rock hundreds of feet high but with passages between them barely big enough for a single man. The narrow canyons wound around in confusing twists and turns, a veritable maze, and by nightfall they had no idea where they were or in which direction they were facing.

The night here, they found, was different as well.

There was a full moon out, but they could not see it, could only receive its refracted indirect light from the narrow band of sky above them. Most of the light died halfway down the striated rock walls, but the remainder filtered into the bottom of the gorge, throwing odd areas into relief, creating shadows where none should exist.

Shadows.

The two of them walked slowly, carefully, saying nothing. The shadows appeared to be moving of their own volition, and though it was hard to tell, an even darker shape seemed to be lurking among them, scuttling from one to another, hiding, a strangely formed being on strange claws that blended with the darkness and whose sounds simulated those of the wind.

They decided not to make camp, but to keep on, to try to find a way out of here. This was not a place where either of them would feel comfortable stopping, let alone sleeping, and they moved forward. Past moonlit silhouettes that should have looked like outcroppings of rock but did not. Past inky pools of shadow that looked both deep and soft, that shifted as they approached and seemed to have weight and heft and some terrible spark of life.

What struck William most about this area was its fundamental wrongness. If the canyon in the mountains had seemed evil, if the monster they'd found and the thought of a creature that had been able to kill it seemed frightening, that was nothing compared to the feeling generated here. For these narrow interconnected canyons were like an antechamber of hell, and as they pressed on it became increasingly hard to remember that they were somewhere in the unannexed western territory of the United States. Dread weighed upon them from all sides. They continued on, trudging through endless identical passages, and it was as if the land itself was conspiring against them, building itself as they moved forward in an effort to trap them here forever.

And then the canyon opened up, and the bluish light of the moon spilled upon them. The shadows disappeared and with them the unseen creature of darkness that had been hiding in their wake.

But the single shadow that remained on the rounded rock wall ahead was far worse than anything they had seen previously.

It was the shadow of his mother.

Goose bumps rippled over his skin. William was not easily frightened, not with the powers he had, but he was frightened now, more frightened even than he had been at his mother's execution, and as he stared at the shadow, it started to move.

It started to dance.

His mother had never danced in public, had never dared to do so, but she had often danced at home, in front of him. It was a form of expression for her, was her favorite way to conjure, and her movements were unique and individual, so specific and stylized that they could not possibly be duplicated by anyone else.

And that was exactly how her shadow was moving now.

Jeb was frightened as well, he sensed, but for other reasons. The other man could not possibly feel the depth or resonance of his own fear. William stared. The outline of his mother's form was perfect, down to the stray strand of hair that had always flipped up when she danced, and he remained rooted in place, unable to pull his gaze from this unnatural sight.

He muttered a quick spell, words of banishment and words of protection, but the twirling shadow did not disappear. He did not feel safe or protected at all. He felt vulnerable and afraid, weak and helpless.

A hand grabbed his sleeve, and then Jeb was pulling him away, chanting words of his own, words of power that William recognized but could not quite seem to place.

Whatever evil was here, he knew, was doing everything in its power to keep him from leaving. He forced himself to look away, brought to bear the full strength of his energies on repelling those influences that were focused so hard upon him.

There was a lessening of pressure, a definite easing in the strength of the malevolence being directed at them, and they quickly moved around the rock wall, steering clear of the dancing shadow, heading in the direction they suddenly knew to be south.

Amazingly, they were back in open country, where the stars were in their proper places, the moon was sinking in the second half of the sky, and there was a lightening on the eastern horizon where, in a few hours, the sun would arise.

Before them, in the now unthreatening darkness, illuminated by pure and innocent moonlight, stood a lone horse. William's horse. They hurried toward the small copse of scrubby trees where the animal stood waiting, its pack tilted on its back but still secured.

William unfastened the pack, and for the first time he and Jeb both climbed atop the horse, holding the supplies themselves as the animal carried them swiftly away from this cursed country.

Not until some time later, when the horse had slowed from a gallop to a trot, did William hazard a look behind him. All he could see was inky blackness, and he felt cold as he once again faced forward. He had the sense that if they had not left, they would have been trapped in those dark lands forever, in canyons where night never ended and only the shadows were alive.

A little over a week later, they reached a much bigger canyon, a wide, rugged gorge through whose bottom ran a quiet river, where pine trees and cactus coexisted along the sandy banks and birds twittered in hidden crevices among the rocks.

It was the land they had been deeded by the government, land at once remote and accessible, wild and peaceful, and William thought at that moment he had never seen anything quite so wonderful. In his mind sprang up a town of the future, their town, and he could see where homes would be. Shops. Taverns. Public buildings.

And now it was a reality. They had a settlement of their

own, their safety and sovereignty guaranteed by the United States of America, and more of them were on the way. It had almost been worth all the suffering and persecution, the trips through lands of nightmare, and he turned away from the kitchen sink and walked outside, looked up into the blue, blue sky, and smiled.

2

Winter passed. And spring. And summer. And fall. Winter rolled around once more, and before he knew it summer had arrived yet again.

Jeb had never been so happy in his life. The work was hard, the days were filled with the mundane chores of everyday living, but there was something exhilarating about being able to live so normally. He did not have to hide here. None of them did. They could be themselves, without constantly looking over their shoulder, without worrying that some small misstep would give them away.

And Wolf Canyon was growing by leaps and bounds.

He did not know how word was spreading, but it was, and witches from back East were making their way west, coming like pilgrims seeking sanctuary. Many of them wept when they finally saw the town. Many others yelled for joy.

They had decided to name the town after its location. It was a common thing to do out here, and "Wolf Canyon" was anonymous enough that it would not attract undue attention.

Although there was something satisfyingly humorous about it, a sly hint in the "Wolf" reference that appealed to both him and William.

There were two streets now, a main street and a cross street, and within a year there would probably be one more. It *looked* like a real town, and it was that appearance more than anything else which always gave him a feeling of real accomplishment. He remembered when Wolf Canyon had been nothing more than a piece of paper from the government and an idea in William's head, and to see it actually take shape, to be a part of its foundation and growth, was truly both inspiring and humbling.

Jeb looked up at the midday sun, then stood up from his chair, stretched, and walked across the dusty street to the bar, where he ordered brown-label whiskey.

"How goes it, Jeb?" the bartender asked, pouring his drink.

"Same as always, only more so." Jeb plopped a coin on the bar.

"You want change?"

"No, just keep 'em coming till it's gone."

One of last year's arrivals, an old dowser by the name of Herman, had canvassed the area with his stick and had announced that he had found significant silver deposits. So they'd dug a mine, found men to take turns working it, and for the first time money was coming into the community. They sold the ore to the government, and now, instead of bartering for goods and services, they had bills, they had coins, they were able to use currency like civilized folks.

Jeb smiled to himself. Pretty soon they'd have their own goddamn opera house.

Swinging hinges creaked behind him, and Simon walked up to the bar, sat down next to him. "I'll have what Jeb's having," he announced.

The bartender brought over a shot glass, filled it, and Jeb saluted his friend. The two of them downed their drinks in one quick swallow.

He'd made a lot of new friends here. Simon. Martin and Olivia. Cletus. George and Jimmy. Hazel, June, and Marie. Madsen. They'd been thrown together at first by their common nature, by the shared experiences of oppression and persecution, and that bond had seen them through the tentative early days, had enabled them to establish a sense of community.

But they *knew* each other now. And, more important, they liked each other.

William was still his best friend, and although there was no official hierarchy, the two of them were the de facto decision makers by virtue of the fact that they had been the first. William was in charge—it had been his idea and initiative, after all, that had gotten this thing off the ground—and Jeb was his second in command. They'd bandied about the idea of holding elections, but there was no real push for it. The outcome was a forgone conclusion, and they had the sense that things would be better left as is, at least for now.

He'd wondered at first how it would be, living with people like himself. Would there be feuds and fighting? Would people be reading each other's minds, jinxing the endeavors of their rivals, using their gifts for venal purposes, to fuel those petty jealousies that inevitably popped up whenever a group of people lived together in close proximity?

Thankfully, no.

None of that had come to pass, and if someone just wandered into the canyon and stayed for a few days, like as not he would not even realize that they were witches. Their powers were not hidden, but neither were they exploited. He and the others lived the way they'd always wanted to live—just like everyone else. Magic was used when it was needed, but it was only one tool among many, and it was only employed when appropriate.

From outside the bar came the sound of voices and feminine laughter, followed by footsteps on wood as a group of women strode along the walkway toward the new park at the edge of town.

Today was Independence Day, July fourth, and while the holiday had never meant much to Jeb back in the old days, here in Wolf Canyon it meant a lot. They finally had their own independence; they were finally free to be who they were. It was he who had first suggested that they all stop work on this day and celebrate, pool their talents to create the biggest celebration any of them had ever seen.

Last year had been the first. There'd been conjured fireworks the likes of which had never been seen even in China, as well as spirit shows and a spectacular display of ground light created by all of them concentrating on a single effect and using their powers together.

This year things were supposed to be even better. Jeb didn't know what William had planned—his friend had been keeping it a secret from *everyone*—but mention of it always brought a smile to his face.

"Simon?" he asked, turning to the man next to him. "What's your favorite thing in the world?"

Simon thought for a moment. "The unbathed private parts of a mature woman."

The answer was so unexpected that Jeb simply stared at him for a moment. Then he burst out laughing. Soon they were both laughing, clapping each other on the back and ordering one more round.

Afterward, Jeb walked outside, went for a long slow walk around the town to clear his head. The park was filling up with people, the women bringing food, the men bringing appetites. From June's kitchen came the warm, fragrant smell of fresh bread. One of the advantages of witchcraft—the ability to cook without fuel or fire. He passed by Martha's house, waved at her through the window. She was just placing a pie on the sill, and he offered to carry it to the park for her, but she said it had to set awhile first.

He felt good. A couple walked past him, hand in hand, and he watched them for a moment. The only thing missing from his life was that he had not yet found a woman. A lot of the men had. A lot of witches of both sexes had

met here and gotten married, and while he was always happy
for them, he could not help feeling a little sorry for himself.

Of course, no one he'd met really interested him.

Because he was still in love with Becky.

Even after all this time, he thought of her often. In his
dreams, she came to Wolf Canyon. Sometimes she was a
witch who had only just discovered her powers. Sometimes
she was not but had trekked halfway across the continent
because she missed him and wanted to be with him. But always they ended up together, and while he knew that was
just a foolish fantasy, it prevented him from even thinking
about anyone else.

"Jeb!"

He looked up at the sound of the familiar voice to see
William hurrying across the dusty street toward him, a big
smile on his face.

"I've been looking for you."

Jeb stopped, waited. "What is it?"

"I need your help."

"With what?"

William's smile grew even broader. "Something I've been
working on."

"For tonight?"

"I'd rather not discuss it here." William clapped an arm
around his shoulder. "Come on. Let's go to the picnic first.
We'll talk about it later, back at the house."

Jeb grinned, nodded, and the two of them made their way
down the street toward the park.

Now

1

He'd called his sister the night before, and told her about their father.

It could be put off no longer, and Miles didn't beat around the bush but told Bonnie exactly what had happened. She'd grown extremely quiet, for once in her life not interrupting him, and when he was finished she said simply, "Where is he now?"

"Still at the coroner's." He answered her next question before she even asked it. "They have him restrained, but he still seems to be . . . animated."

"Are you sure he's dead?"

"I'm sure. We're all sure. We just don't know . . . what it is."

There was silence after that.

"I think you should come down," Miles told her.

"For the funeral?"

He was growing exasperated. "Obviously, we haven't scheduled a funeral yet, but Dad is dead and I thought you might care enough to—"

"All right," she said. "I'm coming." But she sounded annoyed, put out, and after promising to call him once she'd booked a plane, she hung up.

She'd called back an hour later, saying that she'd be flying to L.A. In the afternoon. He asked for her flight number and the time, but she refused to give him either.

"How am I supposed to pick you up?" he asked.

"You're not. I'll take a cab from the airport. I need some time to think."

"You won't have enough thinking time on the plane? Come on, Bonnie, this doesn't make any sense. There's no reason to waste money on a cab when I can easily come and pick you up. The airport's fifteen minutes from my house, for God's sake."

"I want to be alone."

"Bonnie—"

"Stop trying to boss me around all the time. I have some things to sort through. Can't you understand that?"

She was getting ready to hang up on him—he recognized the signs—so he backed off and they parted, if not warmly, at least amicably.

Now she'd called him from the back of the cab, telling him she was on her way, and he assumed that meant she had a cellular phone. She'd never mentioned it to him, but she and Gil were yuppie enough to invest in such an obvious status symbol, and he reminded himself not to pick on her, to leave her alone, that this was a tragic time for both of them.

Well, a tragic time for him.

An inconvenience for her.

At the sound of a car pulling into the driveway, he peeked through the front window and saw a yellow cab in back of his Buick. He swore to himself that he would not provoke her, that they would not quarrel, and he hurried out to meet his sister.

She looked tired. Her skin was pale, there were large bags under her eyes, and he found that he actually felt sorry for her. He gave her a hug, helped the cab driver remove her luggage from the trunk, then carried her suitcases inside as she followed him into the house.

He put her bags in the guest bedroom, then walked back out to the living room.

Bonnie took off her coat and sat down on the couch.
"You want something to drink? Water? Tea? Coke?"

"No, thanks."

He nodded, sat down in the recliner to the right of the couch. "So how are you doing?" he asked.

She shrugged. "Fine."

He looked at his sister, suddenly aware of how much she resembled their mother. She was thinner, her movements were different, but her features and especially the expressions that passed over her face were their mother's exactly. It was ironic, because Bonnie and her mother had never really gotten along. They were too much alike, perhaps. Both highly strung and self-involved, touchy and defensive, neither of them had possessed the requisite sympathy or patience to ever understand one another. There'd been no reconciliation between them before their mother's death and, Miles suspected, no remorse on his sister's part afterward.

Bonnie smiled stiffly at him, and he smiled back. He realized that he didn't have anything to say to his sister. The questions that popped into his mind, the generic conversation openers he considered and rejected, were all of the superficial sitcom variety—*How's Gil? How are the kids?* He wanted to be able to talk to her, to really communicate, but he didn't know how. She, too, seemed to be at a loss, and they sat there awkwardly, strangers who were siblings.

It was Bonnie who spoke first. "So where's Dad . . . I mean, his body?"

"Downtown. The coroner's office."

"Do you think I should see him?"

"Do you want to?"

"I don't know."

"It's up to you."

Another awkward silence.

"Maybe I will take that drink," she said. "Water?"

"With ice?"

She nodded, and he went into the kitchen, grateful for some time to plan out what he would say. He and his sister had never been that close, but he hadn't realized until now how much they had depended upon their father to keep the conversation alive when they were together. He filled a glass with water and ice and carried it back out.

Bonnie accepted it. "Thanks." She took a sip. "Whatever happened to the nurse? You didn't tell me."

"Audra?" Miles shrugged. "She's still working for the hospice agency, but she doesn't want to speak with me. I've tried, several times. I suppose she's already on some other case, with a new patient." He sighed. "She can avoid me all she wants, but if the police want to speak to her, she'll have to talk to them."

"Police? Are there police involved?"

"Not yet. But they might be." He shook his head. "Who knows?"

More silence.

He thought for a moment. He'd been honest with her over the phone, but there was one thing he hadn't told her about, and he asked her to wait while he walked into his father's bedroom and took out the cardboard carton containing the contents of the safety deposit box.

He set the carton down on the coffee table in front of her and started telling her about their father's dream, his recurring nightmare of the tidal wave and his subsequent trip to the library to pick up occult books. Miles speculated that their dad had known what was coming, that he was somehow preparing for it or maybe even trying to stave it off. He then explained about the paraphernalia he had found in the safety deposit box.

Bonnie didn't seem all that surprised by what he had to say, and that made him suspicious. "That doesn't shock you?" he asked.

She shook her head. "Not really."

Miles pointed at the box. "So what is this?"

"What is what?"

"This!" He picked up a phial of gray powder and shook it in front of her face. He dropped the phial back in the box. "What is all this? Why would Dad keep all of this . . . magic stuff in his safety deposit box?"

"How would I know?"

"I thought he might have mentioned something about it to you."

"To me? If he'd talked about it with anyone, it would have been you. In case you hadn't noticed, we weren't exactly on the best of terms."

"I mean before all this. When we were little."

She stood. "Look, I don't know anything about any of this. I don't know what this crap is, and I don't care. I don't think it has anything to do with anything." She looked at him, shook her head. "And I don't understand why you're so worked up about it."

"Because our father is in the morgue and he's dead and he's still walking around! Is that clear enough for you?"

She sat back down.

They looked at each other—glared, really—but there was more fear in their expressions than anger, and the animosity could not be sustained by either of them. Bonnie broke first, and she reached her hand up to him, and he took it, and then they were hugging. "I'm sorry," Bonnie said.

"I'm sorry, too," Miles told her.

They held each other tighter. She started crying, sniffling at first, then wailing, and he rocked her and whispered reassurances as she sobbed into his shoulder like a baby.

In the morning, Bonnie was gone. She'd written a long apologetic letter, a rambling screed covering six double-sided pages, telling him that she could not handle this right now, that she needed some time, that she would be there for the funeral if one ever took place, but until then she just wanted to be with her family, with Gil and the kids, far away from all this.

He wanted to be angry with her, but he wasn't. She was not to blame for what was happening, and though it would be easier to hate her for her cowardice, he could not find it in himself to condemn her. After everything was said and done, she was still his sister, and there was no reason she should have to wait around for her reanimated dead dad to stop walking around and finally die like he was supposed to.

No one should have to do that.

Miles had been absent since Monday, and rather than sit cooped up in the house for yet another day, he decided to return to work. His hands were sweaty as he rode the elevator up, and he perfunctorily accepted the condolences of the other people in the office, thanked Hal for his offer to be a sympathetic ear. Not until he was safely in his cubicle, in his chair, at his desk, surrounded by the familiar mess of paperwork, though, was he finally able to relax.

He had not realized how stressful staying at home was, and he felt relieved here, almost happy. It was as if a great weight had been lifted from his shoulders, and though Naomi told him that several days of bereavement leave were still available to him, Miles was glad he'd made the decision to come in. Work would help him forget, hopefully take his mind off his personal problems.

Marina's case was the only one of his that hadn't been parceled out, and it was the only one in which he was really interested. He spent an hour or so trying to track down addresses and phone numbers, attempted to talk to Liam and was promptly hung up on, called Marina and gave her what little information he had.

Then it was lunchtime.

On an impulse, he drove out to Palm Springs, to the home

of Hubert P. Lars, the fifth man down on Liam's list, the one with the disconnected phone. As he'd suspected, the house was abandoned, and when he questioned the neighbors, he learned that Hubert had passed away six months back. Natural causes, they said. In his sleep. But Miles wasn't so sure. Every death seemed suspicious to him now, and as he drove back to L.A., past the fields of oversize high-tech windmills that spread across the hot breezy desert of the San Gorgonio Pass, he tried to imagine some reason or rationale that did not involve the supernatural.

But he could not.

He thought of his father. It was as if the walls of reality were breaking down, as though the world had shifted away from the logical, physics-governed place with which he was familiar.

There were no messages waiting for him when he arrived back at the office. He gave Liam a quick call, and in the few seconds allotted to him before the old man hung up, he blurted out that Hubert P. Lars was dead. There was a click and a dial tone, but he knew that Liam had heard him, and he hoped that the information would work on him. The men on his list all seemed to be either dead or dying, and if Liam had any sense at all, he would start cooperating and talk so that he could avoid a similar end.

Of course, maybe he thought it was inevitable. Liam was definitely frightened and did not want to die, but perhaps he believed that his fate was sealed and what was coming could not be undone.

Just like Bob had?

The parallels were a little too close for comfort, and Miles pushed the thought aside for now. He wanted to work on this case, but he did not want to think about his dad. He shifted his focus from the general to the concrete, once again busying himself with tracking down addresses and phone numbers.

On the way home, he'd planned to stop by the coroner's office, but he could not bring himself to do it. He circled the block three times, telling himself that if a parking spot opened up, that would be a sign and he'd take it. But when a space did open up on his third pass, he didn't pull in and instead drove quickly off, heading straight home.

He heated up a frozen macaroni and cheese pie, and sat down in front of the television to eat. The house seemed empty and cold, and for some reason he thought of Claire. He didn't know why, but he had been thinking about her quite often lately, and it occurred to him that he should let her know that his father had died.

No, he told himself. He might be able to rationalize it and claim that he merely wanted to inform her, but somewhere down in the mix was the fact that he would like to speak to her again, would like to hear her voice, and he refused to exploit the tragedy of his father's death for his own personal gain.

He would not tell Claire.

But the idea would not go away. He watched the news, then a syndicated tabloid show, then a sitcom, and more than once, during the programs and during the commercials, he found himself thinking of how she'd react to the news, how sad and upset she would be, how she would want to know.

He looked over at the clock. Eight-thirty. Claire had always had a prohibition against answering any phone call after nine o'clock at night, figuring that if someone called that late it was probably bad news, and she'd rather sleep through the night not knowing and find out in the morning.

Should he call? Would she even care? He wasn't sure. She had always liked his father, but the breakup had been bitter, a lot of harsh words had been exchanged, and there'd been no communication between himself and his ex-wife for nearly five years.

He wasn't even sure he had her current phone number.

But he felt obligated to at least make the effort to contact her. Death was so much bigger than everything else; it superseded all other problems between them.

And a death like this . . .

He searched through his old personal phone book until he found her number. If this wasn't good, he could use the agency's resources to track her down—though he wasn't sure he was willing to do that.

He dialed the number. The phone rang once. Twice. Three times. It was picked up in the middle of the fourth ring. "Hello?"

Claire.

Her voice sounded different than he remembered, softer, lower, less strident, but he recognized it immediately, and for one weird moment it felt as though no time had passed, as though they were still together and he was merely calling to check in with her.

"Hello," he said, keeping his voice even. "It's Miles."

There was silence on her end, and he was tempted to hang up, but he pressed forward, talking quickly, not wanting her to cut him off. "My dad had a stroke about a month ago, and he's been bedridden ever since, partially paralyzed. And . . . and now he's dead. He died. I just thought you might want to know."

His hand was trembling almost as much as his voice, and he gripped the receiver tighter, trying to steady his grip, but that only seemed to make the shaking worse. He realized when he felt a building tightness in his chest that he was holding his breath, waiting for her response, and he exhaled, the sound amplified loudly in the earpiece of the phone.

"Oh, Miles," she said, and the genuine sadness he heard in her voice, the concern that was imparted through those two simple words, made him ache with a loss that cut clear to the bone. He understood for the first time how much he had truly missed her, and he closed his eyes, trying to hold back the tide of emotion that threatened to wash over him.

"Are you okay?" she asked.

He took a deep breath. "I'm fine."

"I really liked your dad. He was a great guy. I . . . I've missed him."

Miles tried to swallow the lump in his throat. "Yeah."

There was a brief silence, and Miles thought he heard a sniffle on the other end of the line.

"Was it . . . ?" This time the sniffle was definite, and it was accompanied by a catch in her breath. "Did Bob suffer much?"

"I don't think so," he said. "But . . . I don't know."

He wanted to come clean, wanted to tell her everything, but they were no longer married, she was no longer a part of his life, and this wasn't her problem.

That was probably the one good thing about them not being together anymore: the fact that she didn't need to know what had really happened to his father.

"When's the funeral?" she asked.

"We, uh"—he cleared his throat—"we haven't scheduled a time yet."

There was an awkward pause that turned into an extended silence.

"Are you . . . would you like . . ?" He heard the nervousness in her voice, heard her suck in her breath in order to imbue herself with resolve, just the way he remembered her doing. "Is it all right if I come over?"

His response was a beat too slow.

"I understand if you don't," she said quickly. "I just thought—"

"Yeah," he said. "That'd be great."

"You want me to come over?"

"I'd like to see you again."

Neither of them knew what to say after that, and for a

few seconds Miles thought he had screwed it up. Then she said, "I'll come by in an hour or so. I assume you still live in the same place?"

"Same place."

"All right. I'll see you then."

They said their good-byes and hung up quickly, neither of them wanting to jinx the plan. As soon as he hung up the phone, he started furiously cleaning the living room and kitchen, trying to get the house in some semblance of order before Claire arrived. He barely had time to put on new clothes and comb his hair before the doorbell rang.

He went to answer it, his heart fluttering, his palms sweaty, his hands trembling.

She looked even prettier than he recalled, as though his memory had rounded her off to a lower level of beauty, not wanting him to suffer any more than he did already. But now she was here, in glorious 3-D technicolor, and she was as attractive to him as she had been the first time he'd met her. Whatever spark had originally ignited their feelings for each other was still there, at least on his side, and he stared at her stupidly, unable to think of anything to say other than, "Hi."

There was a moment of indecision, then she was throwing her arms around him, hugging him, crying, saying, "I'm sorry . . . I'm sorry . . . I'm sorry . . ."

He hugged her back, feeling his own tears well up. He had not cried since his dad died, but Claire's presence somehow gave him permission to feel grief, and he sobbed now as he had not sobbed since childhood.

She talked about his father as she cried, and each recalled memory brought forth a renewed burst of tears. It was painful to think about, but the pain felt good in a way, searing, cleansing. For the first time since his father's death, he allowed his mind to think about the old days, the good days, the days before the stroke. He had been concentrating only on the here and now, afraid if he let himself dwell upon better times in the past, he would sink into an emotional abyss from which he could not crawl out.

After a while he was all cried out, and soon so was she. They broke apart, sat down on the couch, and for the first time since the divorce, they talked.

He was still in love with her, he realized, would probably always be in love with her, but they did not speak of that. They did not talk of their marriage or their former life together, though that was a subtext under everything they said. They did not talk of their current lives or their possible futures.

They talked about Bob.

The shadows lengthened, the house grew dark. They turned on lights but made no effort to move. Miles did not offer Claire anything to eat or drink, and she did not ask for anything. They remained in place, remembering the life of a man they loved, until well past midnight.

It felt strange not straying from that topic, but it felt right. Miles knew that any attempt to broaden the conversation might break the spell, might disrupt the tentative rapproachment they had forged, and that was something neither of them wanted, so they continued sharing their memories, good and bad, happy and sad, until each of them had said everything they had to say.

They both had to work in the morning, and Claire got up to leave. She asked if he was all right, asked if he needed her to stay, and he told her he was fine. She said good-bye but promised to return tomorrow, after work, and she gave him a quick kiss on the cheek before walking out to her car.

He watched her drive away, still standing in the doorway, staring at the empty street long after her taillights had disappeared around the corner.

Claire.

He was not sure he understood what had just happened.

They had not seen each other since the divorce—and at that time she'd made it clear that she never wanted to see him again—but she had raced over at the news that his father had died, and had even offered to spend the night if he needed someone to be with. It could have been just kindness. Maybe, for some reason, she thought he might be suicidal and was showing him the same consideration she would show anyone in mortal distress. Maybe she simply loved her ex-father-in-law and wanted to share her feelings with someone else who had known and loved him and would understand.

Maybe.

But he had the sense that there was something more going on here, and while he usually did not allow himself to cling to false hope, he wasn't sure this hope *was* false, and in his mind he could see the two of them together again.

Miles fell asleep thinking about how nice it would be to once more wake up with Claire under the covers next to him.

He was awakened in the middle of the night by the sound of ringing, and it took his sleep-fogged brain a moment to sort through its catalog of sounds and identify what the noise was. By the time he finally picked up the receiver, the phone had already rung at least ten times. With a sinking feeling in his stomach, he spoke into the mouthpiece. No good news ever came from someone so desperate to get ahold of a person at this ungodly hour. "Hello?"

"Mr. Huerdeen?"

His heart rate accelerated. Formality was never good either. "Yes?"

"This is Smith Blume, deputy county coroner. I work the night shift here, and I've been assigned to your father's case." Blume cleared his throat embarrassedly. "I'm afraid there's been . . . well, not exactly an accident, but . . . we have a small problem with your father."

Miles gripped the phone tightly. "What are you saying?"

The coroner took a deep breath. "I'm saying, Mr. Huerdeen, that your father has walked out of here. He's gone."

2

Liam dreamed he was running through the desert, being chased by a horde of homeless people with raggedy black clothes and glowing blue faces. It was a very lush desert, and he kept getting scraped and stabbed as he ran between the closely growing cacti. Ahead was a small shack, a ramshackle building barely bigger than the Unabomber's cabin, and though there were no windows, the door was open and standing in the doorway, silhouetted by the yellow-orange light of a fire, was a hunched old woman.

The woman scared him, but the mob behind him scared him more, and he ran toward the open doorway. As he drew closer, he could make out details of the old woman's appearance. There was something strange about the crone's features, something unearthly in the makeup of her face.

She was his only hope, however, and he ran up to her. "Let me in!" he yelled. He turned to look over his shoulder, saw the blue faces of the homeless people running toward the shack.

"Eat an apple." The old woman held forth a shiny red apple, and he understood that the only way he would be allowed into the hut was if he took a bite of the fruit. He recognized the scene—it was from *Snow White,* the Disney version—but there was a real sense of menace here, an intensity that Walt Disney never could have invested in any movie.

He didn't want to eat the apple, was afraid to even touch it.

"Let me in!" he screamed.

"Eat the apple."

The old woman handed him the fruit. He had no choice, the mob was almost upon him. He bit into the apple.

Immediately he regretted it. He felt warm wetness in his mouth, and he tried to spit the piece out, but it was moving on its own, and it wiggled past his tongue and down his throat. He looked down. The apple was filled with veins of pumping blood. He could see them running through the whiteness of the interior fruit, beneath the shiny skin that now looked like real skin, human skin.

He whirled around. The desert was empty, the mob was gone.

They had been chasing him *here,* he realized. The old woman was in charge of the homeless people, and as he swallowed the bite of bloody apple he saw her change. She stood straighter, grew, the years dropping from her. She was now a gorgeous, statuesque woman, and though the features of her face were now young and beautiful rather than old and ugly, they were no less terrifying.

"It's time," the woman said, smiling in a way that made him want to scream. Behind her, the fire went out, all light disappearing from the shack. She grabbed his midsection, pulled him with her into the darkness, and they fell into water that was black and cold . . .

He awoke drenched with sweat, shivering. He'd left a window open, and the damp beach air had permeated the room. That was not what had instigated the nightmare, though. He knew that sometimes the outside world dictated the conditions of his inner night thoughts, that his brain incorporated snatches of dialogue from the television when he napped, or set him down on a tropical island when it was summer, but that had not happened here, he was sure of it, and though he couldn't say why, he knew with unshakable certainty that the impetus behind this dream was nothing so benign.

The phone rang, but he was afraid to answer it, and he let it ring and ring and ring until the ringing finally stopped.

He took the phone off the hook.

Why was she playing with him? Why didn't she just get it over with?

She?

Where did that come from? His dream, he supposed, although it felt more substantive than that. It seemed more like something he'd always known but until now had not been able to recall, and the picture in his mind was of the statuesque woman standing in the doorway of a shack in Wolf Canyon.

Wolf Canyon.

It always seemed to come back to that.

Liam got out of bed and walked into the bathroom to get a drink of water.

He'd felt, even back then, that Wolf Canyon had been more than just an accident or a tragic mistake, and that feeling had grown, not diminished, over the years. He felt responsible, yes, but he'd known even at the time—they'd all known—that there'd been more at work here than the physical facts of the event. And the lack of information they'd received from the government, the fact that no charges had ever been brought against anyone, that the incident had never been acknowledged and that no word had ever leaked out about it, only confirmed his suspicions.

Still, he knew that he and his crew had the direct responsibility for what actually happened, and on some level, he supposed, he probably thought he deserved to be punished for it.

Maybe that's why he was resisting Marina's detective, why he wasn't making more of an effort to enlist help in defending himself.

He got his drink, then walked back out to the bedroom. On an impulse, he opened the curtains and looked outside.

He would not have been surprised to see either a band of homeless people standing on his lawn or a long black car parked in his driveway, but there was neither, and he crawled back into bed and spent the rest of the night sleeping dreamlessly.

Then

1

He met Isabella two days out of Cheyenne. She was wandering westward, allowed, through fear rather than charity, to leave the town in which she'd been practicing instead of being executed.

William first saw her on the trail far ahead, a dark dot in the distance, and he hurried to catch up, spurring his horse onward.

He reached her quickly. She was pretty, he saw as his horse pulled next to hers. Beautiful in fact. But it was a wild, dangerous beauty, frightening somehow, and totally unlike that of any woman he had ever seen. Her black hair was long even by Territory standards, and though it framed her face in an unkempt tangle, it looked somehow natural.

She greeted him with a tired unsurprised smile, a remarkably mundane expression that seemed inappropriate on the otherworldly features of her face. "I thought I sensed another," she said simply.

"My name is William," he told her.

"I am Isabella."

She had no destination in mind, was merely following the setting sun, having heard of more tolerant communities in the West, places where people were less judgmental of those who were diffcrent.

She'd come from Fallbrook, a tiny settlement three days east of Cheyenne, where she'd lived for the past several years, acting as the town's unofficial healer and midwife.

No one there had peered too closely into her life or examined too carefully what she did—not because they didn't suspect anything but because she was too valuable to the community and they thought it better not to know.

All that had changed with the coming of the missionaries. Three closely knit Pentecostal families had moved into the valley in an effort to save souls, and they had known what she was immediately. The townspeople feigned ignorance, staved off the inevitable as long as they could, but soon they were pretending to be outraged and pretty soon their outrage became real.

They came for her one night, a mob, the whole town almost, trampling her herb garden and demanding that she come out and repent for her sins.

They did not want her to repent, Isabella knew. They wanted her to pay for her sins. But she had been ready for this, and she scattered them with a windstorm while she gathered together her belongings. She had no horse of her own and had to steal one, but a man at the stable saw her and ran to fetch the others.

She'd escaped only by killing a baby girl and threatening death for all other infants, blight and disease for all crops and livestock.

A baby girl.

William didn't like that, but though he could not imagine himself ever doing such a thing, he realized that these were desperate times for their kind. He had not been there. Who was he to judge? Besides, maybe he too would be capable of such an act if it meant his own survival.

Maybe.

But he didn't think so.

He would have found some other way to demonstrate his power.

He watched Isabella as she rode along the barely discernible trail. There was a hardness to her—the familiar hardness of whores—but something else as well, something solid, icy, and unfathomable that penetrated the deepest center of her being. She was not like anyone he had ever met, and though that made him wary, it also attracted him. He was enticed by her mystery and her strength as much as by her beauty.

She glanced over at him. "Where are you from?" she asked. "And where are you going?"

He told her about Wolf Canyon, how he'd come up with the idea and gone about getting a grant of government land, how it offered a place of safety and refuge for those of their kind, a chance to live in peace without having to always worry about exposure. Her eyes widened at the news, and he saw in her face the excited wonder and anticipation he had seen in so many others when they first learned that they had a community of their own.

He was returning from a meeting in Cheyenne with a government representative, he told her. The mine in Wolf Canyon had proved to be quite profitable, and there had been some question as to whether the government had to buy the mined ore from them or whether it was entitled to the ore outright since the land deed specified occupational rights, not mineral rights. The official with whom he'd met had signed a document granting the residents of Wolf Canyon all land rights and agreeing to buy at full market value any ore mined.

Isabella grinned. "Did you force him into signing?"

William was puzzled for a moment. "Did I—?" Then he understood what she was getting at. "You mean, did I use magic?"

She nodded.

"No. Of course not."

"Would you have? If you needed to do so?"

"I hadn't thought about it."

"Think about it now."

He was uncomfortable with this line of thought, but it took him only a moment to declare emphatically, "No, I would not have used magic."

"Hmmm." She nodded, saying nothing else, and they continued on for a while in silence.

He knew what her answer would have been, and while it disturbed him, he could understand her feelings and was not entirely unsympathetic.

They were soon talking once again, and of course she asked about the town. He invited her to accompany him, to visit if she wanted, to stay if she so desired, and Isabella quickly agreed to come.

Most witches did not realize how alone they were, and the existence of Wolf Canyon captured the interest of all of them, offering a sense of true community. Isabella was no different. She continued asking about Wolf Canyon, and he delighted in telling her stories of the people and the places, introducing her to individuals she had yet to meet. By the time they finished the long trek to Arizona Territory, she would probably know the town as well as anyone who lived there.

The day passed quickly. Isabella was a wonderful traveling companion, and the more time he spent with her, the more impressed he was with her wit, her intelligence, and her remarkable beauty.

She gave herself to him that night, on the ground, under the stars. There was a dark strangeness to her desires, and a willingness to assert herself, that made him embarrassed and uncomfortable but with which he willingly went along. She touched him in places he had never been touched before, both literally and figuratively, and by the time it was over and they were lying in dirt that had since become mud, he knew that he loved her.

* * *

Jeb was not so easily won over. Neither were most of the other people in town. They were nice to Isabella, friendly up to a point, but she seemed to elicit suspicion and misgivings of a type that none of their previous settlers had. William put it down to jealousy for the most part. He was, after all, the town's leader and founder, and it was only natural that his older friends would feel left out because of the amount of time he spent with her.

But that didn't explain all of it, and the uneasiness that the others seemed to feel around Isabella was, he had to admit, not entirely absent from his own thoughts.

A baby girl.

Still, she was one of them, and it was easy for him to overlook in her what in someone else might be serious cause for concern.

Besides . . . he loved her.

She moved directly into his house, and though he made a pretense of offering her a room of her own, Isabella informed him bluntly that they would be sleeping together.

There was no period of adjustment for her. If she noticed the reservations other people seemed to have, she gave no indication. She behaved as though she had been born here, immediately inserting herself into the life of the community, planting spontaneously germinating flowers along the streets in town, bringing her considerable powers to bear on the struggling apple orchard, transforming William's house from the spartan living quarters of a bachelor to a beautiful happy home.

She was more assertive than the other women in town, more like a man, and that seemed to unnerve a lot of the residents. She had a regalness to her bearing, a self-confidence that bordered on arrogance and set her apart no matter how much she tried to fit in. So when she started taking extra duties upon herself, it seemed perfectly natural.

The truth was, William was happy to have someone with

whom he could share the pressures of his position. Jeb was his right-hand man, and the two of them talked over everything, but the final decision was always his to make. He was grateful for Isabella, grateful to have someone more intimate than a friend or an adviser who could understand and share his feelings and often help him come to a decision.

She'd been in Wolf Canyon for nearly half a year when she first made the choice to act independently. Their settlement was far off the beaten track and they rarely had outside visitors, but it had happened once or twice before, and this time a trio of men heading to Yuma were passing through and stopped.

As always, the residents were on their best behavior. They had discussed this among themselves in numerous town meetings, and they'd unanimously decided to hide all evidence of magic from outsiders, not wanting word to spread. Their rights were legally protected by the United States government, but the territories were far from Washington, and out here legal protection and real protection were often two different things.

So the people on the street smiled at the three men as they rode in and waved at them, pretending as though there was nothing out of the ordinary here and they were just typical settlers.

William was standing with Jeb outside the livery stables when they heard the excited commotion and turned to see the strangers passing through a growing crowd of townspeople. They were obviously headed for the saloon, looking to wet their whistles, and William felt more than a little proud that there *was* a place where travelers could get some whiskey.

He looked at Jeb, and the two of them started down the street.

"Don't say anything," Jeb told him.

"I never do."

The men had tethered their horses and were about to walk into the saloon when Isabella appeared, as if from nowhere, and barred their way. The man in the lead, a burly bearded fellow wearing about three days' worth of dust on his leather hat and clothes, stopped short, confused. He nodded at her, tipped his hat, tried to smile. "Pardon me, ma'am."

Isabella remained in place.

"I'm sorry, but we need to get into the saloon here."

"No, you don't." She looked at him. "Why don't you just turn around the way you came?"

Her words carried clearly in the still air, and the rustle of the crowd settled into silence.

For the first time since coming to Wolf Canyon, William was at a loss. He didn't know whether to intercede, to stop Isabella and apologize to the men, or whether to let the situation take its own course. His first impulse was to slink away and pretend he had never seen any of it—and that disturbed him. He was not a coward and he had never before shied away from confrontation, but his gut instinct told him to stay away from this.

The bearded man looked at his friends, then looked back toward Isabella. "Excuse me?"

"Get out. This is no place for your kind."

It was said with supreme disgust, in the way she had no doubt heard similar words addressed to her for her entire life, but there was still something off-putting about it. William had experienced prejudice, too—they all had—but he felt no sense of satisfaction hearing the words spoken by one of his own kind. He could tell from looking around that most of the others in town felt the same way.

He should have stepped in at that point. Everything afterward could have been avoided.

But he did not.

All three of the men started laughing, deep rough angry laughs, and there was nothing at all humorous in the sound.

"Out of the way," the bearded man said, attempting to push Isabella aside.

He was thrown into the street, landing flat on his back.

The other two men followed, pushed by an unseen force, and Isabella advanced down the saloon's single step toward them.

William was aware once again of her fundamental strangeness. He had gotten used to her in the time they'd lived together, but once more he saw her as she'd appeared to him that first time: an untamed beauty with unknown potential power and a clear capacity for chaos.

The smallest and dirtiest of the three looked up at her. "What the hell's going on here?"

"We're witches," she said, smiling slyly. "You're in *our* town now."

The man drew his gun and tried to shoot her, but with a flick of her wild mane, the weapon flew from his grasp, twirled in the air, and fell impotently to the ground.

All three of the men were trying to scuttle backward and scramble to their feet, all the while keeping an eye on her. The bearded man looked wildly around at the assembled crowd. "Is that true?" he demanded. "You're all witches?"

"Now you know," Isabella said. "That is why you have to die."

Before anyone could stop her, she was chanting and moving her hands in the air. The bearded man, on his feet now and drawing his gun, suddenly exploded outward. His guts burst through his stomach and flew like a bloody pink lasso, unraveling until it reached the end, and then falling lifelessly into the dirt. The man's mouth opened and closed, greenish bile running out and down his beard, but no sound issued forth, and he fell face forward onto the dirt.

The small man was frozen in place, shaking with tremors. His eyes widened as his arms were jerked above his head. He started to stretch, started to grow, but it was not a gradual process. It was as if his feet were affixed to the ground and some invisible giant was yanking on his arms, trying to pull him up quickly. He was still shaking, only now he was screaming, and his body actually did lengthen before it finally gave way and popped open, the bones breaking loudly, the skin ripping apart. The screams stopped abruptly, and the man's legs slumped to the ground as his torso continued upward for several seconds before being dropped back down onto the pile of bloody entrails that had fallen out and onto the dirt.

The third man had his pistol drawn and was running straight toward Isabella, shooting, but with each attempted shot, his hand would jerk up or away, the fired bullets soaring harmlessly over the buildings or into the wood of the structures. She continued to walk toward him, and when they reached each other, he attempted to hit her with the pistol, but she caught his hand in hers, and the pistol melted, hot metal dripping over his fingers, searing the flesh, eating through to the bone. He screamed in agony. Smiling, she touched his forehead, and it was as if her hand itself was hot metal. His skin started smoking. She caressed his cheek, put a finger to his lips, trailed her hand over his throat. Wherever she touched him, the skin started to burn, and before she had even gotten below his neck, he had fallen to the dirt, thrashing around on the street, his head dissolving, until he was finally still.

All of this took place quickly, and it was over almost as soon as it started.

William stood there, stunned.

The bodies lay in the center of the street, blood seeping into the dusty gravel and hard-packed dirt. The world lay enveloped in a huge conspicuous silence. Most eyes were still on Isabella, but quite a few were focused on him as well, and even those who weren't specifically looking his way were directing their thoughts at him. He knew what they expected. He was the leader of the town, and she was his woman. It was up to him to put a stop to this. But he did not know how, and truth be told, he was afraid to do so. This was not the Isabella he loved. He did not know the woman who had murdered these men. He was not even sure he *could* do anything to her. Clearly she was possessed of a power he could not hope to match.

What frightened him, though, was not the strength of her powers. It was not her magical abilities that made his blood run cold.

It was the delight she seemed to take in torturing the men, the relish she exhibited in killing them.

A baby girl.

He looked at her, and she was still smiling, a strange crazed glee lighting up her features.

Then she met his eyes and the expression vanished.

She immediately burst into tears. Crying, she ran between the saloon and the general store, back toward the house. He stood there, looking around at the townspeople. His gaze met Jeb's, held it for a moment. Then he turned away and, with his head down, hurried off after Isabella.

He found her in their bedroom, on the bed, sobbing.

He didn't know what to do. He did not want to put his arms around her, but she was clearly in pain. Despite his revulsion and horror at what she had done, he sat on the bed next to her and touched her hair. "Isabella?"

"It got out of hand," she said. "I didn't mean to . . ." The words trailed off into tears and sobs and sniffles.

He didn't believe that. She'd done exactly what she meant to do, and even if she really was feeling remorseful now, at the time she had intended to kill those travelers.

And she'd enjoyed it.

He said nothing, not knowing what to say. He continued to stroke her hair as he waited for her sobs to quiet down.

Isabella rolled over, wiped her eyes and nose. She faced

him squarely. "I knew those men," she said. "They didn't recognize me, but I knew them from Kansas City."

"Kansas City?"

"It's where I was born and grew up. Or where my parents abandoned me after they found out what I was. The owner of a brothel took me in and raised me, and eventually I started . . . working for her." She took a deep breath. "That's where I met those men. They . . . hurt me. They made me do things I didn't want to do. And when I ran out of the room, crying, the woman who'd raised me, the woman I considered my mother, took their side, and made me go back, where they beat me and cut me and almost killed me.

"I ran away after that.

"And today, when I was walking to the garden to pick vegetables, I looked up and there they were. The men who had almost killed me. I . . . I couldn't help myself. I couldn't resist."

He didn't believe it.

William looked away. He didn't doubt that it could have happened—and there was no way he could know for sure because he couldn't read her—but it seemed to him implausible. He had a hard time imagining Isabella ever submitting to the will of another, and there was no way he could picture her being hurt and abused without using her powers to strike back.

He wasn't sure he even believed that her parents had abandoned her. Or that she'd ever been in Kansas City.

"I'm sorry," she said, starting to cry again. "I'm sorry."

He held her and patted her back and told her it was all right, but it was not all right. Although he loved her and would always love her—he could not help that—he was still appalled by what she'd done. He tried to think of a way to smooth it over for the town, to somehow bring her back into the fold and make everything the way it was before.

"I'm sorry," she sobbed.

●

He would accept her story, he decided, and he would tell it to everyone else, let everyone know. That would make her actions more understandable, more forgivable.

At least to the other people in town.

That night, in bed, she was energized, creative beyond even her usual standards, and as she screamed, as she climaxed, he looked down at her face, and the expression he saw there was the same one that had been on her features when she'd killed the last man with her burning touch. He recognized the same fervid, intense excitement he'd seen in her on the street, and he closed his eyes and quickly finished without looking again at her face.

Now

1

His father had dropped off the face of the earth.

It was impossible, but it seemed to be the case, and as the days passed and neither the police nor the agency could find any trace of the body, Miles began wondering if he would ever learn of his father's ultimate fate.

He kept expecting to be visited by men from some top secret government agency, well-dressed individuals wearing business suits and sunglasses and small earphone transmitters, to be told that all information concerning his father was classified and that he was forbidden to continue his search on the grounds that it was a threat to national security. But real life was not the same as the movies, not even here in Southern California. No mysterious agents came forward to inform him that his father was part of some secret experiment, and he was left with just the blind, dumb search for his dad's walking corpse.

Maybe he would never know. Maybe the body would never turn up, there would never be a funeral, and he would go to his own grave never finding out whether his dad had finally succumbed to a proper death or was still some sort of zombie.

The only thing good to come out of all this was Claire.

He still did not know where they stood, but she came over after work each day, bringing dinner, and they ate together, talked and enjoyed each other's company. He was happy to be with her, it was almost like having her back, and he didn't want to jinx it by discussing the status of their relationship.

He *had* talked to her about Bob, had told her everything, and with the type of trust that is only born of intimacy, she completely believed his account of events. She was concerned and worried by what had happened, but she did not appear to be scared, and for that he was thankful. He was frightened enough for both of them, and it was nice to have a shoulder he could lean on.

Together, they looked over the magic paraphernalia from the safety deposit box, and Claire theorized that Bob had in his younger days crossed swords with some sort of satanic cult or coven of witches, and that he'd attempted to use this stuff to protect himself against them.

"If that's the case," Miles said, "it looks like he failed. They won out in the end."

"Maybe," Claire admitted.

Both of them refused to believe that Bob himself had been involved in the black arts, that he had in any way brought this upon himself. They knew him too well. He was not that kind of person. He had been a good and kind man, a loving father, and to implicate him in all this would have meant that his whole life had been a lie, that he had deceived everyone into thinking he was someone he was not, and neither of them could believe that that was the case.

Miles found it a little disconcerting, the ease with which Claire accepted all of this. Without any proof she believed a man could continue to walk after death. He asked her if she had ever encountered anything supernatural before. The way things had been going lately, he would not have been surprised to discover that all along she'd been part of some underground group of conjure wives. But to his relief she said that, no, this was her first encounter with the supernatural, and she hoped to God that it was her last.

As the days passed and there was still no sign of his

father's body, as his morning and evening calls to the police and the coroner's office became less and less urgent, more and more resigned, Miles kept expecting Claire to cut him off, to determine that he was stable enough to handle this situation on his own, and to resume her normal life, to tell him that it was nice seeing him again, but...

That didn't happen.

If anything, they became even closer as the pressure, inevitably, lessened.

They were kissing each other good-bye, hugging their hellos, snuggling together on the couch when they watched TV, all actions that could be interpreted in a variety of ways. He knew how he wanted to interpret them, but that was precisely the way he was afraid to interpret them, and he chose to pretend that they were just friends, grown-ups who behaved in a civilized adult manner without ascribing emotional significance to every meaningless touch.

Still, she was once again a part of his life, and they now had a relationship where before there was none.

On Wednesday, they met at a restaurant after work. Matta's. The Mexican restaurant where they'd gone on their first date and many dates after and that had eventually become "theirs." He had not chosen it for that reason. He had merely wanted to take her out as a change of pace, to thank her for cooking him dinner so often over the past few weeks. He decided on Matta's because it was close, cheap, and he knew that they both liked the food. The sentimental symbolism of the restaurant did not occur to him until she showed up and they were led to one of the small back booths, just like the old days. The knowledge put something of a damper on the meal, inhibiting conversation, making them both uncomfortable, and they ate quickly, in a hurry to leave.

After, it was still early, and Claire came back home with him. They settled in front of the television to watch the news. Their earlier awkwardness was gone, and once again they were close and comfortable with each other, commenting on the news of the day, making fun of the superficial anchors on the entertainment program that followed.

Miles went to the kitchen and returned with two glasses of wine. He handed one to Claire, and she sipped it carefully, smiling in thanks.

They sat in silence for a few moments. Miles picked up the remote control and flipped through channels until he found something he wanted to watch, an old Humphrey Bogart movie.

"You know," Claire said, "one of my clients should become one of your clients."

"Yeah?" he looked over at her, and he could not help smiling. He hadn't realized how much he'd missed the give-and-take between them, these casual discussions of their work and their jobs that somehow managed to be more intimate and more interesting than any conversation he'd had with any other woman. Claire was a clinical social worker, and when they'd lived together, she'd often tell him about the drug-addicted single mothers she'd be trying to steer straight in order to reclaim child custody, or the developmentally disabled she had to teach to shop for food and necessities so they could live on their own. He'd always enjoyed their talk of work, it had always made him feel close to her, and it was only after their breakup, during the bitter divorce proceedings, that he realized she considered this part of his pattern of avoidance. She'd wanted to focus on their lives together, not their lives apart. To her, their conversations were more proof, as if proof was needed, of how far they had drifted apart. But to him it meant just the opposite, and now as she told him about her client and talked of her work, he felt a pleasant sensation of déjà vu, and he allowed himself to speculate that perhaps they would get back together again.

Maybe he *had* picked Matta's for some reason other than mere convenience.

Claire finished her wine, put the glass down on the coffee table. "He's been diagnosed as a paranoid schizophrenic, a diagnosis he accepts, but he's still convinced that he's being stalked, even though he has no objective proof to back him up. He says he's been getting weird phone calls, he's been chased on the street, cars have attempted to run him down. We've tried to tell him that no one is stalking him, that what he sees as a series of interconnected events are, if they even occurred, random coincidences, but it seems like the only thing that would put his mind at rest would be to have an actual detective investigate whether someone's after him."

Miles' heart had started to pound halfway through her story. "What's his name?"

"Why?"

"Hold on a minute." He got up, rushed out of the room to the den, and returned with a copy of Liam's list. "Is his name on here?"

Claire scanned the paper, read to the bottom, shook her head. "No. Why? What's this about?"

"Are you sure?"

"Of course I'm sure."

He took the paper from her. "My current client is being stalked. Phones, cars, everything you described. He made up this list, and one by one the people on it are being picked off, killed."

"Then, this is some kind of hit list."

"Some kind. But not all of the people have been murdered. Some have died of natural causes. And some have died in ways that . . . well, that can't really be explained."

"And you thought my client might be connected to this?"

"The story's similar."

"Yeah," she admitted. "It is."

"So I thought this might be tied in."

She nodded. "I understand why you might think that, especially after what happened to Bob, but you have to be careful not to start reading import into everything. Pretty soon you'll be seeing patterns in unrelated events, making connections where there are none. Don't let your father's situation color everything."

"This is something similar to the case I'm working on. That's all. It has nothing to do with my dad."

"Doesn't it?"

He turned away, folded the paper. "No. And I suggest you keep an eye on this guy. My list is not foolproof. Just because your client is not on the list doesn't mean that he's not a target. Don't automatically discount his fears."

"I won't," she said.

They were silent for a moment.

"So what about Bob?" she asked.

"Wasn't that a movie?"

"I'm talking to you seriously."

Miles took a deep breath. "What about him?"

"Do you think—?"

"I don't know what to think."

"What are you going to do?" she asked.

He shrugged. "What *can* I do? Wait until his body turns up, I suppose."

"Do you think it will?"

"It has to sometime."

But he didn't sound convincing even to himself, and he was glad when Claire dropped the subject and put her arm around him and they settled back into the couch to watch the movie.

Finally.

One of the other men on Liam's list lived in the Los Angeles area, and with the help of Hal, who had a good memory as well as a recurring client who ran an adult bookstore, Miles found the work address of one Owen Brodsky.

Brodsky was a porno distributor, one of the third-tier middlemen who sold videos through ads in raunchy magazines and smutty newspapers. His office/headquarters/warehouse was a two-room rental in one of the nearly condemned Hollywood buildings that was sinking thanks to the subway being dug under the street below. Subway construction was the bane of Hollywood's tourist office but a boon to small business owners like Brodsky, who could now afford rent in places that before would have been priced far beyond their means. A Hollywood zip code was all-important, and Miles understood why Brodsky would covet a Hollywood location, particularly in his business.

Downstairs, Brodsky's building housed a movie-themed bookstore, a closed tattoo parlor, and an open-fronted shop carrying gaudy Mexican merchandise. The upper offices were reached by a narrow stairwell located behind a door sandwiched between the bookstore and the tattoo parlor, and Miles climbed up the steps, walking down the hallway at the top until he found the closed door with the cheap plaque reading: *Brodsky Productions*. He knocked, heard no answer, then tried the knob. It was unlocked, and he opened the door, stepping into the office.

The room was crowded and messy and looked more like an abandoned storage locker that had been ransacked than someone's office. A grossly overweight man with a pile of Der Wienerschnitzel wrappers on the cluttered desk in front of him looked up when Miles walked in but did not stop sorting through what looked like a sheaf of order forms in his hands. Miles glanced around, saw stacks of videocassettes and their extremely graphic covers piled on tables, cabinets, and the floor. A doorway leading into another office revealed boxes and cartons and even bigger piles of

stacked tapes, as well as a dirty floor littered with magazines and yellowed newspapers.

"Mr. Brodsky?" Miles said.

The man's eyes narrowed. "Who are you?"

"I'm a private detective. Are you Mr. Brodsky?"

"Yeah, I'm Mr. Brodsky. What can I do for you?"

Miles held out his hand. "Hi there. I'm Miles Huerdeen."

The big man declined to shake, continued sorting through
the forms. "Call me Fred."

"Fred?" Miles frowned. "I'm looking for a Mr. *Owen*
Brodsky."

"You're looking for my dad."

"Oh. Do you know where I can find him?"

"Forest Lawn."

He had a sinking feeling in his chest. "You mean he's—"

"He died about a year ago. Heart attack. Why? What'd
you need him for?"

Miles sighed. "I'm investigating a stalking case. My
client's father has been threatened numerous times, and his
life is possibly in danger. He drew up a list of names, and
quite a few people on that list have died under mysterious
circumstances."

"I told you: my dad had a heart attack."

"I understand that. But I was hoping to speak to your
father, if he was alive, to see if he knew of any connection
between the names on the list, if he knew of any reason
someone might be going after any of them."

"You might want to look up Hec Tibbert. He was one of
my old man's buds. The two of them went way back. If
anybody'd know about that kind of shit, Hec'd know."

"You have any idea where I might be able to find him?"

Brodsky shrugged. "Phone book, maybe."

"You got one here?"

"Yeah." With considerable effort, the fat man bent down

and opened one of the bottom desk drawers. He took out the White Pages and dropped the thick book onto the desk.

Miles turned to the T's and quickly scanned the row of names. "Is Hec his real name? There's an L. Tibbert in Torrance and a Peter Tibbert on Fairfax in L.A."

"Naw. Hec lives in Monterey Park or San Gabriel. Somewhere around there."

"Did your dad have a personal phone book? Someplace where he kept the names and numbers of friends and family?"

"There might be one back at the house."

"You think we could go over there and check?"

Brodsky gestured at the mess around him. "I'm kinda busy here."

"Twenty bucks."

The fat man scowled. "Look, I don't know you from Adam. I told you what I know, let you look at my phone book, but that's it. It's time for you to go now."

"Twenty-five bucks."

"I've wasted enough time with you. Get the fuck out of my office. This conversation is over."

Miles met his eyes. "Twenty-five bucks, and I won't report the existence of those golden shower videos"—he nodded toward a stack of pink jacketed cassettes—"to my friend Manny Martinez on the vice squad."

Brodsky stared at him for a moment, as if gauging his seriousness, then shrugged and pushed himself away from the desk, making the Herculean effort to stand. He was almost as wide as he was tall, Miles saw, a physical attribute that gave him the appearance of a cartoon character.

"Do you want me to drive?" Miles asked.

"We'll take our own cars so we can go our separate ways afterward. No offense, but I don't want to spend my entire afternoon on this fucking thing."

"Your call." Miles followed him out of the office and

down the hall to a key-operated elevator. He'd been wondering how Brodsky would be able to manage the steep steps. The pornographer did not look like someone who had climbed stairs within the past decade.

"Where're you parked?" Brodsky asked.

"Out front."

"I'm out back. I'll swing around the block and you follow me. It's a red Lexus."

The elevator doors opened, and Miles took his leave, heading back down the stairs the way he'd come. A few minutes later, Brodsky's red Lexus made a slow crawl along the lane closest to the building, incurring the honking wrath of an impatient driver who swerved into the left lane around him. Miles pulled in behind the fat man's car, and the Lexus sped up, circling back around the block at the next intersection.

They headed north. Brodsky drove like a maniac, imparting to his vehicle an agility he himself would never possess, darting in and out of traffic at speeds well exceeding the legal limit, almost daring Miles to keep up.

The house was a generic tract home just over the hills in Studio City. The fat man took only a moment to sort through a pile of papers and notebooks in a cupboard next to the phone before he came up with a black-bound organizer containing his father's personal address book.

Miles tried to call first, from Brodsky's phone, but there was no answer, so he wrote down the number and address, peeled off a twenty and a five, and thanked the pornographer for his generous help before setting off for Monterey Park.

Hec Tibbert was waiting for him in a folding chair on the dead weed patch that was the lawn in front of his house.

It had been awhile since Miles had driven through this area, and he was not surprised to see that the Chinese presence seemed to have increased even more. This section of the southland had become a major Chinatown—a real one, not the kind that tourists came to see. Now the population was so heavily weighted toward emigrees that even American institutions like banks and gas stations had signs written in both English letters and Chinese characters.

Brodsky must have called again after Miles had left, because Tibbert was clearly expecting him. The ramshackle house was sandwiched in between a run-down single-story apartment complex and a brand-new multistory office building. The old man stood and walked to the sidewalk as Miles got out of his car.

"Mr. Tibbert?" Miles asked.

"Hec," the old man said, extending a hand. "Freddy told me you'd be coming."

Miles shook Tibbert's hand. "I'm sorry to bother you. I tried to call, but no one answered. I just have a few quick questions."

"Don't apologize. At my age, I'm grateful for any visitors." He scowled at two cute little Asian girls skipping down the sidewalk, laughing happily. "Especially if they're white. Come on, I got some coffee on the pot inside. Sit a spell."

Miles followed him across the nonexistent yard into the house. There were piles of newspapers in the hall, a leaning broken-legged table covered with overturned beer cans in the living room, but the kitchen was surprisingly clean, and at Tibbert's insistence, Miles sat down on one of the bright yellow chairs arranged around a sparkling Formica table.

The old man stared out the window as he cleaned out two cups in the sink. "Get out of here!" he yelled at someone outside, and Miles heard the sound of giggles and running feet.

Tibbert poured coffee and brought the two steaming cups to the table. "Damn slopes are taking over. Whose country is this anyway? I remember when this used to be a nice town to live in, before they ran all the white people off."

Miles tried to smile politely. His gut reaction was to berate the old buzzard for his racist stupidity, but he couldn't afford to antagonize the man.

"Owen used to say that the chinks weren't as bad as the niggers or the Mexicans, but living here sure showed me that ain't true."

That was his cue. Miles cleared his throat. "Speaking of Owen, I'd like to ask you a few questions." He pulled out the list, scanned it quickly—

—and spotted Tibbert's name.

He looked up at the old man in surprise. For some reason, it hadn't occurred to him that Tibbert would be on the list, too, and he hadn't bothered to so much as look at the paper since he'd left for Hollywood.

Miles thought for a moment. He wasn't sure how to bring up the subject, and finally he simply handed the paper over and said, "There's a list here. Made by the father of my client. You and Owen are both on it. Could you tell me why you're on it, or what you have in common with the other men on the list?"

The old man looked at the piece of paper. There was no pause for thought, no racking of his brain, only a slight puzzlement. "Oh, yeah," he said. "We all worked on the dam."

She's going after the dam builders, too.

He'd almost forgotten about the crazy old lady in the mall, but the words of the homeless woman came back to him now, and a chill passed through his body, a shiver of cold that began at the back of his neck, wrapped around his heart, and continued down to the tips of his toes.

He stared stupidly at Tibbert, not knowing how to broach what he didn't even understand. A crazy old woman in a mall, a series of bizarre deaths, a list predicting the murder of men who worked on a dam but now all lived in different parts of the country.

Montgomery Jones had been killed near a dam, he remembered.

It almost made sense. Almost. But the connections were still not quite tangible, and he could not for the life of him figure out what was going on here.

He was scared, though, and the most frightening thing was that the crazy woman in the mall had called him by his father's name.

Bob!

Tibbert was looking down at the list, his finger following the silent movement of his lips as he read the names one by one. Every few seconds he would look quizzically up at Miles, but Miles still did not know what to say.

He gathered himself together, took a deep breath, placed his own finger at the top of the paper. "Several of these men," Miles said slowly, "have been killed recently. I've been hired by the daughter of one of them—Liam Connor—to find out why he is being stalked, why attempts have been made on his life. The list does not seem to be in any particular order, there's no way to predict what's going to happen, and that makes this whole thing a crapshoot. That's why I have to try and get to the bottom of this as soon as possible. I can't just stake out someone's house or put a round-the-clock guard on someone, because I don't know who's next or even if someone will be next."

Tibbert nodded. "Liam Connor. I remember him."

"What can you tell me about Liam? Do you have any idea why someone would be after him? Why someone would be after *any* of these men?"

"Wolf Canyon," the old man said.

"What?"

"It's not just the name of the dam, it was the name of the town."

"What town?"

Tibbert suddenly looked much older. The sun was streaming through the kitchen window, emphasizing the lines on his face, but that was not what had affected his appearance. It was emotion that had added the weariness of years to his features.

"We dammed the Rio Verde," he said. "It was about twenty miles downriver of an existing dam, and between the two was a small town. Wolf Canyon. The people there fought the dam project tooth and nail, but they lost, the courts ruled in the government's favor every time, and the dam went up. Finally, the project was completed, the governor and some senators and the vice president came out for the grand unveiling, and . . ." He shook his head. "It was all ready, everything was a go, only Wolf Canyon . . . the town . . ." He trailed off.

"What happened?" Miles prodded.

Tibbert leaned forward. "It wasn't evacuated like it was supposed to be. There were people there when they let in the water."

Miles shook his head. "I don't . . . I don't understand."

"We killed them," Tibbert said. "We flooded the town and killed them all."

The picture was starting to come together, though he still could not claim he understood it.

Apparently, someone screwed up and forgot to make sure that all of the people were out of the town before water was released from the dam upriver. The water flooded the new reservoir, killing everyone who had not been evacuated. The force of the raging water drove them through the canyon— in many instances knocking them out of their shoes or clothes, breaking their bones—and their existence was only discovered a day later, after the ceremonies were over and the dignitaries were gone, when scuba divers went down to examine the new dam and found the bodies crammed against debris screens, mixed in with the mud. All total, over sixty men and women died.

And now someone or something was taking revenge for it, picking off people who had worked on the project. Supervisors, from what Tibbert told him of the names on the list. People in charge.

The old man leaned back in his chair, drained his cup of coffee. The expression on his face was unreadable, and though he met Miles' eyes, it was only for a second; then he pretended to focus his attention on a bowling trophy atop the refrigerator.

It made sense, Miles supposed, but it was fantastic, and the scenario brought up more questions than it answered. If this was some sort of curse, why had it waited until now to kick in? And who was behind it? Was this part of some ancient Indian thing, or was it instigated by the relative of one of the people who'd drowned?

Miles stood, perfunctorily thanked Tibbert for the coffee and for answering his questions, told him he'd be in touch soon with some follow-ups, then quickly hurried out of the house and over to his car. On the sidewalk two Asian girls were playing hopscotch, and from the porch Tibbert told them to get the hell away from his house and play in their own yards. The shouting brought Miles' mind back to the here and now, and he turned back toward the old man, still standing on the front steps. "Be careful!" he called out. "You know what's happening. You might be next."

"Don't worry about me," Tibbert said, but Miles heard the fear beneath the bravado.

He stepped back up the walk. "You want me to have someone watch you? Maybe stake out your place here in case something happens?"

Tibbert shook his head.

"You have someone you can stay with?"

"I'll be fine."

Miles nodded. He wasn't sure that was the case, was not even sure Tibbert himself believed it, but he knew when not to push, and he sensed that the best thing to do right now was to give him a little breathing room. He'd call the old man back in a few hours and check in, see what he wanted not to do after he'd had time to soak this all in and think about it.

Miles walked out to the car, got in, and started the engine. He gave Tibbert one last look, then pulled into traffic.

Magic. Curses. Mysterious deaths. It was crazy, but he bought it all, and he realized that what was really throwing him for a loop was the old lady from the mall.

She's going after the dam builders, too!

The crazy woman had mistaken him for his father, had called him by his father's name. Did that mean that Bob was somehow connected to all this? Miles refused to credit that. He accepted that some supernatural force was being used to avenge the deaths in Wolf Canyon all those years ago, but linking that to his father's . . . resurrection did not make any sense.

Or did it?

He drove out of Monterey Park and onto the Pomona Freeway, troubled.

2

Liam Connor pushed open the sliding glass door and walked outside to light up a cigarette. Even with Marina gone, he still felt guilty smoking in the house, and he stood on the back patio, inhaling deeply, staring into the darkness.

There seemed something strange about tonight. He could not put his finger on it, but it made him antsy. This was already his fifth cigarette of the evening, though he had vowed to limit himself to three a day.

The backyard was big, but night expanded its parameters even farther. Light from the house illuminated the patio and a half-circle section of lawn, but the outer flower bed, the bushes beyond, and the wooden fence that marked the edge of his property were hidden behind a curtain of black that erased all boundaries.

It was a quiet evening, and the ocean seemed unusually close. The cars on PCH were loud enough for him to differentiate individual vehicles, and he could make out male and female voices from the sidewalk in front of the bar and shops. He could not hear the sound of waves, but he could hear the cries of gulls, and the air was tinged with the briny scent of the sea.

It occurred to him that he was standing very near the edge of the continent and that, beyond that, water continued halfway around the world, traveling so far that at the other end it was already tomorrow.

Water.

He thought of Wolf Canyon.

There was a sound from the bushes beyond the perimeter of house light, a crack of twig that made him jump. He nearly dropped his cigarette but caught and kept it at the last moment, immediately bringing it to his lips to take a long calming draw.

An apple came rolling out of the darkness.

Goose bumps appeared instantly on his arms and the skin at the back of his neck. He looked out across the lawn toward the section of blackness from which the apple had come, and another one rolled across the grass toward him, bumping to a stop on the concrete edge of the patio. He heard laughter on the wind, a low giggle barely discernible in the slight breeze that had suddenly materialized.

He dropped the cigarette, ground it into the cement with his shoe, and turned, reaching for the door handle. He tried to slide the door open, but it was stuck, and though he wiggled it back and forth, jerked it with all his might, the door remained closed, almost as though someone had locked it from inside.

This was it, he realized. This was the night he was going to die.

He wanted to cry out, but his throat was constricted, and instead he tried to run around the house to the side yard. If he could just get out to the front, he could dash over to one of his neighbors' houses. Or get in the car and drive away.

But he had not even gotten off the patio before another apple flew out of the darkness. This one did not roll across the lawn but came sailing through the air, hitting him on the side of the face. His head was rocked back by the impact, and the stinging pain made his eye immediately tear up. He looked down at the apple, and it split open at his feet. The individual pieces wriggled off the cement and onto the grass, burrowing into the dirt.

His heart was thumping wildly in his chest. He had to get out of here before she showed herself, before she emerged from the shadows and attacked him.

She? How did he know it was a she?

Because it *was* a she, just as in his dream, and he thought of the woman's voice harassing him over the phone—

I'll pull your cock out through your asshole

—thought once again that he ought to know who she was, that he should understand why this was happening and why she was coming after them.

The laughter came again, and though it was an evil, unnatural sound, he recognized it as definitely female. He held a hand over his burning left eye and dashed across the grass, past his bedroom window, toward the side of the house.

She floated toward him out of the darkness.

She came from the spot toward which he was running rather than the area that had been the source of the apples, and he stopped dead in his tracks. Both eyes were teary now, but still he saw how truly terrifying the woman before him was. She was naked, her considerable attributes on full display, but there was nothing even remotely sexy or arousing about her. Her skin was white and dead-looking, and the harsh angularity of the bones in her arms and legs struck him as horribly wrong. Her head did not seem to match her body precisely, and even through his tears he could see the horrible cast of her features, the unearthly anger and rage that had somehow been twisted by will into a mirthless smile. He experienced an immediate abhorrence of her, and he staggered backward, instinctively trying to move away.

But she kept coming.

She held in her hand an apple, but she did not offer it to him, did not even speak. Instead, chuckling slyly, she glided directly up to him and shoved the fruit as hard as she could into his mouth.

His head was slammed back by the blow, and he both heard and felt several of his front teeth shattering and breaking off.

He dropped to his knees, screaming with the pain, swatting her hand away, spitting out blood and teeth and the small pieces of apple that had been dislodged.

He looked up at her. He still did not know who she was or why she was doing this, knew only that it was because of what had happened back in Wolf Canyon, and he started crying, blubbering. "It wuth an ack-thident! We didn't know! No one knew!"

Even as he cried out the words, he understood that they were incomplete, not the whole story. True enough, they hadn't known people remained in the town when they let loose the water, but they knew afterward, and still they did nothing. None of them had stepped forward to take responsibility, and the government had never held any of them accountable for what happened. The whole thing was covered up and forgotten about, and he'd known even then that it was wrong. He understood that that was why he was being made to pay now.

Who was *she*, though?

He was not going to find out. He was going to die not knowing.

Her touch was a cold breeze against his face, and the coldness moved through his bleeding mouth and settled in his throat.

He could not even scream as he was forced across the lawn into the darkness of the night.

Then

1

Jeb stared hard into the mirror, concentrated.

Nothing.

He sat back down on the bed, his head hurting. Something had happened to his power. It was as if it was draining slowly out of him—or being drained out of him. He'd noticed it over the past few months, but only in the last week had the effects become obvious enough to be worrisome.

Now he could not even conjure a simple alternate scene in a mirror.

Next to him, Harriet rolled over. She opened one eye and smiled lazily, pulling down the covers to expose her naked body. He looked down at her large lolling breasts, at the triangle of thick black hair between her ample thighs.

"Get back under here," she said. "You paid for the whole night, you might as well take advantage of it."

Jeb forced himself to smile back at her and lay down, resting his head on the pillow, allowing her to pull the covers over both of them. He never had found a wife or a woman of his own, but since prostitutes had set up shop in town, he had seldom been without companionship when in the mood.

And he was often in the mood.

Both he and William had been surprised at the range of occupations followed by those of their ilk. In the beginning there had been only settlers: hardworking men and women willing to do anything in order to get this community started and establish new lives for themselves. Back then their conception of the future town had been an idealized one, filled with selfless, caring, dedicated witches like themselves, all of them ready to be assigned the specific tasks and duties that would make Wolf Canyon a real community. But it took all kinds to make a world, and soon the people arriving were not so dedicated, not merely the peaceful and persecuted who were interested in creating an alternate society.

Now there were drunks and whores and gunfighters and swindlers. The world of witches was no more egalitarian than the world of normal people, and though they were all welcome and accepted, all granted residence by virtue of what they were, it was clear now even to William that some were not as desirable to the community as others.

Jeb rolled onto his side, feeling Harriet's magic hands grab his manhood and once again bring it back to life. He was never sure if it was her power that reinvigorated him so quickly or if she simply drew the power from him, but whatever the source, her hands were able to arouse him faster than any other woman in town. In fact, faster than any woman since . . .

Since Becky.

Only Becky hadn't needed to touch him in order for him to become aroused. Just seeing her, just being next to her, just talking to her had excited him in a way that was at once animal simple and spiritually profound.

"Come on," Harriet said. "Get it in."

He rolled on top of her, she guided him, and he began moving, circling his hips, grinding against her, gradually increasing the speed. Soon the magic was flowing back and forth, from her to him, from him to her. He could sense her excitement reaching its peak, and he began thrusting hard, attempting to hasten the culmination of his own pleasure.

She thrust back in return, pressing herself tight against him, and that simple act of greedy desire made him explode.

He spent himself inside her, spurting with abandon until his loins were emptied, and she held him in, obtaining her own gratification, before finally allowing him to pull out.

She let out a sigh, looked over at him, smiled. "Maybe I oughta pay you instead."

He fell asleep happy and contented, and it was only in his dreams that his worries once again reasserted themselves.

He dreamed that he was freezing, in the snow, and a pile of sticks was in front of him and he could not even conjure a fire.

In the morning, he rode out to the mine, where work had stopped due to a dispute over wages. He thought of the early days, when there had been no wages, no money. Everyone had contributed to the community, and everyone shared equally in the community's bounty. They'd come a long way since then, but he was not sure this was progress. There seemed to be too many factions now. The selfless spirit that had once united them had degenerated into a selfish individualism which threatened to undermine the common goals of the townspeople.

Jeb hopped off his horse, tethered it to a cottonwood tree. Outside the entrance of the mine, several men were arguing, one burly, bearded fellow shaking his fist at another man who removed his hat to wipe the sweat from his forehead. William had chosen Jeb to settle the dispute because of his good relationship with most of the miners, and indeed the argument abated as he approached up the pathway. This close, he could see that the bearded man was Lyle Siddons and the other man was Wade Smith.

"All right," he said. "Let's settle down. Ain't nothing here we can't work out if we just talk things out in a reasonable way."

In fact, finding a solution turned out to be easier than he thought. The major bone of contention was that the drill operators felt they should be making more money because their job was the only one for which it was not feasible to use magic. The heavy-duty tunneling could be done only with the help of traditional mining equipment, and they felt that they should be compensated for their manual labor. Jeb agreed, and over the protests of some of the others who considered the use of magic in their respective positions to be equally draining, he declared that a standard wage would be received by all, with those required to perform extra duties getting additional pay. The definition of "extra duties" would be ironed out later, and he did not rule out the possibility that it would refer to heavy use of magic as well as physical labor; but for now, he told them, the wage demands would be met and everyone should get back to work.

There was some minor grumbling, but the drill operators were ecstatic and the complaints from others seemed to be voiced mostly out of obligation. The truth was, they all thought they were performing "extra duties," and they could all see the prospect of increased pay in their future, and Jeb left the miners much happier than he had found them.

Returning to town, he stopped off to tell William. He was starving and could use a drink, but he knew William would want to hear the outcome as soon as possible and to discuss it with the vendors who sold the ore to the government.

As he rode up to William's house, he saw Isabella, digging in her garden. She waved to him as he passed, smiling against the sun.

He tipped his hat, nodded.

He'd never admit it to William, but he'd felt a small surge of pride and the faint seductive tickle of revenge as he'd watched Isabella take care of those three strangers in front of the saloon that day. They were probably not bad men, not in the ordinary sense, but they were ignorant and intolerant, belligerent bigots, the type of people who had for years been persecuting their kind, and it was nice to see them finally get a taste of their own medicine.

William, of course, had been shocked and outraged, torn in his reaction despite his unwavering devotion to his wife. That's what made him William. But Jeb was more ambivalent, less sure of the morality involved, and while he'd offered his friend a sympathetic ear as always, secretly he'd supported Isabella's actions.

William's wife was growing on him. He hadn't liked her at first, he could admit that, but unlike most of the other people in town, he had come to appreciate her unusual charms. He supposed it was because he and William were so close. He was the only other person who had really gotten to know her, and he now understood what his friend saw in Isabella. She was not only beautiful but intelligent, and she was not afraid to speak her mind or act on her impulses. He admired that.

Most of the others did not see it that way. To them, she was a usurper, a temptress who had seduced their friend in order to achieve her own nefarious ends. The way she had dispatched those three strangers and had gotten off scot-free, without even a reprimand, when William's policy had always been to attract no outside attention, proved that.

Jeb could understand their concern. The fact was, however, she hadn't done anything else to engender any mistrust or suspicion in the townspeople. They simply did not like her, resented her because of how close she and William had become in such a short time, and he could not help thinking that they were behaving just as people had always behaved toward them, with prejudice and a reckless disinterest in the truth.

Maybe it was inevitable. Maybe that's what happened when people lived together. Hell, maybe they'd all be better off if they just spent their lives moving from one place to another, living a nomadic existence as they had before.

Jeb hopped off his horse, tethered it to the porch rail. "William!" he called out.

A tap on the window of the den captured his attention, and behind the glass William motioned for him to come inside. Jeb nodded and walked in the house, traipsing through the parlor and into his friend's room.

William was standing next to his desk, waiting for him, and Jeb told him how he'd gone out to the mine to see what was what, and how the drill operators wanted compensation for work that involved manual labor rather than the use of magic.

The use of magic.

For the first time since last night, his attention was brought back to the fact that his own ability to use magic seemed to be slipping away. He paused for a moment in his narration, and William looked at him quizzically, waiting. Jeb was suddenly tempted to tell him about the strange and gradual diminution of his power. He looked into William's face and knew that his friend would understand, that he might even be able to come up with a solution for it. He was about to broach the subject, but then he heard the front door open and close, heard heels on wood, heard Isabella's throaty voice ask if either of them wanted anything to drink, and decided against it. The situation was probably only temporary. He was wrong to panic. His magic would probably come back on its own. Hell, for all he knew, this was a natural occurrence. Maybe the power ebbed and flowed. Maybe it even began to fade as one got older.

As quickly as it had come, the impulse disappeared, and he sat there silently as William asked his wife to bring a bottle and two glasses, waiting until Isabella left the room before continuing his story of the miners.

2

Ten years.

Wolf Canyon was coming up on its tenth anniversary, and

William wanted to do something special for the occasion. A celebration. He wanted to involve the entire town, from the first settlers to the most recent arrival, but he also wanted it to be a surprise. This was something he wanted to do *for* the town, and he thought that it would be nice to be able to dazzle them with something entirely unexpected.

Still, he could not pull off what he had planned by himself, so he had, out of necessity, involved Jeb and Isabella, the two people to whom he was closest in the world. He could trust them not to talk. Isabella had thrown herself into the planning with fervor, getting into the spirit of the occasion, but Jeb had seemed somewhat preoccupied lately, distant, not quite himself. William had asked what was wrong numerous times, had even tried to reach out and read him, but his friend remained stubbornly closed off. What worried him the most was that there seemed to be a touch of anxiety behind Jeb's recent reticence.

Not for the first time, William looked up the street and down. He consulted his pocket watch. A quarter of an hour late. Jeb was supposed to have met him this morning in front of the assaying office, but he had not yet shown. William found that worrisome. Jeb was seldom late, and when he was, the reason was always serious.

He walked through the narrow space between the assayer's and the fire brigade to Back Street, seeing if perhaps Jeb had misunderstood and was waiting at the rear of the building, but no one was on the street save Grover Farland, sweeping the wooden walkway in front of his small shop.

William walked up to the haberdasher. "Morning, Grover. You seen Jeb this morning?"

The other man stopped sweeping, shook his head. "Can't say that I have." He scratched his beard. "You looking f r him?"

"He was supposed to meet me—"

Isabella's scream sliced through the morning stillness. What had been curiosity accelerated instantly into fatalistic dread as William ran across the dusty gravel and down the street. The scream came again, and he increased his pace until he thought his muscles would snap, dashing between buildings and across Main until he had reached the front yard of his home. He ran around the side of the house to the source of the scream.

Jeb was lying on the back porch.

Or, rather, something that had once been Jeb was lying on the back porch.

For the dried white form that lay spread over the weathered boards only vaguely resembled a human being. It was naked, but all gender identification had been obliterated by whatever had vacuumed out the insides of the body. Crinkled milky skin was stretched over a partial skeleton. The features of the face and body had somehow been wiped away, leaving only a uniform blankness. He was reminded of the monster he and Jeb had come across in the canyon all those years ago, and while anger and agony battled for supremacy in his heart, terror overtook them both and settled in his gut.

Isabella screamed again.

"What is it?" Grover called, hurrying around the corner. He had followed William through the town and a crowd had come with him, concerned and curious people who had heard Isabella's cries.

William shook his head, looked at Isabella. She was staring down at Jeb's unmoving form, and she glanced up, her eyes meeting his. She ran over to him, through the garden, not bothering to watch her step, trampling flowers and vegetables in her hurry to reach him. She threw her arms about his shoulders, and held him trembling.

"What's *that*?" someone asked, voice hushed.

"It's Jeb," William said. He disengaged himself from Isabella's embrace and walked onto the porch, over to the body, touching it, opening himself to it, trying to read it.

Nothing.

More people were arriving. All of them stopped at the edge of the house as they saw Jeb's empty corpse. It was as though an invisible shield kept them from entering the backyard, and William could not help noticing the way they regarded Isabella with suspicion and trepidation.

He turned toward her. "What happened?" he asked. "Did you see who caused this?"

She shook her head. Her voice was hesitant, tentative. "I was walking out to pull some carrots and radishes, and I found him. I just came through the back door, and there he was. I didn't know who it was at first—or what it was. Then I saw that it was Jeb . . . and I screamed and you came running over here."

William looked down at the bleached, dried form. "You didn't . . . hear anything? You didn't see anything or sense anything?"

"Do you?"

He shook his head. Neither of them had been on the back porch since the previous day. Jeb could have been killed and dumped here hours ago or minutes ago. There was no way for them to know.

But who could have killed him? And who could have done . . . *this* to him?

Who?

Or *what*?

He licked his lips. What. For no human, not even a witch, could have so completely destroyed a man as powerful as Jeb.

Isabella seemed to be reading his mind.

"I have heard of this before," she said quietly. "My mother told me stories."

"About what?"

"In Europe," she said, "they are called 'vampyrs.' "

Vampyrs. He glanced around at the gathered crowd. It was not a word with which any of them were familiar, but something about it rang of truth, bespoke a reality they might not know but that existed nonetheless.

"They are monsters. Creatures that draw out the essence of a man—or a woman—and draw sustenance from it."

"Bloodsuckers," Susan Clement said.

"Yes."

William had heard rumors of such things, and he recalled his own mother telling him of monsters that fed upon human flesh, shape-shifters that drank blood and lived forever.

"What do they look like?" he asked.

Isabella shook her head. "Those who have seen them have not lived to tell."

He walked about the yard, looked for signs, checked the dirt for footprints, tried to sense any psychic residue, but both the porch and the backyard appeared to be clean. Whatever this thing was, it could protect evidence of its existence even from their advanced senses.

"Can they fly?" Grover asked suspiciously.

Isabella nodded. "Some say they can."

There were vampyrs here in the West, William thought. It made sense. It explained the emptied monster he and Jeb had found in the canyon. It explained what had happened to Jeb here today. The only thing that puzzled him was the fact that none of them had sensed its presence. It had been able to sneak in and out of the town as easily as if it had been wind.

Or perhaps it was still here.

Hiding.

Waiting.

He thought of the Bad Lands. The evil there had been strong, and perhaps that was where these vampyrs originated. After all this time he doubted he could even find that area of the country again, but a part of him wanted to set out with an expedition right now, mustering all of the magic at their disposal, and lay waste to the land, putting their power to the ultimate test, using it not merely to change or alter but to destroy.

That was unrealistic, though. And it went against everything he stood for. If there was a vampyr in Wolf Canyon, they would find it, hunt it down and kill it. But they would not go out and attack some unknown assailant or wage war against an enemy that might or might not exist on the pretext of avenging the death of a friend. They would defend themselves, but they would not take the offensive.

William walked around the yard one more time and found himself again on the porch, looking down at the dried white body that had been his friend. His thoughts were all muddled, and he admitted to himself that he did not know what they should do.

Isabella began to herd people out of the yard, and for that he was grateful. He was the leader of the town, but Jeb had been his right arm, his coleader, and the thought of continuing on alone was daunting. Besides, he did not feel like much of a leader right now, and he did not want to set aside his own feelings in order to reassure others. He wanted the freedom to grieve, to see to his own personal needs for once rather than putting the town first.

Grover was the last to leave, and he asked William if there was anything he could do, but William merely shook his head, offered his thanks, and promised to call a town meeting later in the day.

The haberdasher left, and William squatted down on the newly painted boards of the back porch. He lifted his friend's lifeless and nearly unidentifiable body and carried it into the house. Jeb felt too light even for his newly shrunken size, as though even the heft of bones had disappeared, and

William had no trouble opening the door with one hand and supporting the corpse with the other.

He placed the body on the couch in his den, looking down at it with sadness and pity and a soul-deep ache.

"Jeb," he said softly, taking the corpse's skeletal hand. "Old Jeb."

By the time Isabella walked in, he was crying.

The funeral was attended by all. Jeb was liked, if not loved, by everyone, and though there was no obligation to appear, people did so out of admiration and friendship.

William sleepwalked through the ceremony. Their kind had no death rituals, and they certainly weren't about to adopt the customs of Christianity, so they invented new rites of their own. It was a dignified ceremony in which they attempted to contact Jeb's ghost before silently consigning his body to the earth.

They had not had a cemetery up until this point, had not even designated a specific plot of land for that purpose, and William had been forced to determine where the graveyard would be.

Jeb was the first person to be interred there, and those who felt up to it took turns addressing him, letting him know how they felt, how much he meant to them. Afterward, they all joined in silent communion, expressing simultaneously a single predetermined wish of support that they willed to his bodiless spirit.

The odd thing was that no one had any luck in communicating with him. Not that day, or the day after, or the day after that. They were able to contact the ghosts of Indians who had gone before, but it was as if Jeb had never existed. His spirit could not be reached.

Had the vampyr eaten his soul?

The question haunted William. The terror he had felt after first coming upon the shriveled body of his friend had never entirely abated, and the complete absence of Jeb's afterlife presence suggested that his fear was not unfounded.

They combed the town, the canyon and even the top of the cliffs over the next week, the next month, separately and in groups, but no indication of anything abnormal was found. There were no more attacks, not even any suspicious animal deaths, and it appeared as though whatever had killed Jeb had been after him specifically, had targeted him and then left, never to be seen again. Rumors were whispered about, and though they were not spoken to William's face, he was aware of what was being said, and it disturbed him.

At home, the sex with Isabella was unusually charged. They had always had a very active love life. Isabella was a supremely sensual woman, and sex with her was imaginatively vigorous and daring, comprised of acts that even to most witches would probably seem unnatural and perverse, but since Jeb's death the intensity had been increased tenfold.

One midday, after some particularly grueling lovemaking, they lay in bed, trying to gather their energy and rest their sore muscles. Isabella stood, looked at herself in the mirror for a few moments, then turned back toward him. "They're afraid of me, William. I can feel it. They think I killed Jeb, and you know I could never do such a thing. I cannot take back what I did to those men after I first arrived, but I should not have to suffer forever for doing what any of them would have done if they were in my place."

This was all a surprise, and he was not prepared for such a conversation. His brain was still numb, thinking about what they had just done, and he sat up in bed and shook his head, trying to clear it. "What?"

"They are all talking about it. Everyone in town. I have heard them, whispering behind my back. They think I killed Jeb. They blame me for his death."

William stood, padded over to her. "No, they don't," he

lied. He put his arms around her, held her close. He had hoped to be able to keep this from her.

"Yes, they do," she said. "And they are afraid of me."

"No."

Her voice dropped. "Maybe they should be afraid."

"Isabella!"

She sighed, pulled away from him. The expression on her face was unreadable and emphasized that wild beauty which had so enchanted him on first meeting her. He realized that he did not know her any better now than he had then. He loved her, but he didn't know her.

"People are frightened," he told her. "They do not know what killed Jeb and that scares them, something which is entirely understandable. They are upset."

"Upset enough to undo all that you have done for them?"

"What are you talking about?"

"They no longer trust you because you are married to me."

"That's nonsense."

"Some are even thinking of leaving!"

The words hit him like a physical blow. He sat down hard on the bed, not wanting to believe what she'd said but instinctively recognizing its veracity. He stared down at the floor. His dream was unraveling. The anniversary of the town had passed without comment or acknowledgment, his celebratory plans derailed by Jeb's death. Now people were threatening to tear asunder all they had worked toward over the past decade due to fear and suspicion and unfounded allegations. There was an empty hole inside him, and he admitted to himself that perhaps his idea for a town where those like himself could live in peace, without fear of persecution, was doomed to be a noble failure.

"This is wrong," Isabella said. "We cannot allow decisions based on lies to destroy all that we have worked for.

Their fear of Jeb's death will render the actions of his life meaningless if we do not hold together."

She was right, and he felt a renewed sense of pride, a reinvigorated determination to keep Wolf Canyon from tearing itself apart. He had been wrong to ignore the rumors and whispers. That was not the way for a leader to act. He should have allayed people's fears, should have made it clear that no matter what outside threat confronted them, they would stick together and he would lead them.

"Yes," he said.

"We need to convince them to stay. It's for their own good. It's for the good of all of us. We must all hang together, else we shall all hang separately."

He smiled. "You are right," he said. "We will convince them to stay."

She leaned closer. "If they do not want to stay, they are traitors. If we let them go, if we let them escape, they will betray us. We must keep them here."

He shook his head. "This is a free country and a free town. That is why it was founded. We do not want people who do not want to be here."

"They *are* here. It is time for them to take some responsibility for their actions, to support others of their kind who do want to be here."

"I will call a town meeting," William promised. "I will talk to everyone. I will convince them to remain."

"And if we cannot convince them, we will make them."

He looked at her.

"We will make them," she repeated more strongly. And though her words frightened him, he found himself nodding in agreement.

Now

1

Miles dreamed he was swimming in a pool and the water around him was gradually darkening. He popped his head above water and he was no longer in a pool but in a lake. His limbs were tired, the closest shore was several hundred yards away, and he knew that if he did not get started now, he would not be able to make it. He began paddling as hard as he could, but when he looked up again, there was no shore. There was no land. He was in the middle of an ocean, and the water was black. Above, the sky was gray and cloudless. He felt something cold touch his feet, felt something slimy slide past his midsection. Then hands grabbed his limbs and dragged him down into water that lightened from black to the deep crimson color of blood. His lungs were about to burst from the pressure, and involuntarily he opened his mouth to breathe, but there was only the red water, and he sucked it into his lungs and knew that he was about to die.

He awoke to feel an arm around his midsection, and he opened his eyes, looked next to him—

—and saw Claire.

He smiled, reached over, touched her cheek. She stirred in her sleep, rolled onto her side.

Claire had spent the night, and they had gone to bed together. They had made love. It was something he'd been thinking about ever since he'd called her, and he still couldn't believe that it had actually happened. The experience had been tremendously exciting, but it had also been comfortable, a combination he had never before encountered. Their past had informed their present in a way that was wonderfully liberating, and their lovemaking had been exhilarating.

They had still not talked about where they were in their relationship, whether they were getting back together permanently or if this was just a little fling, a nostalgic visit back to the good old days. They'd talked of everything else, conversing with a candor that had never been possible during their marriage. But somehow they could not seem to broach the subject of their feelings for each other. It was as if both of them were afraid the spell would be broken.

Miles glanced over at the clock on the dresser.

Seven-fifteen!

He kicked off the covers, leaped out of bed, and shook Claire awake. He had forgotten to set the alarm last night, and they were going to have to hurry like hell if either of them hoped to make it to work on time.

"Get up!" he said. "It's fifteen after seven!"

Announcement of the time jolted her into action in a way his shaking of her had not, and for five minutes they ran around the bedroom grabbing clothes and putting them on, practically bumping heads, like some silent screen comedy duo. She was faster than he was, having gathered her hair into a quick ponytail while he wet his head under the sink faucet so his hair would be manageable enough to comb. She kissed him on the cheek as he was brushing his teeth, said good-bye, and promised to come by after work. Before he could even rinse and spit, she was out the door and gone.

Traffic as usual was horrendous, and he had plenty of time to think while he sat in an unmoving line of cars that followed the path of the freeway downtown.

He had opened up to Claire about his visit with Hec Tibbert, telling her the story of Wolf Canyon, even talking about the homeless woman in the mall and the possibility that his father was tied up in this somehow. She suggested that he stake out the shopping center or the streets around it and see if he couldn't find the old lady again. A lot of homeless people were territorial, so the woman might be still hanging around.

He himself thought it would be more productive to confront Liam once more, this time taking Tibbert with him. Liam obviously knew a lot more than he was telling. It was highly likely that he knew what was behind all this, and if Miles could get the two men together and start them talking, perhaps he'd be able to squeeze some information out of the cantankerous old buzzard.

He reached the office, parked, walked inside. Naomi flagged him down the second he stepped off the elevator. "Where've you been? One of your clients has been frantically trying to get ahold of you all morning."

"All morning? It's only eight-thirty."

"And she's been calling me every five minutes since *seven*-thirty, when I got in. I wouldn't be surprised if there are fifty messages lined up on your voice mail." She handed him a stack of pink call slips. "Here."

Miles glanced down at the top slip.

Marina Lewis.

He knew the feeling that settled into his midsection. It was the same one he'd had when the coroner called to tell him his father had walked away. He hurried over to his cubicle, ignoring the blinking message light on his phone, and immediately dialed Marina in Arizona. She answered, too fast, on the first ring. "Hello?"

"It's Miles Huerdeen. I got your messages. What's wrong?"

"My father. I think something's happened to him."

It was as if she'd been holding her breath, damming up her emotions, because while her voice started out strong, it ended in almost a sob, and he suspected that hysterics were very near the surface. She'd obviously been stressing out over this all morning, perhaps all night, and he did not want to be the one to push her past the breaking point, so he said simply, "Tell me."

"I can't get ahold of him." He could hear the panic in her voice. "He's not answering his phone, hasn't answered since I started calling last night. He never goes anywhere, and even if he did, he'd be back this morning. Something's happened. I already called the police, but they won't send anyone down. Could you go over there and make sure he's all right?"

"Of course," Miles said. "I'll head out right now. It should take a half hour to forty-five minutes, depending on the traffic. Don't worry. I'm sure he's fine. I'll call you from there."

"Thanks."

He hung up. But the feeling in his gut told him that Liam Connor wasn't fine, that he was in fact dead.

The drive out to Santa Monica seemed endless. Traffic wasn't as bad as he'd expected, but every second seemed to drag out interminably, and each stoplight or slight delay caused him to hit his steering wheel in frustration. If something was wrong, he was no doubt too late to do anything about it, but he could not shake the irrational feeling that if he arrived in time, he might be able to save the man's life.

He pulled into Liam's driveway at precisely nine o'clock, according to the all-news station on the radio, and he hurriedly got out of the car, ran up to the front door.

He rang the doorbell, waited.

Rang again.

Waited.

He knocked loudly. "Liam?" he called.

No answer.

This was going to be bad. Whatever it was, it was going to be bad.

He tried the door, jiggled the knob, but as he'd suspected, it was locked. He had tools to get around inconveniences such as that, but he had not brought them with him. He stepped around the side of the house, intending to try the back door before searching for a loose or open window.

He hurried around a hydrangea bush, over a brownish weedy section of lawn, and ducked under the thorny branches of a low-growing lemon tree. "Liam?" he called.

The old man was in the backyard.

On the fence.

If Miles had had any doubts about the supernatural aspects of this case, about the power of curses or witchcraft or voodoo or whatever it was, they were instantly dispelled.

For Liam Connor had not merely been affixed to the fence, he had *merged* with it. He was naked, placed in a pose of crucifixion, and his body had melded with the boards, his skin taking on the whorled texture of the redwood, the outlines of knotholes visible beneath the hair on his arms and legs. In an area where a fence slat was clearly missing, Liam's form had been poured into the breach, approximating the shape and grain of the board while still retaining the coloring of human skin. The joining was so seamless at several points that it was impossible to tell where Liam ended and the fence began.

Only his head had escaped this synthesis. It hung forward, onto his chest, and did not touch wood even at the neck. The expression permanently etched on his static features was one of terror and indescribable agony, and his wide-open eyes stared unseeingly down at the ground.

Miles remained rooted in place, shocked into inaction. He flashed back to the sight of Montgomery Jones' torn body—although even that, gruesome as it was, could not compare with the insanity of this. Confronted with the enormity of a power that could not only kill a man but *transform* his flesh into something entirely inhuman, Miles was suddenly filled with a feeling of hopelessness.

Part of him was tempted to walk across the lawn, reach

out, and touch the sections of Liam's body that had become one with the wood, but though he was almost positive that whatever had done this was gone, he was still afraid, frightened to the core of his being. He turned and ran, unable to remain alone for even a second longer in that backyard.

He'd left his cellular phone in the car. He yanked open the door and grabbed the phone from its place on the passenger seat. He knew he should call Marina first, but he wasn't sure what to say, didn't know how to break the news to her. With trembling fingers, he pressed 9-1-1 instead, calling the police. He spelled out the pertinent facts in a voice that sounded far stronger than it had any right to be, and promised the woman questioning him that he would remain on-site until the authorities arrived.

Talking to the dispatcher helped organize his thoughts, gave him the chance to go through a trial run, and immediately after terminating the call to the police, before his courage failed him, he punched in Marina Lewis' number to tell her that her father was dead.

2

Janet Engstrom was afraid of her uncle.

She tried to tell herself that it was a fear of death, it was because his condition was worsening, because he was obviously going to die, that she felt so scared when she was near him. After all, her parents' deaths in the accident had been traumatic, and not a day went by that she did not think of the way they'd looked when she'd gone to identify their bodies.

But that was not why she was afraid of her uncle.

No, it was because he was changing, because he was becoming someone she didn't know.

The strange thing was that she felt closer to her uncle than to anyone else in her family, even her parents. He was the only one to whom she had admitted that she'd been molested as a young teenager. She'd told him of her parents' Halloween party, how she could hear the increasingly loud sounds of the party goers through the closed door of her bedroom, how she'd sneaked out to go the bathroom and had been sitting on the toilet when the clown staggered in. She'd tried to pull up her pajama bottoms, started to yell at him to get out, but he'd lurched across the bathroom, shoved a hand over her mouth, and hit her hand away from her crotch. Then he was pushing her onto the floor, spreading her legs, and he was on her and in her and then it was over. She thought it was Mr. Woodrow from down the street, but it was impossible to tell behind the clown makeup, and afterward she could never be sure.

Her uncle had listened and offered her a shoulder to cry on. He had told her it was not her fault, that she was not used goods but the victim of a violent crime and that one day she would meet the man of her dreams and all of this would be merely a dim and distant memory.

She had never met the man of her dreams, but she had grown up to be a healthy, normal, fairly well-adjusted woman, and if her life did not have a fairy-tale ending, it was not due to the ripple effect of the rape. In fact, what sanity and happiness she possessed was probably due in large part to her uncle's supportive influence.

So when she learned that he had cancer and that it was inoperable, she had immediately returned to Cedar City, vowing to take care of him. She'd been prepared to quit her job, but The Store had arranged to transfer her to their Cedar City outlet and had even helped her find an apartment. Her uncle told her she could stay with him, but until he became so sick and weak that he required round-the-clock care, she wanted to have a place of her own so she could have at least a little privacy.

She'd been cooking for him for the past four months,

cleaning his house, taking him to his chemo sessions, keeping him company, being there for him the way he had been there for her. Other relatives called once or twice a week, a few had even stopped by Cedar City for a quick weekend visit, but she was the only one with him day in and day out. It was emotionally draining, and she'd felt sad and angry, depressed and guilty, all of the usual emotions a person experienced sitting helplessly by, watching a loved one die.

But now she was also afraid.

Because now he was walking.

She didn't know what to make of this, didn't know what to do. He was fading fast. The color in his face was, if anything, even worse than it had been before: white and pale and drawn. But he was now pacing around the perimeter of his room, when for the past six days he had been unable to get out of bed at all. He looked like death warmed over, and the juxtaposition of his cancer-ravaged body with this strong purposeful stride that seemed not to be his but appeared to have taken over him, forcing his body to go along with its aggressively inhuman rhythm, terrified her.

The hospital had support groups for relatives of cancer patients, doctors and psychologists who were willing to provide advice and assistance, but the thought of turning to one of those people about *this* was out of the question. At work, she thought about telling Donise, the only person at the store with whom she was at all close, but Donise had her own family problems, and the two of them were not yet intimate enough that she felt comfortable imposing upon her friend.

She should really be talking to his doctors. This was not a feeling or an emotion. This was something physical, concrete, an action that could be seen and measured and documented. He needed to be examined by a professional, and it was her responsibility to call the hospital and tell someone.

But she didn't want to.

She was afraid.

He had started walking the day before yesterday, and she did not think he had stopped since. It could not be good for his condition, but she still did not want to alert the doctors. She had the sense that this was entirely unconnected to his cancer, that its cause was above and beyond anything with which she was familiar, and that no doctor on earth would be able to tell her what was happening.

She did not want to hear that.

And she did not want to know what was behind this unless it was simple, logical, and completely ordinary.

The truth was, she wanted her uncle to die.

It was a hard thing to admit, but at this point, she honestly felt that death would be better for him, for her and for the rest of the family. He had nothing to look forward to other than increased pain and decreased quality of life.

She drove straight home after work. She could see from the street that there was a crowd of kids gathered around the duplex, and the queasy feeling in the pit of her stomach told her that it had something to do with her uncle. Sure enough, he came walking around the side of the house, wearing nothing but his pajama bottoms. The kids started laughing and yelling, throwing dirt clods at him. One hit the side of his face, another clump of mud spattered against his bare chest, but he seemed oblivious and kept walking, never varying in his stride.

Janet slammed to a halt in front of the driveway and ran out of her car, furious. The kids scattered at her approach, and she yelled at them that she was going to tell their parents.

Her uncle had disappeared around the east side of the duplex, and she chased after him, catching up to him in the backyard.

"Uncle John!" she called, but he did not stop or slow down. He continued walking, moving past the stunted juniper tree and around the opposite side of the duplex. She ran and caught up with him.

"Let's go inside. Come on." She reached out, grabbed his wrist, but then instantly recoiled. His skin was cold and rubbery, lifeless, and the muscles beneath felt lax and totally without tension.

He was dead.

She knew it instinctively, and she was filled with horror and revulsion as she dropped his hand and backed away. He continued walking, ignoring her, his dead eyes staring at a fixed point in the sky, his mouth hanging slightly open, a hint of tongue poking between parted teeth.

She followed him to the front, ran up the porch steps into the house, closed and locked the door.

Only then did she start to scream.

Then

1

Outside, winter winds were howling through the canyon.

William lay awake in the darkness, next to the sleeping Isabella, feeling her comforting warmth beneath the quilt. Her skin was so smooth, she seemed so soft when she was asleep, but there was an inner core of iron within her, and whether this was hardness or strength he had never been able to tell. Her gifts were obviously powerful, very powerful, greater perhaps than his own, but this he knew only through conversation and observation. She had told him of conjurings she'd performed, and he had seen her do magic that was beyond the capabilities of anyone else in Wolf Canyon. But he could *sense* nothing from her. He felt no power, could not read her or in any way gauge her abilities objectively. She was a cipher to him—to all of them, he suspected—and there were times that he wished he had never brought her back to Wolf Canyon.

But he loved her, loved her deeply, passionately, obsessively, and that made up for all doubts and questions, overcame all regrets.

He closed his eyes, tried to sleep. He was riding up the canyon tomorrow. According to Joseph, who had just returned from a cattle-buying trip to Prescott, a family in a wagon had set up camp at the head of the canyon next to the river. Ordinarily, that would not be a problem, but Joseph said that it looked like this family was fixing to stay. The man had all sorts of gold-mining equipment, sluice boxes and the like, and was planning to stake a claim on their land.

Isabella had wanted to go, but William had overruled her and said that *he* would take care of the problem. She'd known why he didn't want her to accompany him, and she'd only looked at him in that hard way she had and said, "Make sure you *do* take care of it."

"I will," he told her.

His greatest regret had always been that Isabella was not able to bear him children, that even their combined powers had not been enough to create life from their loins. But for the first time he thought that that might be for the best. He was not sure what kind of mother she would be and was not at all certain that he wanted to see the type of child she would produce.

The night wore on, the wind eventually dying down, but he could not seem to fall asleep naturally, so William wove a spell about himself, inducing sleep and guaranteeing that he would awaken just before dawn.

He set out immediately after a quick breakfast of steak and eggs. Isabella warned him once again that he had better get rid of the interlopers, and he assured her once more that he would do so.

It was a half-day's journey to the head of the canyon, and he followed the path of the river, passing through narrow marshy stretches where ferns grew high above his head in the cracks of the rock walls, riding over wide sections of sand and boulders as the canyon expanded outward, the trees and plants remaining close to the cliffs, the open middle area arid and dry save for the banks immediately flanking the flowing water.

It was nearly noon when he reached his destination.

There was indeed a family camped at the head of the canyon. They were living out of their wagon, but foundation space for a cabin had been cleared next to a small stand of cottonwoods, and it seemed obvious that they were planning to settle here.

A woman was kneading dough on a flattened board stretched between two rocks, while a young boy watched her from his perch atop another rock. A heavy, bearded man was standing shirtless and shoeless next to the river, attempting to push a large wood-and-metal contraption into the water.

"Hello!" William called, dismounting from his horse.

All three looked up, and the bearded man scowled, abandoning his device and picking up a rifle from behind a small bush. William made his way straight toward the woman, who stood, dusting off her hands on her dress. The man hurried over as the boy quickly jumped off his rock and ran next to his mother.

"What do you want?" the man demanded, brandishing the rifle.

William removed his hat, bowed to the woman. "I merely stopped off for a friendly visit. My name is William. I live farther down the canyon, in town."

"Town?"

"Yes. The town of Wolf Canyon. I am the mayor. In fact, that is the reason I have come to see you. If you would like to camp here for a few days—"

"Camp here? We're settling. This is going to be our home."

"If you would like to camp here for a few days," William continued, "you are welcome to do so. But you cannot live here."

"Who says so?"

William looked at the man. "What is your name, sir?"

"I don't have to tell you my name."

He was starting to become annoyed, but William tried to remain calm and reasonable. "You must leave," he said gently. "This is not free land. It belongs to us."

"Who is 'us'?" the man asked belligerently.

"The town of Wolf Canyon."

"Yeah?"

William smiled. "We are witches."

The man and woman exchanged a frightened glance. The boy grabbed the edge of his mother's petticoat. It was the reaction he'd expected, and William could not help feeling a twinge of satisfaction as he saw fear overcome the bluster in the man's face.

"You're—"

"We're all witches. Everyone in Wolf Canyon."

The man took a step forward. "*You* are the ones who must be gone from here," he said bravely, brandishing his rifle. The woman grabbed his coat, tried to pull him back. "The Bible says, 'Thou shalt not suffer a witch to live.' I suggest you leave here now before I shoot you as you stand."

"We have been deeded this land by the United States government," William said.

"And it will be taken from you by—"

The man's oratory was cut off by the rifle flying out of his hand and sailing through the air to land against the wagon. William looked at the man, met his eyes levelly so he would know that he was the cause, then let his gaze wander over to the river. There was a sound of thunder, and the mining equipment that had been so carefully set up in the sand burst apart, the pieces falling into the water.

"Begone," William said in a low ominous voice.

He was tempted to add an explicit threat, to tell the man that if he did not hurry, his wife and son would be next.

That was what Isabella would do.

But that was exactly why he had come himself. He would not make threats he was unwilling to carry out. He would not kill the woman or the boy—and would only kill the man if forced to do so in self-defense. His goal was merely to frighten the family away.

"You have until dawn," he said.

They *were* frightened, and he swung back atop his horse, heading slowly back the way he'd come. Before disappearing around the bend, he stopped, turned the horse, and for several moments watched as the family started to gather up their belongings and hurriedly pack the wagon. Satisfied that they really were leaving, he pushed the horse into a trot and headed back through the canyon toward home.

He heard Kate's screams even before he reached the corral outside of town. He willed the horse forward and held on as the animal galloped over the dusty road between the buildings.

Outside Kate's cottage, a small crowd had gathered. The young woman's face was a splotchy angry red, streaked with bloody scratches. Her enormous mane of hair was tangled and flying out in all directions and looked almost as wild as her eyes. "I wanted that baby!" she screamed. She threw herself at Isabella.

Isabella smiled. In her hand she clutched a bloody lifeless infant. Even from here he could see that the blood was not from the birth but from long slices which ran along the length of its small body.

She stepped easily aside, and Kate went sprawling into the dirt. Grabbing the other woman by the hair, Isabella lifted her up and threw her back toward her husband, Randolph. Her grip on the baby tightened, and William saw blood streaming down Isabella's arm as she squeezed the dead child.

A chill passed through him, and he jumped off the horse and hurried over. "What's going on here?" he demanded.

"She killed my baby!"

"One hundred," Isabella said quietly, "is a magic number."

"What?"

"We have one hundred people in town. Until one of us

dies or moves on, no new members will be brought in, no babies will be born."

"I would have moved!" Kate screamed.

"Then we would have been ninety-nine."

"Damn you!" Kate tried once again to attack, but her husband held her back. He and the rest of the onlookers seemed frightened.

"Isabella," William said sternly.

"One hundred is our number," Isabella repeated, giving him a look that brooked no argument. She hugged the dead baby to her chest, blood soaking into the white fabric of her dress.

They disappeared in the night, Kate and her husband. Isabella wanted to go after them, hunt them like animals, but this time William put his foot down. There would be no chase, no punishment, no retaliation.

He made sure the others in town knew of their differences, made sure they knew that he had prevailed, that he was still in charge.

It was too late, however. Whatever reputation he had had among the people of Wolf Canyon was gone now, and if he was still their leader it was because he had installed himself in that position and not because they wanted him there.

He was a tyrant.

He and Isabella.

This was not what he'd wanted, and if he had known it would come to this, he would not have approached the government with his petition in the first place. His dream had been to provide a home for their kind, not to establish a fiefdom of his own. He'd wanted to liberate his people, not enslave them.

But it was too late to turn back. Whether he liked it or not, the wheels had been set in motion, and he could not backtrack now.

He wished Jeb were here. He'd be able to talk this over with Jeb. His friend had always been the most effective sounding board when it came to matters of governance . . . and matters of the heart.

Right now he needed advice on both.

For he no longer wanted to lead the people of Wolf Canyon—but he would. And he no longer wanted to love Isabella—but he did.

He did not even know what Isabella had done with the newborn's body. He was not sure that he wanted to know.

What if, he thought, by some miracle, she finally found herself with child? Would she kill their baby too?

It was a disturbing question, and like too many questions these days, it was one for which he had no answer.

2

Mary left in the middle of the night. Joseph a few weeks later in the middle of the day, when everyone was busy. Olivia died of a mysterious blood ailment that even magic was unable to cure. Martin fell down a well.

It took awhile for William to realize that all of the original settlers were gone. The men and women who remained in Wolf Canyon were those who had come later.

He knew why Mary and the others had left. They hadn't told him, but they hadn't had to.

Isabella.

They did not like what Wolf Canyon was becoming. He understood completely. He himself had grave misgivings about what was happening here. This was not what he had envisioned, and he held no resentment toward those who had left.

And the others, the deaths?

Accidents, he told himself, and he made himself believe it.

William sat on his horse and surveyed Wolf Canyon from the top of the upper trail. From up here everything looked the way it always had, but the truth was that the whole tenor of the town had changed. Isabella was not alone in her feelings of anger and hatred toward those who were not witches. Many of the other townspeople, particularly the newer ones, felt the same way and were not shy about expressing their opinions in public. He understood that there'd even been some sort of meeting in the schoolhouse, a sort of strategy session to decide what to do should the "normals," as people had taken to calling them, discover Wolf Canyon. He had not been invited to the meeting, but he assumed Isabella had gone.

He had not asked her. He had not wanted to know.

If this had been a democracy, and if Isabella had been a man and allowed to run for office, he had serious doubts as to whether he would be able to beat her in a fair election.

He willed the horse onward, toward the town, hoping that Isabella was at home, in the kitchen, cooking his midday dinner.

But he had the feeling she wasn't.

They killed the first rancher on All Hallow's Eve.

The man had done nothing wrong. He was not even aware of the fact that they were witches. But Clete, returning home from a sojourn east, saw the settler's crude hut and makeshift corral on his return trip and promptly informed Isabella.

Not him.

Isabella.

The raiding party went out the next night, dressed in black garb and armed only with magic. Isabella said nothing to him, was not there when he arrived home after a long day of overseeing operations at the new tunnel over at the mine, but William knew where she'd gone, knew what she was doing, and he was filled with an anger so pure and strong

it made his hands shake. He strode through the darkened
streets of Wolf Canyon, his rage growing as he saw how
quiet the town was, how deserted the bar. A lot of them had
accompanied her, and he resolved that when she returned
home he would lay down the law. This was his town, damn
it, and wife or no wife, she had to abide by his will like the
others. They all did.

His resolve fled when she arrived, however, covered with
blood and singed by fire. What was left of her clothes was
torn and blackened. She leaped from her horse, victorious,
and grinned at him. "We did it!"

William's mouth was dry, the words he'd intended to say,
the lecture he'd intended to give, forgotten.

"It was glorious," she said rapturously. "We came out of
the night like demons, and he obviously thought we were
such, for he started shooting even before we had arrived."
Her smile broadened, and William could see the blood on
her teeth. "We took his animals first, making the cow wither
in front of his eyes, roasting the pig alive, turning his chick-
ens into statues of dung. He continued shooting, and we
burned his corral, set fire to his cabin.

"Then we went in."

She touched his face, showed him, and William saw the
scene through her eyes, saw the bullets reflected back at the
shooter, saw Isabella cause the rancher's Bible to explode
as he fell to his knees, praying, waiting for the end. He
cursed her, cursed all of them, and they took turns with their
spells, Isabella going first, popping off his fingers one by
one. Daniel followed, clouding over one eye. Thomas turned
the man's teeth to plantflesh.

And on and on.

She let go, and William stepped back, flushed. Against
his will, he felt some of the same satisfaction she had, the
same righteous sense of justice, but he didn't know if these
were his own feelings or if she had imparted hers to him.

She bathed in the river, and afterward they made love outside, like in the old days. What she prompted him to do would have made a normal woman sob with shame and humiliation, but Isabella loved it, and he loved it, too. The surrounding world disappeared for him as their bodies intertwined in ways unspeakable, and as wrong as it was, he realized that he would not oppose his wife in anything she did so long as this passion continued.

She read him, she knew this.

And that was the start of the purges.

Now

1

Miles sat in his cubicle, slumped in his swivel chair, staring at the unfunny *Dilbert* cartoon one of the agency's computer nerds had tacked up on the cloth wall of the room divider for his amusement.

The case was over.

Marina Lewis had had what was left of her father's body transferred to Arizona for burial as soon as the coroner had finished with the autopsy and the police had completed their paperwork, and she and her husband had gone back as well. Miles told her she didn't owe anything and let her off without a bill, although he wasn't sure how he was going to justify that to Perkins. It was the right thing to do, the only thing to do. He'd failed to protect her father, and while, strictly speaking, that wasn't his mandate, it was what he had expected of himself, and he felt as though he'd let Marina down.

He spun slowly around in his chair. He was at a loss because he didn't want to let the case go. There were other jobs he should be working on, a whole host of new clients from which to choose, but he wanted to stick with this.

Because it involved his dad.

That's what it came down to. Yes, he was concerned for the safety of Hec Tibbert and the other men on Liam's list. Yes, he desperately wanted to know what was behind these deaths, wanted to put a stop to this before it went any further—if that was at all possible. But it was his father's involvement that gave everything an added emotional dimension, that personalized it for him and made it so pressing and immediate.

The police had promised to investigate further—after having been warned of the danger Liam Connor was in, having been given the list, and having watched as Liam became another casualty, as predicted, under their very noses. But he had his doubts that they would follow through. There were too many other, more immediate crimes. Los Angeles was a perpetual wellspring of wrongdoing, with new murders, rapes, and robberies popping up every day. It was all the police could do to keep up with new crimes, let alone get started on the backlog.

But *he* could do it. He *wanted* to continue this investigation. It was his moral and ethical responsibility. What kind of detective would he be, what kind of human being would he be, if he did not follow through and act on what he knew, what he'd learned?

Except he'd be fired if he used the agency's time and resources to continue working on the unfunded case of a client who had not paid in the first place.

It was a lose-lose situation.

Miles felt a pencil nub hit his shoulder, and he glanced over to see Hal leaning forward in his chair, attempting to snap him out of his gloom. "What would you rather do," his friend asked, "perform analingus on an incontinent Ronald Reagan or eat out your sister?"

Miles had to smile. It was a game they'd invented several years ago when the recession had cut into the private investigation business and they were stuck in the office for long periods of time without any work to do. It had started out simply, asking each other which of their female coworkers they would most or least like to have sex with, and had gotten more outrageous over time, graduating to gross-out proportions as they expanded one another's tolerance for insults and honesty. It was based on the premise that, faced with two heinous choices, there was always one option that was less intolerable than the other. They'd never had a name for the game until one time Hal had tried to squirm out of answering—Miles had asked whether he would rather fellate Clint Eastwood or be cornholed by Tom Cruise—and the other detective had replied, "Neither. I'd rather die."

"Death is not an option," Miles told him.

Hal's face lit up. "That's it!" he exclaimed.

"That's what?"

"That's the name. 'Death Is Not an Option.' "

They'd discussed, only half jokingly, pitching Death Is Not an Option as a game show idea to HBO or one of the cable channels where there were no restrictions on language. "We could even add nudity," Hal said, "for higher ratings."

Since then they'd ritualized the game, and though they'd often mentioned bringing in others, letting Tran play, for instance, it had remained their own private entertainment.

Miles looked over at his friend, smiling. "I guess I'd have to eat out my sister."

Hal cackled with delight, as he always did, tickled, even after all this time, at hearing such an admission. He walked over to Miles' cubicle. "You okay?"

"I'm fine."

"You sure?"

"I said I'm fine."

Hal held up his hands in surrender. "I'm just asking."

Hal's attempts at cheering him up were as disjointed and disorganized as ever, but in a strange way, he found that comforting. He did feel a little better after talking to his friend. Maybe there *was* a way to keep the investigation going. After everything that had happened to him the past two months, Perkins would probably be willing to give him a leave of absence if he asked, some time off without pay.

As if reading his thoughts, Hal said, "Still no news on your dad's body?"

Miles shook his head.

"What do you think happened to him?"

He'd told Hal and everyone else that his father's body had been stolen, not wanting to share the truth of what had happened, knowing that they wouldn't believe him even if he did. And of course the coroner's office had kept it under wraps as well. They'd had enough scandals recently. The last thing their department needed was for word to leak out that they were losing bodies because the bodies were getting up and walking away.

"I don't know," Miles admitted.

"I hope it's not some psycho sicko who's doing, you know, sex stuff."

"Thanks. That's just the image I need in my head."

"Sorry." Hal headed sheepishly back to his cubicle, and Miles started sorting through the stack of files Naomi had given him. There was a sixteen-year-old girl who had run away with the forty-year-old manager of the Taco Bell at which she worked, a woman who suspected her husband of having an affair with another man, a dowager who wanted someone to track down her stolen poodle because the police hadn't been able to find the dog, a man who suspected one of his employees of smoking marijuana even though the worker had passed numerous random drug tests. None of the potential cases appealed to him, and he thought for a moment, then went out to talk to Naomi and see if she could get him an appointment with Perkins this afternoon.

He was going to ask for some time off.

Two weeks without pay.

It was a week less than he'd asked for but a week more than he'd expected, and hopefully it was all he would need. He finished out the afternoon, tied up a few loose ends, and made arrangements to contact Hal each day so that they could keep each other up on what was happening.

The telephone was already ringing when he arrived home, and he dashed through the living room to answer it.

Claire was calling to say that she'd be late—after seeing her last client, she had to attend a budget meeting with her boss, his boss, and a representative from the county board of supervisors. She told Miles he'd have to make his own dinner, but she'd be back by nine.

He warned her to drive carefully and hung up. It was going to be a long evening without her, and he walked into the kitchen, already feeling lonely. He opened the refrigerator, leaning on the door, but the metal shelves were bare save for an old half-empty container of milk, a package of butter, and a bottle of ketchup.

He realized that he hadn't done any serious grocery shopping since his dad had . . . died.

The house was silent save for the electronic hum of the refrigerator, but he could hear in his mind the rhythm of his father's footsteps. Boot heels on wood. The sound still reverberated in his brain. There had been something coldly impersonal about the rigid regularity of the tapping on the bedroom floor, and even thinking about it now made him feel frightened.

The house suddenly seemed much darker, much creepier.

He needed to get out of here, and shopping for groceries gave him a practical excuse. Switching on all of the lights on his way out so that he would return to a well-lit home, Miles hurried outside and quickly locked the front door behind him. Only here, in the open air, away from the claustrophobic confinement of the house, was he finally able to breathe easy and relax.

He looked up at the beautiful sunset created by the haze of pollutants in the air above Los Angeles, and he wondered whether right now his father was walking somewhere under this same sky.

He drove to Ralph's—

the same store in which his father had collapsed

—and got a shopping cart, but he was not in the mood for shopping. His fear had fled, leaving behind an uncomfortable melancholy, and he wanted only to get the groceries he needed for tonight and tomorrow, then get out of here as quickly as possible.

He sped through the overstocked aisles as fast as was seemly, grabbing a frozen pizza, a gallon of milk, a gallon of orange juice, a loaf of bread, and some lunch meat.

The registers were all crowded, but since he had less than ten items he could use the express line, and he pulled his cart behind that of an old woman wearing a too bright dress that *might* have been flattering to her when she bought it back in the 1960s. He glanced over at the tabloid news rack next to the checkout stand

and felt his heart leap in his chest.

MY UNCLE DIED . . . BUT WON'T STOP WALKING!

He grabbed the newspaper and stared at the banner headline. Underneath that was a grainy black-and-white photo of what looked like a typical middle-class house. A teaser for another story announced that Bigfoot was a descendant of Ancient Astronauts. Miles' hands were shaking, and he did not notice that the old lady had moved forward until he was nudged by the shopping cart behind him. He began placing his items on the black rubber conveyor, still holding onto the tabloid, working on automatic.

He opened the paper, riffled through it until he found the article he wanted. The story was a page long, with one bad photo of a stunned-looking young woman in the center. He didn't have time to read the whole thing, so he quickly scanned the first few paragraphs. Apparently, a woman in Cedar City, Utah, had come home from work one day to

find her uncle dead and walking in a circle around the outside of their duplex. It had taken six men to stop him and
tie him down to a gurney and transport him to the morgue.

At the sound of a throat clearing, Miles looked up. The
clerk had already rung up his food items and was waiting
for him to either buy the paper or put it away and pay for
his groceries. Miles plunked the tabloid down in front of the
boy, then paid the total displayed on the register's readout
and hurried outside, where he sat down on a bench in front
of the store and read the article all the way through.

Then all the way through again.

The details of what this woman had experienced with her
undead uncle were remarkably similar to his own. If the article could be believed, Janet Engstrom had recently moved
to Cedar City in order to take care of her Uncle John, who
was dying of cancer. She returned home from work one day
to find her uncle dead, wearing only his pajamas, walking
around the outside of their duplex in a continuous circle
while neighborhood kids threw things at him. According to
Janet, he had started walking inside the house several days
before his death, and she had not informed anyone because
she wasn't sure what to do about it. Six men—three attendants from the coroner's office, the coroner himself, and two
policemen—had been required to subdue the dead man and
strap him to a gurney so he could be transported to the
morgue. A "source close to the investigation revealed" that
the coroner could not stop the corpse from moving long
enough to perform an autopsy, and that the body had been
cremated in order to prevent the "disease of the walking
dead" from infecting any more dead people in the area of
southern Utah.

Apparently, Janet Engstrom had approached the *Insider*
because she could not find out what happened to her uncle.
The county coroner's office would not release any information to her or the family and was denying that there had

been anything out of the ordinary in John Engstrom's death. As were the police. Even the parents of the neighborhood kids who had been throwing mud at the walking dead man seemed to have bought the explanation of the experts rather than the eyewitness accounts of their own children and were now telling Janet that she was merely suffering from "stress."

Miles drove home, dialed information for Cedar City, and surprisingly, Janet Engstrom's number was listed. When he called her, though, he was informed by a prerecorded voice that the number was out of service. He had a hunch she'd been besieged by calls from every wacko in the country who had read the tabloid story. The article didn't say where she worked or even what her occupation was, so he couldn't call her employer. He dialed information again, got the phone numbers for the local hospital, but as he'd expected, no one at the hospital was willing to give out any information concerning Janet or John Engstrom. The coroner's office and the police were both forcefully unforthcoming.

But Miles was undaunted. He was strangely excited, and if he had believed in ESP, he would have said that this situation spoke to him on that level, that it was calling out to him.

If he had believed in ESP?

He was trying to get a hold of the subject of a tabloid story about the walking dead, and he was doubting the existence of simple extrasensory perception?

He had to laugh, despite the horrific circumstances, and for the first time he felt optimistic, as though answers and solutions were finally within reach.

He knew what he had to do. He had to get over to Cedar City and talk to this woman. He did not think she was in any danger—like himself, she was a witness, not a participant—but it was impossible to tell how things would go down. People connected to this situation seemed to be dropping like flies, and he wanted to speak with her while he was still able to do so.

Miles had no idea how big Cedar City was, but he was sure he could catch a plane there, and he used his computer to sign on to an online travel agency and look up schedules. American had a direct flight to Las Vegas, with a connecting jump to Cedar City, that left from L.A. at six o'clock in the morning. He'd arrive at Cedar City by eight and even get fifteen percent off the regular price of an Avis rental car. He booked himself the deal using his Visa card number and accessed the site again to confirm it.

Done.

He wondered briefly if he should have waited until he talked with Claire, if perhaps she would like to go as well, but he told himself that he'd done right. She wasn't involved in this. And whether she wanted to accompany him or not, this was something he needed to do himself. It might sound like boneheaded macho posturing—*a man's gotta do what a man's gotta do*—but if that ESP was still kicking in, it was telling him this was a journey he had to make alone.

Well, maybe not alone . . .

He called Hec Tibbert. The phone rang three times, five times, ten times, twenty.

He hung up, wanting to believe that Tibbert had gone to the store or to a movie or to Fred Brodsky's house, but knowing that the old man was probably dead. The excitement he'd been feeling faded, replaced by the familiar dread that had been his constant companion for the past two months.

He thought for a moment, then called the coroner's office. Luckily, Ralph had not yet gone home, and Miles told his friend what he'd found, what he planned to do. The coroner was not as skeptical of the tabloid story as he no doubt would have been before, but he would not go so far as to trust in the article's veracity.

"You called Graham yet? What does he say?"

"I haven't talked to him."

"If I remember right, didn't you specifically tell him to keep this out of the tabloids?"

"The *Weekly World News*. This is the *Insider*."

"Are you going to tell him about this?"

"Maybe when I get back."

"So you just called to get my blessing."

"Basically."

Ralph sighed. "Go ahead, do what you have to do, but be prepared. If, by some chance, there is something to it and you do find out information, give me a call as soon as you return. At this point, I'd be grateful for anything."

"Think I should call the police, too? Let them know?"

"Wait until you find out if it's real. Besides, if they're any good, they have their own detective tracking down tabloid stories."

"Are you making fun of me?"

"I wish I was."

Claire arrived shortly after nine, and Miles filled her in on the plan. She grew quiet, but she did not beg him to tag along, and the fact that she instinctively understood that he wanted to go alone made him realize how lucky he was to have her in his life again. Even after all this time, even after the years apart, they understood each other.

"Be careful," she said.

"I will."

There was a pause. Claire held his gaze. "I love you," she told him.

Miles took her in his arms and hugged her tightly, feeling the warm softness of her breasts against his chest, feeling the fragile vulnerability of her shoulder blades beneath the palms of his hands. He could not remember the last time she had said that to him, and in spite of the situation, he found himself smiling absurdly. "I love you, too."

2

Dan Dyson laughed.

Because if he didn't laugh, he would scream.

Dan placed a hand on the strapped-down leg of the decedent and felt the thrum of hard muscle working beneath the skin, loosening and tightening, stretching, causing the exposed testes of the corpse to jiggle slightly and shift from side to side.

It was outrageous. A week later, and John Engstrom's body was still attempting to walk. There had been no lessening of effort in all that time, not a single second of relaxation. The corpse had not yet started to decay, either. There was not even the slightest whiff of corruption from the flesh. By all rights, decomposition should have begun. True, the room was refrigerated, but the embalming process had been held off, no preservatives had been administered, and nothing had been done with the body other than to strap it down to the autopsy table.

Yet there was no decomposition.

And the leg muscles continued to move.

Dan had been the county M.E. for the past decade and deputy examiner for eight years before that, and in his experience this was totally unprecedented. He'd scoured records and textbooks, trying to find a case even remotely similar but to no avail.

He'd ended up contacting the FBI and CDC because he didn't know what to do. Ever since that damn tabloid story had come out earlier in the week, his office had been inundated with phone calls and faxes from the weirdos of the world, many of them offering ghoulish suggestions on how to deal with reanimated corpses. Some were even predicting that this was the first sign of the apocalypse.

Thank God, the paper had printed that the body had been cremated. He did not even want to think about the hysteria he'd have to deal with if people knew that not only was John Engstrom's body still extant—but was still walking.

Or would be walking if it wasn't strapped down.

Dan had called for help from the coroner in Salt Lake City, from the coroner in Las Vegas, from Dave French, a friend of his who taught pathology at the university here in Cedar City, but no one had been able to offer any advice. They were just as stymied as he was; only he had to actually make a decision and take some action. Finally, out of desperation, he had contacted the FBI and the Center for Disease Control in Atlanta. The FBI's medical personnel were probably more used to dealing with bizarre deaths than anyone on the planet. And while he had doubts that any diseases were at work here, the CDC was sending someone out anyway. It couldn't hurt to have more than one opinion.

Dan moved away from the autopsy table and busied himself making sure all of the necessary surgical implements were on hand and in place. As embarrassed as he was to admit it, he dreaded coming into this room. Familiarity had not bred complacency, and after a week of this he was more frightened of the corpse than he had been at the beginning. He kept the radio permanently on, tuned to a country station, because if there were no other noises here, he would hear the sounds of Engstrom's legs: the subtly creaking strain of the straps, the arrhythmic tick of shifting muscles against the metal tabletop.

The lights remained on, too. He'd had more than one nightmare this week of returning to work, opening the exam-room door, and flipping on the lights to find the body gone. Or standing right in front of him, freed of restraints, hands outstretched and ready to kill.

Both the CDC doctor and the FBI agent were supposed to have been here five minutes ago. Dan was about to leave and wait in the outer office, unable to find more busywork and unwilling to remain in the same room with that twitching cadaver any longer, when the swinging doors to the exam door opened and two men wearing scrubs and surgical masks came walking in.

"Dr. Dyson, I presume?"

Dan nodded, not sure which man was speaking.

"I'm Dr. Hovarth from the CDC." The shorter man in front nodded as he approached the autopsy table. "This is Dr. Brigham from the Bureau."

Dan exhaled as an almost physical wave of relief washed over him. He had not realized how much the pressure had been weighing on him. This opportunity to pass the buck and hand over his authority made him feel much lighter.

The three men shook hands, and Dan gave them a quick rundown of what had happened. They'd both read the reports and documents he'd faxed to them, and he skimmed over that portion of the story, but he went into detail about the past week here in the coroner's office, the minor tests he'd performed, the stubborn consistency of the so far unexplained reanimation.

Hovarth wanted to start on the autopsy immediately, and Dan deferred to his judgment. He had been reluctant to cut because the corpse . . . still seemed like it was alive.

That was the truth. Even surgeons operated on people who were unmoving, under anesthesia, and he himself had never even cut into a live body before. The prospect of opening the chest of a dead man whose legs were still moving made him extremely queasy.

"I'll lead," Hovarth said.

Brigham nodded. "I'll assist."

That meant that Dan would only be backup and probably wouldn't have to cut at all, just observe. For that he was grateful.

They washed up, put on gloves, turned on the video cameras and tape recorders. Hovarth moved the instrument tray next to the table and began a running commentary as he first measured the body, carefully examined its exterior, then picked up a scalpel. The muscle movement did not seem to faze him, and he did not even hesitate as he made the first incision and inserted a catheter.

Dan stood next to the CDC doctor, saying nothing, hearing the muffled thump of blood in his head, feeling the discomfort of sweaty palms against latex gloves.

The blood was drained, but there was no discernible change in the movement of the corpse's legs. Beneath the straps, the muscles still strained in alternating order: left foot, right foot, left foot, right. When the chest had been opened and Hovarth began removing organs, weighing them and bagging them, those restless limb muscles mindlessly continued to exert themselves. The sight caused chills to surf down Dan's arms. It was the most unnatural thing he had ever seen, and even in this lighted room, surrounded by state-of-the-art medical equipment and two other doctors, he was frightened.

"We're going to amputate the legs," Hovarth said finally, after the cranium had been opened, and the brain tagged and bagged. The body was little more than an exposed empty husk, but still the legs worked.

They had a quick discussion as to what would be done with the limbs, who would get to study them. As per procedure, samples of the organs would be taken by both Hovarth and Brigham while the organs themselves would remain frozen in the custody of the coroner's office until such time as all three agencies agreed on disposal, but the legs were different, and Dan quickly made it clear that he thought the best idea would be for the CDC to take one for examination and for the FBI to take the other. After a short back-and-forth, Hovarth and Brigham agreed, and Dan found in the supply closet two plastic airtight receptacles big enough to hold Engstrom's legs from femur to phalanges.

Here, finally, the other two doctors exhibited some trepidation. Hovarth's hand as he installed a new blade on the roto-saw was not quite as steady as it should have been, and as Brigham examined the legs and drew cut lines on the tensing skin, he looked uneasy.

"Amputating left leg at groin," Hovarth said into the recorder before starting up the whining saw and drowning out all hope of hearing anything else.

The saw sliced through skin and flesh, muscle and bone. Dan half expected to hear screaming, to see Engstrom start thrashing around beneath the restraints, or to perhaps break the restraints like Frankenstein and lurch to his feet, but nothing like that happened, and the unwired jaw and unsewn eyes both remained open and dead.

The left leg was severed, Hovarth trimming off the last of the bottom skin.

The leg was still moving.

It was the freakiest thing he'd ever seen, and Dan's first impulse was to cut the amputated limb up into little pieces or burn it in the incinerator. But in his mind he saw little cut-up leg pieces moving independently of each other, still informed by some strange sentience, saw a charred bit of bone wiggling amid ashes.

Unattached to a body, the leg slid out from under its restraints and fell to the floor, where it lay on its side, bending and unbending at the knee, moving itself in a circle on the linoleum as it vainly attempted to walk.

It was his responsibility to place the leg in the receptacle, but it took all three of them to subdue the limb, pick it up, and finally lock it in the plastic box. Dan placed the container in the freezer along with the other organs. The leg was still kicking against the side of the plastic, and he hoped to God that freezing would at least slow it down, if not stop it entirely.

He walked back to the autopsy table.

Then they did it all over again.

It was nearly three o'clock, six hours after Hovarth and Brigham had first arrived, that everything was finished, the table scrubbed down, the camera and recorders turned off. Dupes were made of the video and audio cassettes as the three of them retired to Dan's office, had a drink, exchanged paperwork, and discussed the autopsy. Hovarth admitted that he had never seen anything like this before and that he was at a loss as to how to explain the postmortem activity. It was the repetitive nature of the animation, the fact that it was so focused and precise, that Brigham found most intriguing. He had no clue as to how it was occurring, but that specificity implied a reason, a purpose. Neither man expressed any doubts as to the cause of Engstrom's death—the cancerous tumors were so far advanced and metastasized that they all agreed it was a miracle he had lasted as long as he had—but the cause of his *after*life was beyond speculation.

They left having resolved nothing, Hovarth and Brigham both promising to bring to bear the extensive resources of their respective organizations and to schedule a conference call within the week.

The CDC took one leg, the FBI the other. The remainder of the body was his, and it was really and truly dead. As simply as that his problem was solved. Dan typed up an autopsy report and released what was left of John Engstrom to the mortuary specified by the family.

He watched the mortuary attendants wheel out the bagged body—or what was left of it—on a gurney. He recalled the feel of the moving muscles under his palm. He had laughed at the sensation this morning, alone in the exam room, but he could not recall now why he had done so.

He shivered.

It wasn't funny.

There was nothing funny about it at all.

3

It was on his desk Monday morning. Delivered anonymously, as these things always were.

The name printed on the file sticker was WOLF CANYON.

McCormack stared for several moments at the manila folder before opening it. The last time he had received one of these, two years back, it had been to inform him that Todd Goldman, his right-hand man and liaison with local law enforcement on Wolf Canyon, had killed himself.

Wolf Canyon.

He was the one who'd been in charge of the investigation. Or what was officially *referred* to as the "investigation." For there'd been no real effort to determine what had happened. No one was interested in finding out why the residents of the town had not been evacuated or, indeed, who was responsible. The priority had been to maintain secrecy, to keep the existence of the community quiet and to make damn sure that no one outside—particularly no one from the press—got wind of the fact that the United States government had been not only harboring but actively supporting a community of witches.

The phrase "plausible deniability" had not yet been coined, but the reasoning behind it had been in place for quite some time, and that was their goal: to ensure that if word somehow did leak out about Wolf Canyon, everyone above a certain level in the chain of command could plead ignorance. The fact was, in those early days of the Cold War, a sitting president could not afford to be seen as the patron of a band of godless witches. The heathen commies were bad enough, but supporting a secret society of spell casters here at home, with tax dollars, in the Grand Canyon State no less, would have been grounds for impeachment.

The operation had been a complete success. Not only had no one found out about the witches—not even the men from the dam project—but neither the press nor the general public had ever learned about the drownings. No one connected with Wolf Canyon had ever spoken publicly, had even leaked enough to bring about congressional hearings, closed door or otherwise. *This* dam had held.

He himself still had questions. Despite the fact that he'd led the investigation, he had never fully satisfied himself as to whether the drownings had been accidental or intentional. Their true mission had been to hush everything up, not ferret out the truth, and they had followed their assignment to the letter: they had seen the site, examined the bodies, spoken with the workers, and quietly closed the books. It was not inconceivable that someone somewhere within the bowels of the Eisenhower administration had learned of the existence of Wolf Canyon, judged it a political liability, and determined that the town had to be destroyed, its people silenced. It *was* rather unusual to have two dams built so closely together, and though the reasoning sounded plausible, he could also believe that there had been an ulterior motive, that the decision had been made to neutralize what could have been a political atomic bomb in those Red-baiting times.

Hell, maybe Tricky Dick had even been involved.

So, over the years, he'd put out unofficial feelers, curiosity taking the place of circumspection as he rose through the ranks, letting it be known to trustworthy individuals in the various agencies involved that he was interested in any news related to Wolf Canyon.

Now another folder had been delivered, and McCormack sorted through the document copies provided. His mood darkened as he scanned the material. As before, there was nothing concrete, everything was circumstantial, but the connections to Wolf Canyon lent it all an ominousness that would not otherwise be there.

He read one death certificate and autopsy report.

Two.

The truth was, he had never really believed in witches. Oh, he had believed that they believed they were witches, but as far as magical powers and mystical potions and all of that hocus-pocus mumbo jumbo, he'd thought it was a load of crap. It was a remnant of the seventeenth century, not something that anyone would take seriously here in the latter half of the twentieth.

At least that was what he'd thought until now.

He was not so sure anymore.

Several weeks ago, Russ Winston, one of the undersecretaries at Interior, had been killed here in D.C., in his own garage, in what had been characterized for the press as an "unusual" manner. In reality, it was far more than that. He had been torn apart, and both his son and grandson had told investigators that the perpetrator was a small creature, a hairy toothy thing that had lain in wait for Winston and had disappeared immediately afterward.

A monster.

Monsters and witches. These were the elements of children's fairy tales, not things that should be taken seriously by a government agency. But the government was taking them seriously and once again was doing everything within its power to shield the public from information that it felt its citizens would not be able to handle.

He had known Russ Winston from Wolf Canyon. He'd interviewed him as part of the investigation. Russ had been one of the shift supervisors, and he'd been sharper than most of the others, more helpful, more observant, which explained why he'd made something of himself in Washington. Over the years they had kept in touch in that superficial way casual acquaintances do, but neither of them had ever talked about Wolf Canyon again, and McCormack now wished that they had. He'd always been under the impression that Russ felt guilty about the drownings, that he'd blamed himself and never really gotten over it. That was one of the reasons

McCormack had never brought it up on the rare occasions that the two of them spoke. But he wondered now if the undersecretary had known more than he'd let on and if his guilt was based on knowledge rather than misplaced blame.

The other casualty was a man from Utah, an accountant who had died of cancer. There was nothing connecting the accountant to Wolf Canyon, but a local coroner had brought in the CDC and the FBI because the man had continued walking even after his death.

Apparently, whoever had left him the folder thought there might be a connection.

He did too, and McCormack perused the provided information, including two newspaper articles, one from a local Utah paper and one from a tabloid. There was a leg, apparently, that was still animate. The Bureau's top men were examining it now. Southern Utah was not that far from Arizona and Wolf Canyon, and it wasn't much of a stretch to think that there might be a relation.

Was this stuff real?

The Soviets had always been rumored to be studying ESP and psychokinesis and Kirlian photography and all that. If there was any truth to psychic phenomena, perhaps the United States should have followed suit. Maybe they should have let the Pentagon have a crack at Wolf Canyon, used those witches as a resource, instead of just burying all trace of their existence beneath a man-made lake.

But whether as a result of accident or policy, it was too late now.

He called Greg Rossiter, over at the Bureau. Rossiter had some experience with this paranormal shit, and whether it was true or not, he'd set himself up as an expert. He'd recently obtained black-budget funding to install a new database, cataloging unsolved cases by possible supernatural explanation, which would have made him the laughingstock of the FBI if not for the fact that Rossiter had actually put to rest a host of unsolved murders dating back decades, proving fairly conclusively that they had all been performed by the same murderer and that that murderer was a vampire who had been hiding out in the Arizona desert. He had been part of the party that had dispatched the monster, and while there'd been no body, there'd been enough circumstantial evidence and eyewitness testimony to substantiate his claims. Not everyone believed Rossiter's vampire story, but enough of the higher-ups did that he had been promoted out of Phoenix and was now working here in Washington. McCormack knew him from countless seminars and workshops, and though Rossiter was not one of the people to whom he'd put out feelers regarding Wolf Canyon, McCormack thought that it might be time to bring the agent in on this.

Rossiter arrived after lunch, and after a quick informal greeting, McCormack handed over the folder and asked for his take on the information presented. Rossiter sat down and sorted through the documents. He looked up. "I know that area," he said. "Arizona. My old stomping grounds."

"Keep reading."

McCormack stared out the window at the traffic on the street below. The only sound in the office was the muted rush of the ventilation system pumping in heated air and the occasional sound of pages turning as the agent read through the folder.

When Rossiter finally finished, he stood up, and McCormack could tell from the way he began pacing around the room that he was excited. "What's the background on this? And what's your interest? There are Bureau papers here, so you obviously have some contact feeding you information, but why? And why call me in?"

McCormack gave him an abbreviated rundown of the "Wolf Canyon Disaster," as they'd been prepared to call it if any information leaked to the press. He explained how the town had been set aside as a community where witches could avoid persecution, and how, when the town was flooded after completion of the Wolf Canyon Dam, it had not been completely evacuated and sixty-three people had been killed. He'd been with the Justice Department and had been assigned to head the investigation by the Attorney General himself. No news of what occurred had ever leaked out, and he'd closed the investigation after two weeks, ruling what had happened an accident, but there'd been more to that situation than met the eye, and he had retained an interest in it ever since, keeping tabs on Wolf Canyon news for all these years.

"Let me guess," Rossiter said. "You're still curious because you were never allowed to reach any real conclusions. Your job wasn't to investigate, it was to deny complicity, to prepare a report that would exonerate all branches of government from any wrongdoing in connection with those deaths."

McCormack looked at him, said nothing.

"I understand that you can't talk. That's okay by me. It's probably what's gotten you where you are today. But let me tell you that from what you've told me and from what I read in that folder, that wasn't just some town populated by wackos who thought they could ride broomsticks and consort with the devil. There was something powerful at that place, and it's still viable and it's reaching out." He shook his head. "I know what a lot of the brass thinks of me. I know I'm not exactly everyone's idea of a model agent. But I also know what I've seen, what I've experienced firsthand. I know what kind of things are out there. It's not a black-and-white world we live in, and if the Bureau doesn't get with the program, we're going to find ourselves falling even more behind than we are already. We need to actively investigate incidents like this, not just sweep them under the rug and invent some bullshit explanation that will appease the powers-that-be. We need to start coming up with strategies to deal with these situations."

"What are you saying?"

"I want to go out there. I know the local law enforcement, and I know the area. As you may or may not know, I made my bones in that part of Arizona, and let me tell you, there are some strange things going on out there. I think I could find out what you want to know."

"That's an excellent idea. In fact, to be honest, it's what I hoped you'd say. It's why I called you in. I wanted you to look into it."

Rossiter looked at him skeptically. "I need your help, though."

"My help? Why?"

"Because you can authorize this. Make a call to the Bureau chief and specifically request that I head a task force or an investigative team. With someone from Justice asking for it, it'll happen."

McCormack balked. "Why can't you just go on your own? The Bureau's already studying the leg from that accountant. It's an open case. Get yourself assigned to it."

"First of all, I can't just assign myself to cases. They have to be assigned to me. Second of all, I'm not exactly the most respected member of the FBI team at this point. In case you hadn't noticed, despite my documented success, despite what I was told and what I was promised, I am on a very short leash here. I can't exactly write my own ticket." He leaned forward, and McCormack saw excitement mixed with ambition on the younger man's features. "That's where you come in. I need legitimacy. I need someone who'll go to bat for me. Someone above reproach. Someone respected and powerful and influential who'll back me on this."

"I don't . . ."

"You don't what? You don't want to get involved? You are involved. And if you ever want to find out what really happened—what's really happening—you'll sponsor me. This is a rare opportunity. In your position, this isn't going to make or break you. Win, lose, or draw, you'll come out of it the same. You're so close to this that your perceptions are skewed, but believe me, this isn't the Oklahoma City bombing. This is not a major case. It's a forty-year-old closed investigation in which some of the peripheral participants have recently died. No one'll give a damn if you quietly authorize a new investigation into events after the fact."

McCormack licked his lips, which were suddenly dry. "I don't know."

"What's not to know? You called me in to ask me about this, and I'm giving you my opinion. You should use your authority to open a new investigation, concurrent with the Bureau's case, and request that I be in charge."

"I—I can't accept that responsibility."

Rossiter nodded. "I had a feeling you might say that." He tossed the file back on McCormack's desk. "But don't come crying to me if you never learn the truth."

McCormack met his eyes, said nothing.

The agent waited a moment for a response, then started out the door. "You know where to find me if you change your mind."

McCormack wanted to say something, wanted to stop Rossiter from leaving, but in his mind he saw the stacked waterlogged bodies of the men and women they'd been able to dredge from the lake.

And he was afraid.

He stared at the door for several minutes after it closed.

Maybe, he decided, he didn't really want to know the truth.

He turned on the paper shredder next to his desk and, picking the folder up off his desk, fed the pages of the file through, one by one.

Then

1

The world had changed.

Territories were turning into states, and the wild untamed West was being crisscrossed by tracks and trails and roads. In the cities, telephones now allowed friends and relatives to speak across great distances by means of a mechanical device.

People weren't afraid of magic anymore.

Science had made magic commonplace.

William did not like this new world, and when he went into the cities to trade or buy goods, when he traveled to Phoenix or Albuquerque or Salt Lake City, he felt uneasy with the casual acceptance of what before would have elicited gasps of astonishment. Even the former charges of heresy and blasphemy and consorting with the devil seemed preferable to this bored resignation, and he found himself mentally condemning the cheapening of the miraculous.

Science had usurped the role of witches. Men could now perform their own miracles. In Denver, he had heard discussion of a scientist named Darwin who postulated a "survival of the fittest," who apparently believed that nature provided what was needed and discarded what was not, "natural selection" determining which animal species survived.

Perhaps he himself had helped ensure the extinction of his own kind by isolating them, by providing a haven of safe shelter. They were no longer needed, no longer performed any useful function. They simply existed, and without a larger purpose, they had broken away from the main thrust of life on earth, had become a still, dying pond on the side of a great rushing river.

He lay in bed, staring up into the darkness, needing to move his bowels but unwilling to walk out to the privy in this cold. It was at night when these doubts always came to him, and they seemed to be coming more and more frequently.

This was not how he had imagined it would turn out. His intentions had been noble, his motives pure, and in those long ago days when he'd been expelled from the last town and was riding west, searching in vain for a world that did not exist, he had even deceived himself into thinking that he was an important man and had come up with a great idea that would change the lives of his people forever.

Time had put the lie to that, however, and he now regretted that he had ever come to this place, that he had ever attempted to found a town.

That he had ever met Isabella.

Yes. He regretted that most of all. She was the source of his problems, and if he had never met her, everything would have turned out differently.

He rolled onto his side, his muscles straining and complaining. He winced as he struggled to sit up. He had gotten old and feeble. His powers were as strong as ever. If anything, they had increased with age. But his body was wearing down. He could no longer walk without pain, and if he did not weave himself a strengthening spell, his hands shook when he held something even as light as a pen.

Isabella had not changed.

He glanced down at her, lying next to him in the old brass bed. She remained as youthful as ever, her skin as smooth as alabaster, her face still informed with that wild beauty which had so captivated him on the trail outside Cheyenne all those years ago. Asleep, the covers pushed down below her breasts—round and perfectly formed, exposed to the crisp night air, nipples jutting up proudly—she was still the most amazing-looking woman he had ever seen.

She was not like him, he knew. She was something different, something more.

Something evil.

It had taken him a long time to admit that to himself. Even after she had run off most of his original group, even after the others had died, he had still not wanted to ascribe to her the blame. He loved her. Or thought he did. And with that love came not only an instinctive desire to protect her, but a willful blindness to her failings that prevented him from seeing what had been obvious to so many others.

And when normal people had moved into the region, when she had started the purges and persecutions, when she had built the stakes, he had still refused to acknowledge what was going on, though in the dark private hours he spent alone without her company, he agonized over it all, wondering if the Isabella he saw was the real Isabella or just an idealized image that clouded his view and kept him from the truth.

The last ten years had been hell, as farmers and settlers who came to homestead in the surrounding country were systematically killed or driven off, methodically terrorized, with magic and without, and he had stood by helplessly and ineffectually as Isabella's reign of death spread across the land. Many of the witches went along with this. At least in the beginning. They approved of Isabella's approach, supported it. They and their families had been persecuted for most of their lives, and they relished the opportunity to get back at those who had done so by doing the same, tit for tat. Some did not approve, however, and those dissenters who remained, rather than sneaking away in the middle of the night to take their chances elsewhere, grew increasingly

cowed and silent, intimidated by Isabella's growing auto-
cratic rule.

He had been intimidated, too.

Isabella opened one eye, looked at him, and the lascivi-
ous tilt of her eyebrow reminded him of what they had done
earlier in the evening, acts his poor body was paying for
now. She smiled at him. "Is everything okay, dear?"

He forced himself to smile back and settled onto the pillow. "Everything is fine."

His perceptions had been slowly changing, each new act
of violence eroding his confidence in his wife, but Isabella's
true nature was not brought home to him until the next day.

He spent the morning alone in the house, as he too often
did these days, but when Isabella did not show up to make
his lunch, and when another hour, and another, passed without any sign from her, he decided to go out and search. He
had a bad feeling in the pit of his stomach, and while he
still could not read Isabella even after all these years, his
hunches had never failed him.

She was not in town, not in the bar or the mercantile or
the library or the haberdashery. He did not sense acknowledgment of her among any of the houses in town, and he
saddled up his horse, strengthened his tired body with a spell,
and headed out on the road north.

He found her up the canyon, near the mine's abandoned
first shaft, playfully disemboweling a small girl with a long
serrated knife. The girl was completely silent, either shocked
into soundlessness by the horror of her predicament or rendered mute by magic, and only the wild thrashing and gy-
rations of her mutilated body bespoke the unbearable physical
agony to which she was being subjected. It had been some
time since a raid had been conducted against a settler, and
older scars on the girl's face and legs led him to believe that

Isabella had been keeping this child alive for some time to use as her plaything.

A baby girl.

Isabella turned to look at him, smiled, and pulled out the girl's heart, biting into it. The thrashing stopped.

Until this point he had always been able to make excuses for her. But the sight of her joyously playing with this innocent child shocked him. She was not merely a witch overzealously protecting herself and her people from possible harm. She was a monster.

Something evil.

He realized now what he should have realized long before: that she was the one who had killed Jeb and drained his body.

She was the vampyr.

Except she was not exactly a vampyr. He had read up on such things in the aftermath of his friend's death, and aside from the fact that she did not age and apparently had the ability to drain fluids from a body, she did not possess any other vampyric characteristics. She did not need blood for sustenance, nor was she incapacitated by the day and invigorated by the night. She had no fear of crucifixes, and she loved garlic.

No, Isabella was something else, and what disturbed him most was the knowledge that no matter how long they'd been together, she was a complete mystery to him.

As far as he knew, she was the only one. In all their years together, she had never made mention of missing any people from her past—aside from that story about the brothel in Kansas City, which he had never believed. She'd never appeared to be homesick for a family or any other community, had never indicated that she was waiting for someone else to show up.

He thought of the monster he and Jeb had found in the canyons.

He thought of the Bad Lands.

Maybe she was the last of a dying breed. Maybe the beings that had populated this country before the coming of men had become extinct and she was the only one left, surviving by her wits.

Darwin again.

Everything seemed to come back to Darwin these days.

If he had had the power to go against her, he would have killed her there on the spot. He would have stopped her heart or melted her down or set her ablaze, but he did not have her strength, had never had her strength, and she knew it. She dropped the small broken body on the rocks, and he turned away from the mine, sickened, galloping back the way he'd come. He returned alone to the town, holing up in the house.

Isabella came back many hours later, clean, fresh, and visibly happy. They said nothing to each other about their encounter, and he knew that she was counting on him not to take any action.

They did not speak during supper or after.

He went to bed alone.

Once again he awoke in the middle of the cold night with a desperate need to relieve himself. Although he had gone to sleep alone, Isabella had in the interim crawled into bed with him, and her head lay on the pillow next to his. One of her hands gently cupped his genitals. He sat up, looked down at her, and the expression of perverse contentment on her face twisted his guts into a knot. Originally, he had not intended to do anything about what had happened. Upon returning home, a sort of moral paralysis had descended upon him. But now, thinking about what she'd done—

what THEY'D done

—and seeing her asleep in bed like this, her guard down, vulnerable, he suddenly had the strength to do what needed to be done.

He killed her as she slept.

He killed her, but she did not die.

He put the pillow over her head, held it there, and when he had done so until his arms were aching, he pulled the pillow up.

She was still breathing, still asleep.

And she was smiling.

The chill he felt was not from the outside air seeping in between the cracks of the windowsills, nor from the rheumatism that had permanently settled in his bones. He backed away from the bed, his hands shaking, his mouth dry. He kept waiting for her to sit up, to open her eyes, to acknowledge the attempt he'd made on her life and retaliate in some way. But she remained unmoving, asleep, and only that sly smile on her face let him know that she was aware of what he'd done.

He placed a quick spell on the bed and everything in it, a binding spell, and he rushed around the room looking for a weapon, determined to go through with what he'd decided.

He used her own knife to cut off her head, the long serrated one with which she'd disemboweled the girl. Blood spurted, flowed. He stemmed it with toad powder, he separated the head from the body, but still she lived. The eyes blinked open; the arms moved up to casually scratch her disassociated cheek.

She was playing with him, he realized.

She looked at him and shook her head, the unconnected head rocking back and forth on the pillow, its raggedly severed veins flopping from the open neck like live red worms.

He was covered with blood, as were the bedsheets, as were the blankets, as was the floor. He had never been so frightened in his life, and it was the knowledge in her eyes that was the most unnerving. For he had intended to kill her quickly and cleanly so that she would not know what happened to her, so she would not be aware of his betrayal.

But it had not worked out that way, and her eyes remained wide and seeing, watching each of his awkward fumbling attempts to murder her. Knowing that she was aware of what he was doing filled him with a strange and terrible dread, a terror unlike any he had known before.

With a cry he grabbed the edge of the pillow and yanked it, tossing her head on the floor. He sliced her body in half, said a quick and dirty spell, then stumbled out of the house, breathing deeply, trying to fill his tired old lungs with the clean freshness of cold night air and to remove the taste and smell of blood from his mouth and nose.

He had planned to keep her death a secret, at least for a little while, and then attribute it to natural causes. But the disruption in power must have been sensed because a dozen people were standing outside his fence, dressed in nightcaps and bedclothes. He scanned the faces of those present, expecting to confront the wrath of those who had gone along with her purges. But what he saw instead filled his heart with joy.

Relief.

Gratitude.

They were glad she was gone, thankful that he had killed her.

He staggered down the porch steps, through the small yard, out the gate, and into the arms of Irma Keyhorn and Susan Johnson.

By the time he reached them, his eyes were so full of tears that he could not even see.

They did not wait for morning.

Several of the men accompanied him back into the house. Matthew, Joshua, Cletus, and Russell carried out the two halves of the body, chanting spells to ward off malevolence, spells to protect themselves. William carried her head, having dusted it with invested bone meal in order to render it inanimate, and though his emotions were churning, he had no doubt that he had done the right thing.

By this time most of the town had gathered out front, and they followed silently as the men carried what was left of Isabella up Main Street and out into the wilds of the canyon. The road became a wagon trail, then a horse path as it led farther into the darkness, farther from town.

William felt as though he should explain what he'd done and why, but he did not know what to say, and the truth was that words did not seem to be needed. The people of the town understood somehow, and he sensed nothing but support when he scanned the crowd.

They continued into the darkness.

The cave was up the canyon in the marshy area by the ferns.

He had intended to entomb her there from the beginning. The cave was far from town but still in Wolf Canyon, and it was remote enough that her body would probably never be discovered. His intention was not to keep her corpse from harm, but to keep her from harming others. He had no faith that she was rendered completely disabled by death, that her power had died with her body, and he wanted to make sure that he did everything he could to ensure her permanent incapacitation.

Leading the way, he slogged through the muck and weeds that adjoined this particularly slow-moving section of the river. Underneath an overhang of rock on which grew clumps of green fern shaded from the sun and fed by a trickling spring located somewhere at the top of the cliff, the cave entrance yawned, a low, narrow opening in the rock that disguised a much larger chamber inside. One by one they entered, and someone conjured a sand fire for light.

"We will leave her here," William said. "Place the halves of her body at opposite ends."

He felt movement in his hands, a repugnant unnatural

squirming that startled him into dropping her head. It hit the powdered dirt with a quiet thud, rolling over until the blank staring eyes were looking up. He'd been half expecting something like this, but it still took him by surprise. He stared down at the head, not wanting to pick it up again, afraid to touch it. The eyes blinked, the cheek muscles twitched, and he knew that neither bone meal nor spells were strong enough to block her will.

He backed up a step. The men carrying the halves of her body had dropped them at the opposite sides of the cave, and they had joined the rest of the people near the fire. All eyes were on him.

William heard a whisper, saw Isabella's mouth move. Her eyes shifted to look at him, then took in the rest of the crowd. The temperature suddenly dropped, a chilling of the air that was strong enough to dim the fire.

Despite the absence of a connected body and lungs, Isabella's voice issued loud and clear from between the moving lips of the severed head: "Thou shalt not leave when the waters come. I curse thee. I curse thee and thy descendants, and I shall feed upon thy souls to avenge my death. And woe to anyone who cometh between us, woe to those who bringeth the waters . . ."

She continued to talk, a litany of dark promises that seemed to have no end. William shivered. It was not the curse itself that sent a chill down his spine. It was the words she used, the formality of her speech and the archaic vocabulary. It made him realize emotionally what he had until this point understood only intellectually: she was different, she was not like them. She was far older than he, and stranger in her makeup than any of them could have possibly imagined.

". . . And when I am reborn from the lives of thee and thy descendants, I shall be stronger than thou couldst have

ever imagined. Armies will bow before me. As it was fore-
told, so shall it be . . ."

Marie and Ingrid and several of the others were already
backing out of the cave, attempting to leave without drawing attention to themselves. The utter silence of all who wit-
nessed this scene told him better than could any words the
fear they felt, the impact Isabella's curse was having upon
them.

William looked back at the others, then reached down,
picked up a rock, and smashed her head.

The voice stopped, and the only sounds in the cave were
the echoes of her final words. The large chunk of sandstone
he had dropped completely covered her face, but the veins
of her neck protruded from one end and her wild hair ringed
the rock's upper third. Blood was spreading outward, seeping into the sand, bubbling down.

William said a few words, increasing the intensity of the
fire. Using all of the knowledge and skill he had gained in
his nearly seven decades on earth, he bound her to this place,
warding off intervention from others, containing whatever
self was left of her.

"Get out," he ordered everyone. "Leave. Wait for me by
the river."

He rejoined them twenty minutes later, drained and dizzy.
They sealed the tomb, all of them working together to cause
a landslide that covered the cave entrance, and by the time
the sky above them was lightening with the dawn, they had
left the cave behind and were trudging back to town.

2

In the years left to him, he tried to put the incident behind
him, tried to avoid thinking about Isabella at all, but that
was impossible. She was too entwined with his life, too tied
up in the history of this place, and even avoidance of those

locations most associated with Isabella necessitated thinking about her.

Was her spirit still here, in the canyon, in the house where she had died? He did not know because he made no effort to contact her. Nor, to his knowledge, did anyone else. Such contact could be dangerous, as they were too well aware, and even in Wolf Canyon the magic that had been practiced so freely began to be utilized less and less as they adopted prohibitions on themselves in an attempt to avoid a repetition of the recent past.

The town faded. Several people left, and no new citizens arrived to take their place. The days of persecution seemed to be gone. Wolf Canyon had outlived its most practical purpose. Looking at it now, looking at it objectively, he saw that it was fear that had brought them together in the first place, fear that had enabled them to forge some semblance of society in this wilderness, not a sense of community, not genuine camaraderie. His dream of a utopian village where those of their kind could live peacefully and happily with each other, away from the evil and corruption of so-called civilization, had been only that—a dream. The foolish wishes of an arrogant and overreaching young man.

Still, some stayed on, and many of them had kids, and gradually the flight was stemmed, the population leveled off.

Others settled into the surrounding countryside, hard-scrabble ranchers and family farmers who were not driven off or terrorized but were greeted as neighbors. Whether or not these new people were aware of the fact that Wolf Canyon was a town populated by witches, William had no way of knowing. He had given up all claim to authority after killing and entombing Isabella, had not even voted when the town chose its first democratically elected mayor and sheriff.

He had lived for too long, and when his health began to

seriously fail, he felt only a profound sense of relief. He was more than ready to go.

On his deathbed, he had a vision, a glimpse of the future, something that Isabella had claimed to experience quite often but that had never before come to him. There was no one by his bedside. One of the town's women checked in on him every day, brought him meals in the morning, but he had made it clear that he needed no companionship, that he wanted to be left in peace.

The vision was of a man-made lake, with a wall of smooth stone that rose hundreds of feet to the top of the canyon walls and reined in the waters.

He understood now the import of Isabella's curse. For the town was buried beneath the waters and he knew that the witches down there were doomed, drowned, fated never to leave thanks to her imprecation. Several families had left since Isabella's death, and he knew that they had all assumed this invalidated her curse, since she had decreed that no one would be allowed to leave. But meanings were often elusive, and he realized now that she had made sure whoever remained in Wolf Canyon at the time this lake was created would be killed.

He wanted to let the others know, wanted to evacuate the town and place a spell of avoidance around it that would discourage anyone from living here ever again so that Isabella's plans could never come to fruition.

But he could tell no one.

His breath caught in his throat. He started to choke, stopped breathing.

He died alone.

And when he left life behind and crossed over to the other side . . .

She was waiting.

Now

1

Cedar City was located at the foot of a series of green mountains. Or mesas. He couldn't tell which, with the low clouds planing off the tops to a uniform flatness. It was colder than in California and drizzly, and the high desert vegetation was all a dark blackish green that suited the day.

Miles stepped off the small shuttle plane and ran through the mist to the small building serving as the airport terminal. As he should have expected, no rental car was waiting for him, and he called Avis to confirm that one had been reserved. He had no choice but to wait at the airport until his vehicle was delivered, and he sat down on one of the stained uncomfortable chairs facing the window. He pulled out the piece of paper on which he'd written the two addresses he'd found last night and unfolded the street map of Cedar City the woman at the counter had given him. The city was small, the streets easily found, and he had no choice but to fold up the map and stare out at the drizzle as he waited for his car.

Ten minutes later, a red Pontiac Grand Am pulled up to the curb in front of the airport door, followed by a beat-up pickup. The bald, sad-looking man who emerged from the Grand Am had on a white shirt and an Avis name tag, and Miles quickly gathered up his map and briefcase and hurried outside. There was a form to sign, the sad man took down his driver's license and credit card number, then gave Miles the key to the car and ran back to the pickup, hopping in. The truck roared off, splashing water, and Miles tossed his briefcase on the passenger seat and headed down-town.

He hit it on the first try.

Janet Engstrom was a haggard-looking woman who was probably much younger than she seemed. She lived alone in the front apartment of a single-story complex across the street from the college. Perhaps he should have called first, but since he had not, he simply walked up and rang the bell.

"Are you Janet Engstrom?" he asked the woman who answered the door.

She nodded warily. "Yes."

"I'd like to talk to you about your uncle."

A shadow passed over her face. "My uncle's dead. I'm sorry." She started to close the door.

"I know. That's why I'm here."

Something in his voice must have caught her attention, because she paused.

"His body's missing, isn't it?"

"No."

"No?"

"We buried him on Sunday."

Still, she did not close the door completely, and Miles took that as a good sign.

"Can I come in? I'd really like to talk to you."

"About what?"

"Your uncle. I've come all the way from Los Angeles."

"You're not a reporter?"

"No," he assured her quickly. "Nothing like that. I just want to . . . talk."

"You know," she said matter-of-factly.

He nodded.

She met his eyes for a second, then glanced away and stepped aside to allow him entrance. The interior of the apartment looked simultaneously as though it had been lived in for quite some time and as though she had never fully un-packed after moving.

She sat down hard on the couch. The features on her face remained immobile, cemented into place, but Miles saw tears welling in her eyes. "You know," she said again.

"Yeah." He sat down next to her. "I know."

The first tear escaped from the invisible barrier that had been holding it back, and a slew of others followed, rolling out from beneath her long lashes and streaming down the sides of her face. He reached over to wipe them away, but she pulled back and stemmed the tide herself, using a thin, graceful finger to clear her cheeks.

"Are you okay?"

She nodded, a movement that started another cascade of tears. "It's . . . it's just that it's been so long since I had some-one I could talk to, since . . ." She looked up at him, tried to smile. "You saw the *Insider* article?"

"That's how I found you. I'm a private investigator."

Her body tensed, and she moved back on the couch, away from him.

"No, that's my job," he explained quickly. "That's what I do. It's not why I'm here."

"Why are you here?"

"I want to find out about your uncle. I want to find out about my dad." He took a deep breath. "The same thing happened to my father."

The expression on her face was complex, a look that was at once pained and relieved, frightened and sympathetic, angry and understanding. "I knew you knew, and I thought there was something personal about it. I could tell. That's why I let you in. I had a feeling about you." She looked at him, cleared her throat. "So what happened? Your dad died?"

"Yeah." Miles nodded. "He had a stroke in November, just fell over in the supermarket. They said he would never fully recover, but I was led to believe that he could still live

for quite a while—just in sort of a diminished state. So I
hired a home health-care nurse, who basically took care of
him when I was at work, administered his medications and
all that, did physical therapy." He was silent for a moment,
thinking. "It happened out of the blue. I came home from
work one day and the nurse was gone. She'd barricaded the
door of my father's room with furniture, and he was inside.
Walking."

"In a circle?"

"Yeah. Around the perimeter of the bedroom. And the
bed and dresser and stuff was moved into the middle of the
room. Not because he'd pushed it there but because he'd
bumped into it, forced it over while he walked. I could see
the marks on his body where he'd hit the edges of the furniture."

"So what happened after that? What did you do?"

"I called the coroner's office. A friend of mine works
there. He eventually stopped the walking with some kind of
muscle relaxant and took my . . . took the body. He wanted
to study it, find out what was causing my dad to keep moving even though he was dead. They kept him at the morgue,
kept his body filled with drugs and, I think, strapped down,
but . . . well, one day he disappeared. The coroner was looking for him, I was looking for him, the police were looking
for him, and we all assumed that he'd walked away, but we
couldn't find him. Couldn't find a single trace of him.

"Then yesterday I saw the article in the *Insider*. And here
I am."

"Oh."

Janet's reaction was a non-reaction. She seemed to shut
down at the conclusion of his story, and when it was clear
that she wouldn't be asking any questions and that she
wasn't planning to say anything herself, he prodded her.
"Your turn."

"It's a long story."

He smiled. "I've got time."

She nodded solemnly. "Okay." She licked her lips. "You want something to drink? Water? Coke? Wine?"

He shook his head.

"I think I need a drink first." She stood, walked into the kitchen, emerged a few moments later with a stemmed glass filled with red wine. She sat down again, then cleared her throat and took a loud swallow.

He waited patiently.

"I loved my Uncle John," she said finally. She swirled the wine in her glass, looked down at it. "He started walking before he died, actually. You probably read in the article that he had cancer, and he did, so I guess he was like your dad in that he was bedridden and had a lingering illness. Maybe that had something to do with what happened to them. I don't know. But three days before he died, he started walking. Around his room, like your dad. He hadn't been able to get out of his bed or move at all, really, for the past week, and then all of a sudden he was pacing like a lunatic." She paused, took another sip of wine. Then another. "There was something weird about it, too. About his movements, I mean. It was almost like he was a puppet or a robot—"

"Like something was controlling him," Miles said.

"Exactly."

"I thought the same thing."

"Well, this went on for three days, and I didn't know what to do. I wanted to tell someone, but I didn't know who to tell, and I was scared. Then I came home from work on the third day, and he was outside, walking around the house, wearing only his old pajama bottoms. Some of the neighborhood kids were throwing things at him, mud and stuff, and I chased them off, then ran around the back of the house. I thought he was delirious, and I wanted to get him back inside." She shivered, thinking about it, and finished her glass of wine. "That's when I found out he was dead."

Miles nodded. He understood completely. The memory of touching his father's cold rubbery skin was one that would remain with him for the rest of his life.

Janet shrugged. "That's it, really. The police came, and the coroner. They took him away, did an autopsy, and . . . that's all."

He smiled gently. "See? That wasn't such a long story."

She smiled hesitantly in return. "I gave you the abridged version."

Miles thought for a moment. "So he didn't keep walking after they took him away?"

"I guess not." She shifted uncomfortably in her seat. "I mean, I didn't really ask. I suppose I didn't want to know. He was still moving when they took him. It took several policemen—several *big* policemen—to capture him and strap him down in one of those . . . what do you call them? Not a stretcher but . . ."

"Gurney?"

"Yeah. They strapped him to a gurney and that's the last I saw of him."

"So he'd stopped walking by the time you buried him." She nodded.

"Was it an open casket? Did you see him?"

Janet breathed deeply. "We had him cremated so . . . so he wouldn't come back. We just buried his ashes."

"Are you sure it was him?" Miles prodded gently. "I mean, you didn't actually see his body after the autopsy?"

She shook her head. "I don't know. They said . . . they said we wouldn't want to see him. They said, well, that there wasn't much left that was identifiable."

"Who suggested that he be cremated? Was that your idea?"

"No," she admitted. "It was suggested by the mortuary. But, under the circumstances, I thought it was a good plan.

I'd already had nightmares of my uncle digging his way out of a grave and walking through the city to find me. Cremating him would take care of that possibility." She met Miles' eyes. "You think he walked away, like your dad, and they pawned off some other body on me?"

He shrugged. "It's a possibility. I'm not saying it happened, but I'd feel a lot more secure about it if you'd actually seen his body to make sure it had stopped moving."

There was an awkward pause. Janet stood. "I need another drink. You want something?"

"Maybe some water," Miles said.

She returned a few moments later with a tumbler of water and her refilled wineglass. "You know," she said, handing him his drink, "there's one thing that I've been thinking about. Something that stuck in my mind."

"What?"

"His last words. Or the last words he spoke to me. I was feeding him his dinner. He could barely talk at that point, his voice was just a whisper, and I had to lean close to hear him. After that, about an hour or so after I cleaned him up, he started walking. And he never spoke again."

"What'd he say? What'd he tell you?"

"The last thing he said, before he started walking, was, 'She's here.'"

"'She'? Who's 'she'?"

"I don't know. Maybe he was just delirious, seeing things that weren't there."

"But you don't think so?"

She looked at him. "No."

She's here.

Eeeee-eeear

Miles recalled the noises his father had made in the hospital, the desperate, incomprehensible pleas that had been so earnestly addressed to him. *She's here.* Was that what Bob had been trying to say?

"I've thought about it a million times since they took him away. I've gone over it in my mind, but it doesn't make any sense to me. I don't understand it. I know he was trying to tell me something, but I have no idea what it was. There certainly wasn't anyone else in the room with us, and no woman has shown up since then, unless you count the *Insider* photographer. I've been waiting, hoping—or maybe *not* hoping—that whatever he meant would be revealed to me, but . . . nothing."

She's here.

There was something ominous about the phrase, and Miles gulped down his water. He was pretty sure that that was what his father had been trying to say, and he recalled the panicked urgency of Bob's stroke-slurred voice. His father had been afraid.

"Did your uncle seem, well, *scared* when he told you that?"

Janet nodded. "That's why I haven't been able to forget it, why I keep going over it in my mind. I can't help feeling that it had something to do with his . . . walking."

The homeless woman in the mall, too, had warned him of a "she."

She's going after the damn builders, too.

He wanted to understand, but nothing made sense to him, no facts he could put together, no conjecture he could make that would provide an identity for this . . . woman? . . . girl? . . . witch? . . . goddess?

"Did your uncle leave anything behind?" he asked Janet. "Any diaries? Any item that might give us some clue?"

"Like what?"

"Like witchcraft paraphernalia."

She stared at him. "How did you know?"

He smiled wryly. "I found some stuff in my dad's safety deposit box. I have no idea what it's for or how to use it, but I could tell that it was supposed to be used for magic.

There was a dried, flat frog, a bunch of powders, some roots in bottles." He paused. "And a necklace made out of teeth. Human teeth."

"My uncle had a box in his closet. I looked through it, but it scared me, so I put it in a plastic garbage sack and haven't looked at it since. It's in my hall closet. You want to check it out?"

Miles shook his head. "Maybe later."

"There's no necklace, but there is some kind of arm bone with feathers attached to it. And, like you said, a bunch of powders and . . . potions, I guess."

"No diary, though, huh? No book?"

"My uncle wasn't one for keeping diaries."

"Neither was my dad."

They looked glumly at each other.

"Do *you* know anything about this witchcraft stuff? Did your uncle ever talk to you about it? Do you remember . . . anything?"

She shook her head slowly.

"What about your parents?"

"Dead."

"Any other relatives?"

"Yeah, but they're pretty distant. I mean, I was the one closest to him. If he was going to tell anybody, he would have told me."

"Well, what about friends?"

"I don't know."

"Where did he work? When and where was he born? If I have some background information, I can check up on him, build a profile from there."

"I know he was born in Arizona."

"Arizona?"

"A place called Wolf Canyon."

A shiver feather-tickled the back of his neck, moved down his back, spread into his arms.

Wolf Canyon.

It was all circling back to that.

Miles realized that he did not know where his father had been born, and while he had never thought of it before, he understood now how strange that was. Would Bonnie know? He was tempted to call his sister and find out, but he had a feeling he already knew what the answer was.

He played a hunch. "Did your uncle say anything about dreams he was having before he died? Recurring dreams about—

"—a tidal wave and the end of the world?"

Miles nodded slowly. "Yeah."

"I've been having dreams, too, since he died. Not a tidal wave, exactly, but . . . water."

"Me, too," Miles admitted.

"What's it mean? What's happening?" Janet sounded as though she were about to cry.

"I don't know, but there's more to come." He motioned toward her empty glass. "You might want to get yourself another drink. I have a lot of things to tell you."

He started from the beginning. Marina Lewis and her father. Montgomery Jones and the other men on the list. Brodsky and Hec Tibbert. The homeless old woman in the mall. Liam on the fence.

And, at the hub of all this activity, Wolf Canyon.

When he was through, they were silent for a moment, staring at each other.

"So," she said slowly. "This town, Wolf Canyon. It was—"

"—covered by a lake."

"You think that's where your father walked to?"

Miles nodded. "I'd bet on it. And your uncle too if he escaped and they lied to you about it."

"But why?"

He took a deep breath. "I don't know. Let's go there and find out."

He called Claire at work to tell her what he'd learned and to let her know that he was going to Wolf Canyon. She was not happy to hear it, and when he said he was going with a woman whose uncle had met the same fate as his father, he could feel the tension over the phone. He thought of asking her to come along, but he didn't really want her to and he kept his mouth shut. She wasn't involved in this, not directly, not by blood

blood

and he wanted to keep her as far away from Wolf Canyon as possible. Whatever was out there was dangerous, and he would not be able to live with himself if, through negligence or selfishness or stupidity, he allowed something to happen to her.

"What are you going to do when you get there?" Claire asked. "Just stand there and stare at the lake? Wait for your ESP to kick in and suddenly explain everything?"

"I don't know," he admitted, and he realized that something deeper might be at work here. Claire was right. He had no plan and, logically, no reason to visit Wolf Canyon. There was nothing he could learn empirically from viewing the site where the town was buried. But the impulse to go was strong, and what he had taken for an idea logically conceived was really closer to an imposed thought, an illogical plan that had grown from a casual notion to a definite desire. He still felt as though he had come up with the idea himself, but he also felt like a piece of metal being drawn to a magnet against its will.

"Why does this woman have to go with you?"

"I don't know," he said again. And he didn't.

Claire was silent.

"Trust me on this," he told her. "I don't know what all's

happening, but . . ." The words trailed off as he realized that he didn't know what he wanted to say.

"But what?"

"It *feels* right," he said finally. "I may not know what I'm doing or why, but I know that it's what I'm *supposed* to be doing."

"You're scaring me."

"I'm scaring myself."

Claire breathed deeply, trying to calm down, a staticky sound that only emphasized how far away she was right now. "You really think that Bob went there?"

"Yeah."

"What are you going to do if you find him?"

"I don't know."

"Shouldn't you have some sort of plan? What if . . . ?" She sighed. "Shit. Who knows how to deal with something like this? If someone had told me a month ago that we'd be back together and some kind of curse was killing off everyone connected to a dam in Arizona where your zombie father was headed . . . I mean, Jesus Christ, Miles. What have you gotten yourself into here?"

"I didn't get myself into anything. It came to me. I didn't want it to happen. I didn't ask for it."

"I know, but how are you going to . . . fight it? What are you going to do to get your father to stop walking around and die? With a vampire you put a stake through its heart. With a werewolf you shoot it with a silver bullet. But there isn't anything concrete like that here. There's just a . . . a big jumbled mess, and there's no way to sort it out, and there's only you and some woman against . . . God knows what."

"I know," he told her. "But I have to find out. I can't make a plan because I don't know what I don't know. I just have to investigate and roll with whatever comes."

A welcome wry edge came into her voice. "Part of you is enjoying this, though. Admit it, Miles. You always secretly dreamed of some big exotic movie-like case that you could crack."

"I'm too scared to enjoy it. But you're right. Maybe that keeps me going, keeps me from giving up."

"Just be careful," she said softly. "I don't want anything to happen to you. I love you."

"I love you, too. And I'm always careful."

"Did you bring your cell phone?"

"No. Damn. I forgot."

"Call me anyway when you get there. Use a pay phone. I'll probably be home by then, but if not, call this number. Make sure you call me either way."

"I will," he promised.

"I love you," she said again.

"Me, too."

They said their good-byes and hung up. The sound of the handset dropping into its cradle with a quiet plastic clap had a note of finality to it.

He turned away to see Janet carrying a box out from the hallway and setting it down on the coffee table.

They looked at each other, met each other's eyes.

Janet glanced down at the box. "It's my uncle's magic stuff. Should I . . . ?"

"Bring it," Miles said. "Who knows what we'll need?"

2

Claire took off work early, stopped off to buy some groceries, then headed straight home. She always kept the drapes in the house closed when she was gone, and she put the twin sacks of groceries on the kitchen counter, then opened the front shades to let in some light.

And nearly jumped out of her skin.

She let out an involuntary cry, lurching back and stumbling into the couch. The homeless woman standing next to the window and peering in at her was grinning crazily, both palms pressed flat against the glass. She licked the window, leaving a trail of blurred spittle.

Claire knew instantly who this was—the woman Miles had met at the mall before Christmas—and that frightened her far more than if it had just been some random loony who had wandered into her yard. How the woman had found *her* house she did not know, but she had no doubt that it was intentional, and that added another layer of fear onto what she already felt. She had not seen the old lady while walking in. Had she merely been unobservant, or had the woman been hiding from her, crouching in the bushes?

She refused to let herself be intimidated. Despite her embarrassing first reaction, she gathered up her dignity and strode purposefully out of the house, confronting the woman on the front lawn. "Who are you and what are you doing on my property?" Her voice, thank God, carried exactly the edge of authority she'd intended.

"He's gone there, hasn't he?"

"Who? Who's gone where?"

"Bob's son. He's gone to Wolf Canyon."

Claire's mouth felt dry. She was in way over her head. She stared into a wrinkled, dirty face that seemed both blank and crafty. Whatever this was, it was far beyond her comprehension, and the scope and range of a creature or demon or power that could reanimate Bob's corpse and the dead body of a man in Utah, kill dam workers across the country and lead this homeless woman to her house left Claire feeling small and helpless and overwhelmed. She was terrified for Miles even more than for herself, and although every instinct in her body was telling her to run, to lock herself inside the house and dial 9-1-1, she stood her ground. "Who are you?" she asked again.

"May. I'm here to help you." She leaned forward confidentially. "I'm one, too. Like Bob."

Nothing was making any sense. Either she was getting stupid in her old age, unable to make those large connective leaps necessary to communicate for the first time with people she did not know, or the elements of this conversation were so far off the scale that making coherent sense of them without a shared blueprint was pretty much impossible. "You're one of *what* like Bob?" she asked.

"A witch."

Now it was making more sense.

She still could not completely reconcile Miles' ordinary down-to-earth father with a mystical power-wielding sorcerer, but it explained the collection of powders and nostrums, the mystery of his walking dead body. And if she was going to buy into this witchcraft thing, she might as well take it all the way and subscribe to the notions of good magic and bad magic, white magic and black magic.

Bob would obviously have been a good witch.

But why had he never told this to Miles . . . or anyone else, for that matter? And how had he kept it a secret all those years? In her mind, she saw him waiting until his children were asleep, then chanting paeans to Satan.

No. That was not Bob.

She didn't really know Bob, though. If this woman was telling the truth—and Claire thought she was—*none* of them had really known him.

"Is he at the lake?" May asked.

Claire found herself nodding.

"He won't know what to do by himself. Bob never taught him."

"Never taught him what?"

May flipped up her dirty dress, grinned. "I'm not wearing any panties!"

Claire sighed. Great. Like too many homeless people, this woman obviously had some serious mental problems, and she was going to have to sift through the old lady's words to determine what was truth and what was delusion—not an easy thing to do when the subject was the supernatural.

"Miles—" Claire began.

May snapped her fingers. "That's his name! Miles!"

"Miles thinks his father walked to Wolf Canyon. His father is dead, but he's still walking around and he escaped from the morgue several weeks ago."

"He's going back. They all go back when they die. Or I should say, *we* all go back when we die. It's part of her curse."

"Whose curse?"

The old woman cackled. "Teletype firetrap. Teletype firetrap. Buttfuck Cornelius of love!"

Jesus Christ.

"Isabella," May said, suddenly lucid once again. "She cursed us after she was killed, before she was buried." The old lady smiled at Claire. "Your house is pretty. Can I go in?"

"No." She was starting to get a headache.

"Isabella promised to come back."

"I have no idea what you're talking about. Could you start from the beginning? Who are you? Who is Isabella? What the hell does any of this have to do with Bob and Miles?"

A small wind kicked up, a surprisingly localized gust that swirled about her yard, kicking up leaves and picking up dirt, but leaving the rest of the street and the other yards untouched. May stood at the center of the miniature tempest, her hair blowing wildly, as if this was nothing out of the ordinary. It occurred to Claire that she was causing this, that it was an attempt on the old woman's part to get Claire to invite her inside the house. The wind coalesced into a funnel-like dust devil, and pushed its way through a hedge and into the yard next door. She watched it retreat down the street. A Land Rover drove by, oblivious.

Despite the increased dishevelment of her appearance, May seemed suddenly saner, more grounded and rational. "Wolf Canyon," she began, "was a town of witches founded by a man named William Johnson in the mid-1800s. Like many religious and ethnic groups at that time, witches were persecuted. We were hung, drowned, burned at the stake, and William followed the example of the Mormons, who had headed west to establish their own community."

She smiled widely, reached both hands behind her, started furiously scratching. "Ass itch! Ass itch!"

Just as suddenly, she was all seriousness. "William met and married a woman named Isabella. Isabella was a witch, but she was more than a witch." May's voice dropped. "She was evil. She started taking over the town, molding it in her own image. Those who disagreed with her were punished. She drove some away, others were mysteriously found dead. Finally, they had all had enough. William was old by this time, but his powers were still strong, and he killed her while she slept. He cut off her head, and the people buried her in a cave up the canyon. Before they sealed the cave entrance, her head started talking, and she cursed the people of Wolf Canyon. She vowed to return, stronger, and to wreak vengeance on all other witches, to destroy them all. She said that no one would be allowed to leave Wolf Canyon and that everyone in the town would be engulfed by a wall of water and killed."

May stared off in the distance, almost as though she were in a trance, and Claire shivered.

"Bob and I were born in Wolf Canyon, though we left early. I don't even remember the town, only what my parents told me of it. Isabella's day was long gone, and no one believed by then that her curse would come to pass. Plenty of people had left and returned and left again, and nothing had ever stopped them. But our parents told us of Isabella, warned us of her, and we grew up afraid, fearing and dreading her resurrection and revenge.

"We met each other again after they built the dam. I was living in New Jersey then. I had a husband and a house and a dog and a good life.

"And then I felt it. I felt the screaming of all those souls as they were drowned, as the dam waters flooded in and Isabella's curse came true. I left my husband, left my house, left my dog, and went back to Wolf Canyon. I was drawn there. We were all drawn there, all of us who had escaped the waters, and I met Bob on the shore by the dam, and we both saw the same vision and we talked about what was happening. There were dozens of us, all standing by the water's edge. She was calling to us from down there, laughing at us, and we understood that she had waited a long time for this and that she would wait even longer. She would wait as long as it took for her to escape.

"We made a vow then to fight her, to never let her out. We kept in touch for a while, but then we stopped, like our parents had before us, and maybe that was part of her curse, too. We started new lives, and most of us avoided all thought of Isabella, all mention of magic. Some of us . . . some of us became . . ."

May shook her head, tried to smile, looked for a second as though she was about to say something crazy, then continued on soberly. "Several months ago, it started again. I felt the pull, and I dreamed about Isabella, and I realized that she had grown stronger. She had taken from those of us who'd died over the years and had remained down there, hoarding her power, waiting to use it until she was strong. She was going after the dam builders, too, the ones who had flooded the canyon with water, and she was killing them off one by one, using her powers to find them and hunt them down. She was getting strength from them, as well, even though she was still stuck underwater, in the cave."

May grew silent, and Claire waited for more, but there was no more. That was it.

Now the old lady did smile, and Claire understood that her craziness was the way she dealt with the tremendous mental strain that she was constantly under. Schizophrenia might be somewhere in the mix, but May's outbursts were also part of her defense mechanism, the means by which she coped with the knowledge she was forced to possess. That didn't make things any less unnerving, but at least it explained the homeless woman's bizarre behavior in a way that was somewhat comprehensible.

"Dirty face in a rain chair!" May screamed at the top of her lungs. She looked up into the sky. "Down by feathers of silence!"

Claire looked at her. If May's experiences at Wolf Canyon could transform her from a New Jersey suburbanite to . . . this, what was going to happen to Miles?

That was Claire's real concern, and once again she looked into the old woman's eyes and felt nothing but fear—a feeling she saw reflected right back at her.

The two of them stood on the lawn, facing each other. A car drove by. From down the street came the sounds of kids playing basketball on someone's driveway court. A helicopter flew overhead.

"We need to go back!" May moved forward, grabbed her by the arm. Claire tried unsuccessfully to pull away. She could smell the woman's fetid breath. "We need to go with Bob!"

With Bob.

You mean Miles, Claire almost told her, but she was not at all sure that the old lady *was* confusing Bob with Miles. She had the feeling May meant exactly what she'd said.

Miles, too, thought his father was walking back to Wolf Canyon.

Once again, she felt small and insignificant, caught up in larger events she could only partially understand.

She pulled herself out of the homeless woman's grip, felt a strange tingle in her arm. Was all of this the result of some dead witch's curse? That seemed to be the case, and in a weird way, that gave Claire hope. The ultimate source of everything appeared to be a single entity with a single agenda, and that was easier to fight than the nebulous force Miles seemed to think he was up against.

Perhaps May was right. Perhaps they could help Miles.

"Wait here!" Claire ordered the old woman, and May nodded in acquiescence, mumbling something unintelligible to herself.

Claire hurried inside and used the cordless phone to dial Miles' firm. She asked to talk to Hal, keeping track all the while of the woman in her front yard. She gave her name to the receptionist and, after a few seconds' silence, was put through to Hal.

"Claire!"

"Hi, Hal."

"It's great to hear your voice again! How the hell're you doing?"

"I'm fine."

"Glad to hear it, glad to hear it. I was so happy for Miles when he told me you'd gotten back together—" Hal broke off in mid-sentence, clearing his throat embarrassedly, suddenly aware that he may have said more than he should.

She smiled. "Yeah, well . . ."

He sounded worried. "You're *not* back together? That was just wishful thinking?"

"No, we are."

"Whew! Scared me for a minute. You know Miles; I thought that maybe his plans were rushing ahead of the truth."

"No. We're . . . I don't know what we are, to be honest with you. But we're together again."

"Well, I'm glad you're back," Hal said.

"Thanks," Claire told him.

"So what can I do for you? Miles isn't here—"

"I know. That's why I'm calling. He took two weeks' leave in order to go to Arizona and find out what happened to his dad."

"They found Bob's body? How come he didn't tell me?"

"No," she said. "It's not that." She paused, sighed. "Something's going on. And the reason he didn't talk to you about it was probably because he was afraid you wouldn't believe him."

"Try me."

"All right." She described for Hal the events as Miles had told her and as she herself had seen—Bob and Liam Connor and the woman in Utah—ending with May's mysterious visit and their intended trip to Wolf Canyon. She looked outside, saw the homeless woman grinning at her through the window, palms against the glass.

Hal whistled. "Heavy shit."

"Yeah. I know you probably don't believe any of it—"

"Don't count me out. Miles was asking me my feelings about the supernatural a few weeks ago, and I told him then and I'll tell you now: my mind is open. I don't automatically disbelieve anything."

Claire hesitated. "I don't know exactly how to bring this up, but do you think you could come with me?" She lowered her voice. "I don't want to travel by myself with that woman. She's crazy and she scares me. She said she's a witch, and she obviously has mental problems besides.

"I'll pay," she added quickly. "Whatever your going rate is. I'll hire you to—"

"Fuck that shit. What do you think I am, a stranger? I

have enough sick leave built up. I can take a few days. How long do you think it'll be?"

"One day there, one day back. Two days, probably. Three at the most."

"No problem. I'll get myself together and come right over. Where are you? Miles' place?"

"Don't you have to clear it with someone first?"

"No."

"What about Perkins? Isn't he going to be ticked?"

"Are you kidding? His head's a fecal-containment system. He won't even notice I'm gone. Besides, if worse comes to worst, Tran'll cover for me."

"I'm at my house," Claire said. She gave him the address. "Do you have a cellular phone you could bring?"

"It's my American Express," Hal told her. "I don't leave home without it."

"See you in an hour, then?"

"Or sooner. I don't imagine you want to spend too much time alone with that fruitcake."

"No," Claire admitted, looking out the window.

"I'm on my way."

Then

Isabella was not forgotten.

Leland Huerdeen stood in his yard at the edge of town and looked north toward the flat buttes that defined the east-west boundaries of the canyon. It had been nearly twenty-five years since Isabella had been entombed, and she still cast a long shadow over life in town. Not a day went by that one of her misdeeds was not remembered by the older men, that children did not scare each other with the possibility of her return, that all of them did not tread warily past the abandoned house which had been hers and William's.

Somewhere up there, Leland knew, was Isabella's sealed cave, and though he was not sure of its exact location, like everyone else in town he knew the cliff in which it was situated, and he always sped past the spot on the rare occasions that he passed through that area.

His father, Grover, had been one of the early settlers in Wolf Canyon and the only haberdasher the community had ever known. Leland had taken up the family business several years ago, and though his father was still alive and still managed to block occasional hats for close friends, he had effectively turned everything over to his son.

Hats and Isabella.

Those were the two things his father talked about these days.

Times had changed. Hardly anyone in town used magic anymore, and people kept their powers private, secret.

Though it wasn't official, had probably never even been discussed, the decision had been made to disavow the past, to pretend as though this was an ordinary community filled with ordinary people where nothing unusual ever occurred.

That was all Isabella's doing.

As his father had told him many times, the woman had corrupted the paradise that they had all come together to build. "I was one of the first to see old Jeb Freeman after she'd drained the life out of him, and that's a sight I'll never forget," Grover had been saying as long as Leland could remember. "Jeb was a powerful man, and someone that could do that to him, leave him nothing more than an empty shell, was someone to be feared indeed. We didn't like Isabella, none of us did, but after that we were afraid of her. She still had William hornswoggled, too, and some of the others eventually went in with her. But I never did. I knew what she was."

There was a litany of sins that his father never failed to recite, and Leland had grown up with a fear of Isabella and her seemingly unstoppable powers. Now he had a son, Robert, and his father wanted to indoctrinate the boy as soon as he was old enough to speak, to instill in him the same fear of Isabella's revenge with which he himself had been filled.

"Why didn't we ever leave?" he'd asked when he'd grown old enough to think on his own. "How come we're still here? Other people left. Why don't we?"

"Because this is our home," his father always said fiercely. "We carved this home from the wilderness, and I'm not about to let any *monster* drive us away."

There were rumors that some had seen her: visions in the canyon late at night that terrified horses into running and sent the roughest ranchers into paroxysms of fear. They all knew where the cave was, and a special effort was made by all to avoid that area. It was one of the wider sections of the canyon, several miles across, and though the route was longer, people these days traveled on the other side of the marsh, near the west bluffs, rather than take the old path past the blocked cave entrance.

Leland moved away from the fence, looked down at Hattie's sunflowers, just beginning to poke their heads up toward their namesake after staring at the ground all through the early weeks of their existence. He was supposed to travel to Randall tomorrow for material, a hard hundred miles that covered a lot of diverse territory, not all of it nice. But the truth was that the only part of the journey which concerned him was the trip out of the canyon.

The trip past Isabella's cave.

It was foolish and childish, but he still had the sense that she waited in there, watching, that she could somehow see through the rocks that covered the cave entrance to where he passed by—even though the new trail was miles away. It was as if there were a line across the width of the canyon, and anytime anyone crossed it, she knew.

He'd had a dream the other night that he'd been on the road to Randall and his horse had kicked something in the trail that turned out to be Isabella's head. The hair was filthy and filled with spiderwebs, the skin rotting, the eyes gone, but the bloody mouth worked perfectly and the head flew up into the air before him and began to shriek.

Though he knew it was probably just his father's doing, he still couldn't help feeling some trepidation at the thought of passing by the dreaded place after a dream such as that.

Leland walked into the house, yelled to Hattie in the kitchen that he was going over to see Samuel and visit for a while, have a smoke.

"Supper's gonna be on soon!" she called.

"I'll be back in twenty minutes!" He looked at his pocket watch and headed out the door. She said something behind him, but he didn't hear what it was and it didn't really matter. Even if he was late, she'd hold supper for him.

Magic was still good for a few things around here.

Samuel Hawks was sitting on his porch, smoking his pipe, looking after the slowly setting sun, which would be below both the clouds and the rim of the canyon in a few more minutes. He nodded to Leland, motioned for him to come up and sit a spell.

A spell.

Samuel's wife Maureen was watching the Engstrom's baby John while their next-door neighbors went to the market, and a loud constant crying could be heard from inside the house. Samuel reached back behind him and shut the window as Leland took a seat on the swing next to his friend's rocker. "Thought you was leavin'."

"Tomorrow."

"Be back when? A week?"

"About that." Leland took out his pipe, packed down some tobacco, lit it. "Watch Hattie and Robert for me?"

Samuel chuckled. "Hattie don't need no one watching out for her. That li'l woman can take care of herself." He glanced over. "Which way you headin' out?"

"To Randall? There's only one way."

Samuel said nothing, looked north toward the buttes.

Leland cleared his throat, turned toward his friend. "You saw something out there once, didn't you? Over by Isabella's cave?"

Samuel nodded slowly, was silent for a moment. He took a puff on his pipe. "Wudn't nuthin' specific, you know. Wudn't no specter or spook. I don't know what I told you before, but it was more somethin' I *felt* than saw."

"I thought you said you saw something."

"I did, I did. But that wudn't the scariest part is I guess what I'm tryin' to say. It's what I *felt* not what I saw that scared the bejeebers out a me."

"So what'd you see? Tell me again."

Samuel smoked in silence for a bit, and Leland thought

his friend wasn't going to respond at all, but finally he sighed. "I was gonna go fishing upriver, past that sycamore grove. It was spring, I think, and it wudn't even night, although I think it was a little cloudy." He paused, puffed. "I got spooked around that swampy area. Mighta all been in my head, but I thought I heard noises, and I stopped for a moment and . . ." He shook his head.

"What?"

"I felt her lookin' at me. It don't make no sense, but it was like for a minute she was lookin' *through* me, too. Everything looked brighter. Or darker. Something. Anyway, it felt like I was seein' through someone else's eyes, but I knew it was *her* lookin' through *my* eyes. Then I felt like she was lookin' *at* me again, and everywhere I turned I felt eyes peekin' at me, hidden in that swampy water, behind the grasses, up on the cliffs. It scared the hell out a me, I tell you.

"Then I saw it, over by the bottom of the canyon wall, next to a pile of old rubble that had to be coverin' her cave."

"What?"

"A shadow. But it weren't like any shadow I ever seen. It was kinda human-shaped, female if you want to know the truth, but it din't move right. It sorta twisted in on itself instead a walked. Creepiest damn thing I ever saw. It twisted toward me, and I just hightailed it out a there. Never did go fishing. And I never been back up that part of the canyon since." He looked meaningfully at Leland. "If I were you, I wouldn't go there, neither."

"I have no choice. My materials are in Randall, and until they build a train track to Wolf Canyon, I have to pick them up myself."

There was another long silence as they both smoked, looking up at the darkening late afternoon sky.

"There *is* another way to Randall," Samuel said. "Go south out a the canyon, take the new road from Rio Verde.

It'll add an extra day to your trip, but believe me, it's worth it."

Leland did not respond.

"It's worth it."

Leland walked home feeling even more uneasy than he had on his way over, although perhaps that was what he wanted, the reason he'd gone to see Samuel in the first place.

Supper was ready when he arrived, and he hid his concerns for Robert's sake, eating in silence, letting Hattie talk to the boy and answer his nearly continuous questions. The person he should discuss this with was his father, but he already knew what Grover would say, and despite the comfort he himself would receive from such a discussion, he thought it better not to worry the old man. He'd talk to his dad about it once he returned from Randall.

If he returned from Randall.

Now he was just being stupid.

He left early the next morning but not as early as he'd originally planned. The days were getting shorter already, in anticipation of fall, and when Hattie got up to make breakfast, the sky outside was still dark. It was almost an hour's ride to the section of canyon near Isabella's cave, but he didn't want to take any chances and be caught there before the sun arose, so he dawdled, playing for time until there was a definite lightening in the sky above the eastern walls.

There was no problem on the way out. In spite of all his worries, he inexplicably found himself occupied with the mundane thoughts of haberdashery while passing through the dreaded section of canyon, and by the time it registered that Isabella was entombed somewhere on the far side of this marsh, he was already past the line of her cave.

He spurred his horse on, quickly galloped until that area of the canyon was hidden behind a curve of the landscape. The rest of the trip over was uneventful, his day and night in Randall were fine, and he easily found everything he needed.

He miscalculated the timing on his trip home, however, and before he'd even reached the mouth of Wolf Canyon, he realized that it would be dark well before he reached the marshy area in front of the buried tomb. He briefly considered making camp and starting from here in the morning, but Hattie and Robert were expecting him today, and he didn't want to worry them. He'd also been away from his business for six days, and he couldn't really afford to be gone even as long as he had been. He needed to get back to work.

Besides, he'd be traveling along the opposite wall of the canyon, just as he had on the trip out.

Leland had never been formally taught in the magic arts, growing up in the post-Isabella days, but he instinctively wove a spell of protection around himself, something that, while not perfect, would at least afford him some defense on his journey.

He'd brought with him a lantern, but in the cavernous open space of the middle canyon the light illuminated only the section of trail immediately before him, throwing all else into even deeper gloom. He wanted to put down the fear he felt to imagination, but the horse seemed spooked and jittery, too, and as they traveled farther into the darkness, into the increasingly cold night, it became ever more difficult to pretend nothing was out of the ordinary.

He thought of Samuel Hawks.

It was more somethin' I felt.

Leland felt it, too, and though he knew he would never be able to describe it, he understood now what his friend had meant. For the horror that enveloped him, that seemed to *seep* inside him to his very bones, was the most terrifying thing he had ever experienced. The air itself seemed wrong, the texture of the breeze unnatural. All of his senses were assaulted, and he saw shapes in the blackness, heard soft sounds that should not have been here, smelled wafting odors unlike any he had ever come across, and he tasted in his mouth the foulness of the grave.

And then she appeared.

Her cave was miles away, on the east bluffs, but, as he'd somehow known, hers was a boundary that spanned the entire width of the canyon, and she appeared to him as he tried to cross it on his way home.

At first it was just a light, not greenish like most spirit illuminations but red, like blood. It hovered above the marshy weeds and cattails and slowly solidified into a figure that was almost but not quite human. He kicked his horse, yelled at it, tried to will the animal forward, but his mount refused to budge, as if held under a spell. The red figure floated toward him, wailing terribly in a cry that was somehow translated by his brain into images:

—*Hattie dead and dismembered, lying amid the expelled contents of an outhouse.*

—*Robert nude in the sand, legs spread, screaming, his lap and the ground beneath it covered with blood, his genitals being gnawed on by Grover's head, which was bodiless and sporting raccoon legs.*

The figure's own head dislodged from its ethereal form, turning black in the process. He had thought nothing could be blacker than the canyon at night, but the head was, and despite the darkness, it retained all of its horrible features. He could see clearly the face of a beautiful woman, long flowing hair framing a face that was the most exquisite he had ever seen.

And the most evil.

The laugh that issued from the lightless jet lips sounded like the tinkling of bells.

Leland leaped off his horse and ran. If the steed was stupid enough to remain, so be it, but he was not about to sacrifice his life because of the incapacitation of a pack animal.

He ran down the trail toward town, carrying the lantern, but with all of his supplies and materials still in saddlebags on the horse. He heard a wail, but screamed himself to cover the sound, to keep the images out of his head. Out of the corner of his eye, he saw the black head and the red body reconnect.

He had never run so fast in his life, and he expected at any moment to be grabbed from behind or pushed over or even levitated into the air. Nothing like that happened, however, and by the time he was out of breath and had to stop, choking and wheezing next to a paloverde tree, there was no sign of anything unusual either before or behind him. Even the lantern seemed to illuminate a larger area of ground, and the night seemed neither as black nor as cold as it had by the marsh.

He stood there for a moment waiting, looking back, expecting to see at any moment his horse emerge from the gloom, but there was no sign of the animal, no sound, and it occurred to him that the steed had been a sacrifice.

He started toward town, as quickly as his sore muscles and tired lungs would allow. This was it, Leland decided. He might be his father's son, but he was not his father, and home or no home, he was going to go back, get Hattie and Robert, pack their things, and as soon as the sun came up, get the hell out of Wolf Canyon as quickly as he could.

Forever.

He never wanted to see this place again.

Now

1

Miles had flown to the East Coast and the Midwest, but he had never before been in this part of the country. He was surprised at how cinematic the Southwest was, how closely it resembled those magnificent vistas of western movies. He liked driving through this country, he found, and despite the sparse vegetation and almost complete absence of human habitation, he could see himself retiring here, buying a couple of acres and building a little house.

The ride was long, and they were awkward with each other at first, but when the radio faded out they were forced to talk, and somewhere between Kanab and Page their conversation grew comfortable.

"Who's your favorite Beatle?" Janet asked as they drove through the eroded, Georgia O'Keeffe-like hills that were a prelude to Lake Powell.

"What?"

"That's supposed to be the best Rorschach test around. You can learn everything you need to know about a person by finding out who their favorite Beatle is. Isn't that what they say?"

"John," he told her.

She smiled. "Good choice."

"Yours?"

"Paul. But I like men who like John."

He glanced over at her. "I'm seeing someone, you know. That's who I called from your apartment."

"I'm not hitting on you. I'm just saying that, as a general rule, I get along better with men who like Lennon. And since we have a long trip in front of us, that's probably a good thing."

"I lied," he told her. "It's Ringo."

She laughed.

They talked of trivialities, kept the conversation light. By unspoken consent they avoided discussing what they were doing. It would have made the trip too long, put on them an undue pressure that might dissuade them from completing their journey. They needed to get away from that for a while, and they let the talk drift from movies to television to other equally innocuous topics.

By late afternoon they reached the turnoff. A small brown road sign announced: WOLF CANYON LAKE—22 MILES.

They had not seen another car for the past hour, had not seen a town since Willis, the little city in Arizona's Central Mountains where they'd gassed up, gone to the bathroom, and gotten oversized drinks from a surprisingly modern Jack-in-the-Box.

He felt uneasy being this far away from civilization—
from help
—and he wished he had brought his cell phone, but who knew if it would even work in a godforsaken area like this?

They grew silent. The road to the lake was two lanes, like the highway, but the lanes were smaller and the lines more faded. The asphalt itself seemed washed out, and huge holes in the pavement that had to have been years in the making made Miles swerve from side to side.

They came out of a series of small sandy hills into a flat barren floodplain, and far ahead, on the side of the road, black against the pale sand, he could see a man walking toward some low cliffs. He recognized that walk, even from this far away, the unnatural rhythm, the unvarying speed, and his heart lurched in his chest.

Janet saw the figure, too. "Is that . . . ?"

She did not finish the sentence and he did not answer. They were coming up fast now on the figure.

This close, his eyes confirmed what his gut already knew. It was Bob.

His father was striding purposefully along the gravel shoulder, not trying to attract attention to himself but not trying to hide, either. He was simply walking forward, head fixed, arms unmoving. Miles did not know what to do, whether to stop or slow down, and in a panic he ended up speeding past. The wind from their passage blew Bob's hair and caused the clothes to flap about on his frame.

Miles slowed the car afterward but did not stop, and he looked over at Janet, who was white-faced and staring at him. He knew she was thinking of her uncle. He was remembering the alienness of his dad's movements, the complete inability to communicate with his father or in any way influence his actions.

He did not want to stop the car, he realized. He couldn't do anything for Bob, and the best tack would be to either follow alongside him, or wait for him at the lake to see what he would do next.

Miles chose waiting at the lake. He did not relish the idea of slowly accompanying his father down the road.

Why was his father walking to the lake?

What was going to happen when he got there?

He kept driving, glancing at his father in the rearview mirror until they were off the plain and into the far bluffs and the ragged walking figure could no longer be seen.

They passed others on the road, six of them, men and women, scattered over a stretch of miles.

All dead.

All walking.

Janet's voice was low, subdued. "It's like in New Mexico," she said. "There's this little church outside Santa Fe that's supposed to cure people. It's built on what they call 'miracle dirt,' and every Easter, Catholics from all over make a pilgrimage there. You can see them walking up the highway from Albuquerque. They walk hundreds of miles just to touch the dirt and pray at the church." She looked out the car window, shuddered. "That's what they remind me of. People making a pilgrimage."

"*Dead* people making a pilgrimage."

"To Wolf Canyon."

They looked at each other, and Miles felt an unfamiliar tingling in his midsection. It was a strange sensation, and he thought for a second that he was having a heart attack, since there seemed to be a strange sort of flutter beneath his breastbone. But then it was gone, and he put it down to fear and stress. Perhaps this was considered a "panic attack."

Hell, if anyone deserved to panic, it was him.

The land sloped down, and ahead they could see the lake, shimmering in the sun. The pavement ended, the road devolving into a narrow dirt trail defined by twin tire ruts that zigged and zagged for no discernible reason through the sparse desert vegetation toward the water. Aside from the occasional saguaro or paloverde tree, all of the plants here were low and pale gray, and the rental car bounced along between them on insufficient shock absorbers before finally reaching a dirt parking lot that abutted the northernmost cove of the lake.

To his surprise, an old Jeep was pulled next to a long wooden rail made to look like a hitching post. Miles parked several car lengths away, then shut off the ignition and looked over at Janet. "We're here."

"What do we do now?"

"I don't know," he admitted.

Janet unlocked and opened her door. "I guess we should get out and look around." She glanced over at Miles. "Before they come."

The two of them got out of the car and walked around the front of the vehicle to the railing. Stretched out before them, Wolf Canyon Lake continued almost to the horizon, bounded on the sides by a series of high rocky hills and sandstone bluffs. It had been overcast in Cedar City when they left, and Janet had not brought sunglasses. She stood squinting against the reflected glare on the water. Somewhere under there, Miles thought, was a ghost town, and he found himself wondering if there were still bodies down there, if not all of the corpses had been retrieved.

Maybe the bodies at the bottom were walking, too. Like his father.

Maybe that's where his father was headed.

But why?

She's here.

He looked south toward the far end of the lake. He could not see it from this spot, but he assumed that was where the dam was.

She's going after the dam builders, too.

Nothing quite made sense. There were huge gaps in his knowledge, and if he could fill in those gaps he might reach some understanding of what was going on, but until then he was in the dark, able to guess at some of the more obvious elements of what was happening but completely unable to see the larger picture.

"Let's walk down," Miles said. He stepped over the low railing and held Janet's hand to help her across. The two of them started down a barely discernible, gently sloping path that led to the water's edge.

They were at the end of the path, standing on the sandy lake shore, when Miles discovered they were not alone. He saw movement in his peripheral vision, and when he looked to the right he saw a young man sitting on a rock next to the water—a satchel, rolled-up sleeping bag, and scuba gear spread out on the sand beside him. This was clearly the owner of the Jeep. As the man stood up and looked at him warily, Miles walked over.

"Hey," Miles said. "How's it going?"

"All right."

This close, he didn't look all that young. He had short hair and was clean-shaven, which gave his face a youthful appearance, but there were bags under his eyes and a haunted look in his features. Miles estimated that he could be anywhere from twenty-five to thirty-five.

"You here to do some diving?" Miles asked, gesturing down at the scuba gear. "Water looks kind of dirty to me."

"You can see once you get down there."

"Oh, I'm sorry." Miles motioned toward Janet. "This is Janet Engstrom. I'm Miles Huerdeen."

"My name's Garden. Garden Hawks." The young man looked from Janet to Miles. Their thoughts must have registered on their faces because he said: "You know, don't you? That's why you're here."

"Know what?" Miles asked.

"About the Walkers."

Walkers.

Even the word sent a shiver down his spine. The temporary bubble of unreality that had surrounded him, that had allowed him to keep the truth of why they were here at bay, popped. Next to him, Janet drew in her breath, her eyes widening.

Garden nodded. "I thought so." He smiled wryly. "It's good to know that I'm not the only one. I thought I might be going crazy."

"What . . . ?" Janet stammered. "How did you know?"

"My grampa's down there."

"My father's on the way," Miles said. "We passed him on the road in."

"Two of them have arrived since I got here this morning. I sat in my Jeep and watched them."

"What did they do?"

Garden shrugged. "They walked into the water."

"That's where your grandpa is?"

"Yep. He's down there walking." The young man looked at Janet. "What about you? Are you just here with him, or . . . ?" He left the sentence unfinished.

"It's my uncle," she said. "He died and kept walking."

"Is he here?"

"We don't know," Miles answered for her. "We didn't see him on the way, and he was supposedly cremated, but . . ." He shrugged. "We don't know."

"I see."

An awkward pause followed.

Garden looked down at his scuba gear, looked up at them. "Do, uh, you guys have a plan?"

Mile shook his head slowly. "You?" he asked, though he already knew the answer.

"No. I was just going to play it by ear."

It was Janet who asked the question they were all wondering: "Do any of us actually know what's going on?"

There was another awkward silence.

"Well, let's start with what we do know," Miles said. He glanced at Janet, then turned toward Garden.

He told his story.

Afterward, Janet told hers.

When they were finished, Garden nodded. He looked down at his scuba gear, out at the lake, then took a deep breath. "My grampa went down twenty years ago. It was pretty much like your situations. He got sick from fever, started walking, died, then went into the water. We lived nearby here, in a side canyon, and he kept walking around and around the house—for weeks, wind, sun, rain, didn't matter. There was only me, my daddy and my uncle, and we didn't know what to do. My uncle and my daddy, I think, took turns watching him, but this went on for weeks. He wasn't dead yet, but then he did die, sometime while he was walking, and I remember being so afraid of him. I didn't think he was going to kill me or anything, I was just . . . scared. Can't really say why. Anyway, I went to bed, and I heard my daddy and my uncle talking about—just like you said—a box of my grampa's magic powders and potions and stuff. I never saw it, though.

"When I woke up in the morning, he was gone. We followed his trail to the lake and got here just in time to see him walk into the water. My daddy yelled at him, but he couldn't hear, and he just kept walking into the water until he was gone.

"We never came back to the lake, pretended like it didn't even exist, but I never forgot about it, and when I grew up and went to college, I took a diving class. I think you can guess why. I came back on my break, told my daddy what I wanted to do, but both he and my uncle were against it.

"I went diving down there anyway." Garden licked his lips, obviously unsettled by the memory even all these years later. "The water was dirty, muddy, but I saw him. My grampa was walking. And he wasn't alone. There were several people walking. Through that ghost town down there at the bottom." He shivered. "I guess they lived there."

Miles shook his head, impressed with the boy's bravery. "You've never been back since?"

"Nope." Garden looked down at his diving gear. "Not yet."

"Where're your dad and uncle now?" Janet asked.

"My uncle died a few years back. My daddy lives over in Apache Junction, but I didn't want him to know I was coming here, so I didn't tell him anything. I lied and said I was going hunting over at San Carlos for the weekend."

"All these years you never told anyone? None of you?"

Garden shook his head. "Who would we tell? What would we tell them? There was an old witchwoman who lived here back then. Mother Lizabeth we called her. We were going to tell her originally, but for some reason we never did. I tried to look her up when I first got here this morning, but her shack's gone and I didn't see any sign of her." He scanned the surrounding land. "Everyone seems to be gone."

"Who else?"

"No one in particular. But there used to be little pockets of people living around here in the canyons, on the hills. Maybe this is a recreation area or something now and they kicked them all out, but it just seems strange, like the place is abandoned."

"Like it's cursed," Janet whispered.

Again the wry smile. "I didn't want to be the first to say it, but, yeah, like that."

"What made you come back now?" Miles wondered. "Today? The same time as us?"

Garden shook his head. "I don't know," he admitted. "There wasn't anything calling to me, if that's what you're asking. I didn't see any omens or anything. I guess . . . well, I guess it's because this is the twentieth anniversary of my grampa's . . . of his going down there. Not to the day maybe, but almost." He looked out at the lake. "I've also been dreaming about this place lately, about the water, and probably that had something to do with it, too."

Miles thought about his father's dream. In the nightmare, his dad had been rooted to the floor of the kitchen while a tidal wave crashed over the house. Was that what it had been like for the last residents of Wolf Canyon? Had they stood there, frozen in place, as a wall of water released from the upper dam bore down upon them?

Miles looked around. Where was the upper dam? To the left of their cove, a river snaked away from the lake, up into the hills, and he supposed that the other dam and its attendant lake where somewhere in there.

"We've had dreams, too," Janet said.

Miles nodded.

"About water and drowning."

Garden's voice was quiet. "I drowned in my dream."

"What does that mean?" Janet asked. "Are these premonitions? Does that mean we're going to drown here?" She looked fearfully toward the water.

"I don't think so," Miles said.

"But you don't know."

"Not for sure. But that's not what this *feels* like to me. My father's dream was almost like a recollection of the past, like the flooding of Wolf Canyon as seen through the eyes of someone that was there—even though it took place in our house. But my dreams are different. They're not that literal, not that realistic, and I don't think they have anything to do with a specific event. It's more like a coded message, like something I'm supposed to interpret, only I don't know how."

Janet nodded, apparently understanding, though his meaning was far from clear even to himself. She faced Garden. "Do you really think your grandpa's still down there? You don't think he's . . . rotted by now?"

Garden met her eyes. "No," he said. "He's there. And I'd put money on that."

Miles had no doubt that he was right, but the idea frightened him. He looked over the water. He did not like the lake. Even now, even on a warm weekend, it was deserted. Unlike Powell, Roosevelt, and the other lakes they'd passed, Wolf Canyon boasted no sunbathers, no swimmers, no skiers, no boaters, no jet skiers. Water in the desert usually attracted people, but Wolf Canyon seemed to repel them. The bank opposite, instead of featuring cottonwood and jojoba and the usual desert fauna, was barren, sporting only occasional clumps of dead orangish-brown weeds.

Apparently, the only other creatures at the lake were the

"Walkers," as Garden called them, the witches who have returned to the underwater town.

And, several miles behind them, the new Walkers.

Like his father.

How close was Bob? Miles wondered. He excused himself and quickly dashed up to the parking lot. There was no
sign of his dad, but two of the other Walkers had arrived.
He could see them striding purposefully through the low
brush. One, a woman, bumped into a saguaro but did not
seem to notice the cactus' spines and continued walking,
though at a slightly different angle, toward the lake.

Miles hurried back down to the others. "There are two
of them coming. They're almost to the parking lot."

Janet put a hand on Garden's arm. "Do you really think
you should be going into the water?" She motioned toward
his scuba gear. "Who knows how many of them are down
there?"

"I'd already decided not to go down," Garden admitted
sheepishly. "I was getting ready to put my stuff away when
you guys showed up."

The day was starting to fade. Afternoon was giving way
to twilight, and a portion of the sun had dropped below the
western hills. The sky above was still light, but a large section of the western shore and surrounding countryside had
been thrown into shadow. Through the half gloom came the
two Walkers, not slowing because of the incline, not sliding on the sand, but marching relentlessly, surefootedly, toward the water.

Miles heard Janet's frightened, exaggerated breathing next
to him, but other than that the three of them were silent,
and they watched the corpses—a man and a woman—head
straight into the lake.

"Why are they going down there?" Janet asked. "What
do you think they're doing?"

"Walking," Garden said.

The three of them carried Garden's satchel, sleeping bag and diving equipment back to his Jeep. Another Walker was already heading down the road toward the parking lot.

"You still planning to sleep out here tonight?" Miles asked, putting down the sleeping bag.

"Not next to the water, but yeah." He gestured. "Near the picnic tables probably. What about you?"

"I guess. There don't seem to be any hotels around here."

"I suggest we stay together," Janet said. "I don't think we should separate. Not at night."

"Circle the wagons," Miles said, nodding.

They discussed the sleeping arrangements and other practical considerations, trying to stay away from the real subject, the fact that they had no idea what to do and were simply hanging around pointlessly, waiting for something to happen.

Just before dark the last of the Walkers came striding through the small parking lot.

Bob.

The succession of feelings that passed through Miles made him feel like a frightened child—only he had never experienced anything this intensely as a child. He stood there, stunned into inaction, watching as his dad, the man who had brought him up, the man who had shaped him into the person he was today, the man who had lived with him all those years, brushed against a cactus, stepped on sagebrush.

"Dad!" he called.

His father did not turn his head, did not pause in his walking, but continued forward, down the slope, into the water, until the water was up to his knees, his chest, his neck. He did not float, did not swim, but appeared to be anchored to the muddy lake floor as he walked.

A moment later, there was no trace of him left.

He was gone, but Miles stared at the spot where he had disappeared into the lake, and he continued to stare until the day's light was completely gone and the sky was as black as the water.

2

Greg Rossiter took the week's worth of vacation days he had coming to him and flew to Phoenix.

He knew it was wrong, knew it was stupid, knew that in his current position he could not afford to be a hotdogger anymore, that he had to be a team player. But old habits died hard, and he had not gotten where he was by playing by the rules.

He had gotten where he was by ignoring them.

Or breaking them.

Besides, this was too much to resist. Another "supernatural" case near Rio Verde? How weird was that?

If he had believed in signs, he would have said it was a sign, that some unseen power had arranged this in order to assist him in his career.

Shit. Who was he kidding? He did believe in signs. Why not come out and admit it? After what he'd seen and what he'd done, he had a right to. The fact of the matter was, he'd known immediately after his talk with McCormack that he was going to Wolf Canyon. This case had spoken to him, had grabbed him where it counted, and if that pussy McCormack had just pulled a few of the strings he held instead of jumping at his own shadow and slinking around Washington like a guilty ferret, Rossiter could have been legitimately assigned to this case rather than going off in secret like this.

Still, maybe it had all worked out for the best. If it *had* been a legitimate assignment, he probably wouldn't have been given the lead, would have been one of the team members instead of the team leader, and would not have been given any credit for bringing this case to closure. This way he would once again be the one to crack this thing wide open, would be able to claim all the credit for himself, and would doubtlessly take yet another step up the Bureau ladder.

But what *was* this case?

He didn't know. Not exactly. A man in Utah had become a reanimated corpse, an Interior Department undersecretary had been murdered by some type of monster in his own garage—and forty years ago, government engineers had flooded a town of witches after constructing a damn. Whatever it was, it was big. Not as big as what had happened in Rio Verde maybe, but plenty big enough, and if what he'd gathered from reading between the lines of McCormack's secret report was true, things might be coming to a head pretty damn soon.

He took a taxi from the airport to the Phoenix Bureau office, where he signed out a car. Engels, his old supervisor, was in, but Rossiter made no effort to see the man. The two of them had never been on the best of terms, and when he'd left for Washington, he had rubbed Engels' nose in it, and he was pretty sure the supervisor was carrying a grudge.

A quick lunch at Whataburger, and he was on his way, heading east through Mesa and Apache Junction and then into open country. Like most FBI vehicles, this one was equipped with a radar scrambler, which would keep him from being pulled over and having to explain things to some dumb ass local highway cop, and as soon as it was prudent, Rossiter opened her up, cruising down the two-lane through the barren chaparral at an even hundred. Even at this speed it would be a couple hours before he reached his destination, and he turned on the car's scanner, maximizing the range and listening to the always amusing transmissions of the yokel law enforcement out here in the wild, wild West.

* * *

He approached the dam from the south, passing through Rio Verde. It brought back memories, not all of them good ones, and as he drove by the Chinese restaurant on his way toward the center of town, he considered stopping by the police station, dropping in on his old pal Sheriff Carter for a surprise visit. Rossiter smiled to himself. Such a tweaking would be fun—he knew Carter had no desire to see him ever again—but as much as he would like to hang around and annoy that fat bastard, he had to get to the lake. He had no idea if anything was happening there, or if it was, whether he was late or early for the fireworks, but he needed to go there first and assess the situation.

Maybe on the way back.

Outside Rio Verde the highway followed the river, and twenty miles north the road split, one heading through the desert toward New Mexico, the other winding up a series of plateaus and bluffs to the lake. The road curved around a cliff face, then narrowed to a single lane as it crossed the dam. His was the only car, and Rossiter drove carefully, aware of the inadequate railing that separated him from the water to his right and a precipitous drop to his left. On the other side of the dam, the road was dirt, and it ended at an empty gravel parking area ringed by warped and weathered picnic tables.

He got out of the car, stretching, and walked to the edge of the lake, looking back toward the dam, up the shore, then across the water.

He didn't know what he had expected to see, but he had expected . . . something.

Rossiter stared out at the desert. There were no cars, no people, no vampires, nothing unusual or out of the ordinary. The late afternoon air was silent save for a whooshing rumble coming from the base of the dam where water was released into the Rio Verde.

God, he'd grown to hate this state in the years he'd been

assigned here. And two terms in D.C. had not lessened his antipathy one whit. Who the fuck would live in such a hellhole other than moronic rednecks and inbred hillbillies?

He sighed. He'd start at the dam and work his way around.

Already he was beginning to think that he'd made a mistake and acted too rashly. There was no reason for him to have come. Even if there was some sort of power in this place, he couldn't hope to exorcise it just by showing up. The supernatural wasn't some trained monkey, jumping through hoops on his timetable, showing its face when it was convenient for him.

There was nothing to do about it, though, except continue on as planned, and he looked back at the dam, then started walking along the shore, wishing he had brought some tennis shoes.

3

At night, low whispers.

Miles recognized the soft susurration, the barely audible noises he had heard in the house the night before his father had returned from the hospital. The sounds had scared him then, and he was even more frightened now. Everyone else was asleep—Garden in his sleeping bag on the ground, Janet in the backseat of the car—and Miles wanted to wake one of them, wanted someone else to hear this, wanted some sort of verification that it was not all in his mind, but he did not know either of them well enough to impose on in such a manner, and the truth was that he would have felt stupid waking them up merely because he was afraid of some noises.

The noises were spooky, though, particularly under these circumstances, and somehow he doubted that either Garden or Janet would blame him for wanting company.

He stared into the night sky. The whispers were all around

him, coming from behind the tree, up on the rocks, from the black surface of the lake itself. As before, he thought he could make out words, names: *"May. Lizabeth."*

He was lying atop the picnic table, Garden's jacket wadded up under his head for a pillow, a dirty blanket from the back of the Jeep wrapped around him, mummy-like, against the surprisingly cold night chill.

"May."

What could it be? He didn't know and he didn't want to know. It was what he'd come here for, the reason they'd all been drawn to Wolf Canyon, but now that he was here, now that the answers for which he'd been searching were making themselves known, he realized that he didn't really want them.

"May," the whispers said, and there were other unintelligible words mixed in, backing it up. *"May ... Lizabeth ... Lizabeth May ..."*

He would be less afraid if Garden or Janet were awake, but he still would not allow himself to cave in and rouse them. Instead, he closed his eyes, rolled onto his side, pulled the dirty blanket above his ears and softly hummed to himself in order to shut out the sounds.

It took awhile, but focusing on not hearing the whispers eventually tired him out.

He fell asleep.

He dreamed.

He was back in Los Angeles, at Dodger Stadium, in the middle of the night. The place was empty, all halogens turned off, only the muted glow of city lights under orange-tinged smog offering any illumination whatsoever.

In the parking lot of the stadium was a small plywood shack, a makeshift home made from discarded construction materials. A man stood in the darkness of the shack's open doorway, an old man dressed in chaps and the dusty clothes of a western pioneer. He was smoking silently, and there was something ominous about the way only his arm moved to bring the cigarette to and from his lips while the rest of his body remained as immobile as a marble statue.

The old man tossed his cigarette into the parking lot, turned, and walked into the gloom. Miles understood that he was to follow. He did not want to do so, was afraid of the man and the shack and the darkness, but he had no willpower of his own, and he obediently fell in step behind the retreating figure.

Inside, the shack was big, much larger than was possible given the confines of its outer structure. The old man led him through a debris-filled room to a table atop which was a lit kerosene lamp and a woman's head in a clear cookie jar. Sliced fruit lay at the bottom of the glass container— oranges, peaches, pears—and the head rested upon the slices, bloodless tendons and string-like veins hanging over the clean edges of the skinless fruit. The man picked up an old rusty spoon and used it to sprinkle sugar into the jar from one of two small saucers on the table. He put in another spoonful of mint leaves from the other saucer, and turned to Miles. "It keeps the head fresh," he explained. His voice was high and cracked, not at all what Miles would have expected.

Miles nodded, not knowing how else to respond.

The man picked up the kerosene lamp, walking through another open doorway into a room that looked nearly as big as Dodger Stadium itself. The flickering light illuminated only the small area immediately surrounding them. Strewn about the dirt floor were naked porcelain dolls with painted breasts and pubic hair. Miles followed the old cowboy past the dolls, stopping before a massive opening in the earth. Wide enough to fit a car in lengthwise, the pit descended into an inky blackness deeper than any he had ever seen.

"I dug this hole," the old man confided. "It leads to China."

"What did you dig it with?" Miles asked him.

"My mint spoon."

"Where did you get the spoon?"

"A dwarf gave it to me."

The conversation seemed nonsensical to him, but there seemed to be real significance beneath its lack of literal meaning. Miles nodded sagely as if this was what he'd expected to hear.

The old man put a cold hand on Miles' shoulder. He pressed his face close, and Miles could smell tobacco and coffee and something else, something sweet and not at all pleasant.

"That's where I put her body," the man said. "When the head's ready, it'll go in, too."

Miles awoke with the dawn, and he sat up, the chill of night already dissipating before the warm rays of the rising sun. Janet and Garden were still asleep, and he quietly pulled off his blanket, sat up, and stepped off the picnic table onto the hard ground.

The desert was beautiful in the morning. The monochromatic flatness that would overtake the surrounding land later in the day had not yet arrived, and the rocky hills and cliffs were bathed in sunrise orange, their clefts and indentations shadowed. Tall saguaros, arms upraised and outstretched, stood like surrendering soldiers between the boulders. The sky was cloudless and deep, its gradation of colors spanning the spectrum from orange in the east to purple in the west. Above the top of the nearest butte, a lone hawk circled lazily in the sky.

The lake itself was black.

It was a trick of the light—it had to be—but the effect was nonetheless disturbing, and Miles was grateful to hear the sound of the car door open behind him as Janet got out and stretched.

Garden emerged from his sleeping bag, awakened by the

slamming of the door, and the three of them looked awkwardly at one another, not sure what to say.

"Anyone bring any food?" Miles asked.

Garden nodded. "I have some Pop-Tarts in the Jeep. Blueberry. Hope you all like them, because it's a long drive to the nearest Denny's."

Miles and Janet waited while he dug through the jumbled mess in the back of his vehicle and pulled out a Pop-Tarts box.

The three of them stared out at the lake as they ate. "Any—" Janet cleared her throat. "Any new ones come in the middle of the night? Walkers?"

Garden shook his head. "Not that I heard."

"If they did," Miles agreed, "we *all* slept through it."

Silence.

They finished eating. "So what do we do?" Janet asked finally, rubbing the crumbs off her hands.

"I don't know," Miles admitted. "The problem is, we don't even know what's really wrong. I mean, maybe nothing'll even come of this. Obviously, people have been homing back here for years, decades even. Who's to say that it means anything, that something . . . bad's going to come of it?"

"Because," Garden said, squinting at him, "I feel it. And I'll bet you do, too."

He did, and Miles nodded reluctantly. There *was* a feeling here, an unnamed sense of foreboding that was like a great weight pressing against him. He had not examined it closely, but it was something he'd experienced ever since arriving at the lake, and he realized finally that he *did* have a plan: wait for something to happen and then react to it.

But what made him think that he—that any of them—could react effectively?

Nothing.

All he knew was that they had to try.

"Miles?" Janet said, and he heard a hint of worry in her

voice. He looked over at her, then followed the line of her gaze. A man was walking along the shoreline, an inappropriately dressed man wearing what looked like the black slacks and white shirt of a standard-issue business suit. The dark shades he had on gave him the appearance of a Secret Service agent, and the incongruity of his appearance set off a red flag in Miles' mind. Something about the stranger's bearing bespoke law enforcement, and with a sinking feeling in his gut he thought that they were going to be kicked out, that this area was being closed and evacuated.

The man saw them, apparently catching movement in his peripheral vision, then immediately changed his direction and headed up the slope toward where they stood, looking down at him.

He reached the top fairly quickly and held out a sheathed badge. "Agent Rossiter," he said, identifying himself. "FBI."

"Yeah?" Garden said.

"May I ask what you're doing here at the lake?"

"You can ask, but I don't have to tell you. Unless I'm under arrest or something."

The agent turned toward Janet, who looked furtively over at Miles.

Miles sighed as Rossiter's attention shifted to him. He didn't understand Garden's unprovoked belligerence, but Janet's nervousness was a common reaction to authority. Miles stepped in to speak for them. He nodded politely. "Agent Rossiter? I'm Miles Huerdeen."

"Mr. Huerdeen. May I ask why you're here?"

Miles was about to answer, to give some false, harmlessly generic reason, when the sky changed. Shapeless clouds did not move in but simply appeared without preamble, blotting out all trace of blue, filtering the sunlight to a small white lightening above the suddenly dark desert mountains.

There was a ripple in the water, movement that began in the middle of the lake, moved south, then disappeared, like some Loch Ness Monster surfacing for a moment before diving. They all saw it, and the look on the agent's unintentionally expressive face told Miles everything he needed.

"I think we *all* know why we're here," he said.

Rossiter's eyes narrowed. "What do you know?" he asked.

"You first."

He'd expected stonewalling, but to his surprise the FBI agent stated matter-of-factly that he was here to investigate a series of mysterious deaths that had been tracked in Washington and seemed to have as their only connection strong ties to Wolf Canyon, the former government-sponsored colony of witches that was now buried under this lake.

Colony of witches.

That explained a lot, and in his mind pieces of the puzzle began to fall into place. He understood now the existence of magic paraphernalia, the supernatural aspects of the deaths. Still, it did not explain the source of all the recent activity. Witches had been killed when the town was flooded, and now retribution was being sought. But by whom? Were witches living today or were they coming after those who had wronged them from beyond the grave?

He thought of his father, and found it impossible to believe that Bob was involved in all this, that his dad was a witch.

Rossiter nodded. "Your turn," he said, finished.

Miles spoke for all three of them, describing the situation with his father, Janet's uncle, Garden's grandpa. He explained to the agent that he was a private investigator and told him about Liam Connor's list.

"You have a copy of that?" Rossiter interrupted.

"In the car."

"I'd like to see it."

Miles nodded.

The sky had darkened further. The ceiling of strange clouds kept thickening. The black water of the lake was unnaturally still, undisturbed by wind or bird or fish. The desert warming had not lessened with the disappearance of the sun, however, and the juxtapositon of the Nordic sky and the Arizona temperatures perfectly complemented the goose bumps that thrived on the hot sweaty skin of Miles' back.

"So what's your plan?" Rossiter asked. "What were you intending to do? Why are you here?"

Miles looked from Janet to Garden, unsure of what to say. "I don't know," he admitted. "We were sort of trying to figure that out when you showed up."

"It's—" the agent began, when suddenly there was a disturbance in the lake, a bubbling of the water accompanied by a high keening sound. They all turned to look, and Miles found himself instinctively moving back, away from the slope.

The water parted, not spectacularly like the cinematic Red Sea but cheesily, like Universal Studios' recreation of the event for its tourist tram ride, the section of the lake nearest them opening in a narrow wedge.

Two by two, they walked out of the water, all of the dead who had walked in. The most recent emerged first, including his father, staring sightlessly forward, moving in a march that was somehow more deliberate and controlled than the gait that had brought them here. It was as if the urgency was gone, as though they were no longer striving to reach a destination but had found it and were now operating under different orders. They seemed like slaves, cowed and beaten into submission, and what Miles felt looking at his father was not fear but pity.

The Walkers in front were wearing wet, raggedy clothes, but the clothes were gone on those who came after, and they stepped nude onto the sand, marching not up the slope toward the parking lot but along the shoreline, away.

"I don't see my uncle," Janet kept repeating, her voice a little-girl whisper. "I don't see my uncle."

"I see my uncle," Garden said. "And I see my grampa."
There was dread in his voice.

Rossiter said nothing, but Miles noticed that the agent's
revolver was now drawn, and though he didn't think that
would help, it somehow made him feel better.

More dead men and women emerged from the parted
water.

And *she* appeared.

She's here.

He knew instantly that this was who his father and Janet's
uncle had been talking about. This was the person the homeless woman in the mall had been trying to warn him about.

She walked out of the water, naked. Her head was streaked
with mud, her tangled, stringy hair green with algae, but like
the others, her skin had not been eaten away, and she looked
remarkably well preserved for being so long in the lake. Her
head was tilted at an odd angle, as though her neck had been
broken. While she was inarguably beautiful, there was something terribly off about her face, a wildness, an alienness in
her expression that filled him with fear. He did not know
who she was, but she had an undeniable aura of power.

Isabella.

The name came to him, from where he did not know, but
he understood that it was hers. His feeling that she was somehow behind everything solidified.

She turned her tilted head, looked at him—

*And he was at a crossroads in the moonlight, watching
through Isabella's eyes as she approached the hanging body
of a witch. The woman, a hag with a wild mane of gray
hair, had been stripped naked and was dangling from a
frayed rope attached to a lightning-struck oak. There was a
faint glow about the witch, the remnants of power that were
no doubt invisible to ordinary eyes, and this was what Isabella desired. There were no people anywhere near this
cursed place, and even the lights of far-off villages had been*

extinguished, so late was the hour. She crawled, unhampered and unseen, up the tree to cut down the body, and when it fell, she jumped on top of it. Her lips closed over the corpse's open mouth, and she began drawing in the extant power, at the same time sucking out blood and bile and bits of half-digested food. It was the energy Isabella needed, desired, and he felt the strenghtening within her as her body absorbed the witch's dark force, extracting it from the dead body in the only way possible.

And then he was in an Anasazi village, Isabella taking the community's shaman in front of the shaman's brethren as part of a ceremony, draining the body through the palms of the old man's hands, wanting only the energy, but taking the blood as well in order to support the preconceived notions of the audience. Isabella was nude and moaning, allowing the blood to spatter her breasts, her stomach, her hairy crotch. The people watching prayed and chanted, giving thanks, and as she ingested the last of the man's essence, the shivers of orgasm passed through her loins.

Then the village was gone, and he was in a dark hut in which a man of power practiced his arts. The man was kneeling before a statue he had carved, the statue of a god in the shape of an asparagus. On the floor beside him lay dead women, nude and with their legs spread, stalks of asparagus protruding from their private parts. It was late spring, asparagus season, and outside men harvested the vegetables as their wives and daughters, caged in bamboo boxes, squirmed and screamed and begged to be released.

This was a different earth, an older earth, because the land outside was unlike anything existing today, the mountains on the horizon too tall and oddly shaped, the sky and the dirt of the fields different in color than they should have been.

Isabella had fed recently, so there was no reason to partake of the man's power. Instead, she knelt with him, the two of them speaking in unison, praying to this ancient god, then crawling across the floor to where the prepared bodies lay. She crouched before the first dead woman, said the Words, shoved her head between the cold thighs, and started eating the asparagus.

Then he was in a huge black cave with naked men and women and creatures that had never seen the light of day, monsters that had never been drawn by the hand of man, had never emerged from even the most fervid imaginations of the world's most profane illustrators. The floor was mud, dirt mixed with blood rather than water, and Isabella was standing in the center of the cave, legs spread, arms in the air, howling. The men and women were cowed in terror before her, and she reached down, picked up one of the scuttling creatuers and ate it, crunchy slimy albino skin popping between her teeth as she chewed the unholy flesh. She howled again, grabbed another little monster, ripped it apart with her teeth, and swallowed its essence. She cried out, an inarticulate cry of hunger and pain, and this time she leaped upon a larger creature, a segmented, multi-legged, multi-mouthed, multi-eyed monstrosity that squeuled at her touch and attempted to fight her off. She subdued it easily, bit into the rubbery skin of its back, and killed it.

She howled.

And then the visions were over. He was once again here, himself, and Miles looked quickly around. Only a second had passed. He was exactly where he'd been, nothing had moved, nothing had changed. He felt dizzy, disoriented. He was not sure what had happened, but some sort of connection had been made between himself and this woman. He did not know how or why, but she had allowed him to glimpse . . . what? Her memories? Her fantasies? Her plans? Her past?

A quick look at Janet and Garden and Rossiter told him that none of them had experienced anything similar. Whatever the phenomenon was, it had been reserved solely for him.

Isabella had emerged completely out of the water and was walking on the sand. She turned toward him, smiled chillingly—

And the vision hit.

The dam blew apart, Wolf Canyon Lake draining out in a tidal wave hundreds of feet high, emptying through the mountains and onto the desert below, completely wiping out a small town, the bodies of hundreds of people washing onto the plain.

Destruction spread across the land.

Phoenix was buried under a massive sandstorm that covered the entire Southwest and engulfed Albuquerque and Las Vegas as well. New York was in flames, the teeming streets filled with fleeing people with no place to run. Chicago sank into the ground while the waters of Lake Michigan rushed in to fill the hole. Los Angeles was shaking from an endless earthquake that seemed intent on leveling every man-made structure in the state. . . .

As before, he saw it all through her eyes, and in a flash of insight, he realized that she had lived here at Wolf Canyon. She had been one of the witches buried under the lake when the town was flooded.

The vision faded.

He staggered backward. Part of him wanted to rush her, tackle her, but that was a small stupid part and it was overruled by common sense and good old-fashioned fear. Unlike the other Walkers, she was not merely an automaton. She was not following orders. She was the one giving them, carrying out her well-thought-out plans.

Now he understood. Finally he'd discovered a focal point to the evil that had spread out from this spot, that had reached across the country to kill all those people, that had somehow reanimated his father and Janet's uncle and Garden's relatives . . . and had finally brought them here.

Isabella.

She wanted nothing less than complete revenge. Her power would grow with each loss of life, until she was unstoppable.

The end of the world would not come as the result of Divine intervention or cosmic accident but from the small bitter hatred of an angry witch.

Miles was shaking. With fear, yes, but also from sensory overload, overwhelmed by the intensity of what he had experienced.

He had felt her anger, the white-hot core of hate that fueled her rage, but what remained with him most was the loneliness she felt, and moral imperatives were as nothing before it, minor distractions to be ignored or tossed aside. He remembered, as a kid, watching the Apollo space shots on TV, and what he recalled most clearly was Apollo 8, when American astronauts circled for the first time around the dark side of the moon. For the entire preceding week, he had attempted to imagine what it would be like to be in their shoes, to visualize what they were seeing, to experience what they felt. Loneliness was what he came up with. Everything they had ever known—water, sky, clouds, dirt, plants, animals, mountains, people, buildings, bugs—was a million miles away, encapsulated on a sphere they saw floating far off in the blackness of space while they were crammed into a small metal room surrounded by absolute nothingness. And when they circled around the dark side of the moon, when their radio transmission was cut off until they orbited back around, they were denied even that, stuck with only each other and the silence of space without so much as a glimpse of their blue globe world in the distance. They were alone, completely alone.

What he had felt when seeing through Isabella's eyes was

a comparable loneliness, a similar estrangement from the
currents of life. Only it was somehow worse because it was
something he could not understand. Her emotions and
thought processes were so profoundly alien to him that he
could deduce nothing from them, could make no predictions
regarding past or future actions. The only thing he knew was
that she could not be dissuaded from the course which she
had chosen, that she was unalterably set upon her path and
that there was nothing he or anyone else could do to change
that.

Isabella looked past them, through them, and kept walking, following the others along the edge of the lake.

She didn't know that he'd seen!

His heart began racing. On the edge of despair only a second before, cowed and intimidated by her awesome power,
he now saw a ray of hope. Whatever connection had been
established between them, she was unaware of it. Somehow,
he had tapped into her intentions without her knowledge.

It was not much of an advantage, but it was something.
The fact that she did not know he had gained access to her
thoughts meant that she wasn't perfect, wasn't all-powerful.
She'd looked in their direction after coming out of the water,
but if she'd seen them or noticed them at all, she'd thought
of them as little more than bugs or plants, totally irrelevant.

The constant tingling in his midsection faded as she moved
between the paloverde trees away from them, angling inland
from the shoreline. The other Walkers now seemed to Miles
to be driven before her like cattle.

He knew that if anything was going to be done to stop
her, they would have to be the ones to do it. How they would
accomplish this was another matter. He looked over at the
others, wanting to tell them what he'd experienced, but there
was no way to convey the scope of it all.

Rossiter was still holding his drawn weapon, but he had
not fired a shot, and Miles could tell from the expression

on his face that the agent had been stunned into inaction. Janet was staring blankly out at the water.

Garden spoke first. "What the hell was that?"

"I don't know," Rossiter said.

Miles finally found his voice. "Isabella."

They all looked at him.

"She's a witch who was here when the town was flooded, and somehow she survived. She's behind everything. She's old, older than we can imagine, and she's angry at what was done to her. I don't know if she was killed and struggled back from the dead or if she was just weakened and put out of commission for a while, but it's taken her until now to build up her strength. She reached out and killed the people responsible for the dam, the people who built it, the people who oversaw it, and she's gathered to her the people *from* Wolf Canyon, the other victims." He nodded at Garden. "Like your grandfather." He took a deep breath. "And my dad. I think they're, like, her army, and she's going to use them to help her—"

What? Destroy the world?

It sounded so stupid and childish and melodramatic.

"—take revenge," he said lamely, vaguely.

Rossiter nodded, but that was the only response. No one questioned him, and the irrationality of that made him realize just how crazy things had gotten. There were plenty of questions to ask. Why were Isabella and the Walkers leaving the lake after all these years? Where were they going from here? Perhaps the others didn't want to know more. Perhaps they understood on some instinctive level that what he'd told them was true, and that was enough for them.

Janet shook her head uncomprehendingly. "Did you see your father?" she asked Miles.

He nodded. "Yeah."

She turned to Garden. "Your grandfather?"

"And my uncle."

"Uncle John wasn't there." Her voice was filled with something like relief. "Maybe we did bury him. Maybe he *is* back in Cedar City and he's not involved in all this."

"Maybe," Miles agreed. He wasn't at all sure that Uncle John's fate was so benign, but he wanted to ease her suffering. She did not deserve this. He was sorry he'd brought her along, but he knew that the only reason he could say that was because Garden and Rossiter were here. The truth was, he had had her come along solely because he hadn't wanted to be alone. Now he wished that he had left Janet back in Utah.

Garden was staring at the spot where they had last seen the Walkers heading into the desert, toward the hills. The track of disturbed sand that marked their passing was clearly visible. "What do you think we should do?"

"Follow them," Rossiter said, but his voice lacked conviction, and his face betrayed a complete lack of desire to do any such thing.

Miles shook his head. Logically, that should be their plan, but something about it seemed wrong. It didn't *feel* right, although that seemed like a nebulous objection. "No," he said.

His authority challenged, Rossiter's spine stiffened. "They'll get away. If you're right, they need to be stopped. And we're the only ones who've seen them. We're the only ones who know where they are."

"It's too dangerous," Miles said, and though he didn't know why he thought that, he did.

"You coming?" the agent asked Garden.

The young man looked confused, turned from Rossiter to Miles, licking his lips.

"Fine." Rossiter started off on his own. "I'm not letting them out of my sight." He started down the slope, jogging to maintain his balance until he reached the beach at the bottom.

"Don't!" Miles called after him, and he was surprised by the power of his own voice.

"I have to! They'll get away!"

"Let them. We'll go after them later. We need to talk about this. We need to plan—"

"Nothing to talk about. Nothing to plan. You pussies stay here. I'm going." He was already moving away from shore and was past the first paloverde, heading around the column-like bulk of a saguaro.

"Maybe we should go," Garden said.

Janet shook her head fiercely. "Miles is right. It's dangerous. You saw them."

"I saw my grampa and uncle."

"That's not who they are anymore," Miles told him. He looked Garden in the eye and saw that he was only stating what the young man already knew.

Rossiter disappeared into the desert.

"What *do* we do?" Garden asked.

Miles didn't know. He knew what felt wrong, but he didn't know what felt right. Isabella needed to be stopped. But he did not know how to do that, and it seemed criminal and irresponsible to stand around here, waiting for inspiration to strike instead of taking action.

"What's going to happen to him?" Janet was looking off toward where Rossiter had disappeared into the desert brush.

"I hope nothing."

"But you don't think so?"

Miles shook his head. Until Janet had forced him to confront the fact, he had not realized that he never expected to see the agent again. He was surprised at himself for not feeling anything, and once again he realized what a bizarre turn everything had taken, how . . . off it all seemed.

"Where do you think they're all going?" Garden asked. "Maybe we could call the police. I don't know how strong that Isabella is, but maybe they can be overpowered. Maybe

if we get a group together and confront them we can..."
He trailed off. "I don't know *what* we can do, but maybe
we can do something."

Miles nodded absently. He was listening for the sound of
gunfire, expecting Rossiter to catch up with the Walkers and,
once cornered, use his revolver.

But there were no shots, and the optimistic thought briefly
occurred to him that the agent was trained in this sort of
thing. He might be tailing them without their knowledge.
Maybe he would see something or learn something that they
could use to stop Isabella.

Hope died in his chest as Rossiter emerged from the brush,
shuffling through the sand, hands hanging loosely at his sides,
eyes white and wide, his mouth open in a stunned expression.

His face was bright lobster red.

The thudding of Miles' heart rose to a drumbeat loud
enough to drown out all incoming sounds. Rossiter looked
as though his skin had been doused with red paint, but as
he drew closer, starting up the slope toward the parking lot,
Miles saw that the redness came from a transformation of
the skin itself, like some ultra-extreme sunburn. The agent
looked up at them and began talking, but the noises that
came out of his mouth were like nothing that had ever issued from either human or animal.

Rossiter reached the parking lot and promptly sat down,
his legs folding naturally into a lotus position as he lowered
himself onto the gravel.

Gravel.

That's what his voice sounded like.

Rossiter was still talking, but his mouth closed as his but-
tocks touched the earth. The disturbing noise stopped, and
Rossiter looked up at the sky . . . and froze.

Miles thought of Medusa, the gorgon, who, according to

Greek legend, would turn to stone any man who looked upon her.

Was that what had happened here?

What exactly had Rossiter seen?

Miles was not sure he wanted to know.

He looked down at the agent's unmoving form. Behind him, from the road, he heard tires on dirt, the sound of a car engine.

"Someone's coming," Janet said. Her voice was small and uncharacteristically squeaky.

Miles turned. A car pulled into the gravel parking lot, slowed to a stop. "I know that car," he said. "It's from my firm."

4

It was the longest trip of her life.

Even without May chattering nonsensically in the backseat, Claire would have been anxious and unable to sleep. Ordinarily on a long drive, the rhythm of the wheels lulled her and she dozed. But the homeless woman kept alternately muttering to herself and making sudden absurd pronouncements, making for a long and stressful trip.

Claire stared out the windshield.

Hal was a progressive rock fan, and he had an endless supply of tapes that he played throughout the night: Triumvirat and ELP and Yes and Gentle Giant and PFM. She herself was more of a smooth jazz, New Age kind of listener, and after a while she found the sheer number of notes and the tortured time changes of the music wearying. She longed for something soothing, relaxing, but this was Hal's car, and he was good enough to drive her, and she didn't say a word.

She prayed that Miles was okay, that nothing had happened to him, that he had not found Bob.

Or Isabella.

They drove through the darkness, and by morning they were on a two-lane road that the map said led to Wolf Canyon. May said so, too, but Claire was not sure how much she trusted the navigational skills of the old woman, and not until the water was in sight was she sure that they had reached their destination.

Approaching the lake by a dirt trail that ended in a parking lot, they saw two vehicles and a group of three people looking out toward the water. Something in their manner, in their posture, suggested both defeat and terror, and as they drew closer, Claire saw that one of them was Miles.

Before him on the ground sat a preternaturally still man dressed in a suit and staring upward at the sky.

"Hal—" she started to say.

"I see," he responded grimly.

For the past several miles the sky had been overcast, a strange tempestuous swirl of black-gray cloud cover that reminded Claire of tornado weather. There weren't supposed to be any tornadoes in Arizona.

The car pulled to a stop, skidding in the gravel. Miles caught her eye through the passenger window, and she rushed out of the vehicle and hugged him. His return embrace was clutching and heartfelt, the bear hug of a man who had not expected to see anyone he knew ever again.

"I love you," she said.

"I love you, too."

She pulled back and looked up at him as another door slammed. The relief was evident on his face when he saw Hal, heard his friend's booming "Imagine seeing you here!"

Miles started to respond, but then his eyes widened as the back door opened and May stepped out. "Oh, my God," he said.

"I found her," Claire explained. "Or rather, she found me. She was waiting for me when I came home from work.

That's why we're here." Claire took his hand in hers, squeezed it. "She has some things to tell you, Miles. I think you'd better listen."

The homeless woman stood next to the open car door, looking out at the lake as if searching for something.

"May!" Claire called out.

She glanced up and ran over, dirty skirts flying, leaving the car door open behind her.

"May?" Miles said, as though he'd heard the name before. "Lizabeth May?"

The old woman stopped in front of him, smiled.

Miles looked stricken. "What is it?" Claire asked.

He shook his head.

"Hello, Garden," May said, nodding to the young man standing next to Miles. She smiled. "Dreams," she told Miles. "We should always listen to our dreams. They teach us."

"Yeah, right." Hal had walked up, and he snorted derisively. He glanced around at the others: the young man and woman, the guy on the ground. "Hey," he said in greeting, "what's going on?"

Claire looked down at the well-dressed man seated on the gravel. She hadn't noticed it before, but his face was a bright cherry apple red. "Is he . . . ?"

"I don't know. He just sat down there a minute before you showed up. He was chasing . . ." Miles shook his head. "It's a long story. But he came back all . . . red. And then he sat down here and he hasn't moved since."

She felt his neck for a pulse, found one. "He's alive. We should send somebody out for help."

Claire turned toward the homeless woman. "May?"

"Isabella did this. There's no hospital that can help him now."

Again, Miles looked stricken. "You know Isabella?"

"I know *of* her. We all did. Bob"—she nodded at the

young man to Miles' right—"John Hawkes"—she nodded at the woman,—"John Engstrom."

"You haven't introduced us to your friends," Hal said.

Miles seemed rattled, preoccupied, on automatic pilot. Claire remembered that behavior from the old days: he was thinking, his brain sorting things out. It's what he used to do when he was putting together the pieces of a case on which he was working—something that happened far too often at home, at dinner, in the bedroom, during what was supposed to be their time together. Miles motioned toward the man and woman. "This is Garden Hawkes and Janet Engstrom. Janet's uncle died and kept walking, like my dad. I brought her here with me from Cedar City. The same thing happened to Garden's grandfather years ago. We met him at the lake." He turned around. "Garden, Janet? This is my friend Hal. We work together. This is Claire, my . . . ex-wife. And this is a woman I met once at a mall before Christmas. Apparently, her name is May. I guess it'll be explained to me why she's here."

"That's the witch woman I was telling you about," Garden whispered.

Miles nodded distractedly.

"So who is *he*?" Hal asked, motioning toward the man on the ground.

"Agent Rossiter. FBI."

"No shit?" The detective whistled. "You got yourself involved in a big one here."

"Yeah."

"Come to think of it, you got me involved, too."

"I'm sorry—"

"Don't apologize." Hal shook his head. "Jesus Christ, Miles, when are you going to stop playing Lone Ranger? I learned more from Claire in the one hour before we left L.A. than I did from you the past three months. If we really are friends, you need to include me here. I came all this way, and I don't know what the fuck's going on, but this time you can't just tough it out alone. There are other people involved."

Claire knew exactly what Hal was saying, and she agreed completely, but this wasn't really the time or place, and she could tell from the set of his face and the tightening in his jaw that Miles was closing himself off. She reached out. "What happened to Bob?" she asked softly. "Did you find him?"

Miles sighed tiredly. "Yeah. I found him." Drawing in a deep breath, he explained what had happened since he'd left California. Hal interrupted with occasional questions, and Miles answered them all, Garden and Janet jumping in for clarification.

Claire could not help looking out at the lake as Miles told his story. Somewhere underneath that black water was a submerged town, where drowned witches had spent the last few decades walking and to which the newly dead had trekked. The fear she felt was palpable, a physical sensation like the temperature or the wind.

Miles finished talking, and he held her sweaty hand tightly, as if for support. He was keeping something back, she sensed, and that was what was troubling him. Hal seemed to sense it, too, and she met his eyes and saw, beneath the forced good humor, a reflection of her own worries and concerns.

"So," Miles said dramatically, turning to May, "I guess it's time to hear what you have to say about all this. I assume you know what's going on. I assume that's why you're here."

"It is." May repeated everything she'd told Claire, describing how she'd been a New Jersey housewife *pulled* to Wolf Canyon by the strength of Isabella's will, like a moth drawn to a light. "Of course, I was a witch, too. So I knew all about Isabella."

"She's a witch?" Janet asked.

"She is not a witch," the old woman said. "Well, she is but she isn't."

Garden threw up his hands. "She's not even making any sense!"

"Yes, she is," Miles said. "Listen to her."

"Isabella's a predator, a parasite, a creature who lives off her own kind. She feeds off witches, absorbs their power. Yes, she's one herself, but she's also something more. At least, that's the way we figured it."

"And she was killed when the town was flooded," Miles said.

May shook her head. "Oh, no. Isabella was killed way before that. She might even be the cause of it. See, she was around when Wolf Canyon was founded. She married William Johnson, the founder himself. No one knew where she came from originally. I guess she just showed up one day, and William fell under her spell. So to speak. But she was a bad influence on him. After she came, there were mysterious deaths and disappearances, murders. The entire town changed. There were purges of non-witches in the outlying areas, trials and executions of witches who did not agree with the way William and Isabella were running things. She was an evil creature, hated and feared, and eventually even William figured that out. No one knows what all happened, but he killed her one night while she was sleeping, cut off her head. They buried her in a cave outside town, sealing it up, weaving spells around it to keep her in. She was dead but her head was still talking, and she cursed Wolf Canyon and everyone in it, vowing revenge. She promised that they would drown and die, and that they would suffer even after death.

"And that's what happened.

"She called them back after they passed on, all of the people who'd had a part in disposing of her body, who had been living in Wolf Canyon at that time. And, from what we could figure out, she fed off them, using their energies to fight her way back. She was strong enough thirty years ago to reach out to me all the way over on the East Coast, and she's been getting stronger ever since. Her power has been growing with each passing year as the children of Wolf Canyon die off and she consumes their energy."

Miles nodded. "And when she was strong enough, she reached out to the men who had worked on the dam and killed them, too. Only I don't see why, if they were just doing what she wanted done anyway."

"Because maybe they beat her to the punch. Maybe she's angry that they did what she was not yet strong enough to do. Or maybe not. Who knows? Sometimes there just isn't an explanation."

"Where do you fit in?" Miles asked.

May smiled. "She killed a baby. Back in the town's early days. She thought the population had reached some magic number, and she didn't want it changed: no new people, no one leaving. So when a couple had a baby, she killed it. *Her,* I should say, not *it.* The baby was a girl. The parents left, took off in the middle of the night to escape Isabella's tyranny. Years later, they had another daughter. *That* baby was my mother. And her parents taught her and she taught me about the town—and what went on there. Your father knew, too. He was born in Wolf Canyon, and he lived there until he was ten or so, until his parents moved to Los Angeles. That was long after Isabella, but long before the lake. I met him at the dam after I'd come out from New Jersey. I walked the shoreline . . . and I found your father. I think he'd been called, too. He was here to make sure that Isabella hadn't escaped and was still down there." She nodded toward Garden. "John Hawks, your grandfather, had never left. He'd left the town, but he'd built him a house on top of the plateau." She pointed behind them at a flattened rocky bluff. "He's the one who told us about the people in town who didn't leave, who couldn't get out, and we all figured it was her, keeping them there so they would be drowned. There were several of us, and we kept in touch for a while. We knew the stories, and we waited to see if she would return. But the years passed, and she didn't, and we drifted apart, drifted into other lives."

"I remember you," Garden said. "We almost told you when Grampa died, but ... but we didn't for some reason, and then you were gone."

Claire looked at the old lady. It was as if she'd gotten all the craziness out of her system on the trip over, because she appeared completely lucid.

May shook her head. "Now you say she's come out of the lake. With all of the others." She squinted at Miles. "How many would you say?"

"Dozens. A hundred, maybe." He shrugged. "Maybe more. I didn't count."

"You were called, too," May said. She looked intently at Miles.

"So what's the plan?" Garden asked. "What do we do now?"

May turned to face the young man. "We will hunt her down," she said.

Claire felt peach fuzz hairs prickle at the back of her neck.

"And we will kill her once and for all."

5

Miles stared at the homeless woman, who had suddenly stopped talking and was twirling around with her arms out and her eyes closed, like a little girl trying to make herself dizzy. From where he stood, the immobile FBI agent was directly in front of her, and the sight of the two together hit him hard.

May began screaming crazily, looking up at the dark sky and shouting out non sequiturs.

"I was surprised she held out for as long as she did," Hal whispered. "In the car, she couldn't go two minutes without spouting off some loony nonsense."

Claire gave Miles' hand a small squeeze, then let go and moved forward, trying to quiet May and calm her down.

May.

Lizabeth May.

He remembered the whispers in the night and wondered who had been telling him that name. And why.

He had heard his father's name whispered, and his father had died.

Hal turned to face him. "You should've brought me in earlier, man. Tran, too. We could've helped you on this. I thought your dad was just missing, I didn't know all this . . . shit was going on."

"Would you have believed it?"

"Not at first, probably. But I go where the facts take me. You know that." He leaned in, lowered his voice. "And I'd feel a lot better with Tran here than Claire and these other civilians."

Miles had to agree with that.

Except . . .

Except this felt right, and once more he was confronted with the unfamiliar sensation of trusting his feelings rather than facts. Although, under the circumstances, it didn't seem quite so strange.

"Isabella, huh?" Hal shook his head.

"Yeah."

"Does this super witch have a last name?"

"Would it matter if she did?"

"I guess not." Hal looked over at Rossiter, sighed. "You know, I can't help thinking about the fact that this bitch controls an army of zombies and turned an FBI agent into a brain-dead lobster within a matter of minutes. I don't like the odds here." He quickly held up his hands. "But I'm in, I'm in, I'm not complaining."

"You're just scared."

"Damn right I'm scared."

Miles grinned. "Wuss boy."

"Not ashamed to admit it. And you're glad I'm here, aren't you?"

"Yeah," Miles admitted. "I am."

"That's a start, bud. That's a start."

May was suddenly silent. Claire was standing before her, holding the old woman's arms at her sides, when she pulled away, blinking as if she'd just emerged from a trance. "How long ago did Isabella leave?" she asked.

Miles looked at Garden, at Janet.

"I don't know," Garden said. "Fifteen minutes."

"Ten or fifteen," Janet said.

Miles nodded in agreement.

"She's far enough away, then." May mumbled something to herself before looking up again. "Talismans, spell casters, potions. Your families were witches, they all had the makings. Did you bring them? Do you have the materials with you?"

Miles nodded dumbly. He wasn't sure how he felt about relinquishing authority to a woman who obviously had severe mental problems, but crazy as she was, she'd been involved in this longer than any of them. He had no choice but to listen to her. "There's a box in the car from Janet's uncle's house."

"I'll get it." Obviously grateful for something to do, Janet headed over to the rental car to fetch her uncle's witchcraft paraphernalia.

"May told me to bring your stuff, too," Claire said. "Thank God you didn't put it back in that safety deposit box or there's no way I would have been able to get it out. It's in the trunk."

"I have the keys," Hal said. "I'll go."

May turned to look at Garden.

He shrugged. "I never saw those things. I only heard about them. I don't know what happened to them."

The old lady frowned, mumbled something to herself.

Hal and Janet returned with the materials. Miles took his father's stuff from Hal, who then offered to carry Janet's box. Janet shook her head, held on to the carton, and following May's lead, they all walked down the slope to the water's edge, leaving the unmoving Rossiter behind.

By this time the strange sky looked downright fierce. The clouds were not stormy gray but black, deep black, like the water. Though it was difficult to detect movement in so much darkness, shapes seemed to be forming and unforming and reforming in the roiling currents of air.

Feeling his chest tighten, Miles put the box down on the sand, Janet following suit. May crouched down, quickly sorted through the jumble of items and, smiling as if she'd found some long-lost treasure, drew out a rusty spoon.

The spoon from his dream.

The tightness in his chest increased.

She picked out a large covered jar, a porcelain doll with painted breasts and pubic hair, a kerosene lamp.

He'd dreamed about all these things, and he felt a cold coil of fear wrap around his heart. Sure, the spoon had come from his father's batch of items, and he might have dreamed about it because he had seen it. But that did not explain the jar or the doll or the lamp. Those things had belonged to Janet's uncle. There was no way he could have known about them.

May set those items aside, then began sorting through the things he did remember. She drew out the necklace of teeth, the plastic bag containing the dried, flattened frog.

"Wear these for protection," she said. She ran her hands above the necklace, tracing patterns in the air in a manner that seemed oddly sensual and that, in some strange way, spoke to him, though he had never seen such a thing before. She held the necklace out and he took it gingerly. He had no intention of ever wearing such a thing, but she held his gaze and refused to continue until he put it on. Shivering with revulsion, he obliged.

She performed similar hand movements over the frog, took it out of the bag, and handed it to Garden. "Keep this in the left front pocket of your pants."

Garden looked like he wanted to object, but he did not and pocketed the frog.

Janet received a ring of bone, Hal a carved wood fetish, Claire a bracelet made out of some type of dried weed. May herself opened one of the bottles and ingested a pinch of some foul-scented powder.

"Now—" May began. But she never finished. From the dark, swirling sky came a bright yellow lightning bolt that was not accompanied by thunder and did not flash instantly to earth but descended slowly and deliberately through the charged atmosphere and struck May atop the head. She watched it come for her, made no effort to move out of the way. When it touched her hair she fell, the features of her face hardening into an agonized rigidity. She collapsed forward onto the gravel, her arms flailing spastically, her legs jerking in furious countermovement even as the muscles of her face froze.

"Somebody do something," Claire said, but no one moved forward, and Miles grabbed her around the waist and held tightly to keep her from approaching May's electrically charged form.

The lightning retreated as leisurely as it had arrived, heading back up into the roiling sky like a fishing line being reeled in. Claire broke free from his grasp and knelt next to the now still old woman, putting her hand on May's neck to feel for a pulse.

"She's dead."

Miles pulled Claire back. "No mouth-to-mouth."

She didn't object, and Miles understood just how frightened she was. Claire was a congenital do-gooder, always helping people, always giving of her time and money, doing anything she could to assist someone in trouble. She was also well trained in CPR. If Claire was so easily dissuaded from trying to help May, Miles knew that she had to be truly terrified.

Hal looked from May to Rossiter on top of the slope. "Two down, five to go," he said.

"Not funny," Miles told him.

"Asshole," Garden mumbled.

Claire suddenly jerked backward, and Miles was nearly knocked over, thrown off balance by the surprise movement. "What—?" he started to say.

Then he saw.

May.

The homeless woman was vibrating, a uniform shiver that passed through her form yet did not bring life to any part of her body. Her arms and legs remained frozen at oddly cocked angles, and the wide-eyed agony on her face stayed unchanged.

A powerful shudder passed through her.

She stood.

And started walking.

He knew what was happening, knew where she was going. There were only seconds to decide on a course of action, and Miles took charge. "Grab your stuff! We're going with her!" He scrambled about for the spoon and the jar and kerosene lamp, leaving the doll on the sand, unable to carry it. "Water!" he called out. "Bring water if you have it! It's the desert!"

Garden dashed back up the slope to the parking lot, followed by Hal.

May was striding away, her head tilted up toward the sky, while her feet followed the path that had been taken by Isabella and the other Walkers. In his mind was the image of that slow lightning coming down to strike May, Agent Rossiter reappearing from his chase with a red head and a dead brain, the physical proof of the power they were up against, but Miles knew he was doing the right thing and, running on instinct, he kept his eyes on the dead woman, ready to hurry after her if she got out of his sight.

Garden and Hal came sprinting down to the shore, Garden strapped with two canteens, Hal carrying a six-pack of Dr Pepper.

"Let's go!" Miles shouted. "Follow her!

"Get help," he told Claire, kissing her quickly. "Drive back to a town, bring the police, sheriff, whatever you can find."

"Oh, no, you don't." She grabbed Miles' arm, holding tight. "I'm coming with you."

"I'll go for help," Janet said. "Or I'll stay. Or ..." She closed her eyes. "I just don't want to chase after her. Them. I don't want to go with you."

Miles understood. Her uncle was not here, any personal connection she might have had was gone, and she was too emotionally on edge to continue on. He thought she should go with them, thought the fact that her family had come from Wolf Canyon might have a bearing on the situation, but there was no time to discuss the subject, no time to argue or convince her, and he knew that without major reassurances she would not be able to make it.

Miles handed Claire the lamp, fumbled in his pocket. "Here's the car keys," he said, tossing them to Janet. "Get some help. Tell them about the FBI guy. That should bring someone over here pretty quick."

Janet said something in response, but he didn't have time to listen. May was disappearing behind a big paloverde, and Miles took off after her, pulling Claire with him, yelling at the others to hurry up.

They followed her into the desert.

They stayed several yards behind—just in case. May unerringly took the route left by the other Walkers, maneuvering closely around bushes and cacti with the precision of an amusement park ride on a track. After leaving the shoreline, Isabella had headed between two low hills and then through a narrow eroded canyon. Though the way was easy at first, it became increasingly harder to walk as the sand became deeper and looser, more dunclike.

It was also hot. The sky was still dark, but the absence of sun had no bearing on the heat, seemed to make things more humid and oppressive, in fact. Garden shifted the canteens on his shoulders, taking off his sweat-soaked shirt and tucking it into his waistband. Hal followed suit. Miles would have liked to do the same, but May was moving much too quickly, and he would not have had time to stop, put down the jar, and take off his shirt. He would have lost her. Next to him Claire, still clutching the lamp, used a handkerchief to wipe her brow.

They tromped deeper into the wilderness.

This was a perfect opportunity for them to talk things out, discuss what was happening, settle on a unified approach.

But they did none of that.

The noiselessness of May in front of them and the unnatural quiet of the desert all around made speech seem sacrilegious, intimidated them all into silence, and the only sound accompanying their steps was the heavy breathing of out-of-shape exertion.

Twenty minutes in, Hal passed back a can of warm Dr Pepper, which Miles and Claire shared gratefully. She finished the last little bit of soft drink, handed Miles the empty can, and he dropped it on the sand to his left. He had no idea where they were or in which direction they were headed, but he had the feeling it might be difficult to find their way back, and he thought they might need a Hansel-and-Gretel trail to follow for the return trip.

If there was a return trip.

They passed through what looked like a saguaro forest, an especially dense stand of the tall cacti, and then through a narrow valley so thick with ocotillo that they were forced to walk directly behind May in order to keep her in sight. Around them the land was rising up, gently sloping hills giving way to harsher, higher cliffs.

Miles' legs were hurting, and he could tell that Claire was tiring as well. The Walkers were dead—they would never tire out—and he hoped that they were not planning to march indefinitely, because there was no way the rest of them could keep up.

He had no plan, no idea of what he would do when and if they finally caught up with Isabella. He hadn't even taken along Rossiter's gun, had only some half-assed witchcraft items that May had picked out for protection. Assuming those things worked, what then? Should he jump Isabella? Wrestle her to the ground?

He was suddenly conscious of the necklace against his skin, the coldness of the teeth, and he wondered whose teeth they were, what the purpose of the necklace was, why his father had saved it. And where his father had gotten it in the first place. Had he made the necklace himself? Had he taken the teeth from corpses or from people that he'd killed?

Despite everything that had happened, he still could not reconcile the father he knew with this underground horror-show society, with spells and potions and curses and murders. He saw his father more as a victim than a participant, and though Bob had obviously been in possession of witchcraft paraphernalia and had taken pains to hide this aspect of his life from the rest of the world, it was also clear that he was not particularly familiar with his heritage.

Hell, his dad had had to go to the library to find out the meaning of his recurrent dream.

Which made Miles question May's story. She claimed to have known his father, said that the two of them, along with Garden's grandfather, had been born in Wolf Canyon and had known about Isabella and her curse. Maybe so. But there were details that didn't add up.

It happened without warning.

They were following behind, once again at a discreet distance, since the terrain had become more hospitable and the vegetation sparser, when the dead woman stopped walking in the flat sandy bottom of a dry wash. Abruptly, she flopped onto her stomach, arms suddenly straight at her sides, legs and feet together. Without a second's pause she began burrowing head first into the ground.

Miles, stunned, could not believe what he was seeing. May's mouth was open, and it appeared as though she was eating the sand, using her jaws like a shovel to dig into the soft earth. It was inhuman and should not have been physically possible, but in a matter of seconds, May's face and head disappeared into the ground, followed by her neck, her shoulders, her upper torso, her midsection.

And then she stopped.

He looked over at Hal and Garden, saw expressions of fear and disbelief on their faces that no doubt mirrored his own. Claire's fingers found his free hand, and he squeezed back a reassurance he did not feel.

They waited, watching, holding their breath, but there was no sound, no movement, no indication that May would ever move again. It was as if whatever force had been animating her form had suddenly withdrawn, leaving behind only a dead, discarded body as lifeless as a normal corpse.

Miles approached cautiously, prepared for a sudden resumption of activity, the type of explosive furious movement that always occurred at this point in horror movies. But this was not a movie and nothing happened. He reached May without incident. Her legs were sticking straight up in the air, and he touched one of her rough dirty feet, feeling cold skin, spongy dead flesh. Her filthy skirt had fallen over her legs, and when he looked down he could see her overly hairy crotch.

He looked up at the sky, looked all around. Was this something May had done on her own, some sort of rebellion to kill herself completely, once and for all, to terminate Isabella's hold over her? Or had Isabella compelled May to dig into the sand for a reason, only to have the old woman's body give out at the last minute? He didn't know, but either way May's unmoving form reminded him of nothing so much as a broken piece of farm equipment left to rot in the ground where it had stopped.

Maybe the spell had simply worn off. Or maybe magic had geographical parameters. Maybe Isabella had pulled so far ahead that May was now beyond the reach of her influence.

Maybe.

The tightness in his chest was gone, but the tingling in his midsection was back, and Miles found himself wondering if these were actual physiological responses to the sort of power to which he'd been exposed. He turned to Garden. "Do you . . . feel anything? In your body, I mean. Any unusual physical sensations?"

Hal butted in. "Aside from the fact that my balls have shrunk to the size of grapes and retracted into my abdomen with fear?"

"Thank you for that," Claire said dryly.

"Sorry."

Garden shook his head. "I don't know what you mean."

"Is there, like, a tingling in your gut? Or a tightening in your chest?"

"Nuh-uh."

"Tightening of the chest?" He heard the worry in Claire's voice. "That's the sign of a heart attack."

"I'm not having a heart attack."

"There's no way we could get you to a hospital in time—"

"I'm not having a heart attack!"

"I'm concerned! Is that all right with you?"

They were glaring at each other, but beneath the anger in her expression he could see her concern, and he moved forward to give Claire a quick kiss. "I'm sorry," he said. "I'm sorry."

"I'm just worried about you."

"I know."

"I'm not feeling anything weird," Garden said.

Miles nodded. He accepted that no one else was experiencing the same responses he was, but he still could not shake the feeling that these symptoms meant something. For the first time he wondered if—since witch blood apparently flowed through his veins—he himself possessed some sort of extrasensory abilities. It would explain his newly acquired sensitivity, would account for the recent veracity of his gut reactions.

They did not linger in the sandy wash, and there was no discussion about stopping, quitting, turning back. They silently picked up where May had left off, following the trail of footprints, heading out of the wash toward a long low hill in the distance, Garden taking the lead.

They were on their own now, but no wind or rain had yet arrived to disturb the tracks in the sand where the Walkers had passed, and it was easy to follow the trail of Isabella and her zombies. Hal passed back another can of Dr Pepper.

"This is the last for a while," Miles said. "We don't know how far we have to go, and we need to save some supplies for the trip back."

They reached the hill, walked around it. The sand turned to rock, and they were forced to scramble over and between huge boulders. Finally, the ground leveled out and they were confronted with a massive arroyo that blocked their way and spread like a vine through the flatland beyond.

Miles walked up to the edge and looked down. It was a good two stories to the bottom of the gulch, and the footprints of the Walkers went up to the precipice and disappeared. From where he stood, he could see no path leading to the arroyo floor, and he could only assume that they had continued walking and fallen straight down. There were no bodies, of course, and he looked across the gulch, then into it, both north and south, trying to determine in which direction they had gone, but it was impossible to tell from here.

"What are we going to do now?" Garden asked.

"Well, we only have two choices: down or back. It's pretty clear that *they* didn't go back."

Hal was walking along the edge, and he waved them over. "Hey!"

"What?" Miles called.

"I think I found a way down!"

He had indeed: a narrow but not particularly steep trail that switchbacked down a sloping side crevasse and led them directly into the arroyo. Miles offered Claire his help, but she was more coordinated and in better shape than he was and beat him to the bottom.

There was no sand here, only rock, and it was impossible to tell in which direction Isabella had driven her herd. South *felt* right to him, though, and Miles motioned for the others to follow. "This way!" he said.

Claire was next to him, and Hal sidled up on the other side. "You know I'm carrying, don't you?"

Miles shook his head. "No, I didn't."

"Well, I am. Just in case. Thought I'd let you know."

It didn't make Miles feel any more secure that Hal had a gun—he had the feeling that such things had no power here—but if it made the detective feel better and gave him the confidence he needed, Miles was all for it.

Hal, he reflected, was a true friend, and he regretted not opening up to him earlier. Sometimes two heads *were* better than one, and perhaps they could have avoided this if they'd figured things out before. Perhaps May would still be alive.

He turned toward Claire. "Are you okay?" he asked.

She smiled gamely. "I'm fine."

The arroyo twisted and turned. This was flash flood territory, and he hoped to God it didn't rain while they were stuck down here. The sky was still dark with clouds, and if a rain shower—either natural or unnatural—hit suddenly, they would have very little time to find a way up and out before the floodwaters washed them away. The thought occurred to him that they had been lured down here, that this was a trap, but though he remained on edge, nothing occurred.

An hour or so later, the arroyo opened out onto a flat plain. The land behind them, Miles saw now, was a raised plateau. Before them, on the same level as the arroyo floor, stretched a desert markedly different than the one through which they had passed. There were no cacti here, no bushes, no trees, no grasses. There was only rock. And sand. In the distance, hidden beyond haze and waves of heat, loomed jutting buttes and tall, strangely shaped mesas that made the landscape look like a Dali-esque Monument Valley. Just in front of that, the ground was broken up into what appeared to be a series of tan canyons sunk deep into the earth.

"I think we went the wrong way," Garden said. "I don't think Isabella came this direction."

"No," Hal said quietly. "She was here." He pointed. To their left, bordering what looked like a trail across the flat empty land, were the legs of the dead Walkers, sticking up in the air in V-shaped pairs like a line of huge fleshy scissors. As with May, the men and women were embedded in the ground upside down, and only the bottom portions of their bodies protruded from the hard-packed dirt.

One pair of legs doubtlessly belonged to Garden's uncle, another his grandfather.

One belonged to Bob.

A stinging burnt smell hovered in the air, though there was no sign of smoke or haze. Sulfur, Miles thought, but he didn't want to think about what that meant.

"Let's get out of here," Claire said. Her voice was subdued. "We need to get help. Police, National Guard . . . somebody. We can't handle something like this on our own, just the four of us."

"I'm with Claire," Hal admitted.

Miles said nothing. He began walking across the dirt to where the witches' legs stuck up from the ground. There was room enough between the double rows for him to pass, and he proceeded down the gruesome aisle, looking from left to right, trying to determine which pair of legs belonged to his father—and which to Isabella.

He had the feeling she wasn't here.

Indeed, looking ahead, he saw a single pair of footprints heading out across the hard ground.

Only they weren't exactly footprints.

There were far too many toes, and the tips produced small round holes in the dirt—like claws or talons.

She was in the canyons, he thought, looking into the distance. She was waiting for them there.

She wanted them to come.

The thought frightened him. He didn't know why a creature with her obviously awesome power would wait around, playing hide-and-seek with a small ragtag group of ill-equipped, ill-prepared pursuers when she clearly had much bigger plans in mind. But nothing about any of this made sense, it had been irrational and crazy from the start, and he had no trouble accepting that she was doing exactly that.

The others had followed him and caught up. Hal tentatively touched the sole of one Walker's foot. Claire had refused to pass between the twin rows of dead witches and had circled around the aisle to the opposite end.

"I vote that we bail," Hal said. There was no mistaking the trepidation in his voice.

"Go if you want," Garden said. "We don't need you."

"The hell you don't. I'm the only one here who's armed."

"You think that's going to make one damn bit of difference?"

"Look, I'm not going to leave you here. We're all going. There's no reason for this insanity."

"Fuck you!" Garden said. "Who are you? You just show up here and start giving orders, you self-important asshole."

"Knock it off!" Miles roared, glaring at them both.

Garden glared back, though it looked like he was about to cry. "I came here on my own, and I'm going forward on my own. I don't need any of you—"

"My dad's here, too," Miles reminded him.

That shut him up.

No one said anything for a while, and they stood between the protruding legs, looking for signs of positive identification.

Miles saw a slender feminine foot and ankle, a hairy leg with webbed toes. He saw dark skin, freckled skin—

His father's foot.

He didn't know how he recognized it, but he did, and though it was ragged and water-damaged, he recognized the pant leg as well. It was the pair Bob had bought at Sears and that he'd helped to pick out. Looking down, he saw his father's waist disappearing into the dirt.

Anger was what he felt most strongly. Hatred. His father should not have been subjected to such outrageous indignity after death. He should have been allowed to rest in peace. Such a callous exploitation of Bob's body made Miles furious and all the more committed to catching up with Isabella. Sadness and horror were mixed in as well, but it was anger that motivated him, hatred that spurred him on.

They must have all burrowed in at the same time, he reasoned. May probably crawled into the ground at the exact moment all of the other Walkers had done the same. Which meant that Isabella was probably an hour and a half to two hours ahead of them.

She was moving fast, increasing the distance between them while they dawdled and argued among themselves.

He put down the jar, glanced at his wrist. His watch had stopped. He tapped it, shook it, but the second hand remained stationary, and when he held it to his ear he heard no tick. It occurred to him that though they had been traveling now for several hours, there'd been no change in the position of the sun shining opaquely through the clouds. He cleared his throat. "What time is it?" he asked.

Hal looked at his watch. "I don't know. My battery seems to have run down."

"Mine, too," Claire said.

All four of them shared a glance of understanding that negated the need for words.

"We'd better get going," Miles said.

Garden nodded.

Like himself, the young man was probably torn, not wanting to leave his uncle and grandfather half buried in the desert like this, wanting to either bury them completely or bring them back to civilization for proper treatment. But there was really nothing they could do for the dead right now, and at this point it was more important that they continue their pursuit of Isabella.

Isabella.

The vision hit as before, instantly, totally, placing him in the precise center of the action.

Dams were bursting one after the other, in Arizona, in Utah, in Colorado. He saw them from above, from her point of view, and in serial sequence nearly identical walls of water flooded towns and drowned families in what was the first strike in a massive retaliatory effort.

And then he was in a cave, looking out. He knew this spot. He had seen it before, only then it had been through the eyes of a younger Isabella in an earlier time, and it had been from the doorway of a hut. The area had changed over the millennia, but there was no mistaking the peculiar appearance of the rock formations, no disguising the fact that the country outside the cave was the same unique landscape he had viewed from this same vantage point in an unknown era that predated recorded history.

Above the cloud cover, he heard the roar of a military jet.

And then it was over, he was out, he was once again himself. He was facing the horizon, that surreal version of Monument Valley, and he recognized that this was the area he had just seen in the vision. The angle from which he had viewed it could only have originated in the canyons up ahead.

From that direction came the fading sound of a jet above the clouds.

Once again Miles wondered why he was being shown this. As much as he tried to tell himself that it was coincidental, that he was accidentally tapping into some psychic wavelength like an antenna catching television signals, he could not help feeling that specific knowledge was being provided to him intentionally.

Claire touched his cheek, looked at him with concern. "Are you all right? It looked like you were . . ." She trailed off, not knowing how to describe what he'd been like for those brief seconds he'd been out.

"I'm fine," he assured her. He turned toward Garden and Hal, tried to ignore the legs of his father scissored into the air next to him. "I know where she went," he said. "I know where she is."

Hal's gaze followed the claw-foot tracks into the distance. "How far is it?"

"Those canyons up ahead."

"You think we'll be able to get there before it gets dark?"

Miles glanced up at the filtered light of the unchanging sun. "Even if it takes all day."

They were all silent.

"What do we do when we get there?" Garden asked finally.

Miles picked up the jar, started walking. "Don't worry. We'll think of something."

6

The land here seemed wrong. The geologic formations of the earth itself were odd and disturbing, containing angles and shapes that appeared nowhere else in nature, and even the consistency of the air seemed different the closer they came to the canyons. The cliffs and crags, the mesas and bluffs, all looked similar to what he had seen from the entryway of the cave, and Miles knew they were approaching their destination.

Isabella's tracks—if that was indeed what they were—had disappeared almost immediately, fading into the increasingly soft sand, but Miles knew the direction in which she'd been headed, and he had no trouble staying on course.

They'd been hiking for what felt like the entire afternoon,

but with no working watches and no visual confirmation from the position of the sun, he couldn't tell how long it had actually been. They had finished up Hal's Dr Peppers, leaving the cans as a trail, and now only the water in Garden's canteens was left to slake their thirst.

Well before they reached the big canyon, a massive gorge visible from miles away that, in Miles' mind at least, compared favorably to the Grand Canyon, they came across the dry bed of an obviously seasonal river. The river apparently emptied into the canyon or one of its offshoots, and Miles looked down the sloping length of the sandy bed and decided that they probably would not be able to find an easier entry into the canyon lands than this. After a quick discussion, they decided to follow the empty riverbed down.

Around them, the desert grew tall, with marbled white and red sandstone giving way to grayer granite as they descended into the earth. The riverbed grew smaller, forking off, eventually disappearing entirely in a maze of high, narrow flash-flood canyons that merged into each other and spoked off and wound around in a confusing convoluted labyrinth. They could no longer be sure in which direction they were traveling—the sky above was only an unhelpful slit at the top of the rounded cliffs—but Miles trusted his gut and the rest of them trusted Miles, and holding tightly to the dream jar May had given him, he led them forward.

Eventually, the ravine they were following opened out into a wider canyon. Miles had the sense that they were being watched by something unseen, and he suddenly felt uncomfortable being out in the open like this. The others must have felt the same because no one dared speak, and they walked around tangled washed-out branches and the trunks of dead leafless trees that had been swept here by water and trapped between boulders.

Around a curve of the canyon, indentations in the rock face were home to crumbling rock walls with small window

holes. He'd seen pictures of Canyon de Chelly, with its famous Indian ruins, and that was what this reminded him of.

Only . . .

Only he wasn't sure that these walls had been built by
Indians.

Or anything human.

The canyon widened, spread out, then narrowed unexpectedly just beyond a nearly ninety-degree turn. Here, in
front of the cliffs, a low stone wall was broken up, differ-
entiated into hoodoos and stand-alone columns. The rocks,
he thought, looked almost like people. Whether they were
eroded naturally by the elements into these shapes or whether
they had been deliberately carved and then weathered by the
rain and sand and sun until the edges that granted them
sharpness of definition had been blunted and smoothed, he
could not tell, but the sight was unnerving. He was reminded
of that terra-cotta army that had been found in China—

"I dug this hole. It leads to China."

—and the sensation that they were walking through a
crowd of people who'd been solidified into stone could not
be shaken. He quickened his pace, aware of the fact that for
the first time since they'd started walking he was breathing
heavily, straining for oxygen. He heard Claire breathing next
to him, and he announced, "We're almost there."

No one responded.

He thought of the dream he'd had last night. The tingling
in his midsection had returned, and once again it occurred
to him that by dint of his heritage he was a part of this. He
had been purposefully drawn into this situation because of
who and what he was. Nothing was an accident and, subtle
as it might seem, his dad's death and Marina walking into
the agency office looking for help with her father were all
part of some unseen plan.

The jar in his hand suddenly seemed heavier, the shape
of the spoon in his front pocket pronounced against the skin

of his thigh. The necklace of teeth felt cold on his skin, but strangely enough, it also felt reassuring, and he was glad he had it with him.

Soon afterward they came to a confluence of canyons. The sky was still overcast, and Miles could not determine the position of the sun from this angle, but it seemed darker all of a sudden, as though evening had held off until their arrival. The sulfur smell was back, too, strongly, and next to him Claire placed her free hand over her nose to block the stench.

Miles stopped, not sure in which direction to proceed. On one rock wall was the shadow of a woman that looked remarkably like his mother, but he turned away, not wanting to see, sensing somehow that to gaze upon the form would . . . what? Turn him to salt? Turn him to stone? Render him mad?

He had no idea, but looking upon the shadow figure was dangerous, he knew that much.

"Hey," Hal said. "That's my mom."

"Don't look at that!" Miles ordered, whirling to face his friend. "All of you! Don't look!"

Garden seemed to understand instinctively, and when he spoke his voice was hushed. "What is it?" he asked.

"I don't know. But there are probably going to be a lot of things like it coming up. We need to be careful from here on in. Stay close together, and if there's anything unusual, give out a shout. We have to be on our toes."

"Then, I assume we're going that way," Hal said dryly.

Miles followed his pointing finger. The other canyons spoking off from this hub were typically barren, but the one at which Hal was pointing was different. There were . . . *things* growing here. Objects which must have been plant life but from this perspective could have been statues or could have been creatures, black-gray forms that dotted the alluvial fans adjoining the cliff sides and were scattered along the floor of the gorge, giving the entire canyon a creepily dark and ragged appearance. The stench of sulfur issued from this direction as well, and Miles nodded slowly. "Yeah," he said. "That's where we're going."

Hal took out his revolver, opened the magazine, checked it, snapped it back into place. He did not put the weapon back into his shoulder holster but kept it in his hand. "All right, then. Let's do it."

Miles wished Claire had not come along, wished Janet were here instead, not only because he was afraid for Claire but because Janet was supposed to be here, because Janet was one of them, because she had witch blood.

Claire looked over at him, smiled wanly, as if she could read his thoughts. "At least we'll die together," she said.

"No one's dying," he told her.

But he could not make himself believe it.

The canyon was strewn with black rocks and unknown bones. Ugly weeds sprouted here and there, and stunted trees grew in strange disturbing shapes. There was no easy path, and they were forced to pick their way through what seemed to be an obstacle course placed purposely before them. The sulfur smell grew ever stronger. He could hardly breathe, Claire was gagging, but just when it seemed they would have to stop or turn around, the stench disappeared completely. It was as if they had passed through some sort of unseen barrier, and the air in his lungs was suddenly clear and very cold.

There were dead dogs in the trees, hanging by their necks from bare root branches. Beetles scuttled across the sand below, swarms of them circling the trees in a manner that was frighteningly deliberate. In the recesses of the rock wall were carvings, half obscured and only partially observed, that Miles almost recognized and that caused shivers to race down his arms.

Claire let out a small shocked cry and grabbed his arm

with her free hand. Next to her foot, a small stationary creature grew out of the crevice in a rock. Looking like a cross
between an albino frog and an unshelled oyster, it stared up
at them with slitted eyes and let out a gurgling cry that
sounded like laughter.

They walked far around the creature, giving it a wide
berth.

Miles took the lead with Claire, and after a while he
turned to check on the others. Hal was right behind them—

But that was it.

Miles' heart lurched in his chest. "Garden?"

No answer.

He shouted it out: "Garden!"

All three of them stopped walking, looking around, calling, but there was no sign of their companion.

He was gone.

7

"Garden."

It was his daddy's voice, his daddy was here, and Garden stopped walking, turned, and looked into a long, high
crack in the cliff side.

"Garden."

The voice was weak, barely above a whisper, as though
his old man was trapped or had been here some time without food or water. It made no logical sense—he had left his
daddy yesterday in Apache Junction—but he would recognize that voice anywhere. He stepped over the jagged rocks
and into the cleft, angling sideways for several minutes until
the fissure opened out.

"Garden."

It occurred to him that he was being intentionally led
away from the others, and he wondered why he didn't call
out, let them know where he was going—

was his mind being clouded?

—but these thoughts occurred to him at a remove, as if from afar, and the thought that was in the forefront of his mind was that he needed to find his daddy and get him the hell out of here. His daddy had probably followed him from Apache Junction, wanting to warn him away from Isabella, but he'd been too late, and he'd somehow ended up here, trapped.

Or captured.

Garden slowed his pace, suddenly wary of what might lie ahead. For the first time he thought seriously about going back, getting the others, doing a proper search, but then he heard his daddy's voice again.

"Garden."

And he pushed forward between the high dank walls until he was face-to-face with—

a dummy.

The figure propped in a sitting position against the step-like rock ahead had obviously been intended to look like his daddy, but the resemblance was not even close. The head was the right shape but made of stuffed cheesecloth. The eyes were buttons and the rest of the face was painted on: a piggish nose, a goofy gap-toothed smile. The clothes on the dummy were of a style his daddy had once worn but had not owned for decades. There were no hands or feet.

This, however, was where the voice originated, and as he stood there, staring at it, a slight breeze whistled through the narrow chasm and, filtered through the unseen contents of the cheesecloth head, again whispered his name.

"Garden."

A chill passed through him. This was not right. Everything suddenly shifted into clear focus, and though he felt pressure on his mind, a strange insistent pulse that promised him everything was okay, this was the way it was meant to be, he knew that he had been tricked to get him away from Miles and the others.

He reached into his left front pocket, feeling for the flattened frog that the old woman had given him for protection, but the pocket was empty. There was no hole in the material, and he checked his right pocket, but it was empty, too.

The frog had disappeared somehow, pushed up perhaps through the friction of movement to fall out of his pants unseen as he'd walked. He was filled with a dizzying sensation of panic.

"Miles!" he screamed. "Miles!"

He yelled at the top of his lungs, and the repeated word seemed to echo up the narrow space to the canyon rim, but he was not sure how far in he'd come, and didn't know if they could hear him at all. Because another sound was competing with him, a low guttural rumbling that came out of the earth itself, a sound he recognized but could not quite place.

Water.

He knew it now: the roar of a flood, the rush of a wave. The cleft began to fill with black brackish water. It seeped up from the rock beneath his feet at first, but almost instantly it began pouring in from both directions—the way he'd come and the way ahead. He was alone in this space with that hideous dummy, and it floated up on the tide toward him even as he attempted to find a handhold, a foothold, something that would enable him to climb out of this space before he drowned.

"Garden."

The dummy was still speaking his name, and when he looked down at the painted face, its smile seemed more malevolent than goofy. The right button eye, hanging by a thread, began flipping up and back, propelled by the streaming water, in chilling approximation of a wink.

There was no way to climb out, no way to get up the

narrow cliff, and the water was now flooding in fast. The black liquid smelled strongly of sulfur, and he gagged, keeping his mouth closed, trying not to swallow any of it.

Maybe he could just tread water, float on the rising tide, wait until the chasm filled up completely and then exit through the top.

"Garden."

The winking dummy now looked nothing like his daddy. Even the shape of the head was distorted. The dark water had stained the cheesecloth, and it looked more like a figure out of a nightmare. The dummy pressed against him, bobbed up, then sank and disappeared.

A second later, handless arms wrapped around his legs, feeling soft and spongy and frighteningly alive.

"Help!" he screamed.

And was pulled down into the water.

8

Garden was gone.

They backtracked, looked behind boulders, looked into offshoot ravines, calling out his name, but he was nowhere to be seen, and finally Miles said, "She got him."

"Maybe he just pussied out," Hal suggested.

Miles looked at him.

"All right, it's not that plausible. But it's possible."

"He disappeared," Claire said. "One minute he was there, then I turned around and he was gone." She looked at Miles. "So what do we do now?"

His head hurt. If there was anything to his witch blood theory, they were up shit creek because he was the only one left. While Isabella may not have been aware that he'd been granted insight into her motives and intentions, she obviously knew they were here, and she was playing with them, slowly and deliberately picking them off, one by one.

"Do you still have the things May gave you?" he asked.

Claire held up her hand to show the bracelet of weeds. Hal withdrew the small fetish from his pocket.

"Good. Keep them with you. They've protected us this far, maybe they'll see us through this." He took a deep breath. "We're going on. We're almost there."

"Whatever Garden had didn't protect him," Hal pointed out.

Miles looked at him. "It can't hurt."

Hal hefted his revolver. "Excuse me if I place more of my faith in this."

"If you really think that'll do any good against a dead hundred-year-old monster who's been resurrecting witches and killing people all over the damn country, be my guest."

Hal raised an eyebrow, Spock-like. "You have a point."

Miles smiled—and it felt good. His face had been tense, and this brief touch of gallows humor loosened it up.

"Come on," he said. "Let's try to move quickly.

"And stay close," he warned. "We need to keep each other in sight at all times."

He started forward, moving over so that Claire was walking in the middle, he and Hal on the outside flanks to protect her, all three of them rubbing shoulders. The jar in his hands felt warm, slippery, and he held it tightly, not wanting it to slide from his grasp and shatter on the rocky ground. Claire, too, was clutching the kerosene lamp tightly, and he considered asking Hal to hold it instead, but the truth was that Hal was clumsier than Claire and more likely to drop it.

Rising all around them were screeches and cracks and hums and whistles, the scuttling of claws and the quiet cacklings of madness. Out of the corner of his eye, he saw movement off to the sides, between the boulders and the trees, a darting of shadows that instantly stopped each time he looked at one of the spots full on.

He stepped on something wet and squishy that gurgled in a way which sounded both liquid and alive, but he did not look down to see what it was.

The canyon flattened out in front of them, high cliff sides trailing off into low black ridges that faded into sand dunes. The odd-shaped buttes they'd seen from afar were now front and center, and lightning danced in the clouds over dark distant mountains.

It was the scene from his vision.

Miles felt almost incapacitated by fear. The cave from which he'd viewed this landscape was somewhere close by, off to the right, and he began scanning the dwindling cliffs, looking for an opening in the rock.

He found it.

The cave was much lower than he'd expected, on a small ridge just above the sloping hill of alluvial dirt. It would be easy to walk up there, despite the lack of a path, the shards of stone, and the peculiar spiky cacti, but he didn't want to go. The will and determination that had led him this far seemed suddenly to have deserted him, and he was filled with cold dread as he looked up at that small black entrance in the cliff side.

He tried to speak, but no sound came out. He cleared his throat, tried again. His heart was pounding crazily. "That's it," he said. "Up there. That's where she is."

And Isabella emerged from the cave.

"Look!" Claire cried out.

Isabella, her head still held at a noticeably awkward angle, strode forth from the cave entrance and over the edge of the ridge, continuing several feet until she was hovering in the air above the sloping ground. She stared at them, speaking in some strange unintelligible tongue and making elaborate motions with her hands. The look on her face was one of rage and hatred, and out of the corner of his eye Miles saw that the bracelet on Claire's arm was glowing greenly, brightening then dimming, as if it were being bombarded with energy . . . and absorbing it.

Claire noticed his necklace at the same time, pointing, and though he couldn't see it, he felt the heat on his skin and that area of his neck seemed suffused with a greenish glow. Hal reached into his pocket, and his wood carving was glowing, too. He quickly put it back.

"I guess we're protected," Claire said.

Hal looked toward Isabella. "Let's get her."

That provided the impetus Miles needed, and the paralysis that had temporarily overcome him disappeared as he grabbed Claire's free hand and pulled her up the sloping ground toward the cave entrance.

Both of them jumped as Hal fired his revolver, the sound of the report absurdly, outrageously loud, triggering a small landslide and inducing a muffled ringing in Miles' ears. He thought at first that his friend had fired at Isabella but almost immediately saw the gray-green spiderlike crab creature that Hal had shot. Off-center eyes stared into nothingness while clear viscous goo spilled from a well-placed bullet hole.

"It was coming after me," Hal said.

Miles nodded. "Just make sure you don't waste your shots," he suggested. "That might be what she wants."

Isabella was no longer in the air, she was on the ridge, looking down at them, and when Miles' eyes met hers, she pulled away, moved back.

Was she afraid?

It didn't make any sense, but it seemed that way, and the three of them pressed on, moving up the slope, over the rough, obstacle-laden ground until they ran across the remnants of an ancient trail that led them directly on to the lip of the ridge.

A flash of flesh disappeared into the blackness of the cave entrance.

Had they chased her back into the cave? Or was she luring them on? He wasn't sure, but they were going in. He moved forward, peering into the dimness but seeing nothing. What little light there was in this overcast world died instantly upon entering the cave. They should have brought flashlights. What they needed was . . .

a lamp.

He turned to Claire, handed her the jar, took the kerosene lantern from her.

"Good idea," Hal said.

"Let's hope it works."

Hal had matches, and Miles used them to light the lamp before shoving it into the opening in the wall before him.

Just inside the entrance, Isabella screeched at the sight of the light, a horrible sound like the cawing of crows and the breaking of glass. She retreated deeper into the cave, scuttling backward on legs that were impossibly formed and far too agile. Within seconds she was past the perimeter of the lamp's light. Though the screeching had stopped, Miles heard the clattering sound of hard claws on stone receding into the darkness.

"Whatever you do," he told Claire, "don't drop that jar."

"Don't worry. I won't."

They walked into the cave. Claire's bracelet and his own necklace were glowing, giving off a greenish illumination that would enable them to find each other in the blackness but that shed no usable light on their surroundings. They were entirely dependent on the flame of the lamp. Claire latched on to his belt, holding tight as he moved slowly forward.

There were no stalactites or stalagmites, no columns or rock formations. The walls were smooth, black and glassy. Ancient symbols had been painted on the roof of the cave, pictographs in faded white that shifted and changed with the flickering of the lamp and seemed somehow hideous.

The cave narrowed, and they found themselves in a downward-sloping tunnel, a passageway not wide enough for them to walk two abreast.

"Maybe I should get in the front," Hal suggested. "I have the gun."

"*I'll* stay in the front," Miles told him. "You protect the rear."

They passed alcoves and indentations, offshoot passages, but this was clearly the main tunnel, and Miles moved slowly forward, keeping an eye out for any sign of movement, any—

An arm shot out of the darkness to his right, clawed fingers grabbing his shoulder. He screamed, squirmed, lashed out, but the hand retreated immediately, as if scalded by something hot, and Miles knew it was the necklace that had protected him. The grunting commotion behind him was Hal trying to shove his way around and past Claire, but Miles said, "It's nothing. It's over."

"What happened?" Claire demanded.

"Something tried to grab me."

He lifted the lamp and shone it toward the area from which the hand had come, but there was only a shallow alcove, empty.

"Let me in front," Hal demanded. "I'm not letting you be a target. You're the one who needs to stay in the middle. You're the one who needs to be protected."

Miles did not even bother to answer but, with Claire's fingers grabbing his belt, started forward again, holding the lamp out and clutching it tightly, hyperaware of the fact that if it slipped from his grip or was knocked from his hands, they would be trapped here in total darkness.

He saw more symbols carved on the walls, shapes that he did not recognize but that spoke to him somehow and filled him with dread. The tunnel curved to the left

—and Miles was looking into a room. Not a cave or

a chamber or a tunnel but a large square room with slatted wooden walls and wooden ceiling. A single candle the size of a tree stump, placed next to an open black doorway in the opposite right corner, provided sickly illumination.

"Jesus," Hal breathed.

The room was filled with dolls. Dolls that looked like clumps of asparagus, dolls that looked like scarecrows and kachinas, dolls that looked like a selection of children's toys ranging from the Victorian era until now. They were made from a variety of materials and appeared to be of all ages, the newest a genderless factory-pressed piece of plastic, the oldest a carved piece of driftwood with an oversize male organ. They were arranged upon the floor, placed together on shelves and ledges, suspended by hooks from the walls. Vines grew over and between the figures, impossibly green for having grown in the darkness.

In the center of all this stood the corpse of a dwarf, an eyeless, mummified creature with brown skin and rotted clothes and barely discernible features. The corpse held forth one outstretched hand, palm up.

Claire let go of his belt, grabbed his arm. Her hand was cold and sweaty, and he could feel the tension in her fingers as she painfully squeezed his arm muscles. "Let's get out of here," she whispered, afraid even to speak aloud. Her whisper echoed, grew, became other words, other sounds in the strange acoustics of this room. "I don't like it." She breathed deeply. "I'm afraid."

Hal nodded, whispering himself. "She's right, Miles. This is out of our league."

"Stay there," Miles told them.

He pulled away from Claire and, holding the lamp in front of him for additional light, walked slowly forward, careful not to step on any of the dolls. Glass eyes stared blankly up at him as he passed. The flickering flame of the lamp reflected in their surface gave them the illusion of life.

This close, he could see that a vine had wound around the dwarf's feet and disappeared up the faded, rotted material that had once been clothes. The vine emerged once again on the underside of the arm and ended in the dried, outstretched hand. The vine was mint, he saw now, though mint did not ordinarily grow in a vine, and the way it came to an end just beyond the tip of the mummified fingers made it appear as though the small dead man was offering him a branch of newly picked mint leaves.

He remembered his dream last night, the old man with the mint spoon.

"A dwarf gave it to me."

Not knowing if it was the right thing or not, Miles picked the end of the vine, the branch of mint leaves, from the dead dry hand, and put it in the pocket of his shirt.

"It keeps the head fresh."

Cool, clean air beckoned him from the dark doorway in the corner, and Miles turned back toward Claire and Hal. "Come on," he said, and his voice had no echo but died dully. "We're going out that way. Make sure you don't step on any of the dolls."

He needed to say no more. Claire came first, and she stepped gingerly between the figurines, following almost the same path he himself had taken. Hal gave her a moment's head start before doing the same. Miles waited for both of them to reach him then, single-file, they crossed the rest of the room to the doorway.

Once past the massive candle, darkness closed in again. They entered another rock tunnel, only this time the walls were rounded, as if bored by machine. There were no alcoves or side passages, just this one straight tunnel. Holding his lamp high, Miles led them forward. The ground began to slope upward almost immediately, and soon he was being forced to take smaller steps just to maintain his balance. The passageway continued upward, as steep as stairs. They were all breathing heavily, and Miles was about to suggest that they stop and take a break when he saw the sky up ahead.

Storm clouds.

He hurried forward, coming finally to the end of the rock. They were out.

Logically, they had to be at the top of the canyon, but when they emerged from between two boulders embedded in a hillside, he saw no trace of any canyon, only those strangely formed buttes, jutting upward not from a flat sandy desert but from a huge marsh filled with water weeds and cattails. It was an incongruous sight, like modern buildings positioned next to the pyramids or a luxury resort in the middle of the rain forest, and that only served to heighten the sense of surrealism.

There was a strange shapeless glow above the marsh, not green like the phosphorescence of their talismans but red, like blood, and it winked on and off several times, as though trying to attract their attention. Then it coalesced into something resembling a ball and began floating slowly away, toward the nearest, tallest butte. Beneath the glowing orb, he saw, was a stone walkway, slightly raised, that bisected the swampy overgrown ground.

"Let's go," Miles said.

Hal groaned. "Not again."

But Claire was already moving, and Hal followed behind.

Isabella was leading them someplace, purposefully luring them to some location of her own choosing, for purposes that were not yet clear.

When she had emerged from the lake, when he'd shared her visions, when he'd seen the destruction of New York and Los Angeles and cities all across the nation, Miles had believed her to be at peak power. He hadn't understood why she had not immediately embarked upon her mission but had instead waited around for *them*.

He knew now, though.

She needed them.

Or, rather, she needed *him*.

It didn't make any sense, but he guessed it had something to do with his father, with his heritage. Maybe she needed to absorb the power of *all* of the witches in order to carry out her plan . . . and he was the last. Whatever the reason, she was provoking a confrontation, and there was nothing he could do but see this through to the end.

They moved into the shadow of the butte, and what little sunlight had been filtering through the dark heavy clouds was cut off completely. Around them in the marsh they could hear the rustling, slithering noises of unseen creatures.

The red glow faded into nothingness and only the lamp lit their way, but the marsh was not as large as it looked and the butte was not as tall as it looked, and ten minutes later they were there.

She was waiting for them.

It was a vision of hell. The marsh ended and the ground was smoldering rock. A fence made of burned stakes surrounded a patch of brown tufted weeds and the decomposing corpse of what looked like a deformed elephant. There was a massive hole in the ground—

"That's where I put her body."

—so black it seemed to suck up all available light, and hideous stone carvings lay tipped over and broken all the way to the foot of the butte.

Isabella stood upon a pile of ill-formed bones.

Smiling at them.

Hal shot at her.

He didn't wait for Miles' okay but simply drew his weapon and fired. As Miles expected, the bullets had no impact. They passed through Isabella, ricocheting and sparking off adjacent rock.

You couldn't kill what was already dead.

She floated toward them, her eyes locked on Miles'. They were the coldest eyes he'd ever seen, embedded in a face that was . . . beautiful.

Yes, she was beautiful. He'd noticed it at the lake, but it seemed more pronounced now. She was in her element. This environment flattered her, brought out her best features. She was dead, but he had never seen anyone look more alive. Her beauty was of a type he had never beheld before, a strange exquisite wildness.

The only thing that marred the illusion was that odd tilt of the head, the weird angle at which her neck seemed permanently cocked.

Her eyes were working on him, trying to seduce him perhaps, but either the necklace protected him, or his own feelings were so true and solid that nothing could dislodge them.

He hated her.

She stopped, stood before him, flat on the ground. "Miles," she said. "Miles Huerdeen. I knew you would come." Her voice was soft, musical, but had an edge to it, too. He had the feeling that, like her eyes, her voice was trying to work on him.

"What did you do to my father?" he demanded.

"I was helping your father," she said. "I want to help you, too. We must stick together, our kind. They all want us dead . . ."

She didn't know he was aware of her plans. She didn't know that he knew what she was.

He still had that advantage, at least, and Miles watched her while she spoke, trying to figure out what he should do.

He was not sure what he'd expected. A magic sword to appear? A spell? May had provided them with fetishes of protection, he'd been given visions. Up until now he'd been supplied with whatever he needed, and he'd expected that to continue.

But there was no sword, no magic spell, nothing. He was alone with Isabella, and it appeared now as though he would have to physically attack her if he hoped to stop her and put an end to her plans of mass destruction.

He dropped the lantern and punched her hard in the gut.

Isabella was caught unawares, but she was not hurt. *How could she be? She was dead.* Her astonishment lasted only a few seconds. She spun away from him, out of his reach, causing him to stumble on his follow-up. His chance to use the element of surprise to his advantage had failed. Now they both knew where the other stood.

"You wanted to know about your father?" she said softly. "Bob's in hell. I put him there. He was evil, one of the devil's disciples, and I sent him where he belonged." Her gaze held him. "Do you know why your parents split up, Miles? Do you know the real reason? Do you know why your sister never comes around?"

"Don't listen to her," Claire ordered, grabbing his arm. "Do what you have to do."

What he had to do? He didn't even know what that was.

Isabella smiled. "How many guys do you think Claire fucked while you two were apart? How many huge dripping cocks do you think she sucked and sat on? More than five? More than ten? More than twenty?"

Images accompanied the words: *his father taking his mother anally against her will, sticking his huge hairy hands up Bonnie's nightdress when she was still a child; Claire bobbing up and down between a mustached man's legs, stopping suddenly, her eyes widening as the man ejaculated what was clearly an unexpectedly large amount of semen into her willing mouth.*

The scenes cut straight through to his gut, but he could not let himself be swayed or lose focus. He rushed her, hands out, pushing her hard onto the ground and falling on top of her, punching her midsection.

She was wiry. And much stronger than he would have thought, even though whatever powers she possessed had not been used to enhance simple physical prowess. She withstood his blows and with one knee to the stomach sent him off her, falling sideways, trying desperately to draw breath.

Their positions were suddenly reversed. In one fluid motion she was on top of him. She kneed him again, this time in the crotch, then reached for his necklace, clearly not believing that she would be able to even touch it. But apparently the necklace's power was restricted to witchcraft, and though it could repel spells and conjurings, it could not fend off a direct assault. Her fingers curled around it, and the string yanked free of his neck, coming apart in her hands, the green glow winking out of existence as individual teeth clattered onto the rocky ground.

He saw a look of triumph in her eyes, felt the crackle of power in the air.

Then she was knocked sideways, off him.

And Hal and Claire were upon her.

Both were still protected, Claire's bracelet shining brightly, a glow emerging from the top of Hal's pocket, where he kept his talisman, and they were attacking wildly, like a team of predatory animals, not giving her an opportunity to fight back. Once again, she was not being hurt—

She was dead

—but, not being able to use her powers, she was forced to fend them off. A harsh growl escaped from her lips, a tremendously deep noise that sounded as though it had come from a much larger creature.

Hal held down her arms, head-butted her in the chest.

Claire had grabbed a rock and was sitting on Isabella's legs, bashing in her knees.

Miles still felt the crackle of energy about him, and he had no doubt that she was about to finish him off, to kill him and absorb his life force or whatever the hell it was that she did; but before that happened, he leaped up, ran over, and grabbed her head with both hands. She screamed, began thrashing wildly.

And he pulled off her head.

The break was clean, and he realized her head had not been reattached properly to begin with. That was why it had been held at such an odd angle.

He dropped the head, feeling dirty and disgusted by the sensation of it in his hands: the sliminess of the skin, the coldness of the flesh. Her body had stopped moving instantly, going limp, the thrashing ceasing upon disconnection with the head.

He helped Claire up, grabbing her hand and pulling her to her feet, though she would have had no trouble getting up on her own, and gave her a warm hard hug, kissing her full on the lips, grateful that she was alive, grateful to be alive himself.

"Jesus," Hal breathed, standing and rubbing an obviously hurt knee.

Miles glanced back toward the black hole in the ground. He thought of his dream, the old cowboy.

"That's where I put her body."

Whatever useful knowledge he possessed had come from that dream, and he quickly grabbed Isabella's slack arms. "Pick her up," he told Hal. "We'll throw her in the hole."

There was no argument, no hesitation. Hal grabbed her legs, and the two of them lifted the unnaturally heavy form and staggered over to the edge of the massive pit.

"On three," Hal said.

They began swinging the body back and forth to gain momentum.

"One . . . Two . . . Three!"

They let go, and Isabella's body fell into the hole, disappearing instantly, swallowed by the deep lightless black. They looked down, waited, but there was no flash of light as she was consumed, no sound of thump or splash as she reached the bottom.

She was simply gone.

Or rather her body was.

The head was still there, lying on the smoking ground at Claire's feet.

Miles and Hal walked back to where she was standing. Hal motioned toward the jar Claire had placed on the ground. "What about that? I guess we don't need it any more, huh?"

Miles looked over at the shattered glass of the lantern he had tossed and was about to say no, they didn't need it, when a high keening sound issued from between the lips of Isabella's head. Claire jumped back, crowded next to Miles. Hal's eyes widened.

The head lay on the smoldering rock, and there were no bones or veins or blood in the neck. There was not even an open wound. There was only a smooth bright green gelatinous substance that looked like liquid plantflesh encased in a roll of skin.

Still, the features were moving, eyes blinking, eyebrows raising, lips parting. The keening sound grew lower, separated into words. Isabella began speaking, cursing them, spewing forth a litany of foul promises and invectives that made Miles' skin crawl.

He moved forward. He suddenly knew what he had to do. Reaching down distastefully, he picked the head up by the green algae hair, holding it at arm's length.

"Your children will be born deformed," Isabella said, and her voice was neither male nor female, was not even human. "They will be burned and dismembered by tribes of unbelievers, their entrails scattered to the four winds . . ."

"Open the jar," Miles said. "The lid."

Hal hurried over, pulled off the jar's top.

Miles lowered the head, placed it in the jar. Hal quickly replaced the lid, and Miles took the rusted spoon from his pants pocket, the mint vine from his shirt. He took a deep breath, gathered his strength, then pulled open the lid and used the spoon to sprinkle mint leaves on top of Isabella's upward tilted face. He closed the top again.

With a scream of rage and agony, Isabella's features melted, devolving into separate elements, as though they were unrelated objects that had been held together by glue into a coherent whole. What remained resembled nothing so much as sliced fruit: cherries and pears and peaches.

Miles felt drained. He didn't know what type of witchcraft he had performed, where it had come from, or how it had worked. All he knew was that whatever he had done, it had succeeded. Isabella was no more.

And, hopefully, she was the last of her kind.

This entire odyssey had been a series of vague impulses and half-understood events, things that made no logical sense but fit together on some subliminal level and were granted meaning. He thought of May.

"Sometimes there just isn't an explanation."

He stared up into the dark sky, breathing deeply, his muscles shaking. He had changed, he realized. This experience had altered him in a very profound and fundamental way. His entire outlook and approach was different than it had been. No longer was he a captive to logic, a head-over-heart guy. He was more like his father, and he wished Bob were here so he could tell the old man that he was happy to be like him, that he was proud.

Hal still seemed somewhat jittery as he stared at the closed jar. "What now? Do we dump it in the hole?"

"No," Miles said. "Just leave it here."

"What if—?"

"Nothing will happen."

"How do you *know*?" Claire asked.

He looked into her eyes, took her hands in his.

He didn't.

It just *felt* right.

And for him that was enough.

EPILOGUE

They were still in the canyons when the rescue helicopter found them. Janet had gone for help, and from the town of Rio Verde, the sheriff had contacted the FBI office in Phoenix, which had immediately marshaled the manpower to assist one of its own.

Night had finally fallen, and the strange storm clouds had, if not disappeared, at least reverted to something resembling an ordinary weather phenomenon.

Base camp for the rescue effort was the Rio Verde sheriff's office. Rossiter, still alive but condition unchanged, had been flown back to a Phoenix hospital. The rest of them were questioned in separate rooms in the local lockup about what exactly had happened, and though Miles was tempted to lie and say he knew nothing, they had not gone over a plan in advance and he did not want to contradict anything Hal, Claire, or Janet might say.

So he told the truth.

He had no idea how much of his story would be given credence, but the man talking to him nodded solemnly at the appropriate places and showed no outward sign of amusement. Miles wanted to believe that his story would be routinely filed away and attributed to the effects of heatstroke, but he knew from overheard conversations in the hallway that the half-buried bodies of the Walkers had been found, as had May's. Their stories would be harder to dismiss with corroboration.

And a part of him could not help thinking that someone, somewhere in the government, already knew about Isabella and that weird land beyond Wolf Canyon.

By the time it was all finished and they had each provided their phone numbers and addresses for follow-up interviews, dawn had nearly arrived. The FBI offered to put them up for a day in a local motel, and Janet took them up on that, saying that she was too tired to do anything but sleep. The rest of them decided to get out of Arizona as quickly as possible. Janet promised Miles that she would return the rental car to Cedar City the next day and sign off on it.

"You'd better," he told her. "I know where you live."

She laughed, thanked him, gave him a quick awkward hug. They had explained to her what had gone on after they'd followed May, and though she still seemed disturbed by Garden's disappearance and the fact that he had not yet been found, she seemed less troubled than at any time since Miles had met her, and he had the feeling that she would be okay. He promised to call as soon as he got back to California.

Hal intended to drive Miles and Claire back to Los Angeles, but the FBI offered to pay for a rental car, and Miles decided to take advantage of that. The three of them ate at a Denny's, compliments of the Bureau, and when the local Avis opened, an Agent Madison accompanied Miles, filled out the paperwork, and told Miles that he could drop the car off at any Avis in Southern California.

The agent shook his hand. "We'll be in touch."

Before they parted ways, when Claire was out of earshot, Hal took Miles aside. "Would you rather meet up with Isabella again or have a broom handle shoved up your ass?" he asked. "And death is not an option."

"Broom handle up the ass," Miles replied without hesitation.

Hal patted his shoulder. "Me, too, bud. Me, too."

Miles thought of his father, thought of Bob. The FBI and the other law enforcement agencies involved were going to autopsy the bodies, then, using dental and fingerprint identification, attempt to contact the decedents' families. Miles had already specified his father's approximate location in the lineup and had described the ragged clothes Bob had been wearing. He'd also given them the name of Ralph Barger at the L.A. County Coroner's office, and they'd promised to ship over the body.

His dad would finally get a proper burial.

He didn't want to think about his father right now, didn't want to get caught up in those sorts of considerations. He would do that later, when he was alone, when he had time to think things over and grieve.

Rio Verde was located at the juncture of two state highways, and Miles consulted a road map before choosing to take the route that led northeast across the state. Hal was heading the other way, through Phoenix, and they said their good-byes in the parking lot.

"I'm going in tomorrow," Hal said. "I'll tell everyone you're taking a few days."

Miles hadn't yet decided whether he would take any more days off work, but he thanked his friend. "I appreciate it."

"And I'm telling Tran. Everything."

Miles smiled. "Go right ahead."

Claire gave Hal a hug. "Thank you," she said. "For believing me, for coming with me, for all of it. I don't know what would've happened if you hadn't been here."

"Or you, either," he told her.

Miles put an arm around her. "Thanks both of you."

"What are friends for?"

They got into their respective cars, and Miles and Claire waved to Hal as he started off in the opposite direction.

They hit the highway themselves. It seemed suddenly silent, with just him and Claire—it was amazing how quickly one got used to being part of a group—and Miles turned on the radio as they headed over the bridge that traversed the river and headed into the desert. The radio dial was white noise save for a Mexican station, a right-wing talk program out of Albuquerque, and an all-news station from Las Vegas.

Miles kept it on the Las Vegas station. According to the weather report, a storm system was covering most of the four corners states and heading west, toward Nevada and California. Whether that was from the same dark cloud cover that had started over Wolf Canyon, he did not know, but it would not surprise him.

He glanced over at Claire. He remembered when they'd gotten married. Or when they were supposed to have gotten married. For the wedding had been postponed a day. There'd been a huge thunderstorm, a freakishly out-of-season El Niño downpour, that triggered a mudslide which engulfed the park where the ceremony was to take place. Although they'd been able to laugh about it later, it had been hell at the time and they'd rushed around all morning phoning friends and relatives, telling them about the postponement, while desperately searching for some inside location to host the wedding.

Miles cleared his throat. "How about we get married?"

She looked at him. "What?"

"Will you marry me?"

"No."

"No?"

"Are you crazy?"

"I'm dead serious."

"This isn't a movie, where two people fall in love just because they're thrown together under extreme circumstances. It's us. Me. You. We're together again, yes, but we still have to give this thing time. Who knows where this is going to lead?"

"I do."

"There's still a lot of water under the bridge, a lot of things we haven't talked about, and . . . and it's just too soon, Miles." She put a light hand on his arm.

"What do you say we go to Las Vegas and just play it from there?"

"No."

"Why not?"

"I'm not into those quicky chapel things, if that's your scheme. It's not cute or kitschy or any of that stuff to me."

"I thought you didn't want to get married. If you're not even going to be tempted, then, why not go?"

She smiled at him. "Okay, smarty pants. Las Vegas it is."

He grinned. "Las Vegas it is."

She reached over, shut off the radio, then snuggled close to him on the seat. He put his arm around her as he drove and casually pressed down on the gas, accelerating. He wanted to reach Las Vegas before the storm.

The forecast was for heavy rain by nightfall.

About the Author

Born in Arizona shortly after his mother attended the world premiere of *Psycho*, **Bentley Little** is the Bram Stoker Award–winning author of several novels and *The Collection*, a book of short stories. He has worked as a technical writer, reporter/photographer, library assistant, sales clerk, phonebook deliveryman, video arcade attendant, newspaper deliveryman, furniture mover, and rodeo gatekeeper. The son of a Russian artist and an American educator, he and his Chinese wife were married by the justice of the peace in Tombstone, Arizona.

"A master of the macabre!" —*Stephen King*

Bentley Little

"If there's a better horror novelist than Little...I don't know who it is." —Los Angeles Times

The Resort   212800

At the exclusive Reata spa and resort, enjoy your stay and relax. Oh, and lock your doors at night.

The Policy   209540

Hunt Jackson has finally found an insurance company to give him a policy. But with minor provisions: No backing out. And no running away.

The Return   206878

There's only one thing that can follow the success of Bentley Little's acclaimed *The Walking* and *The Revelation*. And that's Bentley Little's return...

The Bram Stoker Award-winning novel:

The Revelation   192257

Strange things are happening in the small town of Randall, Arizona. As darkness falls, an itinerant preacher has arrived to spread a gospel of cataclysmic fury...And stranger things are yet to come.